Juliana G   edium of
being sentenced to her room,   ice to relieve
the tedium of   actory suitors. Sadly, despite five ye
residence in   exclusive areas of London, she never
             he once sh   a taxi with a future baron.

Juliana's debut romance trilogy, including *A Lady Never Lies*, *A Gentleman Never Tells*, and *A Duke Never Yields*, was largely written when she should have been sleeping. She enjoys dark chocolate, champagne, and dinner parties, and despises all forms of exercise except one.

Praise for Juliana Gray:

'Charming, passionate, and thrilling . . . sets a new mark for historical romance' Elizabeth Hoyt, *New York Times* bestselling author

'A dazzling debut . . . the best new book of the year!' Lauren Willig, bestselling author

'A delightful confection of prose and desire that leaps off the page' Julia London, *New York Times* bestselling author

'Deliciously witty, and devastatingly romantic' Meredith Duran, *New York Times* bestselling author

'Fresh, clever, and supremely witty. A true delight' Suzanne Enoch, *New York Times* bestselling author

'Gray's talent for storytelling and characterization will make her a fan favorite' *Romantic Times*

By Juliana Gray

Affairs By Moonlight Trilogy
A Lady Never Lies
A Gentleman Never Tells
A Duke Never Yields

A Gentleman Never Tells

JULIANA GRAY

ETERNAL
ROMANCE

Published by arrangement with Berkley,
a division of the Penguin Group (USA) Inc.

First published in Great Britain in 2013
by ETERNAL ROMANCE
An imprint of HEADLINE PUBLISHING GROUP

1

Cataloguing in Publication Data is available from the British Library

ISBN 978 1 4722 0483 7

Offset in Times by Avon DataSet Ltd, Bidford-on-Avon, Warwickshire

Printed and bound by CPI Group (UK) Ltd, Croydon, CR0 4YY

Headline's policy is to use papers that are natural, renewable and recyclable
products and made from wood grown in sustainable forests.
The logging and manufacturing processes are expected to conform to the
environmental regulations of the country of origin.

HEADLINE PUBLISHING GROUP
An Hachette UK Company
338 Euston Road
London NW1 3BH

www.eternalromancebooks.co.uk
www.headline.co.uk
www.hachette.co.uk

To the august membership of the Romance Book Club,
without whom my heroines would be nameless.

ACKNOWLEDGMENTS

I am, as ever, indebted to the genius of my agent, Alexandra Machinist, who smoothes all paths and forges new ones.

The enthusiasm and expertise of the Berkley team humbles me daily. To my keen editor, Kate Seaver, and her able assistant, Katherine Pelz; to my copyeditor, who keeps dates, ages, and punctuation in strict order; to the fabulous artists, marketers, and publicists who bring books into the wide world: I am so very grateful.

The romance community entertains, instructs, and inspires me daily. Thank you so much to all the authors, bloggers, and fans who believe so passionately in a happily ever after.

A final acknowledgment belongs to Giuseppe Verdi, whose opera *Don Carlo* inspired many of the elements of the love triangle in *A Gentleman Never Tells*. (Trust me, it all sounds much better when sung in Italian.)

PROLOGUE

London
February 1890

In more than six years of clandestine service to his Queen and country, Lord Roland Penhallow had never before been summoned to the private library of the Bureau chief himself.

It could mean only one thing: He had inadvertently killed somebody.

Roland couldn't imagine how. The last caper had tied up as neat as a bow, with hardly any noise and only a very little blood. *Even the most perfidious villain can be made to serve some purpose*, Sir Edward would intone, pressing one blunt forefinger into the polished mahogany of his Whitehall desk, *but a dead body is a nullity*. Roland had taken that advice to heart as a new recruit, and had lived by it ever since.

Standing now in Sir Edward's shabby Mayfair entrance hall, with the tips of his shoes squared against the chipped marble tiles and his eyes roaming across a series of dyspeptic family portraits, Roland felt the same mild dread he'd known at Eton, when called in by his housemaster to atone for some recent prank. He knit his cold fingers together behind his back and looked upward at the dusky ceiling.

Nothing to worry about, he told himself. *You can talk your way past anything, Penhallow.* Was that a water stain spreading along the far corner? The old fellow really ought to have that looked at; fearsome things, leaks . . .

"Your lordship."

Roland started. Sir Edward's butler stood before him like an avenging penguin. His slick dark hair glinted in the yellow glare of the incandescent lamp on the hall table, and his impenetrable shirtfront held back the advance of his lapels with heroic whiteness. "Your lordship," he repeated, as he might say *your flatulent wolfhound.* "Sir Edward will receive you in the library."

The butler didn't wait for a response. He turned his immaculate ebony back in Roland's face and walked on in the direction—presumably—of the library.

"Thanks awfully," Roland muttered, feeling less like the brother of the Duke of Wallingford and more like a dustman with every passing step.

"Ah! Penhallow!" Sir Edward said, as Roland stalked through the door of the library with as much sangfroid as he could muster. A considerable amount, he judged modestly: He wasn't the Duke of Wallingford's brother for nothing.

"Sir Edward."

The baronet's sturdy hand waved at the ancient wing chair before the desk. "Sit, sit. That will be all, Pankhurst. Oh, wait. Dash it, Penhallow. Have you dined?"

"Yes, at my club."

"Excellent. Good. Off you go, then, Pankhurst. We're not to be disturbed. Sit, I said, Penhallow. Don't stand on ceremony *here*, for God's sake."

Roland sprawled into the armchair with his usual negligent grace, though the nerves along the back of his neck gave off a warning jangle. Sir Edward Pennington, chairman of Her Majesty's Bureau of Trade and Maritime Information, did not typically begin meetings in a stream of jocular pleasantries.

The door closed behind Pankhurst with a defiant thump.

Sir Edward's eyes rolled upward. "Pankhurst. I daresay

I ought to sack him, but on the other hand he's frightfully discreet. A drop of something, perhaps?" He rose and went to the demilune table against the far wall, on which a tray of crystal decanters flashed invitingly. "Sherry? Whiskey? I've a noble port at the moment, last of the ought-nines my father put down for me on the occasion of my birth, ha-ha."

"I shouldn't wish to deprive you," said Roland, who felt the loss of noble ports keenly, even in his present disturbed spirits.

"Nonsense. If one waits for the right occasion, one never drinks it at all." Sir Edward picked up a decanter and lifted the stopper. "Ah! There we are, you damned beauty."

"I say, you're a good deal more generous than my brother," Roland said. He watched with narrowed eyes as Sir Edward poured out one glass and then another, filling each one nearly to the rim with thick ruby port. In the silent book-filled room, the liquid swished against crystal like an Amazonian waterfall. "He never lets me near his vintage."

"Ah, well. Dukes, you know." Sir Edward handed him the glass. "To the Queen."

"The Queen."

The clink of glasses rang amiably in the air, and Sir Edward, instead of returning to his desk, moved to the window overlooking the rear garden. With one hand he lifted aside the heavy burgundy curtains and peered out into the foggy darkness. He took a drink of port. "I suppose," he said, "you're wondering why I've called you here tonight."

"It came as something of a surprise."

"Ah! Circumspect." Sir Edward swirled the port in his glass. "You've come along damned well these past few years, Penhallow. Damned well. I thought, when they first foisted you on me, you'd be nothing but an aristocratic millstone around my neck, with your flashy looks and your matchless damned pedigree. But I was quite wrong about that, to my considerable pleasure. Quite wrong." He turned to face Roland, and all the painfully contrived jollity had faded from his expression, leaving its lean angles even more austere than usual.

"I'm grateful to have been of service, sir," said Roland. "Queen and country and all that. Dashed good fun." He gripped the narrow bowl of his glass until the facets cut hard and cold against his fingertips.

"Of course you are. I don't doubt that for an instant." Sir Edward stared down into the ruby depths of his port.

"Sir?" Roland said, because his dry mouth would not permit anything more fluent. Then he remembered the port, and raised it to his lips for a hearty seamanlike swallow.

Sir Edward cleared his throat. "Here's the trouble. As I suspect you're aware, we're not the only organization in Her Majesty's government charged with gathering intelligence."

"Of course not. Tripping on each other's toes all the time." Roland offered a winning smile, his most charismatic younger-brother effort. "Why, just last month I nearly came to a bad end myself. Stumbled directly into a setup by some damned chaps from the Navy office. The bloodiest balls-up you've ever seen."

"Yes, I read your report." Sir Edward returned to the desk and sat down in his chair. A trace of what might be called a smile lifted one corner of his mouth. "Rather well written, your reports, except perhaps for an excess of descriptive phrase."

Roland shrugged modestly. "Reports would be so dull otherwise."

"In any case, it appears those—er—damned chaps from the Navy office, as you put it, aren't taking things in quite the same spirit of brotherhood."

"No? Hardly sporting of them. They were all quite on their feet again within a week or two." Roland flicked a speck of dust from his jacket sleeve.

"Ah. Still. Despite your tender care, which no doubt met the very highest standards of the service . . ."

"Naturally."

". . . there's talk"—Sir Edward set down his glass and fiddled with the neat rectangle of papers in the center of the leather-trimmed blotter—"that our involvement represented a deliberate attempt to undermine the efforts of a long and prestigious investigation."

Roland lifted his eyebrows. Despite hours of concerted effort, he'd never yet managed to raise one by itself. "You can't be serious. Does the Navy office really think I've nothing better to do with my time than to plot its downfall? For God's sake, my source gave me every reason to think . . ."

"Your source." Sir Edward lifted the topmost paper from the stack and scanned it. "Johnson, to be precise."

"Yes, sir. You know the man. Thoroughly reliable, well-placed at the Russian mission."

"And as of this morning, aboard a steamer to Argentina with a number of small heavy trunks, inhabiting a first-class starboard cabin." Sir Edward looked up. "Surprised, are you?"

Roland slumped back in his chair. "Well, I'm dashed!"

"Dashed. Yes."

"Argentina!"

"Apparently so. Traveling under his real name, of all things."

"The cheek!"

"My counterpart at the Navy is, of course, beside himself. He's convinced you paid off Johnson, that it's all part of some plot on our part to make fools of them, at best. At worst . . ."

Roland shot forward out of the chair and pinned the paper to the blotter with his finger. "Don't say it, by God."

"Pax, you young fool. I wasn't accusing you of anything."

"But someone is." Roland's voice was low, deadly, quite unlike its usual self.

Sir Edward tilted his lean face to one side and considered Roland for a long moment. "Someone is."

"Who?"

"I don't know." Sir Edward frowned. "Look, Penhallow. I shall speak as freely as I can, because I consider myself a fair judge of men, and I know no man more disinterestedly devoted to the welfare of the British nation than you."

Roland's arrow-straight body relaxed an infinitesimal degree.

"Something's up, Penhallow. I don't know what it is. Rumblings, currents. There's always been rivalry, of course; bitter, at times. One expects that, in this line of work, with no great financial benefit, no hero's reception at St. Paul's and whatnot. Power's the only currency. But the things I hear now, the things I sense, odd instances of this and that . . . I can't put it into words, exactly. But something's off."

Roland eased back into his chair, every sense alert. "What sort of thing?"

Sir Edward tented his fingers together atop the fine white paper, fingertip against fingertip. "If I knew that, Penhallow, I'd have taken action by now."

"Then how can I help?"

"That, you see, is the trouble." He drummed his fingertips together; hard, sturdy, peasantlike fingers that matched his hard, sturdy body and made the gentleman-like cut of his superfine jacket seem like racing silks on a destrier. "Tell me, Penhallow," he said, in an even voice, "have you any enemies? Besides, of course, those damned chaps you put out of action a few weeks ago."

"Oh, any number. One doesn't construct a reputation like mine without putting a few noses out of joint."

"Anyone who might wish to ruin you?"

"There are all sorts of ruin to wish upon a man who's beaten you at cards, or stolen your mistress."

"I mean total ruin. Moral, physical. A man, perhaps, who might wish to have you condemned for treason."

Treason.

The word rang about the room, ricocheted off the books and objects, settling at last between them with an ugly clank.

"None that I can call to mind," Roland said quietly.

"And yet," Sir Edward said, just as quietly, "I can say, with near certainty, that such a man exists."

"Name the man, and he is dead within the hour."

"I don't know his name. That, you see, is the mystery." Sir Edward rose and went to the middle of a row of bookshelves near the window, where a small globe interrupted the even flow of leather-bound volumes. He placed one hand, spiderlike, over the Atlantic Ocean. "Have you anywhere you can retire for a month or two? Perhaps more? Somewhere discreet?"

"What, *hide*? Oh, I say . . ."

"Not hide. Not at all. Only retire, as I said, from the limelight for a bit."

"Damn it all, sir, I won't turn tail and slink away."

"Discretion, in this case, is much the better part of valor." Sir Edward turned and skewered him with a rapier gaze from his dark eyes. "The idea is to tease the fellow out in the open. Find out what he's really after. Let him think he's won. An easy triumph breeds overconfidence."

"And I should meanwhile sit twiddling my thumbs in some countryseat . . ."

"Preferably outside of England."

"Oh rot. Outside of England? I've no tolerance for Paris, and no friends anywhere else that . . ." He stopped. A thought began to writhe its way through the currents of his brain, like a poisonous eel.

"What is it?"

"It's . . . it's nothing, really. Only some damned idea of a friend of ours."

"What sort of idea? What sort of friend?"

"A scientific fellow. Burke's his name, a very close and trusted friend of mine and my brother's. He's got some lunatic scheme in the works, proposes to spend a year in a castle in the Tuscan mountains, fiddling with automobiles and whatnot . . . really most ineligible . . ."

"Good God! It's perfect!"

"What's that? Oh, Lord, no. Not at all. Damp, wretched things, castles. And swearing off women and drink and . . . well, everything that makes life bearable."

"Just the thing for you, Penhallow. Marvelous. I shall write the necessary letters at once, open up a line for communication . . ."

"What's that?"

But Sir Edward was already scribbling himself a memorandum. "Beadle, I think, in the Florence office. He shall set you up with everything you need. Tuscany, eh? The land of unending sunshine, I believe they say. Ha. You'll have a splendid time. Most indebted to this Mr. Burke of yours."

Roland watched the motion of Sir Edward's pen along the paper and began to feel queasy. "I refuse to . . ."

"What's that? Oh, rubbish, Penhallow. I shall take care of everything on this end and notify you when it's safe to return. Think of it as a kind of sabbatical. You'll come back to us refreshed, renewed. Full of zest for life and all that."

Roland, who was never at a loss for words or composure, found himself devoid of both. His jaw swung helplessly below his brain.

Sir Edward folded the paper and looked up. "What's that? Oh, come, Penhallow. You look as though you've been passed a sentence of death. Think of all the advantages: sunshine, wine, decent food. Ripe young women who can't speak English."

He rose from his chair, held out the paper, and grinned like a demon.

"What could possibly go wrong?"

ONE

Thirty miles southeast of Florence
March 1890

The boy couldn't have been more than four or five years old. He stood square in the doorway of the inn and stared at Lord Roland Penhallow with a peculiar hostile intensity, his brow frowning into his dark eyes and his thumb stuck firmly between his teeth.

"I say, young fellow," said Roland, with a gentle cough, one foot upon the step, "might I perhaps sidle past?"

The boy removed his thumb. "My father could beat you up."

Roland felt the rain rattle down from the eaves against the crown of his hat. From there it streamed along the narrow brim and into the collar of his coat, soaking the shirt beneath until it stuck, cold and stiff, against his skin. "I daresay he could, old chap," he ventured, gathering the ends of his coat collar together with one hand. "But in the meantime, I should like very much to dry myself by that cracking hot fire directly behind you. If you don't mind, of course."

"My father," the boy said, lifting his finger and pointing it at Roland's nose, "could smash your face and arms and legs and you would cry for *EVER*." The last word was delivered with particular relish.

Roland blinked. He could glimpse, behind the boy's small figure, the inn's common room: its long tables lined with people, with plates of steaming food and bottles of local wine. An enormous fire roared away the dank March air, impossibly inviting. "Of course I should cry," Roland said. "Bitterly, in fact. No doubt about it, no doubt at all. But about that fire . . ."

"Philip! There you are!"

An exhausted female voice called from somewhere behind Roland, somewhere in the middle of that stinking mud-ridden innyard he'd just crossed. An exhausted voice, yes: strained and dry, with a suggestion of incipient hoarseness, but also perfectly familiar.

Roland's back stiffened with shock. Not here, surely. He must be mistaken. Not in the yard of a rustic Italian inn, tucked into a remote hillside, miles away from the civilized comfort of Florence and ages away from the London conservatory where he'd heard those dulcet tones last.

No, he must be imagining things.

"Philip, you're not *inconveniencing* this poor gentleman, are you?" The woman spoke in agonized tones, nearer now, coming up rapidly to his right shoulder.

Good God. He couldn't be imagining her *now*. Could he?

"Sir, I beg your pardon. The boy is dreadfully overtired and . . ."

Roland turned.

"Oh." The lady stopped at once, two or three steps away. Her face was nearly hidden by the brim of her hat, but the lips and chin beneath curved exactly as they did in his dreams. Her plaid scarf wrapped around a neck that he knew would be long and sinuous, would melt into the delicate flesh of her chest and shoulders, covered presently and sensibly by a dark wool coat.

"Roland," she said, in a whisper.

Of course he was dreaming. She couldn't possibly be real. A mere figment of his weary imagination; the strain of the journey, taking its toll on his wits.

"Lady Somerton," he said, making a little bow, so the

rain dropped from his hat in a single sheet. Since it was a dream, he might as well play his part. "What a charming surprise. I have just been making myself acquainted with your son."

Son. The word echoed in his head.

"Lord Roland," she said, dipping her head. She folded her gloved hands before her. "Indeed, a very great surprise. I should not have . . . Oh, Philip, *really!*"

Roland wheeled around, just in time to watch the tip of the boy's tongue disappear into his cherubic mouth.

"I'm so terribly sorry." She swept past him to take Philip's hand. "He's normally such a *good* boy. It's the journey, and his nursemaid was taken ill in Milan, and . . . oh, Philip, *do* be good and apologize to his lordship."

"You told me to wait where it was dry," Philip said, looking up earnestly at his mother's face.

"So I did," she said, bending next to him, "but I never told you to accost unsuspecting gentlemen in the doorway. Say you're sorry, Philip, and let his lordship pass. He's dreadfully wet."

"Sorry," Philip said.

"Philip, *really.*"

The boy sighed and turned his face to Roland. "I'm most awfully sorry, your lordship. I shall never do it again."

Roland bowed solemnly. "Quite all right, old chap. Quite all right. The heat of the moment. I've done far worse myself."

"That's very good, Philip. Very good," Lady Somerton said. "Now let his lordship pass."

Philip moved grudgingly aside.

"Thank you, sir," Roland said, still solemn, and climbed the steps. He turned in the doorway and removed his hat. "Have you just arrived, madam? I understand they're quite occupied tonight."

"Yes, just now," she said, glancing upward, so the full force of her blue eyes struck him like a most un-dreamlike blow to the noggin. "But I'm sure we shall find a room. Lady Morley is speaking to the landlord this instant, and . . . well, you know Lady Morley."

"Lady Morley, by Gad!" He smiled. "Are the two of you taking a tour? Dashed beastly time of year for it."

She straightened, her hand still clutching Philip's. She didn't return his smile. "I suppose you could call it that. And you, Lord Roland? Are you on your way to Florence, perhaps?"

"No, no. Just left it, in fact. I'm here with my brother and . . . and another fellow. We're . . ." *We're off to spend a year in a drafty Italian castle, devoting ourselves like monks to algebra and Plato and God knows what else. Smashing time.*

Her eyebrows lifted expectantly.

Roland gathered himself. "Well, never mind that. I do hope . . . That is, if I can be of any service . . ."

"No, no." Her eyes dropped. "We're quite all right."

"Are you going in just now?"

"No, I'm . . . I'm waiting for someone."

He peered into the darkness behind her. "Can't you wait inside? It's frightfully wet."

"She'll only be a minute." Her voice was quiet and resolute, just as he remembered it. Rather irritating, that: If he were taking the trouble to dream about her, mightn't she do something more dramatic? More fantastical? Tear off her dress, perhaps, and leap into his arms, and engage him in sexual congress against the wall of the inn, with the rain streaming down her body?

Oh yes. *That* would be a worthwhile dream indeed.

"Very well, then." He made a little bow. "I expect I shall see you shortly."

"Yes, I expect so." As if the prospect were about as appealing as an appointment with the tooth-drawer. She turned away, dismissing him, and shifted the boy's hand to her other arm.

From the innyard a voice shrieked, "Lilibet, you'll never guess what I've found in the stables!" and little Philip shouted back, "Cousin Abigail, come look, the strangest fellow!"

The dream was taking a most unwanted turn.

Roland walked swiftly through the doorway and into the busy warmth of the common room, leaving Lady Elizabeth Somerton and her son under the portico.

For God's sake, Penhallow. We've been waiting for hours," drawled the Duke of Wallingford, setting down his cup. His eyebrows shot upward at the sight of Roland's face. "What's this, then? Seen a ghost?"

"I believe I have," Roland said. He tossed his hat on the table and swung his coat from his shoulders in a shower of droplets. "You'll never guess the apparition I perceived outside, here of all the bloody godforsaken innyards of the world. Is that wine?"

"The local swill," the duke said, pouring from the pitcher into an empty cup. "I don't make guesses, as a rule, but I'd venture your ghost has something to do with the Dowager Marchioness of Morley. Am I right?"

Roland slumped atop the chair opposite, his bones sinking gratefully into the sturdy frame. "Seen her, have you?"

"Heard her. We were endeavoring to remain unnoticed." Wallingford pushed the cup toward his brother. "Have a drink, old man. Food should be arriving shortly, God willing."

Phineas Burke leaned forward from his seat next to Wallingford. "She's been arguing with the landlord this past quarter hour," he said. "The most infernal din. They've gone upstairs to see the room."

"Mark my words," Wallingford said, "we'll be tossed out on our ears and forced to sleep in the commons."

"Surely not," Roland said, drinking deep. "You're the damned Duke of Wallingford. What the jolly use is it, being a duke, if you can't keep a room at an inn?"

"Mark my words," Wallingford repeated darkly.

Burke pressed his index finger into the worn wood before him. "For one thing, they're women," he said, "and for another, it's Lady Morley. Carries all before her, the old dragon."

"Hardly old," said Roland charitably. "I daresay she hasn't seen thirty yet. Hullo, is that our dinner?"

A girl wobbled toward them, homespun skirts twisting about her legs, bearing a large pewter tray filled with chicken and thick country bread. A pretty girl, Roland thought idly, slanting her an assessing look. She caught his look and set down the tray with an awkward crash, just as the voice of Alexandra, Lady Morley erupted from the stairs, cutting through the buzzing din of the other travelers in a vicious attack on the Italian tongue. "It isn't at all acceptable, *non possibloe*, do you hear me? We are English, *anglese*. We can't possibly . . . Oh! Your Grace!"

"Mark my words," muttered Wallingford. He threw down his napkin and rose. "Lady Morley," he said. "Good evening. I trust you're well."

Her ladyship stood on the stairs, tall and imperious, her chestnut hair pulled with unnatural neatness into a smart chignon at the nape of her neck. She'd been a handsome girl several years ago, before her marriage to the Marquess of Morley, and was now an even handsomer woman, all cheekbones and glittering brown eyes. She wasn't exactly to Roland's taste, with her strong, bold-featured face, but he could appreciate her, rather as one appreciated the classical statuary in one's formal gardens, without precisely wanting to embrace it.

"Darling Wallingford," she said, continuing down the stairs toward them, her voice shifting effortlessly from commanding to cajoling, "you're just the man I was hoping for. I can't seem to make these Italian fellows understand that English ladies, however sturdy and liberal minded, simply *cannot* be expected to sleep in a room with strangers. *Male* strangers. *Foreign* male strangers. Don't you agree, Your Grace?" She stopped in front of them.

"Are there no rooms available upstairs, madam?"

She shrugged beautifully, her tailored black shoulder making a practiced little arc through the air. "A small room, a very small room. Hardly large enough for Lady Somerton's boy to sleep in, let alone the three of us." Her gaze shifted to Roland and she started visibly, her entire body snapping backward. "Lord Roland!" she exclaimed. "I'd no idea! Have you . . . my cousin . . . Lady Somerton . . . good God!"

Roland bowed affably. Why not? It seemed the thing to do. "I had the great honor of meeting her ladyship outside on the . . . the portico, a moment ago. And her charming son, of course."

A choking noise emerged from Lady Morley's trim throat, as if a laugh were suppressing itself. "Charming! Yes, quite." Her mouth opened and closed. She cleared her throat.

Roland, watching her, felt his own shock begin to slide away, numbness replaced by awareness. You could not deny the reality of Alexandra, Lady Morley. She crackled with reality. And if Lady Morley were real, then . . .

His nerves took up a strange and inauspicious tingling.

It was true. He hadn't dreamt it. Lilibet was here.

Stop that, he told his nerves sternly, but it only made things worse. Only made things more real, only made Lilibet's presence—the actual existence of her living body not ten yards away—more real. He had the disturbing premonition that he was about to do something rash.

Lady Morley wrung her hands and looked back at the duke beseechingly. "Look here, Wallingford, I really must throw myself on your mercy. Surely you see our little dilemma. Your rooms are ever so much larger, palatial really, and *two* of them! You can't possibly, in all conscience . . ." Her voice drifted, turned upward. She returned to Roland. "My dear Penhallow. Think of poor Lilibet, sleeping in . . . in a *chair*, quite possibly . . . with all these strangers."

Burke, standing next to Roland with all the good cheer of a lion disturbed from his nap, cleared his throat with an ominous rumble. "Did it not, perhaps, occur to you, Lady Morley, to reserve rooms in advance?"

Roland winced. Damn the fellow. Old scientific Burke was hardly the sort of man to endure arrogant young marchionesses with patience, and patience was called for just now: patience and delicacy and the utmost exquisite sensitivity.

Because Lilibet was here. Here, within reach.

Lady Morley's cat-shaped eyes fastened on him in the famous Morley glare. "As a matter of fact, it did, Mr. . . ." She raised her eyebrows expressively. "I'm so terribly sorry, sir. I don't *quite* believe I caught your name."

"I beg your pardon, Lady Morley," said the Duke of Wallingford. "How remiss of me. I have the great honor to present to you—perhaps you may have come across his name, in your philosophical studies—Mr. Phineas Fitzwilliam Burke, of the Royal Society."

"Your servant, madam," he said, with a slight inclination of his head.

"Burke," she said, and then her eyes widened an instant. "Phineas Burke. Of course. The Royal Society. Yes, of course. Everyone knows of Mr. Burke. I found . . . the *Times*, last month . . . your remarks on electrical . . . that new sort of . . ." She drew in a fortifying breath, and then smiled, warmly even. "That is to say, of course we reserved rooms. I sent the wire days ago, if memory serves. But we were delayed in Milan. The boy's nursemaid took ill, you see, and I expect our message did not reach our host in time." She sent a hard look in the landlord's direction.

"Look here." Roland heard his own voice with horror. Here it was. The rash thing, unstoppable as one of Great-Aunt Julia's obscene anecdotes at the dinner table. "Enough of this rubbish. We shouldn't dream of causing any inconvenience to you and your friends, Lady Morley. Not for an instant. Should we, Wallingford?"

"No, damn it," the duke grunted, folding his arms.

"Burke?"

"Bloody hell," muttered Burke, under his breath.

"You see, Lady Morley? All quite willing and happy and so on. I daresay Burke can take the little room upstairs, as he's such a tiresome, misanthropic old chap, and my brother and I shall be quite happy to . . ."—he swept his arm to take in the dark depths of the common room—"make ourselves comfortable downstairs. Will that suit?"

Lady Morley clasped her elegant gloved hands together. "Darling Penhallow. I knew you'd oblige us. Thanks so *awfully*, my dear; you can't imagine how thankful I am for your generosity." She turned to the landlord. "Do you understand? *Comprendo?* You may remove His Grace's luggage from the rooms upstairs and bring up our trunks at once. Ah! Cousin Lilibet! There you are at last. Have you sorted out the trunks?"

Roland couldn't help himself. He swiveled to the doorway, desperate to see her, now that he'd recovered his wits; desperate for even a glimpse of her, without all the rain and darkness and bloody damned *hats* in the way. He wanted to know everything. Had she changed? Grown cynical and world-weary? Had her fresh-faced beauty faded under the blight of marriage to the legendarily dissolute Earl of Somerton?

Did he wish that it had?

She was kneeling by the door, unbuttoning her son's coat. Typical of her, that she would make the boy comfortable first, the little martyr. She turned her head to answer her cousin, her voice as even and well modulated as ever, despite the raspy edge Roland had noticed before. "Yes, they've all been unloaded. The fellow's coming in the back." She straightened and handed the boy his coat and began unbuttoning her own.

Roland held his breath. Her gloved fingers found the buttons expertly and slid them through the holes, exposing inch after inch of a practical dark blue traveling suit with a high white collar, pristine and ladylike, her bosom (fuller now, or was that his imagination?) curving tidily beneath the perfect tailoring of her jacket.

He felt a sharp poke in his ribs. "Oh, for God's sake. Keep your tongue in your mouth, you dog," hissed his brother.

The landlord hurried down the steps to assist her. She had that effect, Roland thought crossly. "I take the coat, milady," he said, dipping obsequiously, folding the wet wool over his arm as if it were cloth of gold. "And the hat. The hat. Ah, *mia donna*, it is so wet. You come to the fire, you dry. *Mia povera donna*."

"Thank you," she said. "*Grazie*." She allowed herself to be drawn to the fire, smoothing her dark hair with one hand, pulling young Philip with the other. The light gleamed gold against her pale skin, casting shadows beneath her cheekbones. She looked tired, Roland thought, taking an involuntary step in her direction before he remembered himself. Concern! For Lady Somerton! As if she couldn't take perfectly good care of herself without him. She'd proven that well enough.

Roland looked around and found that both Burke and Wallingford had resumed their seats, and he was standing there like the village idiot, staring after her ladyship's decorously clothed backside.

TWO

For a small folded square of notepaper, it burned with unnatural energy through the material of Lilibet's best navy blue traveling suit to brand the skin beneath.

She ought to have tossed it away at once, of course. Roland had pressed it into her hand in the bustle of greetings before dinner, and she'd been too stunned to throw it on the fire with a haughty quirk of her chin, or whatever her mother would have expected of her.

Now, of course, she couldn't remove it; not with the sharp eyes of Abigail and Philip trained upon her.

Philip, especially. Her son, her innocent angel, her damned stubborn nemesis, the one good thing she'd salvaged from six years of misery.

He didn't want to go to sleep. Not unusual in a boy of five and a half, of course, but Lilibet, who would have given anything to collapse into bed herself, felt almost affronted by his reluctance. "Darling, you're exhausted," she pleaded. "Just lie still and close your eyes."

"I'm not tired," he said, eyes rolling. "I'm not." He kicked off the covers.

Lilibet drew them back.

Philip kicked them off again.

She felt it rising, the tide of her temper, so strong this time it took an almost superhuman strength to muscle it downward again. Be calm, she told herself, as she always did. Dignity. Clarity. She counted to ten, eyes closed, pausing on each number.

There. She opened her eyes.

Philip wasn't on the bed.

She spun around and saw Abigail, laughing, snatching him up in her arms just before he reached the door. "Naughty boy," she said, and rubbed her nose into his tummy. "Naughty, wicked, despicable boy." She blew rude noises into his skin, until he was giggling helplessly, writhing with joy.

"Abigail, you'll overexcite him," Lilibet whispered, and put her fingers to her temples.

How heavy could a piece of paper be? It dragged in her pocket like a stone: the massive, sharp-sided kind they collected in more primitive cultures to lob at adulterers.

"You don't deserve a story, you dreadful rascal, but I'll tell one anyway," Abigail said, tossing him into the bed. "But you've got to eat this bun for me while I'm telling it. It's a magic bun, you see." She drew it from her pocket and held it before him. "A wonderfully magic bun. It lets you understand me, even though I'll be telling you the entire story . . . in . . . Italian."

"Italian! No, you won't. You don't know Italian."

"Yes, she does," Lilibet said, drawing up the blankets. "She knows it perfectly."

"But this bun," Abigail said, rotating it solemnly, "will make the words sound just like English."

"Ha," Philip said. But his eyes narrowed.

Abigail shrugged. "If you don't believe me, then fine. *C'era una volta, viveva un re e sua figlia . . .*"

Philip snatched the bun from her fingers and trained his eyes on her lips.

Abigail said: ". . . *in un castello antico solitario in cima a una collina.*"

Philip bit into the bun.

"The queen had died long ago, and the king was so stricken with grief that he ordered all the ladies of the castle to be banished, so he might never see another woman again," Abigail continued, without missing a beat.

Philip stared at Abigail's lips, transfixed, nibbling away at the bun. Lilibet watched his little body relax into the mattress, his energy fading and settling around him. His eyelids drooped, and his hand dropped against the pillow, still clutching the bun between his fingers. Abigail continued on a minute or two longer, until his breathing became deep and regular and peaceful, the candlelight glowing softly around his round, smooth cheek.

"They look so innocent when they are asleep," Lilibet said softly, brushing the hair from his forehead. "It makes me feel guilty for being angry before."

"You were angry?" Abigail asked, and Lilibet, turning to her, saw that she was genuinely surprised.

"Yes, of course."

Abigail straightened from the bed and smiled at her, a great, wide smile in her oval face. "Even-tempered Lilibet. I don't think I've ever seen you angry."

Lilibet looked back at her son's sleeping face. "All the time," she said. "I'm angry all the time. Only I've learned how to hide it."

"You don't need to hide it," Abigail said. "We'd understand."

No, you wouldn't, Lilibet thought. All that anger, those wicked, immoral emotions, kept in check by a network of fine interlocking threads that strained and cut viciously and yet somehow held against the pressure. *You wouldn't understand at all, Abigail, my artless virgin.*

"Are you angry at *him*?" Abigail ventured. "At Lord Somerton?"

"Of course not," Lilibet lied. "I don't know why you should ask."

"I'm not a fool, Lilibet. Just because I'm not married doesn't mean I don't hear things. And if we're running halfway across Europe just to escape him . . ."

"Eavesdropper."

"Of course I eavesdrop. There's no better way to find out what one's not supposed to hear." Abigail hesitated and reached out to clasp Lilibet's hand. "I know he's a beast, for one thing."

"He's a man."

Abigail's hand squeezed hers. "You'll feel better when we reach the castle tomorrow. Think of it, a whole year to ourselves! You'll be safe, you'll be among friends. No one can get past Alexandra. Everything will sort itself out."

"Yes, of course." Lilibet drew her hand away. She moved restlessly to the wing chair in the corner, oddly out of place against the rustic plaster wall, as if left behind by some English traveler who couldn't pay his bill but happened to be transporting wing chairs upholstered in hideous bile green paisley. She dropped herself into it and trained her eyes on the sleeping figure of her child. "Go back downstairs, Abigail. I'll watch him."

"And leave you by yourself?" Abigail protested.

Lilibet smiled. "Abigail, darling, I know very well that you're desperate to go back down to that common room. Don't think I didn't see the way you were examining poor Wallingford."

Abigail's arms crossed against her ribs. "I wasn't. He's a perfectly ordinary duke. There are *princes* in Italy, Lilibet. *Princes.* Much more interesting than dull English dukes."

"Go, Abigail. I'm all done in, really." She made a whisking movement with her hand. "Go, for heaven's sake."

Abigail left at last, and Lilibet leaned her head back against the chair with a sigh of relief, free at last to let the urgent thought explode across her brain: *Roland.*

The shock had been so great, at first, that she hadn't even felt it. It was as if he were a ghost, conjured up by her exhausted brain. Lord Roland Penhallow, here in a dreary, wet hillside in Tuscany, on the doorstep of the very inn she was about to enter herself, locked in negotiation with her own son? The coincidence was too catastrophic to be true.

Only later, when she'd made the arrangements for the

trunks, gathered Philip to her side, and swept through the doorway of the inn, had the truth smacked her in the jaw. Never in her life had she felt so self-conscious as she had in that moment, removing Philip's coat and then her own, feeling Roland's eyes trained upon her every gesture. Her hands had shaken; had he seen it? Did he care, if he had?

Six years; six and a half, really, since last she had met him. Of course his ardor had faded. It had faded quickly, if reports were true. Lord Roland's bachelor exploits about London were the stuff of legend. Mistresses of preposterous unsuitability, country weekends that had gone on for months, pranks and hijinks of fiendish ingenuity and frivolity. Race-horses in the Prince's bedroom, to her certain knowledge.

The ingenuity she recognized; the frivolity she did not. This Roland of scandal and innuendo could not possibly be the same young man she had met at a river party in Richmond nearly seven years ago; the handsome brother of the Duke of Wallingford, laughing and careless and eloquent, with a knack for verse that might be achingly silly or breathtakingly romantic. She had just come to London, fresh from the schoolroom, and fell in love with him at once. "Darling, here's Lord Roland Penhallow, Wallingford's brother, who's been begging me for an introduction this half hour," her hostess had said. Roland's hazel eyes had gleamed, and he'd bent over her hand, and she was his.

They'd lost little time going conveniently astray in the shrubbery, while everyone else gathered by the tea tables near the water. He'd wanted to know everything about her; she'd told him what little there was to know, and he'd seemed fascinated by every word. "But that's marvelous!" she could still hear him exclaim, into the motionless, pollen-laden May air, his cheekbones faintly flushed and his arm steady and warm beneath hers. "I've been a devoted disciple of Browning for years. I'd no idea there was a girl in the world who'd agree with me."

"He's indispensable, of course," Lilibet remembered herself saying, "but his work suffered badly after his marriage."

"Are you arguing against marriage, Miss Harewood?" he'd asked, leaning toward her, eyes merry.

"I've no intention of marrying at all," she'd said. "I believe there should be no obligation on either partner. In a free union, a genuine union, the marriage vow would be utterly superfluous."

He'd thrown back his head and laughed, all careless, youthful joy, and she'd laughed with him. Later, as they'd emerged from the shrubbery, he'd drawn her back and pressed his lips against the back of her hand, so the heat of his breath penetrated the thin kidskin of her glove and warmed the marrow of her bones. His fingers had brushed once along the underside of her wrist, in the gap of bare skin between her glove and her sleeve. "Do you stay in London all season, Miss Harewood?" he'd asked, quite soft.

"Yes," she'd replied, unable to say anything more.

"Then so I shall, as well," he'd said, and they had rejoined the party, flushed and alive, and the air around them had shimmered with anticipation. Even now, after everything, Lilibet could feel her heart accelerate, feel the thread of excitement in her veins that the memory always awakened. The night before her marriage, she'd burned all the notes and letters, had locked away all the memories, because it was her duty and because they were little use to her, now that she was marrying another man. All the memories, that is, except for the scene of that first meeting. Surely God could not deny her one innocent afternoon, she'd pleaded: a few paltry hours against all the days and months and years ahead of her.

Lilibet slipped her hand into her pocket and fingered the folded edge of the paper there. Such a look he'd given her, dark and meaning, when he put it in her hand. Not an innocent look at all, not the sort of look one gave a woman when offering a note that read *Bread moldy; avoid at all costs* or else *Large stain on back of your dress; suggest immediate soaking in bicarbonate.*

She couldn't control her thoughts entirely; she'd given up on that long ago. But she could control her actions. Whatever her husband had done, whatever the lengths to which she now went to protect herself and her son, her own conduct was spotless, blameless. She should not open this note.

Her hand slid upward and out of the pocket, with the paper trapped between her thumb and forefinger.

She stared at the innocuous white square for a moment, and then at Philip, asleep in his little bed, eyelashes spread like fans against his cheeks.

She turned away from the boy and opened the note.

I have long wished to assure myself of the happiness of my dear friend, whose honour remains sacred to me. If she can spare a moment or two at half eleven, I shall be waiting with all reverence at the end of the stable block.

Unsigned, of course. Considerate, gentlemanly: the Roland she recognized, rather than the Roland of public reputation. The Roland she trusted.

Her Roland.

She read the note again, ran her fingers over the black letters, lifted it to her nose and inhaled the plain, unadorned scents of paper and ink. She folded it and placed it back in her pocket and drew out her watch.

Not quite nine o'clock.

With silent steps she went over to the bed and knelt beside the sleeping body of her son. His hair made little dark whorls on his forehead; she wound and unwound them around her forefinger, savoring the silken feel, fine and strong and unbreakable. Below them, the sounds of the common room drifted up through the wooden floor: muffled thumps and laughter and the low vibrating hum of conversation. People connecting, life going on.

She rose, picked up her book from the table by the bed, and settled herself back in the bile green English armchair to read, with her watch tucked into her lap.

THREE

Abetting man by nature, Roland gave himself about four-to-one odds against Lilibet's appearance at eleven thirty.

Not that long odds troubled him much. He'd faced them often enough. He set his lantern on a wooden shelf and leaned against the stable wall, arms crossed, listening for the sound of human movement through the faint drum of rain against the roof above. The warm scent of the stable filled the air around him: horses and leather and grain and manure, all mingled together, familiar and comforting. The smell of his boyhood, of that authentic Roland who still existed, somewhere, beneath all the layers of frivolous disguise.

Of course Lilibet would have heard all the stories. Much of the energy he'd thrown into his role had come from the angry knowledge that she'd be told of his latest absurdity, his most recent rashness, by some gossiping London countess. She'd hear of his actresses and his pranks, and know that he wasn't wasting away for regret of her blue eyes and ringing laugh. The luminous Lilibet he'd once adored.

And how he'd adored her. He could still picture her in

his mind, that first moment at Lady Whatsit's river party. He'd met pretty debutantes without number, of course; all very charming and that sort of thing, laughing like songbirds into the dulcet spring air. But Elizabeth Harewood had stood out at once. Not just her beauty, though that in itself was endless, flawless, a miracle of color and freshness and symmetry. No, it was something about the amused, half-shy gleam in her eye, the queenly way she held herself, the mixture of reserve and freedom with which she cast her eye about the scene. She had something *in* her, something different, noble and reticent and irreverent all at once. A streak of something earthy and passionate, deep inside her, carefully hidden. And then he'd wrangled an introduction, and led her into the shrubbery and talked to her, and he'd known within five minutes that he couldn't live without her.

He'd courted her properly. He'd intended to wait until the end of summer to declare himself, just to show how steady were his intentions. At the end of August, he'd returned home from his Norway expedition, flush with success, and gone straight to his club for a late supper. He'd intended to present himself at her door at the earliest possible hour the next day, nosegay in hand. He'd just tucked into his capon and Burgundy when Sir Andrew Greentree, that ass, that sneering weasel, had dropped into the chair opposite. *I say, Penhallow, you're taking the news well.* And Roland had answered, stupidly, what news? *Why, that the Harewood girl's gone and engaged herself to Somerton, ha-ha! A Christmas wedding, they say.*

He'd nearly taken off Greentree's head.

He'd nearly taken off his own.

And now? Was he still angry with her? What, exactly, had possessed him to write her that note? What did he mean to say to her, if she came? What could possibly be said, after all these years?

He leaned down to pick up a stray stalk of hay from the bales stacked nearby and twirl it between his fingers. The kerosene lantern cast out a steady golden glow, revealing the empty corner in which he stood, the blanketed heaps of

Burke's machinery sheltered in the next bay, the faint outline of the horse boxes farther up the row. He slipped his
watch out of his pocket and held it against the light. The
soft snitch of wheels and cogs counted out each second into
the silence.

A quarter to twelve.

A movement caught the periphery of his senses.

Roland straightened. His pulse pounded hard and fast in
his ears. He ought to call out, he knew; this was hardly high
danger. But over six long years of training and experience
held his tongue in place.

A small, dark shape crossed the shadows by the doorway and turned to the light from the lantern. "Roland?" she
whispered, the thread of sound like a fist to his gut. "Is
that you?"

He stepped forward. "Yes, I'm here."

She walked toward him in lithe, graceful strides, not
self-conscious at all, no hint of any kind that she might not
be crossing a drawing room to greet a morning visitor, rather
than walking down the aisle of an Italian stable to meet a
man who had once been her ardent admirer. Raindrops glittered and fell from the brim of her hat; she shook them off
with a little toss of her head. "I never thought to pack an
umbrella," she said, coming to a stop a few feet away. "One
doesn't think of rain in Italy."

"No," he said. His mouth dried. Every thought fled his
brain except one: *Lilibet.* Here, before him. Alive and real
and infinitely desirable.

She put out her hand. "How are you, Lord Roland? You
took me quite by surprise on the portico. I hope I didn't seem
unfriendly. It really is a great pleasure to see you again, after
all these years."

Her voice rang in his ears, sincere and amicable. He
took her hand and held it briefly. "Yes, of course. A very
great pleasure. I . . . I'm sorry to have . . . I suppose I could
have found another place to meet you. Somewhere more
suitable."

"Oh no." Her pink lips curled upward from beneath her

hat; he couldn't quite make out her eyes in the shadows. "It's splendid. Proper young matrons don't often have the opportunity for clandestine meetings in Italian stables. I shall dine on it for years."

He swallowed. The curve of her cheek gleamed with rain in the light from the lantern; he could just make out the pale skin of her neck, emerging from the collar of her coat. "I didn't think you'd come, to be honest," he said.

She plucked at her gloves. "Of course I came," she said, shifting her voice lower. "Of course I came. We parted as friends, did we not? I hope . . . I have always wished you well. I have always prayed for your happiness."

"And I for yours."

She said nothing to that. Her head tilted downward, as if she were reading her next lines from the toes of her shoes.

"Have you been happy, Lady Somerton?" he asked softly.

"Of course. My life has been quite full."

"No regrets at all?"

She looked up again. "Of course I have regrets. Who hasn't? But when one makes decisions, important decisions, one can't look back. One can't imagine what might have been, or one would go mad."

He took a single step forward. "And what might have been, Lady Somerton?"

Her lips parted, taking in a little breath. "I . . . I don't know. I never had a chance to know. You were off in Norway, fishing for your blasted salmon."

"Yes. Salmon." His hand clenched at his side. Norway: his first assignment, a whirlwind of excitement. He'd presented himself in Sir Edward's office on a Wednesday, and found himself rowing through a fjord at midnight on Friday.

"You were gone for weeks. I daresay you must have caught enough salmon to feed half of England."

"It was all such an adventure," he said. "I lost track of time, I suppose. But I hardly expected to find you engaged when I returned. To Lord Somerton, of all men."

"Yes. Well. Neither did I. But you were gone for ages, without a word. Not a single word. And everyone was terribly persuasive, you see. My parents, his lordship."

"I daresay."

"I tried to write, but no one knew your direction. I went . . ." She laughed, a thin little laugh. "You'll think me silly. I even went to the Norwegian consulate one afternoon, when Mother thought I was shopping. I asked them for a list of hotels. They must have thought I was mad."

"Oh, God, Lilibet . . ."

"Ridiculous, wasn't it?" She laughed again and walked past him, to where an old harness hung from the wall, its leather dry and curling with age. She fingered it with one hand. "In any case, they weren't terribly helpful."

"If I had known . . ."

"But you didn't. And I can't regret anything, can I? To regret anything is to regret Philip, and he . . . well, I suppose you'll have a child of your own, one day, and you'll understand . . ." Her voice quivered to a halt.

"I'm so awfully sorry, Lilibet. I was a fool, an idiot. I ought to have spoken before I left. I meant to, but our plans . . . well, I didn't have time. I shall . . . I know you don't feel the same, but *I* shall regret it all my life."

"Don't, Roland . . ."

"No, you *must* let me say it. You'll be gone tomorrow, and so will I, and God knows when we'll see each other again. In some damned drawing room, I suppose." He shook his head.

A tremor went across her shoulders. She turned to him, with the lantern light full in her face, illuminating the steadfast blue of her eyes, the gleam of wetness on her lashes. She dashed her hand across her brow. "I shouldn't have come," she said. "This was so foolish. I only wanted to let you know that I was . . . that I'm quite all right. I only meant to be firm and friendly, and now look."

"Don't say anything," he said. "You needn't. You've a son and a husband. I only wish . . . I only want to say that I envy them both. I should have wished to do things differently. I was an idiot, a young fool who thought the world would stand still and wait . . ."

The words stopped in his throat.

Before his brain even became conscious of the disturbance behind him, he leapt forward and put out the lantern.

"Roland!" she exclaimed, the last syllable muffled by his hand over her mouth.

"Hush," he breathed in her ear. "Someone's entering."

Lilibet's brain spun under the shock of Roland's body against hers. His fingers pressed her lips; his broad chest crushed her breasts; his breath, sweet and heavy with wine and some sugary dessert, curled around her face. For an instant she froze.

Roland, she thought. *This is Roland's body, Roland's touch.*

She began to thaw, bit by bit, skin and bone and muscle softening under his.

As if her body's acquiescence were a signal of some kind, his hand relaxed and slipped away from her mouth, just grazing the side of her breast, her hip, before bracing itself on the wall behind her.

She could see nothing. She could hear nothing, except the sound of his breathing.

"Who is it?" she remembered to ask, mimicking his own faint whisper. He was so close, she nearly touched his neck with her lips.

"Hush," he breathed again. "Don't move."

Now she heard it: the rustle of feet against the wooden floor, the faint, careful clack of booted heels that wanted to be silent. Roland was listening, too. She felt the hum of tension in his body, the readiness. He covered her, filled her every sense, and yet he wasn't paying attention to her at all. She might have been a doll, a statue.

The footsteps grew louder and then stopped. She dared

not turn her head to look, but she sensed the intruder was not far away. The next bay, perhaps, with all the blanketed heaps.

A long pause, and then the footsteps resumed, more slowly now, less regular. She closed her eyes and leaned her head against the wall. It hardly seemed worth imagining what this unknown person was doing, as she and Roland rested here in the shadows, unnoticed. Far more agreeable to luxuriate in the nearness of his body, an unexpected gift, a treasure she'd never thought to receive.

She did not raise her arms to enfold him. That would be wrong. She only stood, with her fingertips pressed hard and resolute against the cold wall, and absorbed his body, the way it fit perfectly around hers: her face tucked into his neck, his chest holding her shoulders steady, his hips bracketing her belly. She noted every detail. The rustling continued nearby, odd little noises she couldn't interpret, like a dream at the outside of her consciousness.

Her nose brushed against the skin of his neck. He smelled of wool and clean rain and . . . something else, something familiar . . . his soap, perhaps? She inhaled deeply, quietly, and in a flash she was on the riverbank at Henley again, and Roland had just emerged from the Leander boathouse, bathed and dressed and flushed with victory.

He'd been surrounded by well-wishers, of course: the hero of the hour, having stroked the eight to a heart-stopping half-length win in the Grand Challenge Cup, and everybody wanted to clap his back and shake his hand and steal some taste of his magic. He'd put on his golden smile and nodded and done his duty, but his eyes had roamed about, peering past hats and over shoulders, on the lookout.

For her.

She still remembered the way his face had lit into joy, when at last he'd matched eyes with her. Her mother hadn't let her into the middle of the crowd, of course. He'd had to sidle past everyone, murmuring excuses, ignoring a score of flirtatious glances. And then he was next to her, tipping his straw boater in her mother's direction, bending into her ear: *Did you watch the race?*

Of course, she'd said. *You were marvelous. I lost my voice, cheering you on.*

The hot June sun had beat against her hat, and the crowd around them had hummed with noise. He'd had to lean close to her cheek to hear her words, and her brain had spun with the clean, newly washed scent of his neck, the delicious flavor of his soap. It had seemed somehow scandalous, that she should know such an intimate detail about him. She'd wanted to drink it in, to lick it off his skin.

He'd chuckled, right next to her ear. She'd felt the vibration of his laugh, the brush of his hat brim against hers, and—knowing, she supposed, that her mother couldn't hear him—he'd murmured back: *Sweetheart, I'll lay all my laurels at your feet tonight, I promise.*

Her mother had drawn her away before she could reply, but she'd given him a parting look that said *oh yes, yes*, and the scent of his skin had lingered in her nose all afternoon and all that evening, while he'd waltzed her around his brother's ballroom at the celebration party as if no other woman existed in the world.

For a long, weightless moment, it almost seemed she could hear that white-clothed crowd chattering again, could feel the sun melt the crown of her hat, could see an eternal summer lying before her. Her mother had never drawn her away to shake hands with the heir to a dukedom, and she'd never married Somerton, and she still stood on the riverbank with Lord Roland Penhallow's coaxing voice in her ear and the sweet scent of his soap filling her head.

Roland's body stiffened, jolting her out of her daze, back into the coldness of the present.

The soft footsteps had halted, and new ones entered the building: firm, purposeful, nothing to hide. The feet marched in their direction—even Lilibet could tell that—closer and closer, until she squeezed her eyes in anticipation of discovery and pressed her back into the wall as if it could close around her. Roland held himself preternaturally still, his body forming a shelter around hers.

The new footsteps stopped abruptly. A male voice penetrated the stillness, low and hard. She couldn't quite make out the words, but they sounded unmistakably English.

A female voice emerged, the first intruder, answering him.

Oh God. Who was it? It couldn't be Abigail.

Alexandra?

Alexandra? Meeting a strange man in an Italian stable? Surely not.

A slight quiver moved across Roland's chest. He whispered in her ear: "Lady Morley, by God."

Don't laugh, Roland, she thought. *For God's sake, don't laugh.* She fought the desire herself: amusement and relief and horror, all muddled together. What if she and Roland were found, clenched together in the darkness, in what could only be a lover's embrace?

They were exchanging words, Alexandra and her male visitor. Who was it? Wallingford, probably. Hadn't there been something between the two of them, long ago? Lilibet opened her eyes at last, trying to peer past Roland into the darkness, but his chest and shoulder engulfed her, and the only light came from a pair of dark lanterns hooked near the doorway.

Another quiver shook Roland's chest, stronger this time. He must have known who the other man was.

The voices continued, soft and intimate. Good God, they weren't going to . . . they weren't meeting here to do *that*! Not Alexandra, not with Wallingford.

Were they?

Lilibet rolled her forehead into Roland's shoulder. No. Anything but that. She could not stand here in the arms of Lord Roland Penhallow, of all the men in the world, and listen to her cousin engage in carnal union with the Duke of Wallingford.

Please, Lord. *Please.*

She listened with horrified fascination as the voices rose

and fell, always too quiet to discern, the round English tones floating across the cold air, an occasional word breaking through the murmur: *ravish* and *stepladder* and *devil*.

Damn the both of them.

Lilibet never swore aloud, of course, but in her thoughts she profaned as frequently as the captain of a China clipper, though she supposed not with as much potency and variety. Hers had been a sheltered life, after all.

The voices dropped to whispers. Bloody hell.

And then, without warning, the words stopped altogether.

She held her breath, waiting to hear the rustle of clothing, the telltale groans and sighs and gasps. The sound of flesh against flesh, of bodies thumping on the ground or—she shuddered—against the same wall that supported her now.

But all she heard were footsteps. Footsteps, treading back down the length of the stables, disappearing out into the night.

FOUR

Lilibet sagged into Roland's shoulder, shaking with laughter at last. His arms closed around her, held her upright as he laughed, too, in great suppressed jolts of his body. "Good God," he whispered, "I thought we were finished. Done for."

"I was afraid they would start to . . . oh Lord!" Tears formed at the corners of her eyes; she struggled to raise her hand between their bodies to brush the wetness away.

"Start to what?"

She blurted the words without thought. "That they were lovers!"

He chuckled. "No, no. Not that. I was only afraid I'd lose control entirely and give us away."

"Oh Lord." She covered her face with her hands. "They'd have thought *we* were . . ."

"When of course we were only . . ."

The air turned to crystal between them. Roland's hands dropped away; he took a short step backward. The separation, the loss of him, was like her heart hollowing out from her body.

"We were only . . ." she repeated softly.

". . . saying good-bye," he said. Without the lantern's glow, his voice came out of the void, unmoored from his beautiful face.

She didn't need to see his face. She knew exactly how it looked: how his hazel eyes crinkled at the corners when he smiled, how his golden brown hair curled on his forehead. How his strong jaw met his sturdy neck, how his full lips parted just before he spoke.

How would those lips feel upon hers?

She'd never known. Their years-ago courtship had been long on elegant words and clandestine glances, and short on physical expression. Proper English ladies, dutiful daughters of proper English ladies, did not accept kisses before engagement rings.

But she'd imagined his kisses, more than once, in the lonely dark hours of the night, curled in her bed, eyes dry and aching. She'd imagined more than that. She'd imagined how his body would feel atop hers. She'd imagined how his face would soften with passion as he looked down at her, how his legs and belly would stroke against her, how their limbs would entangle afterward as they drifted to sleep.

Imagined it, and despised herself in the cold light of morning.

No one would ever know, she thought. Tomorrow she and the other women and Philip would be off to hide in a hillside castle, and Roland would be off to Rome or Venice or somewhere equally amusing. They wouldn't meet again for ages, if at all. He was an honorable man; he'd never tell a soul. He'd take the secret to his grave.

Why not?

He was a man. He wouldn't refuse her.

Only God would know. And surely God would understand, would forgive her. It seemed—it almost seemed—that He had arranged this meeting, just for her.

Do it. Do it. Regret it later, if you must. But do it now, before it's too late. Before he's gone forever.

She lifted her hand and brushed his cheek with her fingers. "Yes. I suppose it *is* good-bye."

She couldn't see his reaction, but she felt it: a flicker of rigidity beneath her fingertips.

His hand appeared out of nowhere to cover hers. "Not good-bye," he said. "Never good-bye, you and I."

She was never sure, afterward, who kissed whom. One instant they were apart, his hand holding hers against his cheek, breaths mingling in the dank air, and in the next his mouth brushed her lips, gentle and tender, and his other hand cupped the curve of her head like an infant's.

"Lilibet," he whispered. "Oh, Lilibet."

"Don't say anything. Don't say a word."

He gathered her up and kissed her again, a lover's kiss, working her lips apart and tasting her, his mouth like silk and champagne and every forbidden thing. She could not hold back, not any longer; she met him unstintingly, stroked his tongue with hers, spread her fingers across the sides of his face, strained her body upward into his.

They kissed for the longest time, more than six years' worth of kisses, gentle and urgent and then gentle again: his lips sliding across her face to her ear, her jaw, her neck, and then returning to her mouth to absorb her sigh. Each movement, each tiny detail, rent a tear down some fabric at her core and sent an electric current of sensation sparking through her bones to the extreme tips of her fingers and toes and scalp. *Alive, I am alive*, she thought, and thrust her fingers up through the soft waves of hair at the back of his head.

His hands slipped downward. One came to rest at her waist; the other fingered the top button of her coat, inquiring.

She could not say the word *yes*. But she could arch her neck for his lips. She could drop her own hands to the smooth horn buttons of his coat and work them free with fingers that were no longer cold and numb, but tingling and dexterous. She could spread his unbuttoned coat apart and slide it across his broad shoulders until it hit the hay-strewn floor with a whispered *plop*.

Without words, he returned his hands to her coat, sliding each button out of its hole, his head bent forward and his rapid breath warming her face. Words jumbled together in her head, *darling* and *love* and *please* and *more* and *oh*, but she held them all in and concentrated only on Roland, on his hands uncovering her body and his face bent toward hers. Her eyes, accustomed now to the darkness, could just pick out his features in the ghostly light from the distant lanterns; she could just glimpse the way his lids half covered his eyes, as if he couldn't quite bear to open them fully.

The last button fell free, but he didn't remove her coat. Instead his fingers moved back to her neck, to the fastenings of her jacket, until the two sides hung apart and only her white silk shirtwaist and underclothes lay between them.

Her heart beat in a mad thumping rhythm beneath his active fingers. One by one he undid the buttons of her shirt-waist, down to her waist, his knuckles brushing her flesh, raising goose bumps.

His hand hovered. "Are you certain?" he said, in a reverent whisper.

She could not say *yes*. But she could grasp his hand and guide it beneath the silk of her shirtwaist; she could slide her own hands to his jacket and unbutton it, while her nerves tracked the hot touch of his fingers along the curve of her bosom and beneath the edge of her corset. She could part the edges of his jacket and tear his shirt from his trousers and slide her hands along the smooth skin at his waist, his abdomen. She could throw her head back in a silent cry as his hands—eager now, bold—freed her breasts from her stays and chemise; as he dropped to his knees before her and suckled her fiercely; as his tongue circled her nipple in languorous strokes. She could gasp as his hands found the edge of her dress and traveled up her legs, while his mouth went on caressing her breasts and her skin shivered and glowed and her thoughts blurred into kaleidoscopic joy.

His fingers plucked at the fastening of her drawers and slid the plain, practical cotton downward. Cold air swirled about the bare skin above her stockings, replaced instantly by the heat of his hands on her thighs, on her hips, in the tangle of curls at her center. His mouth had stilled upon her breast; his forehead rested against her, his breath spreading a pool of warmth about her belly. When at last his tentative finger ran along the rim of her inner flesh and dipped inside, his groan vibrated against her skin to mingle with hers.

He rose to his feet in a swift motion and buried his face in her neck. She felt the tremor in his muscles, the damp sheen of sweat on his skin. His voice came husky and beseeching: "Lilibet, my love, my life, stop me, darling, I must have you, I can't stop . . ."

She could not say *don't stop*. But she could unfasten his trousers and draw his member, hard and beautiful, between her hands. She could caress the velvety skin, the curving ridge, and stretch her face toward his; she could kiss him deeply, show him with her tongue what she wanted from him. She could fling her arms about his neck with a gasp as he lifted and swung her downward into the pile of sparse hay on the floor.

"I'm sorry," he whispered. "I'm sorry," and she knew what he meant.

She wanted to tell him that he had nothing to be sorry for, that these rough walls were a palace because he was there. That this haystack was a couch of velvet because he shared it with her, rose above her, parted her legs and her clothing, thrust inside her slippery body and united her to him at last.

But she couldn't tell him that, couldn't tell him that the memory of this instant would live sacred in her mind through all the remaining years of her life, and so she held his big body against her and wept into his shoulder while they rocked together, shuddering, fighting the urge for completion.

But the imperative could not be denied: the need curled around her womb, the friction ached between their matched bodies. At last he rose up on his elbows and began to thrust, gently at first, and then with growing strength, deep inside her, his hips grinding against hers at each plunge, reaching for more of her, all of her. She reached her hands to his face, his cheekbones, his jaw, his hair, as if touching all the precious pieces of his body would brand him on her fingers.

He is inside me, he is part of me, we are one, oh God, let it never stop, let this wave never break, let it keep on building and building forever, oh God.

The wave built and it built, and his thrusts came harder and more urgent, and release began like a slow explosion within her, spreading in long shocks down her limbs and up through her belly and breast to force a cry at last from her throat. He bent and took it into his mouth, where his own shout met hers. The jump of his body, the tremor of his climax, echoed through them both.

Roland's mind, ordinarily a nimble and fluent instrument, seemed to have been drenched by a barrelful of treacle.

Lovely treacle, of course. Thick and dark and sweet, it spread around the folds of his brain in lazy trickles, obscuring all nimbleness and fluency. All that remained was sensation: the softness of Lilibet's body wrapped around his; her honey-rich scent, laced with lavender, filling his nose; the gentle rush of her breath in his ear.

He attempted to lift his head, and discovered that the treacle was also heavy as the devil.

He kissed her ear instead. "Darling. My love, my Lilibet, you . . ."

"Shh." She stroked his hair, his back. "Shh."

Roland closed his eyes and obeyed her, because the treacle seemed to want him to, but after another moment of blissful lethargy he became aware of other and more uncomfortable sensations.

Namely, the hard wooden floor beneath his knees and elbows.

He lifted his head, this time with more success, and gazed at her face in adoration. In the shadows, she looked like a figure from a dream; the faint bluish light blurred her edges, hollowed out her cheeks, caught her loosened hair in a halo about her head. His angel, his love.

There would be scandal, of course. They might have to

live abroad for a time; perhaps for a long time. He'd have to give up his work at the Bureau, or else take on strictly foreign assignments. There was also the small matter of Lord Somerton. Medieval sort of chap, Somerton; a duel might be involved, for formality's sake.

But it would be worth it. Lilibet would be his at last. He pictured a cottage by a lake of some sort, snow-tipped mountains in the background, sunshine gleaming from a red-tile roof. He'd turn his hand to that poetry he'd always meant to write, and she . . . well, she'd do whatever it was women did. Read novels. Warm his bed. Raise children. A tingling feeling invaded his chest at the thought: their child growing in her belly, nursing at her breast, toddling about the cottage, all immaculate and smiling and polite and well behaved. Perhaps even another one, after a suitable interval.

Oh yes. It would be well worth it.

He kissed each of her closed eyelids. "Darling. Sweet love. You're mine at last. Tomorrow we'll . . ."

Her eyes flew open. "Good God!" she hissed.

"Or we can wait until I've paid a call on Somerton," he added hastily, mindful of her notions of propriety. "To make things all right and tight. I'm sure he'll give you a divorce, when I've explained . . ."

She pushed him away and sat upright. "A divorce! No! Good God! What . . . what are you thinking?"

Dear skittish creature. He smiled and leaned forward to kiss her. "That I love you, a thousand times more than before. That the rest will take care of itself. That nothing matters except . . ."

"Except my son! Except my honor!" She shoved her breasts back into her corset and struggled with the buttons of her shirtwaist. Her eyes were wide and horrified. "Do you know what he'll do when he finds out?"

"I daresay he'll be rather put out, but I shall stand firm . . ."

She made a sound, somewhere between a groan and a sob. Her hands shook at the buttons. "Roland, you're a fool. Oh, he'll divorce me, I'm sure, if he ever finds out. But he'll take Philip. I'll never see my son again; he'll make sure of that . . . Oh, these damned buttons!" She covered her face with her hands.

"Darling, darling. Calm yourself. He won't do any such thing. Here." He reached out with tender fingers to fasten her buttons.

"Don't!" She brushed his hand away and stood up. "Don't touch me! Don't . . . Oh God, what have I done?"

He rose, found his trousers gathered rather ignominiously around his ankles, and pulled them up into decency. "You've done—we've done—what we were meant to do all along. I love you, Lilibet. I've loved you from the day we met, and I shall bless you forever for allowing me the chance to redeem myself."

"Redeem yourself? *Redeem* yourself?" She stood there in astonishment, shirtwaist and jacket and coat still ajar, and he couldn't help dropping his eyes to the curve of her bosom: so recently overflowing his hand, and now overflowing her corset with every indignant heave of her breath.

Not his wisest moment, by any means.

"Look at you!" she exploded. "Still ogling me, for God's sake! You've no idea at all what this means!"

He stepped backward. "Of course I do! I shall marry you, Lilibet. I shall stand by you always, take the most tender care of you. I'll be the most faithful of husbands, a loyal old hound . . ."

"Faithful!" she snapped. Her fingers resumed their buttoning in agile jerks. "This from a man who finds a new mistress every week! Who trades women with his Prince over a game of cards! Whose reputation for uselessness and moral laxity is the stuff of legend, even in London!"

His mouth opened and closed. What could he say? *Oh, that. All a sham, you see. A front. To cover up my true activities as an intelligence agent for Her Majesty's government.*

No, really. All in the name of duty.

She watched him steadily, her gaze like a needle into his soul. Her fingers alone remained active, inserting each button into its proper hole, closing off her body from his sight and touch. From down the length of the stable came the sound of a horse whuffling, moving restlessly about his stall. *Yes, Penhallow*, it seemed to say. *Tell us. We're absolutely with child to hear you talk your way out of this one. Good old slick-tongued Penhallow.*

Lilibet shook her head at his silence and glanced downward. Her coat was buttoned, her collar straightened. She plucked a strand of hay from the dark wool. "You don't know what faithful means, Lord Roland," she said. "You're a child, a boy. You don't know."

"I know that I love you." His voice was hoarse, petulant. "I know that you love me. That you loved me once, at least, with the kind of love I *thought*"—he allowed the faintest trace of bitter emphasis—"would live an eternity."

She shook her head. "You don't know."

"Then why *this*?" He gestured angrily at the ground. "Why the bloody hell spread your legs for me on the floor of an Italian *stable*? Just an ordinary roll in the hay for you, was it? Virtuous Lady Somerton! If only London knew . . ."

Her hand moved like lightning, stinging across his face in a loud slap. "How dare you!" she hissed. "You alone know what this meant to me. What it cost me. And you must ruin it, mustn't you? Soil the most precious memory of my life with your vile . . . with . . ." Her voice choked; she turned away.

"Oh, Lilibet. Darling, no . . ." He reached for her, but she was already walking down the row, toward the door. "Wait, love! Don't leave yet!"

She broke into a run.

"Wait! Stop!" He ran after her and caught her by the arm.

"Let me go! I've nothing to say to you!" She struggled against his grip and kicked against his shin. Her eyes glittered in the muffled light from the dark lanterns nearby.

What had she just said? *The most precious memory of my life.*

He grinned with sudden confidence. "Stop it, you little hellcat. It isn't that."

"What, then?" She angled her head away.

"It's just that . . . well, I'd suggest you let me help you with this hay."

"Hay?"

"Yes. Hay. It's all down the back of your coat." He brushed her bottom to illustrate.

"Oh! You!" She knocked his hand away and began brushing herself, twisting left and right.

"Hold still." He plucked and brushed with ruthless efficiency while she stood, frozen with pride, staring at the door. "All done," he said at last, straightening.

"Thank you." She started forward.

He caught her arm again, more gently this time, and leaned into her ear. "I *will* marry you, Lilibet Somerton. Mark my words."

She shrugged off his hand and spoke in her loftiest accent. "The only chance of your marrying me, Penhallow, is if you manage to have yourself ordained to perform the office. At which point hell itself"—she stabbed his chest with her forefinger—"will have frozen over in mourning for its lost soul."

She bolted through the door and into the rain-soaked night. He gazed at the empty space she left behind and brushed his fingertips across his cheek. Her handprint had lost its sting, leaving only warmth behind.

*A*dulteress.

Lilibet hoped the rain would wash away the word, which she could almost feel on her forehead, written in bold scarlet letters, like that poor lady in the book.

What had she done?

She hadn't. She couldn't possibly have just spread her legs for Lord Roland Penhallow on the floor of an Italian stable. She couldn't have held his body inside hers, couldn't have felt the heat of his skin and his mouth on her breast.

She couldn't have. Because if she had, everything she knew about herself—her strength, her honor, her implacable sense of duty—was wrong.

But—oh God!—how could she regret it? She loved him so. For more than six long years she'd hidden that love inside her bones, denying its existence even to herself. And the reality of it, of drawing that love from the darkness and into the sunlight at last, had been more perfect and infinite than her most secret imagination. His touch still echoed on her flesh, would echo forever. On her deathbed, she would remember it.

You've done—we've done—what we were meant to do all along.

No. A beautiful fiction, but only that: a fiction. God had meant her to marry the Earl of Somerton, to bear him a son and heir; to endure all that she could and then to retire and raise that son to manhood.

I'm sure he'll give you a divorce, when I've explained.

Lilibet choked back a laugh and quickened her steps. Oh, priceless. Priceless, the expression on Somerton's face if he were told that he, who had committed infidelities without number—infidelities of the most shocking sort, as her own eyes had witnessed—was now himself a cuckold.

Perhaps, when his rage had cooled, he might divorce her. Perhaps he wouldn't. It hardly mattered: Either way, he would remove Philip from her care, from her sight. If he knew where she stood at this instant, he would send someone to take her son away. And though the separation would rend her apart, it was for Philip she feared most. If she had to, she could endure a lifetime of hollow existence, of the shame of divorce and abandonment, without her boy; but she could never condemn Philip to be reared according to his father's notions of manhood.

The rear hallway was deserted, the common room silent and snoring. Lilibet slipped upstairs to her room and removed her hat, her coat, her jacket, her shirtwaist, her skirt, the snug embrace of her stays. Each article of clothing rasped like sandpaper against her flushed skin and sent ripples of sensation through her stunned body.

In the quiet chamber, the steady tread of breathing surrounded her: the dark shapes of Alexandra and Abigail in the large bed, Philip by himself in the other. The fire was banked; the chill penetrated her shift, making her shiver. Slowly, taking great care to disturb the bed as little as possible, she crawled under the covers next to her son's sleeping body, not quite touching him, the rough sheets heavy upon her limbs. Between her legs, a raw, tender ache throbbed upward to reproach her.

She would never forget those stolen moments with Lord Roland Penhallow.

And, thank God, she would never see him again.

FIVE

S o, my dear brother," said the Duke of Wallingford. "How are you enjoying your year of chastity thus far?"

Roland, overtaken by a fit of coughing, took a moment to reply. "Well enough, I suppose," he said at last, and coughed again into his gloved fist. "It's only just begun, after all." He peered up the rocky track before them, hung with dolorous gray mist. Yesterday's heavy rain had moved on, but the air remained cold and damp, penetrating his clothing to numb his fingers and toes.

Wallingford lifted one hand from the reins to rub his upper lip. "No doubt you had it all out of your system before we left."

"Yes. Yes, of course. Endless orgies and whatnot."

"Excellent. I should hate for you to prove the weak link in our chain. I've no doubt that Lady Morley will hold us strictly to our wager." His tone was dark.

"Wager? What wager?" Roland glanced upward at the unpromising sky and was rewarded with a fat, cold drop of rain in his eye. He wasn't surprised: The weather fit his mood precisely. He'd gone to bed last night full of happy plans for winning Lilibet over, starting with a full-on advance of the legendary Penhallow charm at breakfast the next day. Morning and the innkeeper, however, had brought the information that the ladies had already left, just after dawn, and no, *signore*, the innkeeper did not know in which direction they'd gone.

"Good God, Penhallow." Wallingford let out an exasperated groan. "Don't tell me you've forgotten already. Last night at dinner, after the younger ladies retired with the boy. The wager with Lady Morley."

Roland's brain sifted through the memories of the night before, until light dawned. "Oh, right-ho. Something to do with keeping to our studies."

The sound of Burke's laughter barked out from the duke's other side. "I stand corrected, Wallingford. You're quite right. His head really is lodged between his legs at the moment."

"Not between his *own* legs, I suspect," growled Wallingford.

"See here . . ."

"The wager, if you'll recall," Burke said kindly, "came about after Lady Morley told us that the women are embarked on the same sort of project as we are. A year of study for the two of you, while I work on my automobile design, away from the distractions of London."

"And the opposite sex," added Wallingford.

"Sex of any kind, really," said Burke. "In any case, the winner's the party that . . ."

"I remember, I remember," Roland said, drawing in a deep gust of raw air. The metallic scent of wet rocks washed through his head. "The winner's the one that holds out the longest. And I was quite certain it would be the other side."

"Can't imagine why," said Burke.

Wallingford shrugged. "But they're women. They can't possibly hold out. It's a matter of strength of character. I expect Lady Somerton will have no trouble abstaining . . ."

Roland coughed again.

". . . but Lady Morley is certain to give up after a week of solitude. And as for that provoking little sister of hers . . ."

"Damned odd, you know," said Burke, "that they're doing the same thing we are. At the same time."

"Damned odd," agreed Wallingford. "I don't like it at all. I hope we shall win our wager in short order. In fact, I hope they'll give up the endeavor and clear out of Italy altogether, and we shan't have to concern ourselves with them further."

"Except for the advertisement," said Roland.

"The advertisement?"

"The advertisement in the *Times*. The loser's forfeit, do you remember? I recall *that* little detail quite clearly." Roland winked at Burke.

"Yes, of course. Our stakes." Wallingford cast a sidelong glance of his own at Phineas Burke, who rode along with a grim expression beneath his woolen cap. "Your fault, Burke. Whatever were you thinking? *'I see no reason why the loser should not publish in the Times an advertisement of no less than a half sheet, acknowledging the superiority of the winning side.'*" He said the words in a singsong falsetto. "Just to make sure that all of London knows what we're up to, of course."

"There's no reason the advertisement can't be done anonymously," Burke said reasonably. "In any case, you can't have a wager without *some* sort of stake, and one can hardly wager money with ladies." He removed his hat and ran his fingers through his bright ginger hair, peering up the road through a sudden gust of drizzle. His eyes narrowed. "What the devil," he muttered, and he urged his horse into a trot.

"Dashed coincidence," agreed Wallingford, into Burke's diminishing back.

"Perhaps they have other reasons," said Roland. *Like prying poor Lilibet from the clutches of that damned scoundrel husband of hers.*

"In any case," Wallingford went on, watching Burke move into a canter, "they're long gone, and in the opposite direction if we've any luck at all. By the end of the day we'll be through the gates of this castle Burke's found us, and quite safe from temptation. Eventually, I suppose, your legendary Tuscan sunshine will appear, and . . . Hello! What's Burke up to? What's this?"

Roland looked up the road. He saw them at once: a party of bedraggled travelers, stranded in the mud, unloading trunks from a wagon. Women, from the looks of it. In fact, he could almost swear that . . .

Good God.

He clapped heels to the sides of his horse.

For him, the sunshine had just come out.

The clouds blackened over Lilibet's head.

Or so it seemed, anyway. Surely there could be no darker omen than Lord Roland Penhallow riding up the road to offer his most chivalrous assistance to their wretched mud-bound convoy.

God's retribution, of course. She'd done her best, strained every nerve to get Abigail and Alexandra (both of them sleepy and befuddled to a most inconvenient degree) and her son (clearheaded and energetic, also to a most inconvenient degree) on the road early, before the men were awake. She'd had stale bread and cold water for breakfast. She'd bent her head into the cold and damp. She'd tightened her arms about Philip and fixed her brain on the goal ahead: the castle Alexandra had found for them; the sanctuary, safe from threatening husbands and irresistible lovers alike.

But almighty vengeance had found her anyway, even sooner than she'd expected. Though vengeance, she had to admit, had never taken so fair a form as Roland Penhallow. He swung his broad-shouldered body from his horse with athletic grace and creased his beautiful brow with solicitude. Below his hat, a curling fringe of his golden brown hair soaked up all the meager light in Tuscany.

Oh, that hair, wound around her fingers.

Those curving lips, trailing down her breast.

That lean, taut body, stroking against hers . . .

Stop. No. She shoved the images out of her mind. She

frowned ferociously as Roland reached into the cart and began removing the trunks, lightening the load so the horses could pull the vehicle out of the mud.

Philip struggled from her lap. "Mama, I want to help," he said.

"Don't be silly. Let the gentlemen work in peace."

But he was too quick for her. His light body skimmed over the muddy ground to the cart, right next to Roland's tall riding boots. She staggered after him, mud sucking at her heels, but he was already scrambling up the wheel well and into the cart.

"Stop that, Philip! Get out of that cart at once!" She stretched her arms in his direction.

His little fingers curled around the handle of his own leather-bound chest. "But I'm helping, Mama!"

"His lordship does not require your help, Philip. Come here at once."

"Just the one trunk, Mama!"

"Philip, I said . . ."

"Look here, old chap," said Roland kindly, "why don't you hop back down, there's a lad."

"I can help!"

"Oh, I daresay, but there are chores better left to those with a bit more strength in their sinews, eh what?" He reached one long arm across the cart and took the trunk handle from the boy's hand.

A weighty silence dropped. Lilibet just glimpsed the flash of tears in Philip's eyes, before the boy turned his head away.

"Come here, darling," Lilibet said, and Philip ran toward her and flung himself at her chest. "Shh, love. His lordship is quite right. When you're older and bigger."

She didn't look at him. She let no hint of reproach invade her face, no sign at all that a tiny piece of her heart had just chipped away. But she felt the weight of everyone's attention: Wallingford and Mr. Burke looked studiously away and occupied themselves with the trunks, Alexandra and Abigail examined the mud on their boots. Philip's body burrowed into hers, like a squirrel into its den, stiff with repressed sobs.

"I say . . ." Roland said softly. "I didn't mean . . ."

She shrugged. She couldn't reply. She couldn't think, just now, of Roland's discomfiture. Of her own disappointment, of the failure of human reality to match some unconscious hope she hadn't even realized, until now, she'd held in her heart. She could only wrap her arms around Philip and soak him with her love. "It's all right, sweetheart," she murmured into his hair. "My eager little love. His lordship is quite right. The sooner the trunks are unloaded, the sooner we can be on our way. Isn't it kind of the gentlemen to help us like this?"

A hot sigh penetrated her wool coat.

"Now be my brave boy and thank his lordship for his help."

Philip moved his head against her, wiping his eyes. She didn't press him further, only let him gather his composure, his body still and heavy within the circle of her arms.

At last he turned his head. His voice was firm. "Thank you, your lordship."

"Not at all, my boy," said Roland. "And perhaps, on second thought . . ."

"Philip," broke in Abigail, "do you know, I've just heard the most extraordinary thing. You'll never credit it."

Philip straightened in her arms and craned in Abigail's direction. "What's that, Cousin Abigail?"

"No. No, you won't believe me. Never mind."

"Oh, please! I will so! Oh, tell me!" His body pitched with eagerness, all disappointment shrugged off like a coat.

She shook her head. "No. No, I'm sure you won't."

"Oh, please, Cousin Abigail!" He drew away from Lilibet and stretched his arms to Abigail. "Please tell me!"

"Well . . ." Abigail stretched the word with doubt. She reached for Philip and swung him from the cart and into her arms. "It's about this horse, you see. He just told me . . ."

"Horses don't talk!"

Abigail groaned. "You see? I knew you wouldn't believe me!"

"No, I will! I will! What did the horse say?"

"He said to me, in the most doleful way—cart horses are so universally doleful, you understand—he said that he was awfully, terribly, *excruciatingly . . ."*

"What? *What?"*

"Hungry," said Abigail.

Lilibet watched the two of them move to the horse's bobbing head. Philip held out his hand to stroke its white-streaked forehead, and Abigail produced a miraculous carrot from her pocket.

A few yards away, Roland resumed unloading the trunks. "Dreadfully sorry about all that," he said, in a low voice, reaching in front of her for another chest. "I expect I've lost all credit with him."

"It's all right," she said coldly. "It doesn't really matter, does it? After all, he'll likely never see you again."

She turned and walked away to where Abigail and Philip were feeding the horse his carrot. In a few hours, she told herself, she would be safe inside the castle.

In a few hours, Roland's voice would be gone forever from her ears.

A few hours later

Well, this *is* splendid!" said Roland, in his most affable voice. "Old friends traveling together and all that. An inspired idea; I amaze myself, sometimes."

"Vastly amusing," said Lilibet. *Her* voice sounded distinctly frosty. She tightened her arm around Philip's body, which squirmed before her in the saddle. "I can't remember a more pleasant journey."

The little boy patted the horse's neck, making hardly a sound with his thick mittens. "I think it's splendid! Riding horses is much better than riding in carts."

"I quite agree," said Roland. He spared Philip a benevolent glance. Not that much of the poor little fellow remained visible; he was covered from head to foot against the cold, as if bound in an endless woolen bandage by a particularly thorough nurse. What bits of him did emerge, however, glowed with unquenchable glee, and had been doing just that ever since he'd been set atop the noble steed of the Duke of Wallingford a few hours ago.

Philip's mother, however, appeared considerably less gleeful. Her thickly lashed eyes stared straight ahead and showed not the slightest inclination to spare Roland a glance of any kind, let alone a benevolent one. "It was kind of the gentlemen to offer us their horses, of course," she said, in the same cold tone as before. "Though quite unnecessary. The baggage cart would have come unstuck eventually."

But Roland had faced far less charming challenges before, and with far less hope of success. "My dear Lady Somerton, have pity," he said with a laugh. "We enter our monastic seclusion in a few short hours. Don't deprive us of a last taste of female company."

"You've already had more than you ought," Lilibet snapped.

He laughed again. He welcomed her snappishness: At least she felt *something*. "Dearest Lady Somerton, a single taste is *never* enough."

Waves of anger seemed to ripple forth from her body and rattle the air between them. Her back, already ramrod straight, stiffened even further. "You must endeavor to reconcile yourself to reality, Lord Roland. Our lodging will be coming into view at any moment, and you'll be quite relieved of the nuisance of our company."

"Ah, don't speak of it." He shook his head sorrowfully. "When I've only just had the opportunity to speak with you."

"Perhaps it might have occurred to you that I was avoiding the encounter."

"Then I'm fortunate Nature paid a call on young Philip at the crossroads." He reached out to give the lad a chuck on the shoulder, and found Lilibet's hand wrapped like a vise around his wrist. He dropped his arm and cleared his throat. "No need for thanks, of course, though I tremble to imagine how you might have unwound all those scarves in time, without someone to hold the horse for you. A near-run thing, eh?"

"How gallant of you," she said. "I'm sure *my husband* will be grateful for your tender care of us."

Her husband. Roland scowled at last. "Oh, I doubt his lordship will hear of it. We're *ever so far away* from him, after all."

"Not far enough."

"Oh, I'm sure he'll find out!" piped up Philip. "Father finds out everything. He's . . . He's . . . What's that word again, Mama?"

"Omniscient," she said dully.

Lord Somerton? All-knowing? When it came to whores and drink, perhaps. Roland schooled his voice to nonchalance, however, out of respect. "Omniscient? Really?"

"Oh yes," the boy said, full of importance. "Mama says Father's a real live . . ."

"Philip!" she snapped.

Philip gave an apologetic sigh. "Well, it's a secret, of course."

"Mama seems to be full of secrets, these days," said Roland. "I wonder how she keeps them all straight in her head."

"Rigorous self-control," said Lilibet. "A quality with which his lordship ought to become better acquainted."

"I protest," he said. He let his eyes run down the curve of her back and waist and buttocks, displayed to such disciplined perfection on the back of the horse. She was riding astride, probably for the first time in her life, with her dark skirts gathered like harem trousers about her legs. He drew in a long sigh and stumbled over an unnoticed stone in his path. "I'm exerting the most terrifying amount of self-control, at this very moment."

She made an exasperated noise. He looked at her face just in time to see the color blossom in her pallid cheeks.

"If you'll excuse me, your lordship," she said, "I have matters to discuss with Lady Morley."

She urged her horse ahead, toward the others, leaving him to walk the drizzled road alone, wondering what on earth he was going to do when she walked into her lodgings and out of his life.

He'd think of something, of course. Nothing would keep him from her now: not her bloody bastard of a husband, not her dear misguided sense of honor, and certainly not his own rash vow of monastic seclusion.

But as for what that something might be? At the moment, he was dashed if he knew.

W ell, I'm dashed," came Roland's voice, piercing through the mists of Lilibet's horrified astonishment. "What an extraordinary development."

Lilibet stared at Wallingford in a daze. "Are you quite certain of the facts of the case, Your Grace?"

Wallingford shook his head and looked between the papers. "I can't see another explanation. That damned villain Rosseti—I beg your pardon, Lady Somerton—has leased the castle to both of us."

The castle.

Lilibet turned to the east, where the grim stone turrets rose in a haphazard heap some quarter mile away along the gray brown hillside, fronted by a row of ragged wind-beaten cypress. The Castel sant'Agata, their promised refuge, looked altogether forbidding and impregnable among the mist and rocks and sparse winter grass. Already, Alexandra and Abigail had begun to canter down the track toward it.

"I'm bloody well going after them," said Phineas Burke, striding off down the road.

"It's not possible." Her voice sounded faint, even in her own ears. She cleared her throat and pushed the words out. "Let me see the papers."

"I assure you, Lady Somerton . . ."

"Let me see them!"

Wallingford gave a little start. "If you insist," he said, in his most arctic ducal voice. He thrust the papers into her outstretched hand and peered down the road. "I'm going to set out after them, before Burke makes a cock-up of the entire business."

He headed off down the track toward the castle, and Lilibet dropped her eyes to the papers in her hand. One belonged to Alexandra: She knew the words by heart, had repeated them to herself over and over, to assure herself that this was really happening, that they were really going to live in an Italian castle for a year, safe from her husband and from the sharp-witted curiosity of London society. LEASE AND AGREEMENT, it read at the top, in block letters, followed by, *Whereas the two parties, Lady Alexandra the Dowager Marchioness of Morley, and Signore Alberto Rosseti of Italy, have entered into an Agreement to lease the designated Property for the period of One (1) year, commencing the 15th of March instant, in the year 1890 . . .*

It all seemed quite clear. Alexandra's signature swept across the bottom in an elegant flourish, and Rosseti's appeared next to it. The Castel sant'Agata appeared three times, specific and emphatic, located here in the district of Arezzo in the province of Tuscany. There could admit no doubt, no doubt at all, that she and her companions were the legal lessees of the castle before her, bordered with overgrown cypress, with the heavy iron gray sky weighing upon its many turrets.

She turned to the other paper.

LEASE AND AGREEMENT, it read. *Whereas the two parties, Mr. Phineas Fitzwilliam Burke of London, England, and Signore Alberto Rosseti of Italy, have entered into an Agreement to lease the designated Property for the period of One (1) year, commencing the 15th of March instant, in the year 1890 . . .*

Lilibet let her hands drop to the horse's neck. Philip's hair tickled her chin. "What do the papers say, Mama?" he asked.

"I don't know," she said. "It's all very . . . very strange."

She knew Roland stood behind her somewhere, though he said not a word. She felt him there, the bristling energy of his presence, like a charge of electricity hanging in the air.

"I suppose you had nothing to do with this," she said at last.

"I don't know what you mean." She heard his booted footsteps in the dirt, and he appeared at her elbow, golden and glowing even in the dank gray March air, too damnably handsome for a mortal man, God forever rot him. "Are you implying that I planned this, somehow? Good God, Lilibet . . ."

"I did not give you leave to address me so."

"Lady Somerton. I'd no idea you were in the country at all."

"Oh! I suppose it's all just a very great coincidence. First that damnable inn, of all the places in the world, and meeting us in the road, and now this!" She thrust her hand, still clutching the papers, in the direction of the castle. "To say nothing of the extraordinary coincidence of your devoting a year to academic study in the *exact same manner* as we are! Oh yes! A baffling mystery indeed!"

He laughed. "My dear girl, I'm rather flattered. I daresay you're the only woman in Europe who'd give me credit for enough wits to pull off such a caper."

"Oh, you've wits enough," she said bitterly.

"Oh, I haven't, I assure you. Empty as a . . ." He glanced at Philip. "That is to say, empty as a . . . a milk pail, you see, er . . . well, before the milking, I suppose."

"That's a stupid thing to say," observed Philip.

"See? There you have it," Roland said triumphantly. "From the mouths of babes, and all that."

She risked a sidelong glance, and regretted it immediately. Those damned broad shoulders seemed to beckon her, solid and irreproachable under the impeccable tailoring of a dark wool coat. His hat cocked slightly to one side, exposing his golden brown hair where it curled charmingly about his neck in the damp air, and a smile pushed up the corner of his full mouth. "Don't pretend you're thick," she snapped. "We both know otherwise."

He shook his head. "Blinded by admiration, I see. No, I'm just as you surmised earlier. Scoundrel-about-town. I've had it printed on my calling cards: Lord Roland Penhallow, Rascal and Rake, Frivolous Enquiries Only. So no one mistakes me, you see."

"You're *not* trying to charm me."

He grinned broadly, and it was as if the sun had burst through the leaden sky above. "Of course I'm trying to charm you, my dear. It's what I do."

The ache in her breast bit deep. She rested her chin on Philip's head, anchoring herself to her son. Her voice, emerging at last, had only a fraction of the power she expected it to. "Please don't," she said. "There's no point."

"Oh, I disagree," he said. "After all, if we're to be sharing a castle with one another . . ."

"God forbid it!"

"On the contrary, my dear. God seems expressly to have designed it." His eyes danced at her.

"Or the Devil."

"Oh, Mama!" said Philip. He twisted around to look up at her with wide dark eyes, his father's eyes, black and fathomless as a midnight ocean. "You told me never to say . . ."

"I know, I know." She gathered the shreds of her composure around her. A solution would certainly be found, after all. It *had* to be found. However deep Roland's scheme, whatever his eventual plans, she couldn't let things go any further. What had happened in the stables must never be given the chance to occur again. "Mama's quite wrong. It's been a long and tiring day, dearest, and now there's all this confusion about the castle."

"If the duke stays, too," said Philip, "will he let me ride his horse again?"

Roland burst out laughing. "I daresay he will, old boy," he said. "And if he doesn't, you can certainly ride mine."

"The gentlemen are not . . ." Lilibet began firmly.

"That's all right, sir. I'd rather ride the duke's. After all, I daresay it's the nicest, isn't it?"

"I'm certain it is," said Lilibet. She pulled her eyes away from Lord Roland Penhallow and looked back at the castle. "But it doesn't matter, does it? Because the gentlemen won't be staying with us. Not tonight, and certainly not for the year. It's quite impossible."

She spoke with conviction, to drive away the despair. If she said it firmly enough, often enough, surely she could make it come true.

Roland watched her horse trot toward the castle, hooves clattering on the wet rocks, and made no move to follow. No need for haste, after all. He wasn't a particularly religious man, but he knew a gift from God when he saw it. This time, he wouldn't bungle it. This time, he'd lay his plans with care.

He glanced upward at the grim layer of clouds, the cold incessant drizzle from the heavens. But winter was nearly over, and all things began anew in the spring.

SIX

Castel sant'Agata
April 1890

At first, Lilibet ignored the signs.

So much work to occupy her, so many duties. She studied Greek philosophers with great diligence, she assisted the housekeeper and the maids in the kitchen, and she taught Philip his lessons and took him on picnics.

She took scrupulous care to avoid the gentlemen, of course. This should have been a simple matter, according to plan. After the first night, they had agreed, in a remarkably civilized compact around the heavy trestle table in the dining room, to divide the castle on a north-south axis until Rosseti could be found and the matter resolved, with the east side belonging to the ladies and the west side to the gentlemen. The two parties ought, therefore, to have met only at mealtimes (there was only one dining room, after all) and by random collision outdoors.

The reality was not quite so effortless. While Mr. Burke spent most of his time in his workshop down the hill, and Wallingford usually sulked in the library when he wasn't out riding his horse, Roland lurked about everywhere. She devoted so much thought to avoiding him, she had no trouble banishing unpleasant speculation and calculation in favor of more immediate concerns. Like ducking behind trees while his lordship whistled by on a walk, or slipping into the kitchen until he'd passed through the hallway.

But when she opened her eyes this morning, she *knew*.

"Mama." Philip pushed her shoulder, as he did every morning at half past six. "May I get up now?"

"Yes, my dear," she said, as she did every morning. "Go downstairs and ask Francesca for a cup of milk."

He pressed a wet kiss against her cheek and disappeared. The door creaked and scraped against the ancient flagstones, as it did every morning. She stared for a moment at the dark wooden beams of the ceiling, at the aging yellow plaster between them. How old were they? Centuries, at least. No doubt many women had opened their eyes and took in the same minute details, over the years.

She turned on her side to the window. She'd left it cracked open last night, and now, with the pale early wash of sunlight, the morning air crept into the room: the green scent of new grass, the trace of hay and manure from the stables, the sweetness of the apple blossoms from the nearby orchard. Somebody laughed, not far away, a light, rich sound; Abigail, probably, on her way to milk the goats.

It was all so grossly unfair. Lady Pembroke took a different lover every quarter, as a matter of common knowledge, without producing so much as a new kitten. Lilibet's own husband, Lord Somerton, had likely gone to bed with every whore in London, and not one of those unfortunate women had ever darkened her imposing Belgrave Square doorstep with a bastard in arms.

Lilibet had only sinned the one time. A single stolen reckless moment, an instant of madness, never repeated.

She stood up abruptly from the bed and went to the dresser. A dark-framed mirror lay fastened to the wall above it, the surface somewhat warped and the silvering spotted with age. Her image stared back at her, distorted and ghostly in the pale morning light, blue eyes spread wide.

Why was she so surprised? After all, Philip had been born exactly nine months after her wedding night, to the vast pride of Somerton and the relief of her parents. When she'd stood there in the stable a month ago, buttoning her coat, heart hammering with panic in her ears, she'd felt the warm trickle of Roland's seed down her leg like a tiny serpent: tangible proof of sexual consummation.

She reached for the pitcher of water and poured it into the chipped blue and white washing bowl. With trembling hands, she splashed her face, her neck. The cool water slid in drops down the high collar of her nightdress, down the valley between her breasts, to peter out somewhere on the warm skin of her belly.

Had she imagined she could hide her guilt forever? Had she really believed that if she didn't repeat the offense—didn't lie blissfully, sinfully with Lord Roland Penhallow again, in thought or in deed—it might somehow never have occurred at all?

A soft knock sounded on the door.

Lilibet whipped around. "Who," she began, but her voice was a mere early-morning squeak. She cleared her throat and tried again. "Who is it?"

"Only me," came Abigail's voice, and then Abigail herself, dressed in yellow homespun and smelling of goats.

"Done with the milking already?" Lilibet asked.

"My goats were feeling benevolent this morning. Such a glorious day! Why aren't you dressed?"

"Laziness, I suppose." *Or a possible bloody double-damned pregnancy, throwing all my plans in an uproar, threatening every hope of holding on to Philip.* "Pick something for me, will you?"

Abigail heaved a great sigh and went to the wardrobe. "There isn't all that much to pick from. Why didn't you pack more?"

"I was in a hurry. And it hardly seemed to matter what I wore."

"Hmm." Abigail threw open the wardrobe door and

stood before the meager selection with an air of deep concentration. "What sort of color do you feel like today?"

Lilibet laughed. "I don't feel like any particular color at all. Do you?"

"Oh, always. I felt distinctly yellow this morning, even before I saw that great lovely sun rising in the sky. Yesterday rather green, though I don't own a green dress and had to make do with that rubbishy puce frock I detest."

"If you detest it, why did you wear it?"

"Because." Abigail said it as if the answer were so obvious a child wouldn't have bothered to ask. "Puce." Her mouth pinched with distaste.

"You absurd girl. Blue, then. If I have to choose."

"Blue? You're blue today?" Abigail reached into the wardrobe and pulled out a navy dress with long sleeves and something dangerously close to a bustle behind. She wrinkled her nose. "How old is this dress?"

"Only a year or two. Or perhaps three." Lilibet frowned.

"Well, you can't wear a bustle anymore. Not even the village girls attempt it, and they're lucky to see a single pattern book in a year. Will this one do? It's really more of a violet, but at least the cut won't disgrace you." She turned, just as Lilibet's nightgown slithered to the floor. "Oh! You're so lovely in this light. I should adore to paint you. Well, if I painted, that is."

Lilibet reached for her chemise and laughed nervously. "Not so lovely," she said. "I've had a child, after all."

"Yes, but you're still perfect, you wretch. All that smooth skin and marvelous proportion. No wonder poor Penhallow worships you."

"Rubbish," Lilibet said sharply. She snatched her stays from the drawer.

"Oh, don't be silly. It's quite amusingly obvious, the way he looks at you. And then you give him your haughty look and freeze him out, the dear. Shall I lace you?"

"Please. But not too tightly," Lilibet added swiftly. She felt Abigail's hands at her waist, gathering the strings, and then the swift, efficient tugs stiffening her middle. Was it her imagination, or did a new and ominously familiar fullness rise up over the lace-edged top of the garment?

Were her nipples not the faintest touch darker than before?

Damn, damn. Triple bloody damn.

"There we are! Not too tight, I think. You should still be useful for a tramp down to the lake at lunchtime." Abigail stood back. "Why blue?"

Lilibet turned and reached for the dress, avoiding her cousin's sharp brown gaze. "Blue?" she asked.

"You said you felt blue this morning."

"Oh! Only that I felt like *wearing* blue, you goose. Not that I *was* blue. Feeling blue, I mean. Not at all. Quite the opposite." The frock settled around her shoulders; she turned her back to Abigail. "Would you mind helping me with the buttons?"

"Oh. Well. I suppose I misunderstood." Abigail's voice wore a careful neutrality. Her fingers, swift and experienced, went to work on the buttons. Abigail had never really had much use for lady's maids; they were never up early enough for her, for one thing.

"Thank you," said Lilibet. "Shall we go downstairs for breakfast?"

"Yes, of course. Don't forget your Aristophanes; Alexandra's meeting us in the study for our morning discussion."

Lilibet reached for the books on the dresser and followed Abigail out of the room.

"It's rather odd, though," Abigail went on, as they descended the broad stone staircase at the center of the castle. "Blue, I mean. I was thinking, when I came in, that you looked rather blue. And then you said *blue*, just as if you'd read my mind."

"Very odd. I can't imagine why."

"No reason at all, then? About blue?"

"No." Lilibet put out one hand to steady herself against the wall as she took the hard, steep steps, one by one. "No reason at all."

* * *

The dining room of the Castel sant'Agata—cavernous and stone lined, its trestle table yawning between occupants like the Mongolian plains, its two narrow windows braced like sentinels against a chilling northern prospect—tended to destroy Lilibet's appetite at a glance.

Her pregnancy did not improve matters.

"I say, have you tried the kidneys this morning?" Abigail asked cheerfully. She tucked into her heaping plate with reckless glee. "Swimming in butter, just as I told Morini. Olive oil's all very well, I think, but a good English kidney requires . . . Are you quite all right, Lilibet?"

"I . . . yes." Lilibet nibbled at her toast.

"You look quite green. Or perhaps it's just the light. Philip, you've a hearty appetite this morning. How are those kippers?"

"Splendid, thank you, Cousin Abigail."

"Jolly splendid of them, to find kidneys and kippers for us. I wonder how they managed it."

Lilibet forced down another bite of toast. "I suppose one can order these things. There are hundreds of English in Florence."

"Yes, but how would they *know*?" Abigail leaned forward and spoke in a hushed voice. "Don't you think there's something a bit odd about the old place?"

"I don't know what you mean." Lilibet lifted her teacup to her lips; the fragrant steam seemed to soothe her stomach. "It's an old castle, that's all."

"Really? You don't feel it? As if there are ghosts hanging about every corner?" Abigail swept out one arm, illustrating ghosts, and nearly knocked over her tea.

"Ghosts!" Philip bounced in his seat. "Real live ones?"

"No, darling. Ghosts are generally dead," said Abigail, with a kind expression. "But real *dead* ones, certainly."

"What nonsense," Lilibet said, ignoring the chill in her spine with iron-minded resolution. Old buildings were full of noises and drafts, after all. Quite enough to give one eerie feelings, with no basis in physical fact. "Ghosts, indeed."

A shadow filled the doorway, making her jump: Signorina Morini, the housekeeper. "I have more toast, Signora Somerton, and more of the tea."

"Thank you, Morini," said Lilibet. "Are the gentlemen about yet? Lady Morley?"

Morini marched forward and placed a fresh rack of toast near Lilibet's plate. An impressive woman, Signorina Morini, with her slender figure and her black hair confined by a brightly colored headscarf. From the earliest moment of their rain-soaked arrival at the castle three weeks ago, her capable fingers had taken firm control of the workings of the household. She'd found linens and food, shown them through the lonely rooms, sent word to the village for maids to bring the kitchen to life again. She maintained her benevolent rule from her stately post in the kitchens, overseeing the hive of activity like an all-knowing oracle. "Signore Burke, Signore Penhallow, they both had the breakfast, it is an hour ago. Of the duke, I see nothing."

"Morini," said Abigail, "I wonder if I could have a few words with you on the subject of ghosts."

Morini's hands, in the process of refilling Lilibet's teacup, froze in place.

"Morini! The tea!" exclaimed Lilibet, and the housekeeper straightened the pot just in time.

"Ghosts," said Morini. She looked from Lilibet to Abigail and back again. "Of ghosts, there are none."

"Something else, then?" inquired Abigail. "Because I think the air's humming with them."

"Is nothing, signorina. Only the old stones, the wind rattling the old walls. You are wanting more tea?" She proffered the pot in Abigail's direction.

An instant's silence. Lilibet looked at Abigail and saw her locking eyes with the housekeeper, a queer intent expression on her face.

"I see," she muttered at last, and then, "yes, more tea. I like your blend extremely, Morini."

"But what about the ghosts?" demanded Philip. He reached across Lilibet's plate to grasp a piece of toast.

"Darling, don't reach. There are no ghosts, Morini says." Lilibet found her knife and spread a thick layer of butter over Philip's toast.

"No ghosts," said Morini, in an almost unintelligible mutter, exiting the room in a gust of kitchen-scented air.

"She's lying, of course." Abigail gazed thoughtfully past her teacup to the doorway. "Did you see the look she gave me?"

"Nonsense. Philip, for heaven's sake, don't lick the butter from your toast. It isn't considered at all polite."

Abigail leaned back in her chair and tapped her finger against the rim of her teacup. "Very interesting."

"I assure you, he doesn't do it often . . ."

"Not the *butter*, Lilibet. I mean Morini."

"Why?" Lilibet wiped her buttery hands on a neatly pressed white napkin. The stone walls of the dining room seemed colder and more shadowed than ever; the hint of sunshine from the north-facing windows made no impression whatsoever. She swallowed past the dryness in her throat and looked at Abigail with eyebrows raised. "Surely you don't think she's *hiding* something."

"Of course I do." Abigail's eyes gleamed. She replaced the cup in its saucer with a satisfying clatter. "And I mean to find out exactly what it is."

The groundskeeper glared at Roland with a look that seemed to lay all the world's troubles at his booted feet. "Is a note for you," he said, grudging every word. Not a friendly man, Giacomo; from the very first evening of their arrival, he'd regarded the Englishmen as intruders rather than legal tenants.

"A note! For me! Splendid news." Roland paused delicately. "And have you perhaps got this note conveniently about you?"

The groundskeeper pursed his lips, giving the matter

some thought. He lifted his cap, ran a grimy hand through the hair beneath, replaced the cap, and then thrust his hand into the pocket of his worn tunic. "Is not making any sense," he said, extracting a folded piece of paper.

"What, my receiving a note? Seems perfectly sensible to me." Roland snatched the paper away before the man could entertain second thoughts. A single glance at the seal—brown wax, with a small fox emblem—confirmed his suspicions. He slipped the paper into the inner pocket of his jacket and looked up at the cloudless sky. "Rather warm today, isn't it?"

"The note. The note is not making any sense."

"I'm not sure I follow you, er . . . Giacomo, isn't it?" His eyes slid past the groundskeeper's scowling face to take a thorough inventory of the road behind him. Standing here near the stable entrance, with the sun shining nearly overhead and the air mountain-clear, he could see every detail of the long drive leading to the main road, until it disappeared around the bend where Lilibet had trotted on ahead of him, three weeks ago. "I say, old chap," he went on, "I don't suppose you could tell me who delivered this?"

Giacomo folded his arms. "Is a boy from the village. Why you are having notes with words that are not making meaning?"

For the past few weeks, Roland had kept his brain unnaturally idle. He'd thumbed his way through parts of the library, of course, and endeavored to make some sort of foray into the academic study with which they were, after all, supposed to be engaged. But after so many years of leading a dual life in London, of keeping every sense alert while maintaining the general posture of a half-drunk wastrel, the easy pace of castle life had lulled him into a soporific daze. Or perhaps it was the nearness of Lilibet, whose lavender scent hovered around every corner, and whose image tantalized his every thought. Regardless, his reflexes were not at all what they'd been in the cold haze of London winter.

A second or two passed, therefore, before the cold

prickle at Roland's neck reached the thinking portion of his brain.

Words that are not making meaning.

And just how the devil would the groundskeeper know that?

He spoke with care. "I say, my dear fellow. You'll forgive me. I had the impression—a quaint sort of custom, really, native to my own humble country—that my private notes were, in fact, *private*." He put the faintest emphasis on the final word.

Giacomo made a *pfff*ing sound. Evidently he was not impressed with quaint English customs. "Is my duty, to know everything."

Roland put his fists behind his back, in case they should break discipline and clench. He felt quite appallingly out of practice at this game. "Then perhaps your English isn't up to the challenge, old fellow."

"Is not my English. Is the note."

Roland heard a bird call out behind him, piercing the silence between them with incongruous exuberance. Giving thanks, no doubt, for the annual proliferation of willing avian females. Roland wished he could say the same of the human sort. Instead, he studied the face of Giacomo the groundskeeper, its folds and crags weighed down with suspicion, its small black eyes narrowed almost to slits. The noontime sun cast a straight shadow beneath the short peak of his cap, exactly bisecting his face.

Roland drew the note back out of his pocket. The seal was unbroken. He slipped his finger beneath and loosened the rounded wax with a practiced *pop*, decapitating the fox. The thin paper unfolded easily; the code he recognized at once. "Ah!" he said. "There's your trouble. It's from my grandsire, you see. Quite senile, and probably a bit the worse for a bottle or two of brandy, too, eh what?" He folded the paper again and placed it back in his pocket. "I can't make heads or tails of it, either, to be perfectly honest."

A ripple of doubt cast across Giacomo's face. Roland could have fainted with relief.

He smiled instead.

"Well, then, Giacomo. I'm off to the kitchens to see if I can't persuade them to feed me a spot of lunch. Care to join me?"

The scowl returned to Giacomo's lips, this time even more pronounced. He *pfft*ed again, with vehemence.

"Ah! I shall convey your regrets to the kitchen. Perhaps . . ."

But Giacomo was already stomping back toward the stable, raising a faint puff of dust at every step.

Roland burned to read the note. The code came from Sir Edward himself—a recent one, and fairly complex. The message must therefore be vital. He turned toward the mellow yellow gray stones of the castle's east wing, where the kitchens were located, and walked toward the side entrance with long and purposeful strides.

Well, two or three of them, in any case, before he was brought up short by the sight of Elizabeth, Lady Somerton, with a commodious picnic basket in one hand and his little lordship's hand in the other. She was wearing a deep violet frock that billowed toward him in a gust of fresh breeze from the valley.

She hadn't seen him yet. Her face pointed south, down the long line of terraces, thinking probably of picnic spots.

Roland's mind hovered for a moment, watching her, balancing the two possibilities. On the one hand, Sir Edward's note and his duty to Queen and country, to say nothing of his curiosity. On the other hand, Lilibet.

It was no contest, really.

Sir Edward could go hang himself.

*W*hy can't we go to the lake for a picnic? *Why*, Mama?" Philip's voice veered dangerously close to a whine.

Because I looked out the window an hour ago and saw Lord Roland Penhallow walking in that direction. "Because the water's still too cold, my dear. We're much better off in the peach orchard."

"It isn't either! It isn't cold at all! It's *April*, Mama! Not *winter*!" This time he did whine, a solid respectable whinge, of which any five-year-old child might rightly be proud.

"All the same."

Philip went silent, preparing a new line of attack. "But we don't have to swim, just because it's a lake," he said at last.

"Philip, my dear, I know what little boys are capable of. If we picnic near the lake, you'll wind up in the water at some point. And I've no linens, no change of . . ."

"Lady Somerton! What a delightful surprise!"

Lilibet jumped and turned in the same movement. "Lord Roland! Good God! You . . . what the devil . . ." Her head spun. He was supposed to be at the lake; she'd been sure of it. She'd been safe, secure.

But there he stood before her, broad shouldered and smiling, hatless, the sun spinning gold in his hair. The source—dear God!—of the growing life within her. "Going for a picnic?" he asked.

"Yes, we are, but . . ."

"Let me take your basket. It looks fearfully heavy."

She relinquished the basket, too shocked to protest. Her serene afternoon had crumbled to bits around her. "But you . . . but you can't . . ."

"Can't I? Oh, come, Lady Somerton. You wouldn't turn me away from a picnic, would you?"

"But . . ." She thought of something. "But Wallingford. The wager. We're not allowed to mingle with the opposite . . ."

"Oh, for heaven's sake. My brother and his wagers. I'll tell him I kidnapped the two of you, and take the forfeit myself. Shall compose the advertisement in the *Times* myself, the most abject apology." He grinned at her, the sunlight dancing in his hazel eyes. "Let me join you. I'll be perfectly well behaved."

That damned smile of his. Those crinkles at the corners of his eyes. "I suppose so," she heard herself say. "If you promise not to eat everything yourself."

He gave the basket a little heft. "From the feel of it, there's plenty."

"Are you coming with us, your lordship?" asked Philip. He darted ahead and called back over his shoulder: "We're going down to the lake!"

"To the lake! Splendid!"

"We are *not* going to the lake! We're going to the . . ." Lilibet scrambled forward to catch up.

"Why ever not? It's charming there. Clear mountain water, waves lapping against the shore, and all that. A fine choice."

"But . . ." There didn't seem any point protesting. After all, her one objection to the lake—namely, Roland's presence there—had been made more or less redundant. "I suppose so, then," she finished weakly.

"Excellent. Steady on, Philip!" Roland bounded on ahead after the boy, his tall body shimmering with grace and energy.

She followed the two of them down the terraced vineyards, one by one; across the tender new grass in the sheep meadow; past the apple and peach trees, heavy with rich-scented blossoms. The delicate spring air rushed against her cheek, smelling of newly turned earth, and the thread of anxiety in her belly began to mellow and ripen into something much nicer.

Something closer to anticipation.

SEVEN

Was it fair play to win a lady's favor by complimenting her offspring? Roland pondered the matter briefly, and then concluded as he usually did when faced with questions of delicate ethics: Ignore them.

"He's a fine boy," Roland said, watching Philip arrange the stones on the lakeshore. He paused, searched his brain, and added: "Clever lad."

"Too clever at times," she answered, in a quiet voice. She sat with her back against the sturdy trunk of an olive tree, her gaze pinioned to her son's every move. "Don't go too close to the water, Philip!" she called out.

The boy pretended not to hear. Roland could tell, having utilized the technique on a regular basis as a child. Well, he still did, to be perfectly honest. He leaned back on one elbow and considered Lilibet from the corner of his eye.

She'd been friendly enough. Too friendly, perhaps: the sort of shallow familiarity she'd shown when she first walked into the stables three weeks ago, pretending nothing existed between them. He reached for another piece of cheese from his napkin and let the pungent flavor fill his mouth.

Time to stir things up, he decided.

"Tell me," he said, turning over to face her, "what was your husband like?"

"Is," she said. "He still exists. He's still my husband."

"What *is* he like, then?"

"I'm not sure I know what you mean." She gave him a direct look. "I suppose you know him as well as I do, after all. You move in the same circles."

"Not really. I know him by reputation."

She shrugged. "Well, there you are. Reputations are seldom wrong in the essentials." She reached behind her head and pulled out a single long hatpin. "But I suppose you were really asking what sort of lover he was. That's what you really want to know, isn't it?"

He choked and sat up. "Good God."

She smiled and lifted her hat from her head, setting it on the ground beside her. "You think I can't be daring? That I'm still the same girl I was six years ago?"

"Of course not. And I adore you even more for it."

This time she laughed. "Well, it's no more than you deserve, prying like that. I ought to tell you, just to make you think twice before you ask such things again."

She was just far enough away that he couldn't touch her. He longed to reach out his hand, to make some sort of contact, but her hat sat on the grass between them like a prim, long-brimmed chaperone. Had he really experienced carnal knowledge of that body? Felt those eager hips surge against his?

"Only say what you want," he said.

She returned her gaze to Philip. "What's there to say? I had to put you from my head. I had to. I owed it to Lord Somerton, to the idea of marriage itself. I thought . . . well, I knew his reputation, of course. But I was naive; I didn't know what it meant. What one really did in bed with someone, what that entailed."

"Oh, surely not!" he exclaimed. "You can't have been that ignorant."

She slanted him an enigmatic look. "I knew the essential mechanics. But not everything else."

"The best parts, you mean. God knows I imagined them with you."

"Did you?"

Was that a note of flirtation in her tone? Roland's nerves jumped to attention. *This* he knew how to handle. This was his territory. "My dear Lilibet," he drawled, "if you'd known the sort of lascivious thoughts in my head as I spun you around those blasted ballrooms, you'd have tossed your lemonade in my face."

She didn't laugh, didn't arch her eyebrow, didn't play along. Her eyes made a lightning check on Philip, before returning to Roland. Something in her expression made him lean forward, trying to read the soft blue of her eyes. Nostalgia? Desire?

"You'd have been surprised," she said. "I'd have been delighted to know your thoughts. Girls have desires, after all, even if we don't know exactly what we're longing for."

"You were thinking the same things, then?" He wasn't flirting now. He could barely mouth the words.

She didn't answer at first. She studied him, turning something over in her mind, until finally she said, "Not exactly, I suppose. You were, I'm sure, much less innocent than I was."

He hesitated. "True."

She sighed, her bosom rising and falling beneath the neat, high-cut violet bodice of her gown. "It isn't fair, is it? If you *had* spoken first, if we *had* married, I'd have come to you an innocent, as pure as a lily, while you . . ." She let the suggestion hang there and reached for a boiled egg.

He looked at his hands. "I swear to you, Lilibet, from the moment I met you, I had no thought of any other woman. Only you, all that summer. And if we *had* married, I'd never have . . . there'd have been no ghosts in our bed, no question of others, never."

She nibbled at the edge of the egg and set it back down on her napkin. She spoke with dripping sarcasm. "Oh, these things you men say. These promises of eternal fidelity. Somerton said something rather like that, before we married. I recall being surprised it needed to be said. After all, I would never have dishonored him. I simply assumed it would never occur to him, either."

"Ah."

A flush began to spread over her cheeks, faint and becoming. "I tried very hard. I tried to love him. I allowed him . . . whenever he wanted . . ."

Roland's hand fisted in the grass beside him. He picked up another piece of cheese and turned to stare out at the lake. It didn't help: the image of her body, lithe and naked, entwined in his imagination with Somerton's broad bulk amid the sun-splashed waters before him. Had she enjoyed it at all? Had Somerton excited her, pleasured her? Had she lain there passively, or had she urged him on, ridden atop him, used her mouth on him?

Her voice conveyed only facts. "I . . . I became with child straightaway, however, and after that first month he seemed to think . . . I suppose he didn't want to risk anything, once the doctor had confirmed things. He wanted an heir most acutely." She was firm, matter-of-fact. A breeze drifted across her forehead, riffling a lock of her hair loose from its pins. She brushed it absently behind her ear. "Fool that I was, I thought he was making a great sacrifice for my sake. After all, he . . . I knew his appetites were . . ." She cleared her throat. "He was discreet, at first. It wasn't until after Philip was born that I realized the truth. The scale of it."

Damn it all. Which was worse: imagining her in bed with Somerton, or imagining her shame at his philandering? "I'm sorry," he whispered. The gentle words belied the rage billowing inside him. He wanted to fight Somerton: not with guns or swords or anything so gentlemanly, but with his fists. He wanted to feel the man's jaw pop, feel his nose crush into jelly.

Lilibet went on. "I threw it in his face. We had a dreadful row. I was told, in no uncertain terms, what I should expect from my marriage, and from then on . . . What is it, dear?"

Roland looked up to see Philip scampering in from the lakeshore, eyes huge with excitement.

"Mama!" He waved a rock in her face. "I've struck gold!"

"Oh, let me see!" She rose from the ground in a graceful motion and took the rock from Philip. "Look at that! Astonishing! See how it sparkles!"

"Is it real gold, Mama? Is it? Like those chaps found in California?"

She looked at the rock closely, and then held it up to the sunlight, turning it this way and that. Her brow knit with deep concentration. "Why, yes, Philip," she said. "I believe it is. I can't think what else it would be. A great vein of it, too! You've made our fortunes!"

His face shone. He turned to Roland. "Look, your lordship! Gold!"

Lilibet smiled and handed him the rock. "See?"

Roland took the rock and turned it about. A seam of sparkling pyrite ran through the center and along one side. He looked up at Philip's eager face, at his dark eyes, the same shape and shade as Somerton's. Not an especially handsome fellow, Somerton: rough-hewn bones, olive skin, dark features. Philip favored his mother, for the most part, but those eyes were unmistakable. They reminded Roland of the last time he'd seen Somerton, at his club. The earl tended to keep to a few cronies, as hard-drinking and hard-whoring as he was, who would have been blackballed if they hadn't been peers. As it was, they were pariahs, gambling together in a private room long into the night, invisible to most members, and then disappearing to whatever low den would take them in.

But this particular night, not long after the New Year, most of the club's members had been buried at their country estates, and Roland had been sitting in the leather-scented gloom of the library, tucked behind a newspaper, sherry at the ready, waiting for a colleague to meet him for a confidential chat. He'd felt a looming presence before him and unfolded the newspaper to find Somerton glaring down at him with those cold midnight eyes. *Can I help you, old man?* Roland had inquired politely, and Somerton had looked him over. *No*, he'd said, and set himself into a wing chair at the other end of the room with a neatly ironed copy of the *Times*, malevolence crackling the air around him. MacDougal had appeared soon after, and Roland had managed to exchange his information with the necessary discretion, but the unsettling weight of Somerton's black eyes had lurked in the background throughout, until the man had risen and left a quarter hour later.

"Sir?"

Philip's voice pierced Roland's reverie. He blinked a few times, attempting to dispel Somerton's image from his head, while the boy's uncanny eyes fastened on his face. "Yes, lad?"

"The rock, sir! What do you think?"

Roland glanced down at the object in his hand and spoke without thinking. "Afraid it's pyrite, old fellow. But keep looking. Persistence, that's the ticket."

Philip's eager face drooped before him. Lilibet's gasp came from his left.

"I see, sir. Thank you." Philip turned and trudged back to the lakeshore.

Oh hell.

He glanced at Lilibet and wished he hadn't. The blue flame in her eyes could have melted down the stone in his hand, pyrite and all. She whirled around without a word and went after Philip.

Roland threw himself back in the grass and stared up at the blue Tuscan sky. If his aching loins could speak, they'd have moaned with despair.

No luck tonight, that was certain.

When Lilibet returned to the picnic at last, pockets full of promising pyrite-streaked rocks and Philip's equilibrium restored, she found it had all been tidied up. The food and utensils were packed away in the basket, and the white cloth lay folded atop. Roland stood leaning against an olive tree, arms crossed against his solid chest, watching them both.

"Thank you for cleaning up," she said, reaching for the basket.

He took it from her before she could lift it. "Heading back to the castle?"

She bent to retrieve her hat and placed it back on her head. "Yes," she said, sticking in the pin, grateful for the physical movement to disguise her nervousness. She hadn't meant to be so candid earlier; something about the warm weather and the pleasure of the simple food had wrought an ease in the air between them. A dangerous ease, the kind she'd sought so hard to avoid until now. Where might it have led, if Philip hadn't been there?

She couldn't trust herself.

She went on briskly. "We've a busy afternoon. Philip has his lessons with Abigail, and I'm badly behind on Aristophanes."

"Oh, Mama, do I *have* to do lessons? It's such a smashing day outside."

"Yes, you do. And you like Abigail, so no more complaining. Or else *I'll* give you your lessons, which isn't nearly as nice."

Roland led them away from the lake, picking his way between the olive trees to where the terraces began climbing the hillside. The vines had just begun to sprout their leaves, pale new green under the warming sun, and a few men wandered among them, clipping away shoots and strengthening the new growth with long willow branches. Philip clung to her hand, unwilling to take the lead as he had before.

Roland glanced back and saw them, several yards behind. He stopped until they caught up. "Awfully sorry," he said. "Lost in thought."

"It's no trouble. Go on ahead if you like. We shouldn't be seen like this, after all."

"Oh, I don't mind. Let Wallingford do his worst."

Lilibet glanced down. "Philip, do you think you can run ahead a moment and find a peach blossom for Mama from the trees at the end of the terrace?"

Philip plunged ahead, white sailor's jacket flashing in the sunlight.

"I must apologize," Roland said. "I'm no use at all around children, it seems."

She sighed. "These things seem so obvious to me, but then my whole world is wrapped up in him. I don't suppose you've spoken with a child in years."

"You're splendid at it, on the other hand. How the devil do you learn these things?" He spoke lightly, quizzically. As if it didn't really matter.

"Look," she said, "we really mustn't be seen. I hope . . ." She paused. "I hope I may rely on your discretion. My name . . . If it's known that I'm here, if Somerton finds out, if he knows that *you're* here, too . . ."

"Good God!" he burst out. "You don't think I'd breathe a word, do you?"

Tears started in her eyes, to her frustration. She squeezed them back with ferocity. "He can't know where I am. Please understand. He can't. We've already run the most appalling risk."

Roland's voice dripped with scorn. "Come now. How the devil could Somerton find out? Too drunk to see past his own nose, most nights . . ."

"You fool." She shook her head and stared down at the endless blades of grass passing beneath her feet. How could she explain? "Think of it. The wager, the stakes. An advertisement in the *Times*. Even if the names are disguised, he'll find out. He finds out everything. You don't know what he's capable of."

He stopped under the shade of an apple tree and turned to her, grasping her arm. "Did he hurt you? By God, if he harmed you . . ."

"Stop. It's not your concern."

"It *is* my concern!" His eyes blazed at her; his other hand came up to grip her. He loomed before her, not so immense and forbidding as Somerton, but broad and lithe and vibrating with strength, his checked wool jacket straining along the width of his shoulders.

"Stop it! Someone will see us!"

"I don't give a bloody damn! Just tell me this: *Did he hurt you?*"

The passion in his voice froze her in place. "Not . . . not in that way. Please let go. If we're seen, if your brother and his wager . . . He's determined to win, his pride's at stake, and Abigail goads him so . . ."

He pulled her behind the slender trunk of the apple tree. The heady scent of blossom enclosed them; a heavy-laden branch brushed at her hat. "Why the devil are you so loyal to that man? I'd protect you; I'd fight for you; I'd do anything for you. The damned beast. Why honor your marriage vows, when they mean nothing to him?"

Her throat hurt, looking at him. His beautiful face lit with rage and love and need, nothing like the laughing Roland of summer garden parties and London ballrooms. She dropped her eyes and saw that he'd loosened his necktie, unbuttoned the top of his collar. The skin at the hollow of his throat beckoned her irresistibly.

But she *could* resist; she had to resist. She looked back up, into the hard warmth of his hazel eyes. "If you have to ask that," she said, past the steady ache of grief in her throat, "you really don't know me at all, do you?"

His gaze searched hers. "You're wrong. I know you better than you know yourself, Lilibet." He brushed his fingers against her cheek, as gentle as a hummingbird's wings. "I know that you can't possibly go on living as you have, married to a man like that. The Lilibet I know would tell London's dragons to go hang themselves, rather than stay married to a drunken whoremonger like Somerton."

At the words *drunken whoremonger*, something snapped inside her. She shrugged away from his grasp and hissed, "And do what? Marry you instead, and spend the next six years at home with another baby, while you swive your way through all the beds in London you haven't visited already?"

He started backward, eyes wide with outrage so palpable it stung her face. "What the hell do you mean by that?"

"Oh, you'd be far more charming about it, I'm sure. Lord Roland Penhallow always did have a talent for keeping the ladies starry-eyed." She pointed her finger into his chest. "But underneath you're all the same. You've no more notion of fidelity than a rutting bull. Once you've got what you want, you're on to the next pretty face. The next conquest, the next bit of fun."

He stared at her, shocked. "That's absurd! I'd never . . ." He checked himself.

Her face burned. "Do you think I'm an idiot?" she demanded. "Do you think I don't know? When news of your latest damned escapade was delivered to me in detail by one friend or another every week, for the last several years? Always with the same smug smile, always with the greatest relish. *Oh, my dear, you'll never guess what I've just heard; the most delicious tidbit about our naughty friend.*"

His eyes closed. "I'm not like Somerton, Lilibet. I stand by my promises."

"Oh yes. Just as you stood by me that last summer?"

"That's not fair! That was different. That was . . ." His words trailed off, trapped somewhere in his heaving chest. He searched her face with pleading eyes, and went on, more softly: "I was a boy, then, Lilibet. A sulking, resentful boy, who'd never before had something he loved taken away. I like to think . . . I'd like to *prove* to you . . . that I've grown up a bit, since then."

He looked so humble, so contrite, so vulnerable, as if he were holding out his heart toward her, cradled between his two broad hands. At the sight of his earnest face, the pain inside her grew until it vibrated, ready to snap.

She put her hand up, palm outward. "Enough, Roland. Just leave me be. I have troubles enough already."

She turned and strode up the hill to where Philip stood waiting with his arms full of peach blossoms, an impatient expression on his face.

EIGHT

Roland would rather have torn up the paper in his pocket than read it. Burned it, spat on it, damned its author to a living hell. Preferably with a bevy of large-breasted women dancing eternally naked just beyond his reach. That would be fitting. That would be justice, by God.

He'd never been in such an invidious position in his life. Lilibet casting up his promiscuous reputation in his face, and he unable to defend himself! Couldn't deny it, couldn't explain it, couldn't laugh it away.

Couldn't tell her the truth.

Because of bloody Sir Edward and his bloody secrets and the whole damned rotten intelligence service, blast it all to hell and back again.

Roland burst through the door of the kitchen and dropped the picnic basket on the large center table with a vengeful thud. A large tureen of beans rattled at the far end, as if surprised from a nap.

"Signore!"

Roland jumped and turned. A maid stood in the doorway, her eyebrows arched high and anxious into her forehead.

"What the devil!" he exclaimed. Bloody hell. Had his skills grown rusty so quickly out here in the wilderness? Or was it Lilibet, addling his wits? Many had tried to sneak up on Lord Roland Penhallow in the past few years, but none had succeeded.

Now a simple Italian kitchen maid could nearly empty his bladder with a single ill-timed *Signore*.

Her mouth flailed helplessly. "Signore . . . is basket . . . is Signora Somerton . . ." She looked at the basket, and at him, and the pitcher dropped from her hands to shatter on the floor. "Oh, *Dio*!" she cried. She bent to the ground, face as red as poppies, and gathered the pieces into her apron amid a flood of distressed Italian syllables.

Roland melted. He dropped to his knees next to the poor girl. "There, there. Here, I'll do it. A bit of crockery, that's all." He pushed her hands aside, collected the broken pieces, piled them on the table, and took his handkerchief from his pocket. "See? No bother at all, my dear. Broken any number of plates myself." He gave her the handkerchief, into which she promptly blew her nose with abandon. "Yes. Quite. Er, keep it, if you will. No returno." He motioned with his hand.

She looked up at him and smiled through her tears. A pretty girl, he supposed, all shiny black hair and round rosy cheeks. He smiled back. "You see? All better. *Buon*, I believe."

Her watery dark eyes took on a dreamy sheen. "*Grazie*, Signore Penhallow." She said it charmingly, with a lyric Italian lilt.

"Think nothing of it, signorina . . . er . . ."

Her smile deepened, revealing a well-placed dimple next to her plump mouth. "Francesca, signore. *Mi chiamano* Francesca."

"Francesca! Fine name. My mother was called Frances, rest her soul. Same sort of handle, I believe. Only English." He patted his pockets. The paper crackled beneath his hands. He glanced at the picnic basket on the table. "In any case, I'm off. Just returning the basket. Charming lunch. The cheese was excellent. Er . . ." He looked back at Francesca, whose face had grown even rosier, head tilted slightly to one side, eyes blinking in slow strokes. He cleared his throat. "Er, yes. Well. I'm off."

He sidled out the door and made his escape.

On the first evening of Roland's arrival at the Castel sant'Agata, despite the rain and the confusion and the mind-warping knowledge that Lilibet Harewood (he tried, whenever possible, to banish the word *Somerton* from her name) would be sleeping beneath the same roof for the foreseeable future, he'd still found a moment to manufacture a false back to the third drawer in his ancient Italian dresser.

Into the small space this created, he'd hidden a few essential items: the list of contacts with which Sir Edward had confided him; a rectangular wooden box of gold coins, signed out in triplicate from Sir Edward's meticulous accounts and suitable for bribery as needed; and his codebook.

Such a nuisance, codebooks. Roland usually memorized each new one as it came out; his talent for mathematics was legendary among the small circle of people who knew about it. But it had been a busy few months since that fateful meeting in Sir Edward's library, and he'd had no communication at all from his colleagues since paying a brief visit to Beadle in the Florence office, and one glance at the paper told him it employed a code both recent and complex.

He closed his door, set a chair against the lock, and went to the dresser.

The drawer opened easily, its mellow old wood worn into comfortable grooves and long accustomed to the vicissitudes of heat and damp. Roland reached inside, slid open the false back, and pulled the slim paperbound volume from its resting place.

CAHIER DE MATHEMATIQUES, proclaimed the plain pale blue cover, in a tenuous attempt at disguise, though any counteragent worth his salt would know exactly what it contained if he bothered to look inside. Roland removed the note from his pocket and consulted the wax seal for the proper code. A FOX type, of course; he peered at the animal's right ear until he discovered the number 6 imprinted at the tip, and flipped through the codebook until the pages opened to FOX 6.

The little room had no desk. Roland went to his trunk, got out his travel secretary, and opened the lid. The sweet smell of cedar filled the air. He selected a fine-tipped fountain pen, closed the lid again, and sat down on an old wooden chair, secretary in his lap, long legs propped atop the bottom edge of the bed frame.

Nothing like cold numbers to take a man's mind off his women troubles. The fountain pen scratched comfortably against the paper, a fragrant breeze caressed Roland's cheek from the window, and his brain sank gratefully into the complex puzzle before him. After a moment, the book became unnecessary, and he tossed it onto the bed. The numbers rose up around him like a three-dimensional model, until he could see the solution, the decoded message, in its architecture.

His pen dropped to the floor. "Good God," he said.

Thump thump thump, went the door.

Roland jumped from the chair, just saving the secretary before it crashed at his feet. "Who is it?" he called.

"Your brother, damn it! Open up, for God's sake!"

Roland exhaled. Bloody Wallingford. He chucked the secretary back in the trunk and closed the heavy wooden lid.

"Why the devil have you got your door locked?" demanded Wallingford, by way of greeting. He strode into the room with his usual air of unassailable command, booted heels cracking on the old wooden boards. His handsome face wore an especially thunderous expression, as if he'd just been told his Mayfair town house had been invaded and occupied by a band of cigarette-smoking anarchist squatters in his absence.

"Good afternoon, Brother. Yes, I'm quite well. And

you?" Roland ducked behind his brother's large frame and closed the door with a firm thrust.

Wallingford's voice came dark and alarmed at his back. "Why the bolted door? You don't think they've taken to *spying* on us, do you?"

Roland whirled. "What's that?"

"The women." Wallingford struck his palm with a closed ducal fist. He looked as though he'd just had a bath of extraordinary vigor: His hair hung dark and damp above his collar, and his cheeks shone with the same fresh-scrubbed pinkness as young Philip's. "Bloody hell! I expect you're right! Spying, of course! How else would . . ."

Roland tilted back his chin and laughed. "Spying on us? The women? For God's sake, Wallingford. Been at the opium, have you?"

Wallingford's stern face tightened into a scowl. "Don't be naive, Penhallow. I wouldn't put it past them. Crafty harpies. Do you know, I caught Lady Morley at Burke's workshop this morning?"

Roland gasped and put his hand to his heart. "No!"

Wallingford raised a finger and stabbed it toward Roland's chest. "Damned impertinent cub. Don't you know they're determined to make us break first? That they're determined not just to win the damned wager, but to drive us out of here entirely, before that fellow Rosseti can be found to set things right for us? There was Lady Morley, all but seducing poor Burke before my eyes, and do you know what her ladyship gave me as an excuse?"

"I can't imagine."

"That she was delivering Burke's post. His *post*, by God!" Another smack of the fist.

"The wicked strumpet!"

"Exactly! I told . . ." Wallingford stopped and frowned. "Are you being sarcastic again, you mongrel?"

Roland leaned forward and peered at the hair above his brother's left ear. "I say. Is that a *feather* in your mane, old boy?"

Wallingford clapped his hand to the side of his head. "Where?"

"Just there. Under your hand. Charming little downy white . . ."

"Never mind that!" The duke raked at his black locks with vicious fingers and turned to stride to the window. "The point is, we've got to outsmart them. Beat them to the punch, chase them out ourselves. Before poor old Burke succumbs to Lady Morley's charms and we're hoisted by our own petards."

"Sorry, old man. Don't quite follow you." A flash of blue caught the corner of Roland's eye. He glanced at the bed, where the *Cahier de Mathematiques* lay in bold relief against the faded yellow bedspread.

Hell.

"The *bet*, man! The wager!" Wallingford turned to skewer him with an intense black gaze. "If Lady Morley succeeds, we've got to concede. An advertisement in the *Times*, Penhallow! And once *that* happens . . ." His voice trailed off, as if the consequences of a *Times* advertisement were too appalling for words.

"Once that happens . . . ?" Roland prodded.

"Why, we shall be humiliated before them all! We'd be forced to leave; our lives would be made miserable. More miserable, I say, than they are already."

Roland shrugged. "I'm not miserable at all. I think it's rather charming, having a spot of female company to liven things up."

Wallingford's face, already pink, turned the color of an angry tomato. "Oh, all very well for you, isn't it? You and that damned Lady Somerton."

A sudden gust of wind took hold of the window, flinging it against the wall with a loud bang and ruffling open the pages of the *Cahier de Mathematiques*. Roland took a single step forward. "Do not," he said, with icy precision, "ever say those words again."

Wallingford's mouth opened briefly, and then his eyes

dropped. "Sorry, old boy. Quite in the wrong. She's . . . well, she's a woman of virtue . . ."

"She's the finest woman who ever lived." Roland went to the dresser, placed his fingers against the edge, and leaned backward. Wallingford turned to face him, with his back to the bed.

"Yes, of course." The duke's brow darkened. "You, on the other hand, you weak-willed dog of a fellow. Stay away from her. I'd trust her honor above any of the others, but your damned twitchy co—"

Roland held up his hand. "Watch yourself, Brother."

"All right." The duke sighed. "Shall we say, your propensity for seduction may prove our downfall. Our very *public* downfall. To say nothing of poor Lady Somerton's."

Roland folded his arms. Lilibet's words in the orchard echoed in his ears, her genuine fear of discovery by Lord Somerton. His brain, preoccupied by Sir Edward's note, began to shake itself off and consider what his brother was saying. "Look here, Wallingford. You're not to say a word about her presence here, do you understand? That beast of a husband of hers . . ."

"What the devil do you mean by that?" Wallingford's head jerked to attention.

"Just that he's a damned wretch, and I understand she'd be quite happy if he never got wind of her whereabouts, for the time being."

The duke's eyes narrowed. "Are you trying to tell me we're harboring a runaway wife? Because that's hardly . . ."

Roland leaned forward and spoke in a voice of harsh intensity. "I wouldn't put a dog in Somerton's care, Wallingford, and neither would you! Be compassionate, for once in your misspent life."

Wallingford blinked at the onslaught. "You don't suppose . . ."

"Suppose what?"

"Well, that it's the reason they want us gone? They're afraid Somerton will hear about it?"

Roland let his eyes drop to the floorboard before him. "It's possible."

"Hmm." Silence, and then: "Well, regardless, I shan't comply. Any number of unoccupied castles lying about the area, I'm sure, and the women can damned well find another." His voice blazed.

Roland sighed, still staring at the floor. "Tell me, Wallingford. Why the devil does it matter to you so much? Can't we simply call off the wager and live amicably together?"

"You're joking. Live amicably with the harpy sisters? Oh, I say, Penhallow. *Mathematics*?"

Roland's head shot up.

The duke reached out one long wool-covered arm to the bed and picked up the pale blue codebook. "What the devil? What sort of mathematics is this?"

Roland made a long and ungraceful leap forward to snatch the *Cahier de Mathematiques* from his brother's hands. "Nothing! Just a . . . a pamphlet I picked up in France. A new mathematics. Fascinating stuff. Quite beyond your level, I'm afraid."

Wallingford made a futile swipe at recovering the book. "Look here! I've a decent brain for maths, and that . . . Now, look here . . ."

Roland stuck the book in the top drawer of his dresser and pushed it shut. "Never mind. It's nothing. The point is this . . ."

Wallingford stepped closer. His voice dropped to a silky growl. "Hold a moment, Brother. Tell me more about this mathematics of yours."

"It's nothing. For God's sake. A few numbers on the page. I . . ."

"But it's important, isn't it?" Wallingford leaned his head forward, as if sniffing the air. Perhaps he was, the crafty dog. "You just took the greatest pains to hide it from me."

Roland's heart made an unnatural thud behind his ribs. *Be sensible*, he told himself. *He knows nothing. Remember yourself.* He took in a calming breath and closed his eyes. When he opened them an instant later, he'd schooled his expression into its most charming and empty-headed arrangement.

"Oh rot," he said lightly. "You're just a damned suspicious bastard, Wallingford. What do you think it is? A collection of love notes from mathematical machines? Coded messages from one of those Oriental contraptions, with the . . . the beads and whatnot?" He twirled the first two fingers of his right hand in a helpless gesture.

"Whatever it is, you're taking great pains to conceal it."

Roland heaved a dramatic sigh. "Conceal it? You're joking, surely? Have a look, then, if it means so much to you." He turned and pulled out the book and tossed it at his brother's chest. "If you can make heads or tails of it, I'll give you a fiver."

Wallingford shot him a malevolent stare and ran his thumb along the edges of the pages. "*Cahier de Mathematiques*, my arse," he muttered, selecting a page. His eyes ran over the lines, left to right: one, two, three. A frown furrowed his brow. He lifted one finger and traced along the paper in a long deliberate motion.

He looked up. "I know what this is."

Roland folded his arms and rolled his eyes to the ceiling, pretending to study the pattern of solid wood beams across the plaster. His mind hummed, constructing excuses and scenarios. "Pray enlighten me," he drawled, in his most careless voice.

Wallingford snapped the book shut. "Chemical formulae, of course. Are you helping out Burke with his electrical batteries? Why didn't you tell me?"

Roland's jaw wobbled. "Batteries?"

"Yes. I, er, recognize the equations. Matter and force and . . . er . . . ether and so forth."

"To say nothing of ions."

"Ions, yes." Wallingford held out the *Cahier de Mathematiques* with an air of assurance only a duke could muster in the face of such abject ignorance.

Roland took the book without looking at it and folded it into his hand, against his chest. His gut went hollow with relief. "Haven't told Burke yet, of course. I want to surprise him in a few days. Walk into his workshop and rattle on about charges and sparks and all that. He'll be absolutely gobsmacked, don't you think?"

"Undoubtedly. But about the women . . ."

Roland took his brother by the arm and guided him to the door. "Look here, Wallingford. I've no head for strategy, no head at all. Makes my poor brain spin like a top. And I'm as soft as butter around the ladies. You know that. I could no more plot their downfall than I could plot against our own mother."

"Yes, true. You *are* a damned old romantic," said Wallingford, with patronizing affection.

"You see? So you make all the decisions in that regard, and I'll . . . well, I'll simply hover in the background, I suppose." He smiled his guileless smile. "Sound all right?"

"Ah yes." Wallingford patted his shoulder and reached for the door latch. "I'll put my brain to use this afternoon, and spring it on 'em at dinner tonight. Ha-ha. Give that Miss Harewood and her damned goose down a bit of long-overdue medicine, by God."

"Miss Harewood?" Roland lifted his eyebrows. "Goose down?"

"Yes. Well. Never mind. And look, Penhallow," the duke added, with a final kindly look over his shoulder. "I don't mean to crush you, but I doubt you've the right sort of head for mathematical endeavors. Leave all that higher-level thinking to Burke and myself. Stick to your poetry, that's the ticket."

"Yes! Quite! In fact, I've the most delightful sonnet in contemplation at the moment. Perhaps you'd care to hear it?" Roland offered.

Wallingford blanched. "Yes. No. Perhaps after dinner, old man. I'll . . . er . . . I'll look for you." He bolted down the hallway.

Roland raised his arm. "Right-ho! See you then!" he called.

Wallingford's hand rose up in the air, the last part of him visible as he disappeared down the stairs.

Roland waited another second or two, just to be sure, and slipped back inside the room and closed the door. He leaned against the old wood for some time, eyes narrowed into the abundant afternoon light, mind spinning with the precision of a finely tuned rotary engine. His fingers closed around the paper, crisp and sharp cornered in his pocket.

In the weeks since his arrival in Italy, he hadn't given much thought to the situation back in England. *I'll sort it out*, Sir Edward had promised. *Get to the bottom of things. Ferret out the troublemaker.* Roland hated that aspect of his work: the infighting, the politics, the pitting of one agency against another. It seemed so pointless, so wasteful. He much preferred the excitement and challenge of field-work. If Sir Edward wanted to ferret out the Judas in their midst, he was welcome to it.

Besides, Lilibet's appearance had made dropping out of sight a great deal more delightful than he'd anticipated.

Ah. Yes. Lilibet. Darling girl. What would she make of the information in his pocket?

Roland pulled the paper free and unfolded it. The letters and numbers leapt up at him in perfect English, now that he'd deciphered the code. The message itself was short and direct, as Sir Edward's communications tended to be, and produced a great many more questions than it answered:

> *Triangulation of evidence suggests possible source Earl of S in Navy office. Whereabouts of his wife and son currently unknown. Stay in place and await further instruction.*

It seemed Lilibet's appearance in Italy might not prove a coincidence at all.

NINE

The dining table, like the rest of the Castel sant'Agata, had been divided down the middle. Every evening, the ladies sat along one side, and the gentlemen lined up on the other, a configuration that proved ideal for sparring.

Lilibet, her spirits still in disarray from the disastrous exchange with Roland in the peach orchard, could hardly be bothered to ask for the salt, but the others had no such reservations. Alexandra had apparently been discovered delivering Mr. Burke's post to his workshop this morning, and the duke was convinced that her motives had been sinister.

Abigail, of course, did not agree. "But that's absurd. If you seduced Mr. Burke, successfully I mean, the wager would technically be a draw, wouldn't it?"

Alexandra choked.

"Yes," said Mr. Burke. "Yes, I believe it would."

Abigail turned to Wallingford. "You see? You may put your mind entirely at ease on the subject of seduction, Your Grace. No reasonable person would contemplate such a scheme. Two advertisements in the *Times*! It wouldn't do."

The duke's face reddened alarmingly.

"Dear me, Wallingford," said Lady Morley. "You really

must endeavor to calm your nerves. I fear you will bring on an apoplexy. Have you any medical training, Mr. Burke?"

Mr. Burke selected an olive. "Only a few rudiments, I regret to say. Hardly enough to loosen his cravat."

"I am happy to be the source of such endless amusement. But you"—Wallingford stabbed his finger at Mr. Burke's chest—"and you"—to Lord Roland—"have no idea at all what these women have in contemplation. From the moment of our arrival last month, they've been scheming and harassing us, in order to make our lives here so hellish as to drive us away entirely, and leave them the castle to themselves. Do not, Lady Morley, be so insulting as to deny it."

"I should be very happy to see the last of you, Wallingford," said Alexandra. "I make no attempt to hide the fact."

Lilibet picked up her wine and drank. It was raw stuff, disagreeable. She set it down again and willed Alexandra to keep her tongue in check. From across the table, Roland was gazing at her. She could feel the tender weight of his stare, as if he were stripping her bare, piece by piece.

Wallingford spoke in a cold voice. "Very well, then, Lady Morley. I should like to propose an amendment to our wager. To increase the stakes, as it were."

"Oh, good God," said Mr. Burke. "Haven't you a better use of your time, Wallingford? Reading some of that vast collection in the library, perhaps? It *is* what we're here for, after all."

Alexandra laughed. "He's welcome to join our literary discussion in the salon. We should be pleased to hear an additional perspective, although I would suggest bringing an umbrella, in case of inclement weather."

"No, damn it all! I beg your pardon, Lady Somerton."

Why on earth did everyone think her the guardian of all civilized behavior? "Not at all, Your Grace," she said dryly.

"My proposal is this," said Wallingford. He leaned forward, his dark eyes keen beneath his furrowed brow. "That the forfeit, in addition to Burke's excellent suggestion of an advertisement in the *Times*, should include an immediate removal of the offending party from the castle."

Removal. Lilibet's limbs went cold. She clenched the stem of her wineglass and looked desperately at Roland.

He sat there as calm and insouciant as ever, his golden hair dipping in his forehead, the very picture of confident manhood. He shook his head and whistled. "Hard terms, old man. Are you quite sure? What if it's *us* that's given the old heave-ho?"

"You are, I admit, the weakest link in the chain," said the duke, "but I believe I may rely upon Lady Somerton's honor, if nothing else."

"Really, Your Grace," choked Lilibet. She felt as if she might faint. She tried to gather her wits, to say something that might save the situation, but her head was too dizzy, her stomach too roiling.

Alexandra broke in. "This is beyond absurd, Wallingford, all this talk of conspiracies and whatnot. I assure you, I haven't the slightest intention of seducing poor Burke, and I daresay he has even less desire to be seduced. This is all about this business of the feathers this morning, isn't it? You're trying to have your revenge on us . . ."

Wallingford refilled his glass from the bottle on the table. The rawness of the Chianti seemed to trouble him not at all. "If I'm wrong, Lady Morley, you should have no reason at all to object to the increased stakes. Isn't that so?"

Alexandra looked at Lilibet. Lilibet looked back pleadingly. Surely her cousin wouldn't leap to Wallingford's bait. Surely she had enough sense, enough compassion for Lilibet's plight.

"Of course I shouldn't object." Alexandra spoke with care, picking her words. "Other than a sense of . . . of the absurdity of it all."

Mr. Burke cleared his throat. "Really, Wallingford. It's hardly necessary. I don't see any reason why we can't continue to muddle on as we are. A tuft of goose down, here and there, doesn't much signify. And I'm fairly confident I can resist Lady Morley's charms, however determined her attempts on my virtue." He kept his face quite admirably straight.

Wallingford leaned against the back of his chair and allowed a smug smile to wear across his face. "None of you, then, not one of you has the fortitude to meet my offer? Lady Morley? Your competitive spirit can't be tempted?"

"You always were an ass, Wallingford." Alexandra shook her head.

Lilibet's pulse began to resume its regular cadence against the base of her throat. Alexandra had it well in hand. Alexandra was thinking of something, finding some way to twist the duke's words around, to turn the situation to their advantage. Alexandra would never risk the security of their presence here at the castle.

"Why not?"

The clear voice piped from Alexandra's other side, innocent and ingenuous.

Abigail. Not *Abigail.*

She went on, almost merrily. "I can't speak for your side, Your Grace, but we three are simply going about our business, studying and learning just as we intended. If it amuses you to turn this into a game, to raise the stakes, consider the wager accepted. It means nothing to us, after all. Does it, Alex?"

Next to her, Alexandra traced the handle of her knife where it crossed her empty plate. Her knuckles were white. "No. No, of course not," she said. Beneath the table, she patted Lilibet's knee with her other hand. "Very well. We accept your stakes, Wallingford. Though it hardly matters, as your suspicions are entirely wrongheaded. In fact, your head *itself* seems to be wrongheaded at the moment, and I suggest you turn away from your wild speculations and put it firmly to work as you intended in the first place. We're on Aristophanes ourselves, just now, and my dear Abigail has already reviewed it twice in the original Greek. I'm certain she would have some useful insights for you. Perhaps she can assist you with your alphas and omegas."

With slow deliberation, Lilibet plucked Alexandra's hand from her knee and dropped it in her cousin's lap.

Wallingford prepared to rise. "My alphas and omegas are quite in order, I assure you, Lady Morley. And now, ladies, if you'll pardon the unpardonable, I must excuse myself, and leave you to the far more appealing company of my fellow scholars."

He rose and exited the room, leaving a queasy silence behind him.

Alexandra gave an uncertain laugh. "Now why do I have the distinct impression he's just played us all for fools?"

"Well, well," said Roland. "Amusing, what?"

Mr. Burke folded his napkin and rose. "I think it's time I retired. Ladies, good evening."

Roland heaved a reluctant sigh, but the constraints of etiquette were no match for him. "Yes, quite," he said, rising, too. "Back to those jolly old alphas and omegas in the library. What fun. Ah, this really is the life, isn't it?"

Lilibet considered herself a patient woman. She waited until the gentlemen had left, until their very footsteps had died away in the corridor, before pouncing on her cousin with all claws bared.

Metaphorically, of course.

"What the devil were you thinking?" she demanded, in a decidedly catlike hiss.

Alexandra and Abigail both started and stared at her. She couldn't quite blame them. They'd never heard her say the word *deuce* before, let alone *devil*, let alone anything at all in such a tone of feline menace.

"My dear," Alexandra said, "whatever do you mean?" She leaned aside to allow Francesca to pick up her empty plate.

"You both know exactly what I mean!" Lilibet turned to Abigail and thrust her voice into a singsong falsetto. "*If it amuses you to turn this into a game, to raise the stakes, consider the wager accepted!*"

"Now, wait a moment, my dear . . ." began Alexandra.

"And you!" Lilibet stabbed her forefinger in Alexandra's direction. "*We accept your stakes, Wallingford, though it hardly matters.* Hardly matters, you said!" She let her hand fall to the table in an angry fist. Francesca jumped, nearly dropping the stack of plates in her arm, and scurried out the door.

"Lilibet, dearest," said Alexandra, laying her hand atop Lilibet's like a soothing warm blanket. "You're a dear, sweet, straightforward soul, and don't understand the first thing about gamesmanship . . ."

"Gamesmanship!" Lilibet shot up from her chair and planted her hands on her hips. "Gamesmanship! Is it all just a *game* to you, Alex? Is it? Because I thought—I *rather* thought—it had something to do with my life! With Philip's life!"

Alexandra rose warily and moved behind her own chair, placing her long-fingered hands on the scalloped edge at the top. "Perhaps I used the wrong word . . ."

"Perhaps you did! Perhaps you used the wrong strategy altogether! Because . . ."

She felt a hand on the side of her arm and turned to find Abigail standing there, grave faced, her brown eyes large and round against her pale skin. "Of course we understand, Lilibet. Of course we do. We all love you and Philip. But don't we *want* the gentlemen to leave? Wallingford's proposal plays directly into our hands."

"But don't you see? He aims to win *himself.* He'll be trying to make us crack, so that *we're* forced to leave."

A thump sounded outside the door to the dining room. Lilibet froze, staring into Alexandra's face.

Abigail went to the door. "It's nothing," she said. "Just Francesca, bumping the corner with the plates."

Alexandra tapped her finger against her arm and cast Abigail a significant look across the top of Lilibet's head. "Perhaps it might be wise to discuss this in the kitchen."

Lilibet looked back and forth between her cousins and sighed. "Very well."

Philip sat at the broad wooden table in the kitchen, under the watch of the housekeeper and the maids, finishing his dessert. His gaze lifted from a plate of *panettone* to meet Lilibet's and lit with joy. "Mama!" he cried, and flew into her arms.

She knelt to receive him and buried her face in his warm bread-scented hair. His small limbs clung to her with tenacious strength. "Hello, darling," she said. "Have you been a good boy and eaten your dinner?"

The housekeeper rose from the table, smiling. "He is being such a good boy. He eat his lamb, his *fagioli*, his artichoke. He is growing *forte*, strong." She flexed her white-shirted arm to demonstrate.

"Thank you, Signorina Morini," said Lilibet, returning the housekeeper's smile.

"Signorina Morini gave me an extra piece of *panettone*," he whispered in Lilibet's ear. "Is that all right?"

"If you ate all your dinner, of course it is, poppet." She gave his hair a last tousling and straightened. "Darling, the grown-ups need to have a bit of a chat. Would you like to run along with Francesca and start your bath? Then I'll be there shortly to read your story and tuck you in."

"A bath!" he groaned.

From the corner of her eye, Lilibet saw Francesca heave a desperate sigh. The girl didn't understand much English, but the word *bath* had become painfully evident to her over the past few weeks.

"Yes, dear. No foot-dragging. If you're good with Francesca, I'll read you an extra story tonight." She cast her mind about. "The one about the bunnies. You like that one."

"Mama. Not that one. You've read it over and over. It's for babies."

It took a certain amount of threatening, cajoling, and outright bribery, but eventually Philip made his way upstairs, his hand in Francesca's, and Lilibet collapsed into a worn rush-seated chair at the table, next to Abigail.

"Such a darling," Abigail said. "He told me the most delightful story this afternoon, during his lesson. Something about a picnic at the lake with a certain gentleman of our acquaintance."

"Don't change the subject," said Lilibet sharply. "You're to tell me exactly what sort of plot you're hatching against Wallingford."

"Oh, it's very simple." Abigail reached for the last remaining crumb of *panettone* on Philip's plate and popped it into her mouth. "We're to catch Penhallow seducing you and have them all thrown out."

"What?" demanded Lilibet.

"What?" demanded Alexandra.

"*Che cosa?*" murmured Signorina Morini, from the far end of the table.

Abigail looked innocently about their faces. "Don't you see? I've been needling the poor fellow—Wallingford, I mean—for weeks now, goading him into some sort of step like this. It's perfect. If we catch Penhallow in flagrante, as it were, they'll be honor bound to leave."

Lilibet leapt from her chair. "In flagrante! With Penhallow!"

"Yes, with Penhallow." Abigail lifted her hand, palm up. "Who else? Mr. Burke?"

"Certainly not Mr. Burke," snapped Alexandra.

Abigail ducked her head, hiding a smile. "Yes, of course. I forgot myself. But you and Penhallow, Lilibet—it's perfect! He's desperately in love with you. Crook your finger and he'll be at your side, doing whatever it is men do to seduce women. Tearing at your bodice, I suppose. And . . ."

"I say, where the devil do you hear such things?" demanded Alexandra.

"Novels. And we'll all come bounding in, shouting *Aha!* just like a play." She clapped her hands. "Perfect!"

"But I can't!" said Lilibet. Her pulse pounded in her temples; she dropped back into her chair with a defeated thump. "I can't possibly!"

Abigail reached out to pat her hand. "Oh, we shan't let it go too far, of course. You and your impregnable virtue."

"It's out of the question." Lilibet jerked her hand back and knotted it with the other one in her lap. She took in a deep breath, letting the kitchen scents of rosemary and baking bread spread through her mind, warm and comforting.

"Just a *tiny* tear, Lilibet. I'll mend it myself. Lord Somerton need never know."

"Well, he *will* know, won't he?" Lilibet said, picking at her dress. "When he reads the advertisement in the *Times*."

Abigail waved her hand dismissively. "We'll tell the men the advertisement is unnecessary."

"They'll tell everybody, when they return to town."

"Not if we ask them to remain silent." Abigail smiled. "Wallingford's a bounder, but he's an honorable bounder. More or less."

Alexandra, who had been sitting quietly throughout, eyes fixed to the table, now cleared her throat. "You know, I really don't see that any of this is necessary. The men usually keep to their wing of the castle, and we to ours. What's the difference?" Her voice was oddly soft.

"Because it's such good fun, of course. Come now," Abigail said, turning to Lilibet. Her brown eyes glittered. "Wouldn't it be lovely to have the place to ourselves? To be free of them, once and for all?"

A meditative sound came from the direction of Signorina Morini's throat. Lilibet looked over just in time to catch a small shake of the housekeeper's head, her shiny dark hair escaping her kerchief to curl about her forehead and the nape of her neck. Behind her, the immense hearth glowed with the remains of the fire, hissing and popping in a comforting rhythm; the white beeswax candles in the sconces flickered in warm yellow circles against the plaster walls.

Lilibet put her hands atop the table and drew a circle into the worn wood, acutely conscious of the tiny unknown speck, low in her belly, fighting for survival. In a few months she would be unable to conceal its existence. What would Roland say, what would he do, if he suspected?

She knew the answer. He'd never let a child of his be raised with Somerton's name. He'd confront her husband, force a divorce; she'd lose her son, lose her friends, lose her good name. She'd be left with only this new life growing within her, this new baby, and Roland's fleeting attention, before his passion cooled and his attention wandered. Ostracism, shame, exile, heartbreak: She could taste them in her mouth already, bitter and pungent, a slow poison of the soul.

She looked back up at Abigail's eager elfin face. "So, my dear. How exactly do you propose to arrange this meeting?"

The tiny creak of a floorboard outside the library warned Roland of an intruder.

He went still in his chair, absorbing every detail of the space around him. The musty smells of old leather and damp wood and warm plaster wound through his nostrils; the heavy air hung motionless next to his ears, holding the towering shelves of books in place. Outside the open doorway, a shadow moved against the wall, slight and hesitant.

Roland smiled.

"Come on in, old fellow," he said, placing his thumb inside the crease of his book and closing the pages from view. "It's the man's side of the house, after all."

A small head peered around the doorframe. "Sir?"

"Come in, come in." Roland set the book aside and stood. "Does your mother know you're here?"

Philip took a step forward. "No, sir. Not exactly. I'm meant to be taking my bath just now."

"Oh yes. I quite understand. Baths not at all the thing for a spirited chap like yourself. Glass of . . . er . . ." He glanced at the tray of decanters on the lamp table. "Water?"

"No, thank you, sir." Philip took a few more steps and stopped, straightening his shoulders, fingers plucking at his sleeves. His white sailor's jacket had been removed, as well as his shoes and stockings, but he'd apparently made good his escape before shirt and shorts could be addressed.

"Yes. Well, then." Roland put his hands behind his back. "What seems to be the matter, young man?"

"Well, sir." Philip's throat worked. He put his own hands behind his back, looking stiff and rather touchingly brave. He took a deep breath that seemed to envelop his entire body, and then said, in a rush: "You're the matter, sir."

"*I'm* the matter?"

"Yes, sir. You . . . in the orchard today . . . you made my mother cry."

The floor seemed to fall away beneath Roland's feet. He put out one hand to catch himself on the leather back of the chair from which he'd just risen. "I . . . I'm sorry . . . I *what*?"

Philip's young voice gained strength with the force of righteous conviction. "After she talked to you. I gave her the flowers, and she . . . she had tears, sir. She tried to hide it, like she always does, but I can tell. Sir."

Like she always does.

"I . . . well, I'm awfully sorry." His voice sounded distant in his own ears. His thoughts scrambled about, trying to gain a foothold somewhere, trying to right themselves. "I'd no idea. She seemed all right, at the time."

"What were you talking about?"

"Well, about . . ." *For God's sake, Penhallow. You're a grown man. A damned intelligence agent. Get your wits about you.* "Look here, young man. Perhaps you'd like to sit down a bit." He patted the back of the chair. "Right here, next to the fire. Still a bit chilly, inside these stone walls."

The boy hesitated, tracing a wary glance from the chair to Roland and back. The fire made a loud pop, cracking through the silence, and as if the sound were a signal, Philip drew forward and crept into the chair.

Roland smiled and went to the decanter tray. Among Wallingford's first actions had been the removal of all spirits from the house, though wine had been tacitly saved from this edict and, after some debate, fortified wine as well. One couldn't live in decency without one's sherry, after all. But the library decanter contained only water, fresh and virtuous, drawn from the kitchen well every morning and evening and tasting sweetly of nothing at all. He found a glass and poured off a stiff bumper for Philip.

"Here you are, old chap," he said, handing the glass to the boy. "Thirsty work, wandering about castles at bedtime."

"Thank you, sir." Philip took a cautious sip.

Roland sat down on the nearby sofa and leaned forward,

settling his forearms on his thighs, trapping the fine wool of his trousers in place. "Now then. I expect you know, or perhaps you don't, that I knew your mother a long time ago, in London. Before she met your father."

Philip nodded. "Were you friends?"

"Very good friends. I thought your mother a charming person. I hope . . . I hope I shall always consider her my friend, and she mine."

Philip nodded again and took another drink. "Then why did you make her cry?"

Roland knotted his fingers together, digging the nails into his skin. His gaze fell to the rug before him, old and worn, its colors and pattern long lost to the soles of booted feet. "I didn't mean to. We were talking about the old days, you see, and perhaps she was a bit nostalgic."

"What's that?"

"Well, it's when you remember the old days, when you were younger. The good times you had. And things are different now, not better or worse, just different. But sometimes you miss the old times." Roland looked up. "Does that make any sense?"

Philip's round, childlike face wore an expression of startlingly ferocious concentration. "I don't know. Was that why she was crying?"

"I expect so. I hope I didn't say anything to make her unhappy. I'd hate to make your mother unhappy."

"You'd better not," said Philip. "I'd punch your lights out."

Roland blinked. "Yes. Well. We can't have that."

"My father would find out. He'd punch your lights out, too."

Blood tingled in the tip of Roland's nose and across his cheekbones. "Would he, now?"

Philip sighed. "Yes."

Roland chose his words carefully. "Does he do that sort of thing often?"

A shrug. "Father's always cross. When I was three, or four, four and seven months, I think, I found one of Mama's dolls under the bed and we went riding on the horse together . . ."

"The horse?"

"In the *nursery*. The horse in the *nursery*." Philip's small voice dripped with scorn for slow-witted grown-ups.

"Oh. Oh yes. The rocking horse?"

"Yes! And we rode all across the fields and the roads and Father came up and he shouted . . ." Philip stopped. His eyes went round, and he gave Roland a beseeching look. "You can't tell Mama."

"No. No, of course not. What . . ." Roland swallowed. "What else did your papa do?"

Philip slithered off the leather chair. "Is that a horse book?"

Roland snatched the volume away just in time. "No. No, a dull old grown-up book, not at all interesting." He sprang from the sofa. "Horse books, eh? You like horses?"

"So much. I want to ride in the Derby when I grow up, except Mama probably won't let me. She never lets me do anything amusing." Philip's eyes meandered around Roland's back, trying to glimpse the hidden book.

Roland reached high and shoved the book haphazardly between two treatises on Roman architecture. "Ah, well. Mothers are like that. Anyway, I daresay you'll be far too large to ride the Derby. You've got a solid, broad-shouldered look to you. Ah, here we are. Horses." He pulled down an ancient volume and swiped at the mildew with his sleeve.

"Oh, ripping!" Philip exclaimed. He tore the book from Roland's hands and plopped directly onto the worn carpet. "Warhorses!"

Roland sat down before him, legs crossed, and cocked his head to examine the cover. "*Equus Belli*. So it is."

Philip was already flipping the pages with a fanatic's fascination. "Look at this one! Blimey! What's this mean?" He proffered the page in Roland's direction.

Roland read the Latin caption. " 'Here gallops Bucephalus, steed of Alexander the Great.' A legend, that one. Great black beast of a horse."

"Who was Alexander the Great?"

"Only the greatest general who ever lived, old fellow.

Ruled from Macedonia to Asia Minor. Do you know who tutored him?"

"No."

"Aristotle, my boy. Aristotle himself."

Philip squinted his eyes. "The Greek fellow?"

"Clever lad. They say"—Roland pointed to the engraving—"Alexander tamed the beast when he was ten years old. No one else could do it."

"I should like to try it!" Philip's hand passed reverently over the drawing. He turned the page, his head bowed in concentration, his tousled dark hair glinting in the light from the nearby lamp. The bones of his shoulders poked with determination against the white linen of his shirt.

The fire whispered nearby, growing feeble; Roland rose and added coal from the old iron scuttle. He sat down again exactly as he had before, legs crossed, his knees hovering near the enormous leather binding of EQUUS BELLI and Philip's bowed head.

Somerton's boy. Except that, somehow, in the past several hours, he had ceased being Somerton's boy and became Lilibet's boy. The curve of his cheek, the soft nape of his neck, those sturdy bones straining against his shirt: They were all a part of her. He had grown inside her, nursed at her breast, tucked his body into hers for comfort. She loved him.

Philip looked up with hopeful black eyes, and this time Roland didn't see Somerton in them at all. "Will you read this to me, please?" the boy asked.

Roland cleared his throat. "Ah. Yes. More Latin, you see. Wretched stuff, Latin. Do you know what my brother and I used to say, when we were boys?"

"You mean the duke?"

"Yes. We used to say, *Latin's a dead language, as dead as it can be. First it killed the Romans, and now it's killing me.*"

Philip giggled.

"Used to chant it to our tutor all the time, poor chap."

"What did he do? Did he strop you?" Philip's voice rose with bloodthirsty glee.

"No, more's the pity. He tried to scold us, but we ran off. Eventually my grandfather had to set us straight."

"Your grandfather?"

Roland smiled and chucked Philip under the chin. "The Duke of Olympia. Terrifying fellow."

Philip smiled back and looked down at the page before him. "The Duke of Olympia. I daresay he owns a great many horses, doesn't he?"

"A great many." Roland shifted his body, peered over the page, and began to translate, rapidly and without flaw, Plutarch's account of the taming of Bucephalus.

So deeply engrossed they were, Roland never noticed the rapid drum of footsteps outside the door until it was too late.

*R*oland.
     The word died on Lilibet's lips. She stared, back and forth, between the startled faces of Lord Roland Penhallow and her son, sitting cross-legged on the library floor on either side of a massive book.

Philip recovered first. "Mama!" he cried, and hurled himself across the floor and into her arms.

"Darling, there you are! You had us all worried to death!" She pressed his small lithe body into hers so fiercely, she nearly tattooed him into her ribs.

"Awfully sorry." Roland's voice reached out across the room, lyric and genial. "Should have realized he'd be reported absent without leave."

"You ought to have told me!" she snapped. Her eyes were still closed, buried with the rest of her face in the soft cloud of Philip's hair. She inhaled his scent, sunshine and green things, laced with the warm bakery smell of the kitchen.

"It's not his fault!" Philip's words muffled against her chest. "I asked him to read to me about Bruce . . . Buce . . ."

"Bucephalus," Roland said, still distant. "But your mother's quite right. I ought to have taken you back at once."

She looked up at last. He stood near the fire, his long limbs folded into a contrite pose, arms behind his back and head bent slightly, exposing his cheek to the glow of the fire. He'd unbuttoned his jacket, revealing the lean plane of his waistcoat before it ended at his trousers. That godlike beauty of his, every detail magnificent. "When Francesca sounded the alarm . . ." she heard herself say, her voice unnaturally high.

"Francesca's a silly old girl." Philip wriggled out of her arms. "I told her I'd be right back."

"I daresay she didn't quite make it out, old man," Roland said. "English and all that. Not her native lingo."

Lilibet straightened and gripped Philip's hand. "You ought to have told me at once. You ought to have known we'd be worried."

"I really am most frightfully sorry, Lilibet. Shan't let it happen again, I promise." His eyes met hers, sincere and vibrant, like an electric current between them.

She took a half step backward. "You must let us know instantly if you find him wandering about. I try very hard, but he never stays put."

Roland chuckled. "Boys never do, my dear."

Philip tugged at her hand. "He knows Latin, Mama! Rattled it off like anything! Can I go riding with his lordship tomorrow, Mama? Can I?"

"Certainly not. His lordship is quite busy."

"I wouldn't mind at all." Roland gave a shrug of his broad shoulders and smiled at her. That damned smile of his, drenched with charm, filling the entire room with its crinkle-cornered good humor.

"Perhaps we can discuss it later," she said coldly.

He made a little bow. "I'm at your service, your ladyship."

She opened her mouth to snap at him, but Abigail's voice echoed inside her head, stopping her objection in her throat.

Wouldn't it be lovely to have the place to ourselves? To be free of them, once and for all?

She tightened her hand around Philip's.

Go ahead. It's just a ruse, after all. You don't really mean it.

"Will you be in the library later?" she asked.

His eyes gleamed. "Ah, but it's off-limits, isn't it? You're technically in violation of the rules right now."

"I'm sure we make exceptions for emergencies." She smiled. "We are civilized people, after all."

"Of course. I shan't tell Wallingford if you won't." His eyebrows rose inquisitively, but his feet remained planted in the rug before the fire, moving not one step in her direction.

"Mama, do I still have to take a bath?" said Philip, in his wheedling tone. He leaned backward, gripping her hand, until it nearly wrenched out of its socket.

"Mind your mother, young man," Roland said sternly. "Baths are an absolute nuisance, I agree, but they're essential to civilization."

"I want Lord Roland to give me my bath."

"Oh, Lord, no. You're much better off with Francesca. Charming girl, Francesca. She'll have you rattling away in Italian in no time." He came forward at last, in heavy, deliberate steps, and lowered himself to one knee, looking in Philip's eyes. "Off to your bath, and I'll let you take the book with you, eh what? An offer you can't refuse."

"Oh, may I?" Philip looked up at her, eyes alight. "May I, Mama?"

"Yes, of course."

Roland retrieved the book from the rug and held it out with solemn ceremony.

"Thank you," said Lilibet. She glanced at Philip, who stood with his arm wrapped around an old leather-bound volume, nearly his own size. "You'll be in the library later, then?" she inquired in the direction of Roland's left ear, not quite daring to meet his eyes.

She felt the weight of his smile on her face.

"As I said, your ladyship. I'm at your service."

TEN

The library door stood ajar, one of a pair, its massive wooden surface adorned with a riot of carved lions.

Lilibet placed her hand atop a pair of yawning leonine jaws and paused. Her dressing gown hung in soft rose-colored swags to the flagstones beneath her feet; it gaped open at the top, revealing the lace-trimmed edge of her nightgown and the curving slope of her breasts. Good God! Had it always been cut so low? She clutched the lapels together with her other hand.

And then released them.

All part of the ruse. She was *supposed* to lure him in. A few minutes of flirtation, and she would be rid of him: rid of the temptation he offered her, rid of the threat he cast over her life. Really, she was acting nobly. She was doing the right thing.

She gave the door a firm push and stepped through. "Roland," she whispered.

The room was empty.

She cast her eyes about the room: at the fire, still simmering in the hearth; at the shelves of books, tall and shadowed; at the hulking shapes of the furniture, hardly distinguishable in the dimness. The single lamp had been turned down almost to nothing, a faint pool of light at the far side of the room.

"Roland?" she whispered again, and felt a movement behind her just as the door closed with an almost inaudible snick.

She spun around. Roland was turning the key, slipping it into his pocket. "What are you doing?" she gasped.

"I should hate for Wallingford to barge in and demand an immediate forfeiture of the wager," he said, smiling, "though I expect he'd be gentleman enough to allow you to finish out the night."

"That's not at all amusing." Her heart thumped giddy blood down her limbs. He stood close, too close: His broad shoulders loomed over her, diminished her to nothing, while the clean, leathery scent of him swirled through the narrow space between them.

"Come now, darling. You know I'd never let him do it."

"You mustn't call me that." Her voice sounded fragile in her own ears.

He leaned back against the door, hands resting on the knobs, his warm hazel gaze traveling over her face, dropping down briefly to her chest. The narrow triangle of her exposed skin burned beneath his regard. "Why not?" he said. "You *are* my darling. You're the most precious thing on earth to me. It's a statement of fact, nothing more."

"You must unlock that door at once."

"Do you wish to leave?"

She hesitated. "Not yet."

"Let me know when you're ready," he said, moving off the door, "and I'll unlock it for you." He took her hand. "Now let's be civilized and sit down."

The shock of his touch, of his large, capable hand surrounding hers, incinerated any resistance within her. She allowed herself to be led to the long, wide settee before the fire and settled herself numbly into the threadbare velvet upholstery. Roland dropped down next to her, inches away, pressing her knee with his. Her hand remained enclosed in his palm; she made a feeble attempt to draw it back, but he held on, placing their entwined fingers like a knotted bridge along the crevice between his left leg and her right. The heat of his body reached out and surrounded her, drew her in like a magnet.

"You assume too much," she said. "I only came to . . . well, to thank you for looking after Philip this evening. You ought to have brought him to me, of course, but at least you . . . well, it was kind of you to read to him like that. He loves horses, and . . ."

"Hush," he said. "I quite enjoyed it. An entertaining little fellow, your son. Clever as the devil."

She allowed a slight relaxing of the muscles in her neck. "Yes, he's awfully clever, isn't he? But of course, in the future, he should be brought back to me."

"Why is that?"

She stared at her hand in his, at the way their fingers alternated in a flawless pattern: hers pale and slender, his brown and thick. "Because he mustn't grow attached to you, of course. When you'll be leaving."

He was easing her against the back of the sofa, drawing her somehow against his arm, his shoulder. "What if I don't plan on going anywhere?"

"He *has* a father." She almost hissed the words.

His head shook slowly against her hair. "I know that. I don't mean to take him over. It's just . . . well, I mean as a sort of uncle. He's your son, Lilibet. How could I not want to know him? How could I not care for him?"

Oh hell. She felt the tears form at the corners of her eyes and fought them off with hard blinks. A dull pain froze the base of her throat. Roland put his opposite hand atop hers and drew the near one away, lifting his arm to rest about her shoulders. Somehow, she allowed it. Somehow she'd lost the will to shrug him off.

It was only the ruse, of course. She was just doing it to lure him in, as planned. Except the door was locked, and Abigail wouldn't be able to spring through and shout *Aha!* and stop them.

"It's wrong," she whispered. "You mustn't."

He went silent, allowing the air between them to pulse with unspoken words, with shared knowledge. The fire spread warmth into her toes and up her legs, and Roland's body pressed strong and solid against her thigh, her waist, her ribs. Her head was a hairsbreadth away from resting in the hollow of his shoulder.

"Something's different about you," she said at last, in a low voice.

"What do you mean?"

"You're not . . . the way you were, back then. So sweet and earnest and straightforward. And you're not like you seem now, in public, with the others: careless and light-hearted." Her thumb moved, almost by itself, along the line of his forefinger.

His body stiffened, ever so slightly. "I haven't the faintest idea what you mean. I'm the same man as always."

"No, you're not. I know you, Roland. You forget that. I know you better than anyone."

"Hmm." His forefinger grazed her thumbnail, responding. "Tell me something, darling. How did you discover this castle?"

"I don't know. Alexandra saw an advertisement, I think. It was all rather sudden." She closed her eyes, letting the spell of the moment drift over her. He was behaving so beautifully: reassuring and tender, not overreaching. Nothing daring. Nothing wrong, exactly. Just . . . comforting. Safe, somehow. The secure knowledge that he loved her, that she returned his love, that nothing more was needed than that.

"Sudden? What do you mean? Did something happen?" His voice was neutral, almost careless.

"We had . . . Somerton and I . . . a . . . a row." She opened her eyes. "A fierce row. He accused me of things. And he did things that, afterward, I couldn't tolerate. I could no longer stay with him, in honor."

His arm tightened along her shoulders; she felt a lithe

tension hum along the hard curve of muscle beneath her hand. "Did he hit you? Hurt you?"

"He . . . no." She stared at the fire, at the pattern of black coals and red flame, seething with heat. That last night with Somerton: How could she explain it? She'd tucked the memory away, bound it up with paper and string, shoved it to the back of her mind with all the others. Only images remained to slip, brief and sharp, across her head. His naked flesh, his dark, angry face. The hot burn of his body, ferocious and inexorable.

"What, then?" Roland said.

She took in a long breath and picked her words with care. "He'd quite ignored my existence for some time. I hardly saw him at all. But the night we fought, he was . . . he wanted to prove to me that I was still his wife. And he did. He didn't force me," she added quickly, feeling Roland coil like a spring beside her. "I felt . . . well, that I *was* his wife, and I hadn't the right to refuse him outright. But the next morning, when he'd gone, I realized, I understood at last, that I *did* have that right. That he'd forfeited whatever claims he once had to . . . to physical intimacy with me." She picked up the sash of her dressing gown with her other hand and slid her thumb along the silken weave, up and down. She whispered: "I simply couldn't bear it any longer. I decided. I had a duty to myself and my son that went higher than the vows I'd made to my husband, long ago, in my innocence and faith."

"I'll murder him . . ."

"You won't!" She twisted in his arms. "You won't! You won't do anything! This has nothing to do with you, Roland Penhallow. I won't exchange my husband for a lover. I won't do it."

"You already have," he said fiercely.

She sprang from the sofa. "I haven't. That was a mistake, an idiotic mistake. The wine at dinner . . ."

He rose to loom over her. "Not so very much wine." He spoke with resonance, self-assurance. His genial smile had disappeared; his brow flattened into severity. His eyes seemed to bore right through the mask of her face, to read the truth written on her bones.

"You don't understand, do you?" she said hotly. "I wasn't thinking of the future, that night in the stables. I was only thinking of the past. I wasn't making love to *you*, Roland. I was making love to the young man I adored more than six years ago. That sweet and lovely boy, who wrote me poetry and swore he'd love me an eternity. An eternity, it turns out, that only lasted a month or two."

"That's not true. I love you still. I always have."

Words, always words. Lovely, meaningless words. Anger bubbled inside her, rising through her body like a head of foam. "Oh yes. No doubt. Tell me, did you love me when you were in bed with all those women afterward? Did you love me when you lay naked with them, when you took them with your body? Did you?"

He took her shoulders. "Did you still love me when you lay with your husband? When you let him bed you, take you?"

The words bolted through her chest.

"How dare you!" She was so angry, her voice emerged as hardly more than a squeak. Her eyes overflowed, tracking tears down her cheeks; she brushed them away with her fists. "How dare you! I married him because I had to, because I hadn't any choice. Papa's debts, and Mama . . . and you were gone, left! I'd no one to help me. No friend or ally of any kind. Alexandra was off on her wedding trip, and . . ."

He was slipping his arms around her, drawing her into his chest, absorbing her sobs into the lapels of his woolen jacket. "Hush, hush. Ah, I'm sorry, darling. I didn't mean it. Hush."

"And then you came back, and I kept hoping. Hoping you'd come to me, go to my parents, sway them somehow. Your brother or your grandfather; any of them! But you were silent, all of you. You left me to him." The words tumbled into his chest, muffled and broken. His jacket smelled of smoke and outdoors, masculine and comforting.

"My stupid pride. Ah, damn! What an ass I was, an unpardonable ass. Forgive me, darling. Stupid, stupid ass." His lips pressed into her hair, over and over, punctuating each word.

She went on quietly. "And then I heard all the stories. Your debauchery. And I thought I was well rid of you."

"I'm sorry." His voice stirred her hair. "I'm sorry."

The mad tide of rage receded within her. "Don't be. I had no claim on you. My pride was hurt, of course, but I couldn't blame you for it."

His hands stroked along her back, slow and tantalizing. Her nerves traced the movement, up and down; long, lazy circles, rippling her skin. "Can we not start anew, darling?" he asked. "Put the past behind us, and begin again?"

That persuasive voice of his, low and alluring. How she loved it; how she hated it. It made her want to believe impossible things: that he was sincere, that he wasn't like other men, wasn't the fickle aristocrat he appeared; that he would put aside all those women and be faithful to her alone. But she knew better. Out of spite and hurt pride, he'd let her marry Somerton. Out of pure faithless desire, he'd then plunged himself into endless rounds of women and pleasure.

She couldn't endure that again.

She laid her cheek against his chest and felt the beat of his heart into her ear. Her eyes rested on the spot where Roland and Philip had sat an hour ago, flipping through the pages of a book on warhorses. Philip, sleeping upstairs in the trundle next to her bed, cheeks flushed and curls tumbling.

Nothing was worth the loss of him. Not even the chance of it.

"No," she said.

"No? Really, Lilibet?"

She rubbed her thumbs against his back, unable to help herself. When might she have another chance, after all? "We can't, Roland. It's too late."

"It's not too late. I'd brave any scandal for you, Lilibet.

Find any way to make you mine." His arms tightened; his voice took on a note of pleading. "Won't you . . . Can you not do the same for me?"

"I can't." She drew back and met his eyes, and something in her chest dissolved at the sight of him, at the expression of impassioned tenderness in his features. She had to end this, before her weakness betrayed her, before she let him seduce her again. She had to find a way to make him bolt.

She could think of only one thing.

"We can't, because I have a husband, a husband who has the right to take away my son, if I betray him with another man."

"Then I'll take us all away, where he can't find us . . ."

She held up her hand. "That's not all. We can't, because . . ." She swallowed, gathering her courage, hating herself. "Because I'm carrying his child."

A whirling buzz descended around Roland's ears. Lilibet's face gazed up at him, blue eyes wet and shining and guileless. She couldn't be lying.

Could she?

All the long afternoon he'd been turning over the coded message in his mind; wondering exactly how Somerton fit into the picture, wondering whether Lilibet wasn't making a fool of him. He'd gone back through the terraced gardens to the shore, to the exact spot where he'd shared a picnic with her. He'd stripped his clothes and plunged into the lake, into the frigid grasp of the new meltwater; he'd stroked across and back, his brain tracking every word he'd heard her speak, every gesture, every expression. He'd considered her possible perfidy over dinner, theorized her intentions in the library.

Could she possibly have plotted with Somerton? Arranged her travel to coincide with his; seduced him deliberately in the stables, then withdrew her affection in order to evade suspicion? Was she luring him in, trying to gain his confidence?

He'd agreed to meet with her in the library tonight with the firm intention of having it out of her.

But one look at her, at her blue eyes dark and huge with apprehension and her hand fisting nervously in her dressing gown, and he'd known she wasn't in league with Somerton. No actress could perform her role with such consummate artlessness; no honey trap he'd ever encountered could execute such dizzying reverses, luring him in and pushing him away at the same time.

But now this.

"Carrying his child?" he repeated. His arms dropped away from her.

"Yes."

Images filled his brain, loathsome images of Somerton's body heaving over hers, his greedy eyes devouring her breasts, his broad hands pawing her skin. Roland shoved them ruthlessly away. Not relevant. Not useful. Emotions clouded the intellect, and he needed to think, needed to encompass this new information. He kept his voice steady. "Are you . . . are you quite sure?"

"Quite sure."

He glanced down at her belly, flat and small beneath the belt of her dressing gown. His eyes narrowed. "When are you expecting?"

Her voice faltered. "I . . . I think . . . in the fall."

"December, perhaps?"

"Yes, I suppose. Yes, December." Her Adam's apple rose and fell along the column of her throat.

He placed his hands on her shoulders. "Then it might be mine."

"No! No, of course not." She shrugged off his hands and pulled away.

"Yes, it might. If the dates are that close, you wouldn't know for certain."

"Of course I would!"

"No." He was unequivocal; if she thought she could rely on a general male ignorance of female biology, she was quite wrong.

She tossed him a defiant look. "November, then. I miscounted."

"No. Your waist is tiny, and your breasts"—he stole a look down the front of her nightgown, quite without shame—"are still the delightful peaches I remember from nearly a month ago."

"They're not." She took another step backward and crossed her arms before her chest.

"I'm an impeccable judge of these things." He studied her for a moment, a smile growing across his mouth. She stood near the lamp, and the faint glow lit her clear skin into purest ivory; her hair, coming loose from its pins, curled around her face like a dark cloud. "It might certainly be mine."

A blush spread upward from her neck, glowing across her cheeks. "Of course it isn't," she whispered. Her hand went to her belly and fiddled with the sash of her gown.

What had she said, a few moments ago?

He'd forfeited whatever claims he once had to physical intimacy with me.

I decided I had a duty to myself and my son that went higher than the vows I'd made to my husband.

Ah. Beautiful Lilibet. Brave, frightened Lilibet. She was not a citadel to be stormed by force; he must conquer her bit by bit. He couldn't convince her to be his wife, not yet. She wasn't ready for that. But she'd taken the first step already. She'd separated herself from Somerton, both in body and mind. Whatever she might say, however she might protest, she no longer, in her heart, considered the earl her husband.

Which meant Roland was free to seduce her.

Right now, and as often thereafter as it took to convince her that her future belonged with him.

He stepped toward her, smiling. "Really, Lilibet. Did you really think to push me away with that?"

"You can't possibly want me now."

"But I do. I want you terribly."

Her lips parted with a little gasp. She backed away: one faltering step, then another. "It's indecent."

"It isn't indecent. It's the most decent thing I've ever contemplated." He matched each of her steps with one of his own, driving her slowly to the bookcase. "I love you. You love me."

"I don't love you. I loved you once. I loved the man you were." She bumped against the bookcase and gripped the edges of a shelf with both hands. The impact loosened one of her hairpins, and a few dark curls tumbled onto her right shoulder. Her chin tilted upward defiantly.

"Lilibet." He reached out and took her hand and placed it against his jacket, over his heart. The soft pressure made his loins ache, made every filament of his body long to join with her. "Look at me. I'm still that man."

"No. You're different."

"Not in the essentials." He felt her fingers curl around his lapel and smiled. "You see? You remember."

She jerked her hand back to the shelf.

He leaned closer. He could see the little changes time had wrought in her face: the tiny lines about the corners of her eyes, the new tautness of her skin against the elegant bones of her face. No longer an apple-cheeked schoolgirl, but a woman. Her breath caressed his face, sweet and warm, the only sound in the still air between them; her black lashes drooped downward as her eyes considered his lips.

Roland bent his head toward her ear, nearly brushing her skin with his mouth. "Only you, Lilibet. Only you know me as I really am. You're the only one who knows me like this." He slipped his hand to her waist and rested it there.

"I, and a hundred other women over the past few years," she said huskily.

"No." He kissed the tip of her ear, brushed his lips against her cheekbone. "You understand me, darling. Every inch of me. You always did."

"Once. A long time ago." Her words were a breath of air.

Slowly, deliberately, he raised his other hand to the sash of her dressing gown. "Do you remember," he said, nibbling at her temple, at her forehead, with tiny gossamer kisses, "when we first danced together?"

"Lady Pembroke's ball."

What a delightfully exact memory. "Yes. Only two days after we met. You were wearing the loveliest dress of pale pink, as was proper for a debutante"—he tugged, ever so gently, at the end of her sash—"and you stood under the lights, with your fan waving like a hypnotist's watch in front of your bosom. I lost my breath at the sight of you." The sash slid undone; with patient fingers he parted the edges of the wrapper and found the thin silk of her nightgown. "And I came up to you and demanded your next waltz."

"Which was already taken."

"That sort of thing could hardly deter a chap who'd just discovered his future bride." He slipped his hand under the dressing gown, around her waist; his other hand rose to lift her hair from her shoulders and expose the tender skin of her neck. "We danced two waltzes, I recall. And I tried to lead you out on the terrace, but you had better sense." He kissed a slow path from the lobe of her ear to the hollow of her collarbone, tasting the salty-sweet tang of her skin, the faint essence of lavender that drifted from her clothing.

Her breath sang out in a sigh. She sagged against his hands. "Better sense?" she repeated.

"Yes. Because if you had, I might have tried this." He put his hand firmly on her cheek, settled his mouth on hers, and captured those round lips at last with a slow and purposeful kiss. He felt her startled protest melt almost at once into cooperation; her lips began to move with his, lingeringly, allowing him a fraction deeper, and then a fraction more. Her breath tasted sweet, decadent: He remembered the *panettone* and dried fruit at dessert, and the tiny glasses of grappa.

"Roland, please," she said.

"Hush." He kissed the corner of her mouth and let his hand drop from her cheek to the edge of her dressing gown. With his thumb he brushed the bare silken flesh of her chest.

"I shall hate myself."

"Darling." He slid the gown over the smooth ball of her

shoulder and kissed her there, through the nightgown. Her skin hummed with warmth beneath his lips. "What adorable scruples you have. I shall take great pleasure in divesting you of them, one by one." He gave the gown a little tug with his other hand, and it slipped to the floor with a heavy sigh. "Do you know what I think?" He placed his lips in the hollow of her throat and ran the tip of his tongue along her delicate skin. "I think you're far more wicked than you let on."

The soft weight of her hands came to rest at the back of his head, threading through his hair. Her neck arched; her eyes closed. "Don't say that. Don't say I'm wicked. Only weak, horribly weak . . ."

A tear glittered on her cheek; he licked it away. "Is that what they've let you believe, all this time? Somerton? That damned tyrant mother of yours, God rest her rigid soul?" He returned his lips to hers, kissing away her objections, parting her lips with gentle insistence to brush the tip of her tongue with his. "You don't need to be a paragon with me, darling. You don't need to be perfect. Only be yourself. That daring, passionate soul of yours. I know what lies inside you, Lilibet, and I adore it."

She shivered and clutched his hair. Ah, God, she was beautiful! He could hardly think for the lust roiling inside his body; every instinct screamed at him to *take her, take her*, right up against the bookshelf, on the sofa, on the floor. His hand shook with the effort of self-control as it edged aside the low neck of her nightgown. "Forget their damned silly rules, Lilibet. Be free of them." Her breast spilled out into his hand, round and ripe and heavy. He glanced down.

"Good God."

She spoke in a blurry whisper. "What is it?"

He weighed the breast in his hand, ran his finger over the wine-dark nipple, and watched the tip pucker into a hard, perfect, mouth-ready knob. His cock pushed frantically against the sturdy wool of his trousers.

"I stand corrected, darling," he said in awe. "No longer peaches."

Befuddled as it was, his brain didn't perceive any signs

of danger. The instant of hardening tension in her body went entirely unnoticed; he welcomed the motion of her hands to his chest as a caress. Or—even more promising— an attempt to shed him of a wholly superfluous jacket.

So it came as a shock to find himself flying through the air to land with a thud on his arse before the fire.

"What the devil?"

"Damn you for a seducer!" spat his angel.

He looked up. Her face was lit with rage, and—even more crushing—her breast had already been stuffed indignantly back into her nightgown.

"I am not a seducer," he said, endeavoring to sound a trifle less petulant than he felt. Damn it all, what had he said? He'd only inferred a divine hand in the luscious architecture of her breast, if he recalled correctly. Most women would consider that a compliment.

Evidently not Lilibet.

"*No longer peaches*, indeed. No doubt you have a wide range for comparison! Apples, mangoes, melons." She picked up her dressing gown and shoved her arms in the sleeves. "Perhaps even a few wretched grapes, from time to time, when your famous luck deserts you."

"You've no bloody idea of my range for comparison," he said. "And in any case, a small bosom can be quite elegant." He rose from the floor with as much dignity as he could summon, resisting the urge to rub away the ache on his backside.

To say nothing of the ache in his groin.

She was retying the sash of her dressing gown, taking care to bring the lapels together as closely as physics allowed. "To think I let down my guard for an instant. After I'd promised myself . . ."

"Now look here, darling . . ."

She planted her hands on her hips. "I am *not* your darling!"

"You are forevermore my darling, and you know it."

"You've no shame at all, do you? When I'm carrying another man's child!"

He reached out to grasp her arm and spoke seriously.

"You might or might not. But regardless of the seed, my darling, I claim the fruit as mine. As *ours*. I consider myself as bound to this child, Lilibet, as I am to you. Remember that."

Her eyes widened into round blue pools. "Damn you, Roland. For God's sake."

She pushed his hand away and fled to the door, dressing gown swirling behind her, and grasped the knob.

And rattled.

He came up behind her and took the key from his pocket. "You'll be needing this," he said, and slipped his arm under hers to unlock the door.

ELEVEN

Abigail exploded into the dining room halfway through breakfast, to deliver her apology.

"The most dreadful emergency," she said. "Morini brought word right after you left for the library."

Lilibet set her teacup into her saucer and looked up. "Brought word about what?" she said icily. "What could possibly have been so important as to make you forget your duty? And is that *hay* in your hair?"

Abigail put a hand to her head. "No, straw," she said. "From the chicken run. I . . ."

"The chicken run?"

"I was gathering eggs, for the priest's arrival. He's going to be here in an hour, a sort of Easter ritual, and he's got to bless the eggs." She picked the straw out of her hair, strand by strand, and shoved it into the pocket of her worn home-spun apron. "Luckily the hens have cooperated, the dears."

"Bless the . . . ?" Lilibet shook her head and put up her hand. "Stop. No more. Only tell me why you never came to the library last night."

"I did come, later. Only it must have been after you made your escape, because the room was quite empty. I felt most abjectly wretched." Abigail snatched a plate from the table and went to the buffet at the sideboard. Though their usual proper English breakfast was not in evidence this morning, Signorina Morini and the maids had still made a credible effort, with eggs and cured ham and cheeses, in addition to toasted Italian bread and a tantalizing selection of fruit preserves from last year's orchard yield. "Did he ravish you extremely?" she asked, over her shoulder.

Lilibet choked on her tea. "No. No, he did not."

"Really? How awfully disappointing. I think it might be quite nice, ravishment by Penhallow. If one had to be ravished at all, of course."

"I've never had any complaints, Miss Harewood," said his lordship, sauntering into the dining room at precisely that instant: almost as though he'd been listening at the door, which would not have surprised Lilibet in the least. "Perhaps we might consult your diary and arrange for an appointment?"

"I'm afraid not, thank you," said Abigail, heaping a reckless dollop of peach preserves atop her mountain of toast. "The priest is coming this morning, and we've so much to prepare for."

"What's ravishment, Mama?" asked Philip, through a mouthful of egg.

Lilibet concentrated on the arrangement of food on her plate: ham in the middle, egg standing to attention in its cup, toast balanced precariously on the edge. It kept her from drinking in the sight of a freshly scrubbed morning Roland, his combed wet hair gleaming in the daylight and his cheeks pink from a recent encounter with the business end of a razor. For an instant, it almost seemed she could smell his soap, echoing through her memory. "Don't speak with your mouth full, dear," she said.

"Ravishment, my dear boy . . ." began Roland, from the sideboard.

"Your lordship!" snapped Lilibet.

". . . refers to a long and spirited encounter between a man and a woman," Roland went on placidly, filling his plate, "in which the chap inevitably finds himself vanquished by the lady's superior art. Thus the term *ravished*, you see. To wit, conquered. Undone." He settled down in his chair, morning tweeds stretching neat and flat across his shoulders, and flashed his brilliant smile across the table to Lilibet. "Annihilated."

Philip's brow furrowed. "But if *you* ravished Mama, that means *you* won the argument. Doesn't it?"

"Merely the polite way of phrasing it." Roland picked up his knife and fork and sliced at his ham. As he glanced down, a lock of damp tawny hair fell away to curl charmingly on his forehead. "To buck up a poor fellow's spirits after such a thorough bolloxing. The teapot stands by you, Lady Somerton."

She passed the teapot to Abigail, who relayed it to Roland—the maids had disappeared in a flustered dash this morning, directly after laying out the food—and then Lilibet stood. "Come, Philip," she said. "We must be off for our morning walk."

He looked up. "What morning walk?"

"The one I've been meaning to initiate for some time." She folded her napkin by her plate and held out her hand.

"But I've only just sat down," said Roland, with a damned saucy wink. "You mustn't leave on my account."

"I wouldn't dream of it. We leave on our own account. Come along, darling," she said to Philip's mutinous face, forcing her voice into coaxing tones. "Perhaps we can go on a picnic, later."

"Can Lord Roland come, too?" Philip slid off his seat with wary reluctance, ready to bargain.

"I shall be delighted to accompany you," said Roland. "Name the hour."

"His lordship cannot accompany us, of course," Lilibet said triumphantly, "because of the wager."

"Oh, Wallingford. He'll never know." Roland glanced at the doorway, with perhaps a trace of nervousness. "Where is the old fellow, by the way?"

"I don't know. I haven't seen him. Lady Morley left

before you arrived, and Mr. Burke is, I presume, at his workshop." She took Philip's hand. "If you'll excuse me."

"Don't be too late!" called Abigail, as she hauled her son out the door, before any further arrangements could be suggested. "You'll miss the priest! And the egg-blessing! It's a jolly ceremony, really!"

"Wouldn't miss it for the world," Lilibet muttered.

"Do I have to wear my jacket?" asked Philip.

So the women *were* plotting against them.

Roland shoved his hands in his pockets and tramped along the meadow grass with a broad grin on his face. The darlings. Wallingford, of course, would be pleased to hear this nugget of information, not that Roland planned to let it anywhere near his brother's grasping ears.

He'd heard just enough from Abigail and Lilibet before entering the dining room to make the sequence of last night's events quite clear. Poor Lilibet! No wonder she'd blanched when he'd locked the door. He'd ruined her plan in a single stroke. His smile broadened at the thought of Miss Harewood, occupied by whatever God-given emergency had arisen in the kitchen, while he'd caressed Lilibet's luscious bosom in perfect safety, surrounded by the fire-warmed intimacy of the castle library.

For a second or two, anyway.

Of course, he saw no reason to let them know he was aware of their scheming. The legendary empty-headedness of Lord Roland Penhallow had served him well in his official clandestine activities, and he imagined a similar strategy should reap even more delectable rewards in a private capacity. With any luck, Lilibet would continue to draw him into intimacy, in the hope of being discovered, and he would continue to ensure that discovery eluded them.

Child's play, for him. Useful, in fact, to keep his wits from dulling into utter uselessness while he waited for further word from Sir Edward on the matter of . . .

Roland stopped in midstride, his foot poised above the low stone wall separating him from the next terrace.

Somerton.

Good God. He should be shot. He'd had the perfect opportunity, last night, to learn more from Lilibet about her husband's activities; instead, once he'd satisfied himself that she wasn't in league with her husband, he'd shifted all initiative from one head to the other. He hadn't troubled his brain any further, to perhaps try a few more pieces in the puzzle, to see whether they fit.

Pieces, for example, like that odd conversation from the road to the castle. He'd noted a flash of interest in Lilibet's words at the time, and set it aside: Now his memory, a well-trained and flexible instrument, scrolled backward through its logbook.

What had Philip said?

Father finds out everything . . . Mama says Father's a real live . . .

Philip!

Well, it's a secret, of course.

Roland sat down heavily on the terrace edge. A real live . . . *something.* Something secret, apparently. Something to do with . . . what was it? *Omniscience.* That was the word she'd used. He could hear her dull, defeated voice pronouncing the syllables.

Somerton was omniscient.

Bloody hell. Right there before his nose. How much did Lilibet know about it, then? How had she come across the knowledge?

More to the point, *what* knowledge?

Surely, if Lord Somerton were involved in Navy intelligence, Roland would have heard of it long ago. It was just too delicious a piece of information for the gossipy intelligence community to keep secret, at least within its own boundaries.

Tell me, Penhallow, have you any enemies? Anyone who might wish to ruin you?

No. Surely not. Somerton had won the game, had captured the queen, over six years ago. Strictly speaking, Roland hadn't so much as wronged the earl's leftmost toenail until that fateful night in the inn. If anything, *he* should be the one wreaking ruin on Somerton.

And yet . . . it was a damned odd coincidence.

Sir Edward didn't believe in coincidence. Dig deeper, he would say, and you'll find the link. Dig as deep as you must.

The damp coldness of the stone wall penetrated Roland's trousers to numb his backside. He stared out at the tops of the nearby orchard trees, at the long rows of vines to his right, their tiny green shoots still invisible from this distance. A golden morning light drenched every living thing, every new leaf and bursting blossom; gilded the entire valley laid out before him, and the yellow-walled village huddled comfortably in its center. Heaven, paradise, only he wasn't really a part of it. Could not quite reach out his hand and touch it.

Did he tell Sir Edward, or not?

He'd promised Lilibet he wouldn't reveal her location. Sir Edward would be discreet, of course, but inevitably the source of his information would get out. It always did.

He was a match for Somerton. He'd no doubt that if the earl came galloping down to Tuscany to retrieve Lilibet, he could defend her.

But he'd promised to keep her secret. And there was Philip, and the baby growing inside her: the baby they'd perhaps created together, he and Lilibet.

Or perhaps not.

Oh yes, Sir Edward, and by the way, I've had Lord Somerton's wife under my roof the entire bloody time! Seduced her, in fact! Possibly even got her with child! Frightfully sorry I didn't help you along with your investigation and all that, but I did tell her I'd keep it all quiet, if you see what I mean.

No doubt the Bureau of Trade and Maritime Information would see his point of view perfectly. No doubt Sir

Edward would shrug his massive shoulders and figure that
Lady Somerton's presence under Roland's castle roof was
of no relevance whatever to his investigation.

A sticky wicket indeed.

Roland stood up and turned, nearly pitching himself
into the wiry chest of the groundskeeper.

"Good God, man!" he exclaimed. "Could you not have
announced yourself?"

Giacomo folded his arms with a belligerent air. "Is
Signore Burke. He is needing your help."

"Burke? Needing *my* help? You're joking, surely."

"In the workshop, down by the lake."

"Yes, I know where he works. But why the devil would
he need my help? The fellow's soldiered on well enough
before." Roland spared a glance down the terraced hillside,
in the direction of the old carriage house where Burke had
set up his automotive works, or what there was of them.

Down by the lake.

Lilibet was down by the lake.

Roland turned a questioning eyebrow back in the
groundskeeper's direction and found himself the object of
a rather fierce and staring frown, as if Giacomo were trying
to communicate something too subtle for words.

"Really, old fellow. You must try to make yourself
clearer." Roland tapped his forehead. "Not too much rattling around in there, I'm afraid. Gentle hints have a trou-
bling habit of getting lost, and needing to ask for direction."

Giacomo heaved a sigh that encompassed the entire race
of Englishmen in its despair. "*Before*," he said at last, "there
was no *women*." The heavy and disapproving emphasis he
placed on the word *women* was about as gentle as a club to
the backbone.

Roland's ears lifted. Women, was it?

Burke, you old rascal.

All of Wallingford's bluster about seduction aside,
Roland had known for some time that a frisson of attraction
existed between Phineas Burke and the Marchioness of
Morley. He'd rather enjoyed observing it in action, in fact.

The charming and beautiful Lady Morley was also a snob of the highest order, and watching her pant like an over-heated lapdog after his untitled and unglamorous friend Burke—a handsome fellow, he supposed, though rather too tall and carrot-topped and taciturn for most women—had proven deeply entertaining.

But had things really gone so far? Had the Marchioness of Morley, darling of London society, really succumbed to Mr. Phineas Burke of the Royal Society? Or, as Wallingford suggested, was she trying to seduce him into forfeiting the wager?

And had poor Burke fallen in love with her himself?

Interesting development, indeed. Perhaps even useful.

"Ah," Roland said. "Now we speak the same language. Do you know, I was just headed down to the lake myself. Perhaps I might stop for a look-in."

He tipped his hat to Giacomo and headed down the hillside.

A bit of sport was just the thing in times of psychic anguish.

TWELVE

Lilibet hadn't meant to fall asleep. What mother does?
  She'd known she was weary, of course. One didn't lie awake half the night, staring at the play of moonlight on one's roof beams, burning with longing for tawny-haired English rascals, without feeling a bit out of sorts the next day.

But the cool breeze blowing off the lake had invigorated her. Philip, holding her hand, had dragged her along the shore at a smart pace; they had scrambled over the damp pebbles, laughing, the wicker picnic basket bumping against the curve of her calf, and settled at last near the spot of yesterday's outing. She'd rested against the very same tree and watched as Philip played about on the shore; she'd pictured Roland's long body reclined on the red-checked picnic cloth, just as it had yesterday, and her nerves had danced with an electric awareness. Sleep had been the furthest thought from her mind.

Until she'd opened her eyes some unknown time later, her back rough and aching from the bark of the tree, and Philip nowhere in sight.

She scrambled to her feet. "Philip!" she called out.

Ripples fanned out across the water before her, and an instant later the breeze lifted the hair from her forehead. A friendly white cloud passed overhead, casting a moment's darkness over the landscape.

"Philip!" she called again, more loudly, willing her voice to remain calm.

Behind her, a pair of birds took up a frantic argument, cracking the silence. She heard the rustle of leaves as they jostled for position, the flutter of feathers.

She ran to the edge of the lake. "Philip! Philip!"

Her voice echoed back to her, faint and ghostlike, from the rock outcropping on the opposite shore.

Her heart thumped in her ears in a hard, rapid rhythm, like the pounding of feet in the grass. The water looked so still, so innocent, shedding tiny tranquil ripples that couldn't possibly defeat a five-year-old boy.

She whirled around and scanned the shoreline: the short pebbled beach, the scattering of olive trees, the glimpse of the vineyards and terraces between the dark-leaved branches.

"Philip!" she called, with all her strength.

The warm spring air returned no answer.

From the guilt settled deep into the lines of Phineas Burke's face, Roland hadn't arrived a moment too soon.

He strode through the doorway of the square stone building with decisive strides, giving Burke no chance to refuse him entry, and looked about. No immediate signs of connubial activity. No discarded corsets, no abandoned shoes. No other occupant visible at all, in fact.

Not yet, at least.

Better and better, if the lady were hiding. Cabinet on the wall, hulking great shell of an automobile on blocks in the center of the room. Any number of likely spots. Roland nearly rubbed his hands with anticipation. Aside from appreciating the usefulness of discovering Burke's secrets, he was terribly fond of intrigue.

He started things off briskly. "What the devil sort of hovel is this? And why have you got it all locked up?"

"Security," said Burke. "A competitive lot, we motor enthusiasts."

"Ha-ha. And rather useful for keeping seductive marchionesses at bay, eh what?" Roland came to a stop in the center of the room. From the corner of his eye, he caught sight of two teacups sitting on the worn worktable off to the side. A hint of steam drifted upward from the white porcelain.

"That, too, of course." Burke's voice was decidedly grim.

Roland grinned and turned around. "What do you think Wallingford was on about last night? I hardly recognized the man. All that business about goose down."

Burke's face relaxed. "I suspect, old boy, that your brother's got troubles of his own in that quarter," he said, with a condescending smile, looking for an instant as if he might even venture a wink.

Roland whistled and made his eyes go round with surprise. "You don't say! Wallingford and Lady Morley! I suppose it's a natural match, both of them high-tempered schemers and whatnot. And it explains last night's doings, all those accusations about her seducing you. Jealousy, from my brother! Ha-ha. Very good."

He watched with satisfaction as the color rose in Burke's cheeks. Ginger-haired chaps never could disguise their choler.

"I don't mean Lady Morley," Mr. Burke said.

"What's that? But who—good God, you can't mean Lilib . . . you can't mean Lady Somerton! Damn you for a slandering . . ." He took a menacing step forward, for good measure.

Burke forced out a laugh and maneuvered his way to the worktable. "Pax, old man! Not her ladyship. Good God, no."

Now thunderstruck. "What, then? Not Miss Harewood! You can't be serious."

"Mere speculation." Burke leaned against the table,

blocking the teacups from view. His eyes slipped past Roland for an instant, down to the ground.

Roland wanted to shake his friend's shoulders and teach him a thing or two about clandestine activity. As it was, he was rather disappointed. Shooting a sitting duck was no sport at all.

He liked Phineas Burke a great deal, quite aside from the private fact of their family relationship, which came—rather awkwardly—on the wrong side of the blanket, through Roland's maternal grandfather, the Duke of Olympia. For one thing, Burke was the only man he considered his intellectual superior. For another, he managed to remain a decent fellow, despite his genius.

Not so decent, however, that Roland couldn't have a bit of fun.

He cleared his throat. "Hmm. Miss Harewood. Any port in a storm, I suppose. But what has goose down to do with it all?"

"Haven't the slightest," said Burke. He made a show of taking out his watch and glaring at the face. His hair caught the light in a ferocious orange explosion. "Look, have you got a genuine purpose to your visit, or have you only come to harass me? I've got rather a lot of work to do."

Ha-ha. No doubt, you dog. Work indeed.

"Yes, yes. Of course." Roland turned about with slow deliberation, as if taking in his surroundings for the first time. "So. This is it. The workshop of a genius, where mere mortals fear to tread. All sorts of . . . of doings . . . and . . . I say, what's *that*?" he said, making his voice crack like a whip.

A muffled noise came from beneath the automobile.

Burke stepped hastily forward. "A few spare parts. Look here, Penhallow . . ."

Lord Roland turned with ceremony to the enormous machine in the center of the room, and took a few appreciative steps backward, as if trying to encompass its grandeur. Yes, there it was: a tiny splash of blue beneath the chassis. Good old Lady Morley. What a sport she was.

Though, truth be told, he was rather disappointed to find her fully clothed. "And this! The machine itself! Absolutely marvelous! Really, old chap. I'm floored. Er . . . is that the engine?"

"Yes, I'm almost certain."

"Ha-ha. The old sense of humor, eh? What a card you are." He inhaled a deep gust of air. "Do I smell lilies?"

"Penhallow, for God's sake. Leave me in peace. Save it all for the dinner table."

"Burke, you ass. I've come for a friendly visit, to buck up your spirits . . ."

"My spirits don't need bucking," snapped Burke. "Out."

Roland knew he should leave. Masculine courtesy demanded it, if nothing else. And he'd gotten the information he wanted: Burke (or Lady Morley, or both) were technically in violation of the wager, which might prove useful later on. But outside that door waited the unpleasant decision about Sir Edward, whereas inside . . . well, baiting Burke was too jolly amusing. Besides, he rather liked the idea of keeping the elegant Lady Morley pinned under an automobile in fear for her reputation and her life, no doubt in that order.

"Damn it all, Burke," he said, letting his voice break almost to a sob. "It's the most confounded coil. Last night . . . all that nonsense about raising the stakes . . . oh, you must know I'm most frightfully in love with her."

"Oh, for God's sake."

"I know you can't possibly understand, you with your cold scientific heart and all that, but . . . well, damn it all, I had to confess to someone! And you're such a brick, Burke. You'd never tell my brother, or the ladies. My secret is perfectly safe with you." Roland considered putting his hand to his heart but decided against it. Sir Edward had often cautioned him on the perils of overacting his part.

"Perfectly. Now if you wouldn't mind . . ."

A faint strangled noise issued from the direction of the automobile, like an asphyxiated mouse: the sort of sound that would have gone unnoticed by any other ears, except for the well-trained pair owned by Roland Penhallow.

Dear me. Dust. How unfortunate for Lady Morley. And spiders, perhaps? The space under the automobile looked a perfect heaven for spiders.

He concealed his smile behind a doleful shake of his head and carried on, without a pause. "That damned beast of a husband of hers, I know he's treated her badly, but the dear soul's so loyal and honorable . . ."

"Penhallow, another time perhaps. I'm really quite busy."

"But now that Wallingford's taken this notion into his head, anything I say or do might cause her to be tossed out entirely. And that shrew"—he said it just a trifle more loudly, with just a trifle of emphasis—"that shrew Lady Morley, taking Wallingford up on his wager! I should have rebuked her. I meant to, but Lilibet . . . but Lady Somerton gave me *such* a look."

Burke's color deepened to an unholy shade of crimson. "Lady Morley is not a shrew."

"Well, that's charitable of you, old fellow, considering how she's done her best to lure you in, ha-ha. A handsome woman, of course, but one can't imagine sitting across from her at the breakfast table." Roland threw in a chuckle for good measure.

Burke gritted his teeth. Fairly bared them, in fact. "Penhallow, I'm deeply sorry for your troubles, but you really must see me another time. The battery . . ."

A muffled choking cough.

Roland started and whirled about. "What's that?"

"Nothing. Hydraulics," Burke said swiftly. "As I was saying . . ."

Another cough. Poor dear Lady Morley. Really, he was beginning to feel rather sorry for her, though not nearly enough to stop.

"There it is again!" Roland cried. "What the devil sort of hydraulics have you got in there? It don't sound at all healthy."

Mr. Burke cleared his throat and pulled at his collar. "A mere . . . simply to do with . . . the braking system. A new design I'm trying out. Quite trying, involving the most immense concentration, and rather dangerous at that. I shall really have to ask you to leave." He began walking in the direction of the door.

"But see here, Burke. That's exactly what I came to speak with you about. I was thinking . . ." Roland paused, mind racing. "I was thinking that perhaps you might take me on as your assistant. To keep me busy, to keep me out of her way, you see. It's the most honorable course."

"My assistant?" Burke's tone conveyed such an immense amount of skepticism, it nearly sank under its own weight.

"Yes. Don't you need another pair of hands to . . . well, to help sort out . . . all this . . . this whatnot you've got here?"

Burke released a vast sigh. "Penhallow, old man. Do you have the *slightest* idea how an electric battery works?"

"Well, no. That is, I have some notion that . . . the sparks rather . . . well . . . no. No, I haven't." Roland hung his head.

"Can you even distinguish one end of my motor-car from another?"

Roland turned toward the automobile, just in time to see a piece of blue-swathed elbow disappear from view. "I daresay . . . one would think that . . . well, if I should hazard a guess . . ."

"Precisely," said Burke. "Now if you'll be so good as to return to the library and resume your quest for knowledge. Perhaps compose a verse or two, cataloging the anguish of doomed love. And if the delights of that endeavor should pall, you might consult with Giacomo regarding the cheeses in the stables, as a more practical matter."

"The cheeses?" This time, Roland was genuinely puzzled.

"He'll tell you all about them. But for God's sake, Penhallow, whatever you do, *leave . . . me . . . alone!*" Burke jerked open the door, green eyes blazing.

"I say, Burke. That's hardly sporting."

"Really? How ungentlemanly of me."

Roland picked at his sleeve. "In any case, old Giacomo sent me down here to begin with. Said you needed help. It's what gave me the idea."

"Did he, the old bugger?" Burke folded his arms, straightened to his full six-and-a-half feet, and pierced Roland with a narrow-eyed glare. "Now *that's* hardly sporting."

"Very well. I take your point. But just remember, Burke . . ." Roland walked through the door, straight into the determined prow of his brother, sailing into the workshop under full steam. "Oh, hullo there, Wallingford! Out for a stroll?"

"No, by God. That damned groundskeeper sent me," Wallingford growled. "Told me Burke was in desperate need of assistance."

"Well, that's the devil of a coincidence!" Lord Roland said brightly. "He told me the same thing, about Burke wanting help in his workshop, and I thought to myself, Penhallow, old man, that's just the ticket . . ."

Burke broke through in a furious voice. "Giacomo was entirely mistaken. I'm in no need of assistance. Quite the opposite."

Roland had to admire his spirited defense of Lady Morley. He supposed he ought to relent: Burke could certainly handle Wallingford on his own.

He was, after all, the brothers' natural uncle.

Roland smiled and tipped his cap. "Yes, yes. You've made yourself quite clear on the subject. I'm taking myself off directly, and I'd advise my dear brother to do the same."

Once clear of the workshop, he paused. Up the verdant hillside stood the castle, its gray yellow stones reflecting the sunlight in a comfortable glow; inside that building lay his codebook and his writing desk, ready for use.

To the right lay the clear waters of the lake, and Lilibet picnicking with her son.

He took off his peaked cap and ran his hand through his

hair. A dainty breeze tumbled from the trees by the lake, cool against his temple.

England expects, old boy.

He replaced his cap and began walking, with heavy steps, toward the Castel sant'Agata.

L ilibet slipped along the pebbled shoreline, scanning the trees, her breath scraping against her throat.

How long had she been asleep? Not long, surely. Only a few moments. She stopped and reached in her pocket for her watch. Eleven thirty-three. When had they left the castle? Well after breakfast, well after morning lessons. He couldn't have gone far.

"Philip!" Her voice was hoarse, painful, desperate. "Philip!"

She glanced again to the lake. Philip knew he wasn't allowed in. He would not have disobeyed her so directly. He'd no swimming costume, no towel. He was a remarkably self-possessed five years old, quite sensible enough not to frolic in a bitterly cold lake.

Wasn't he?

Her veins went light with panic.

No. Be reasonable. She drew a long breath and forced her brain to calm. He wouldn't have gone in. No sign of shoes and stockings on the shore: Even in the full throes of reckless enthusiasm, he'd never have tried to swim with his shoes on.

Would he?

Oh God. Search the water now, and waste precious time while Philip lost himself further in the trees and the valley?

But if he was in the lake, had stumbled somehow, had climbed on the rocks and fallen in . . .

"Philip!" she screamed with all her might. Surely he must hear her. The wind carried from the lake. If he heard her, he would come toward her. If he were in the trees, and not in the lake.

The old boathouse loomed a hundred yards away, its rust-colored paint peeling in the sun. She broke into a run, pebbles digging through the leather of her sturdy shoes, breath coming hard and fast in her aching lungs. Her muscles had flooded with energy; she flew down the shoreline, pumped her legs, lost her hat.

She threw open the boathouse door. "Philip!"

A starling flew into the rafters with a shocked rattle of feathers. Dust motes drifted in lazy circles among the piles of old wood, the coils of rope, glittering in the unexpected sunlight.

Every muscle in her body sagged with despair. She turned away and ran to the edge of the water. To her left, a pile of boulders stretched a broad short toe into the lake.

Philip loved climbing rocks.

She scrambled up without thinking. The soles of her shoes slipped against the speckled stone; her fingers bruised, digging for purchase. With inhuman strength she hoisted herself atop the highest boulder and staggered out to the edge.

A perfect diving spot. A perfect place for a curious boy to lose his footing and slip into the water.

She peered over the side, scanning the water, horror and desperation shooting through her blood, shaking her fingers. Unreasonable, she was being unreasonable, she ought to be looking in the woods, this was absurd. But something drew her out, begged her to look. Premonition? Fear? Morbid imagination?

The water lapped below her, clear and empty, mottled rocks shifting under the ripples. A school of tiny fish flickered past, catching the sun for a sparkling instant.

"I see you've found my favorite swimming hole."

Lilibet spun about, nearly falling from her boulder.

Lord Roland Penhallow gazed up at her from the base of the rocks, his warm, familiar smile lighting his face. From atop his lordship's broad tweedy shoulders, Philip stretched his arms toward her and shouted with delight.

"Mama!"

THIRTEEN

S he slid down the rock, she dropped to her knees in the pebbles, she held out her arms, sobbing and crying into his hair.

"I was so worried! Oh, darling! I'm so sorry!"

"I was after this grasshopper, Mama. The biggest ruddy grasshopper you've ever seen. And Lord Roland . . ."

Roland's voice wrapped around her ear, low and concerned. "Were you so worried, then? I'm awfully sorry. I saw him hanging about the trees, happy as a lark."

She looked up. He stood there against the base of the boulder, propped up by one sturdy shoulder, staring down at her with an intense concentration of emotion in his eyes. A tweed cap concealed his hair, emphasizing the impeccable bones of his face, the firm cut of his jaw, the long cords of his neck disappearing into his loosened collar. In the spreading noon sunshine, his skin had turned to gold. He looked like a classical painting, an Adonis in modern clothes, too beautiful to be real.

"I'd fallen asleep," she said, voice hoarse. "I thought . . . I didn't know where he'd gone . . . I panicked . . . the water . . ."

"Oh, Mama," Philip said scornfully. "I'd never go swimming with my shoes on."

She buried her face in his warm, sun-scented hair. "No, darling. Of course not. I was so silly. Of course you were all right. You're a big boy." She lifted her eyes again, hardly daring to look at Roland, lithe and handsome and invincible against his rock. "Thank you," she whispered.

He smiled, and all at once he was human again. "I promised I'd bring him directly to you next time, didn't I?"

"Yes," she said. Philip's curls nestled against her cheek like a cloud of down. "You promised."

He took off his cap, examined the inside, and put it back on again. His eyes cast a considering gaze up to the sky. "I was thinking a chap might have a reward for a job well done."

She couldn't help smiling. "What sort of reward?" she asking, rising to her feet.

"It seems to me a picnic might do very nicely."

"Oh, can he, Mama?" Philip grabbed her hand. "Can he, please?"

She squeezed Philip's fingers. Roland wore an inquiring expression, eyebrows raised, chin tucked inward. No longer godlike, nor even human: rather like a particularly irresistible golden retriever, hoping for a bone.

Relief, deliverance, euphoria still sang in her blood, danced in the tips of her fingers. The back of her head blazed in the warm Italian sun. She was in love with Roland Penhallow; she was in love with the world.

"Yes," she said. "Of course he can."

Three hours later, his shirt collar unbuttoned and his jacket slung over one shoulder, Roland dragged his eviscerated body back up the hill to the castle.

Until now, he'd considered a hard day's hunt atop a vigorous stallion the most exhausting pastime known to man. An afternoon spent chasing a vigorous young boy about a lakeshore had relegated *that* notion to the land of fond nostalgia.

"He needs a father," said Roland.

Lilibet didn't reply. She trudged by his side, between two long rows of grapevines, her face shadowed by the brim of a large hat. Fifty or so yards ahead, Philip ran from vine to vine with the superabundant energy of his species, stopping every so often to check for new growth.

What the devil were they feeding him?

Roland pulled aside his collar with one finger to allow a trifle more air to circulate around his heated skin. "I suppose you would say he has a father already," he continued. "A blood father."

"Yes, he does. He loves his father."

Roland switched the picnic basket to his outside hand, bringing him closer to her body, to the swish of her lettuce green dress. "Is Somerton a good father?"

"Not particularly. But it doesn't matter. Children love you regardless." She was subdued, thoughtful. He couldn't imagine what she was thinking. She'd been so happy and animated at the picnic, almost like the lively Lilibet he'd known that summer in London. Her laughter had bubbled through the warm spring air, had made his heart swell with joy. But as they'd packed up the basket again, an intense quiet had settled over her. She'd folded the cloth and stacked the plates in silence, avoiding his glance, avoiding his touch.

A gentle drone rang his ear, a passing bumblebee, black and fat and drunk with pollen from the orchards. "Perhaps I shouldn't have used the word *father*," Roland said. "I only mean that he's a boy, a growing boy. He needs—I believe he needs—a man about, from time to time."

"It's all right," she said softly. "I know what you meant."

"Do you agree?"

"It depends, I suppose. On who the man might be." She didn't look at him, didn't so much as tilt her head in his direction. Her eyes remained fixed ahead, on Philip's larking figure, the lines and curves of her body snugly encased in her dress. With piercing sharpness, he longed to touch that body, to lie with her, to peel away the layers of cloth between them. He wanted to bury his face in her bosom, to lay his hand atop her growing belly, to plunge his body into hers, to make her weep with pleasure, to worship her.

He brushed the back of her hand with his own, grazing the tips of her fingers for an instant. "And if that man were me?"

"I don't know, Roland." Her voice ached in his ear. "I can't . . . I can't even think about starting again. Even if . . . even if my marriage . . . even if Somerton were magically to disappear, without any consequences, without his killing you or taking Philip, or both . . ."

"I'd never let him do that. You know I wouldn't."

"Even if all these things were to happen, I can't . . ." She checked herself.

"Can't what?"

"You don't know what it's like," she whispered. "You don't know. To be betrayed like that. Oh, I know you've sworn that you're different. Every man says that. But all I have to go on, Roland, is what you've done. All I know is that you've spent the past six years tumbling from bed to bed . . ."

"Oh, for God's sake . . ."

". . . and how can I possibly expect you to change? Even if I were madly in love with you . . ."

"You *are* madly in love with me. As I am with you. Let's not pretend, Lilibet." He stopped and took her arm and turned her to face him. With one finger he lifted her chin. "Look at me. Let's not pretend *that*, at least."

She regarded him steadily, her eyes a startling blue in the bright afternoon light. "Even if I were in love with you, I couldn't ask you to be someone you're not. And I couldn't give another child a faithless man for a father."

The air seemed to empty out of his ears at her words. "I am not faithless," he said, but it sounded feeble, even to himself. "I have not . . . I'm not what you think. I'm not what everybody thinks. I . . ." He stopped himself by brute mental force. *Do not say it. Do not tell her.*

She raised one eyebrow, waiting for him to finish.

He tightened his grip on her arms, willing her to believe him. "This . . . this reputation I have. I won't pretend it doesn't exist. I won't pretend I didn't cultivate it. But . . . the popular rumor . . . the things you've been hearing . . ." He closed his eyes, drew breath, opened them again. Her beautiful face swam before him, intent lines drawn in her forehead. "It is all exaggerated. I swear it, Lilibet. *Greatly* exaggerated."

"How am I to believe you?"

"I swear it, Lilibet. On my honor, I swear it." He slid his hand down her arm to enclose her hand. She glanced up the row of vines to Philip and back again to him. "I swear it," he whispered.

She shook her head and turned to continue up the row. "Rumor is usually wrong in the details, I've found, but seldom in the essentials."

"In this case, both," he said. "In this case, rumor is what I've designed it to be."

"Oh, come," she laughed. "Why on earth would any man cultivate a reputation for promiscuity, without enjoying the reality?"

"I have my reasons."

"Terribly convincing of you. *I'm telling the truth, darling, but I can't tell you why.* Yes, frightfully sound." But her hand remained in his, warm and slightly damp, returning just the smallest amount of pressure.

"Can you not have the slightest particle of faith in me?" he asked.

Philip turned abruptly and began to run toward them. Lilibet dropped his hand like a stone, leaving his fingers empty and grasping for her touch.

"I've learned, your lordship," she said, under her breath, "to prefer deeds over words." She asked Philip, "What do you have for me, darling?"

Philip shook his head and held up his hands in Roland's direction, closed together in a ball. "It's not for you, Mama. It's for Lord Roland. Look! It's a grasshopper!"

He opened a crack between two fingers and Roland peered inside. "Egad! Look at that fellow! He must be an inch long, at least!"

"His name is Norbert," Philip said, looking in his hands himself with a fond parental gaze. "I'm going to make a cage and fill it with grass and keep him in my room."

"*Our* room," said Lilibet, "and you won't do any such thing."

"Oh, Mama! Please! He's really a well-behaved grasshopper! He let me catch him without any trouble!"

"Nevertheless. No inch-long insects in my room, if you please. Not even well-behaved ones."

Philip's lower lip trembled. "Please, Mama! I'll feed him myself!"

"Look here," said Roland, unable to withstand that trembling lower lip, "I'd be happy to keep the little fellow in with me. *I've* no objection to inch-long insects. Properly caged, that is."

The sun burst out onto Philip's face. "Oh, sir! Would you? Would you really?"

"With pleasure," Roland said, "properly caged."

"Really, Lord Roland, it isn't at all necessary," said Lilibet.

He smiled at her. "My dear, it's quite necessary. Every young man should have a pet of some kind. Why not a grasshopper?"

"That's right, Mama! Norbert's a lovely pet."

Roland held up his hand and ticked off his fingers. "Doesn't require meat. Doesn't require daily walking. No hair on the upholstery. No puddles on the Aubusson." He brandished his closed fist triumphantly. "A most eligible pet. Don't know why I don't keep a flock of them myself. Or . . . or is it a cloud?"

She was laughing. "Oh, very well. But you'll have to sort out the cage yourselves. A very *sound* cage, if you please."

"I believe we can manage that all right, can't we, Philip?" Roland chuffed the boy's shoulder.

"Yes, sir! I'm sure Abigail will help us find some chicken

wire." Philip dashed on down the row. His words floated behind his racing body, growing faint. "I think I shall train him up for a flea circus!"

"Oh God," Lilibet said.

Roland took her hand again, and she didn't resist. They were drawing near the end of the row; in a moment, they would be out in the open, with only a short meadow between them and the flagstones of the kitchen courtyard. "May I see you again later?" he asked quietly.

"For what purpose?" She gave a nervous laugh. "Another attempt to seduce me?"

"If you like. I'd be more than happy to oblige."

Another laugh. "You're trying very hard, aren't you?"

Philip had disappeared around the end of the vine row. Roland stopped and turned to face her, taking her other hand in his, her palms smooth and fragile against his fingers. At some point during the walk, her hat had shifted a bit to one side; he reached out and straightened it, brushing her cheek with his thumb. "Is it working?" he asked.

His heart thumped in his chest, waiting for her answer.

Her blue eyes slipped for an instant to his lips, and back up again. "After dinner," she said. "I'll ask Francesca to keep watch on Philip, or Morini."

"Who's Morini?"

"The housekeeper. She won't mind." She spoke a little breathlessly; her hands tightened around his. He could smell the lavender of her skin, the sweetness of her breath. Her round pink lips beckoned irresistibly.

And really, why resist?

Before she could object, he took her face between his hands and buried his lips in hers: not gently, not inquisitively, but as if he were devouring the delicate flesh of a peach from the inside out. He stroked her tongue, the roof of her mouth, the satin sides of her cheeks; he inhaled the scent of her like a drug, shooting through his veins. After a single shocked gasp, she arched her back and leaned into the kiss, returning the stroke of his tongue, her hands *Good God!* grasping the curve of his buttocks with a firm, possessive grip and pressing his hardened cock into the curve of her belly.

She made a hungry growling sound from somewhere deep in her throat; he thrust his fingers into her hair, beneath her hat, and moved his feet to trap her legs between his.

"*Mama!*"

Philip's voice drifted over the rows of vines.

Lilibet stumbled backward with a little cry, pushing him away.

"Coming!" she called hoarsely. Her hands went to her hair, pushing the pins in place, straightening her hat. Her eyes held his, wide and round, the blue so intense he wanted to crawl inside. "I must go," she whispered, and turned away.

"Wait." He gripped her hands. "Tonight."

Her chest heaved for breath, breasts straining beneath the thin linen of her dress. He could see the tick of her pulse where it jumped in her neck. "Yes, tonight."

"What time?"

"Late. Eleven o'clock, perhaps. Outdoors, where we can't be found."

"I'll think of something. I'll send a note."

She nodded, drew her hands away, and hurried down the row, disappearing almost before he could move. His stunned brain took a moment to review what it had just learned.

Tonight. Outdoors. Note. Eleven o'clock.

If he could survive that long.

FOURTEEN

*G*uilt. Shame.
Her ears rang with it; her pulse throbbed in her neck, her wrists, her chest.

"Mama, do I have to study with Abigail this afternoon? I think building a cage is enough learning for one day, don't you?"

Trollop. Adulteress. No better than you should be.

"I suppose it depends on how long the cage takes," she said, "and how busy your cousin Abigail is this afternoon."

Abigail was delighted to build a cage for the grasshopper. No, it wasn't too much trouble. They'd pick up their writing and sums again tomorrow. Certainly, she had some chicken wire. Only perhaps the loops were too large to hold in a grasshopper, even one of so magnificent a size as Norbert? Well, they'd find something. Come along.

A kiss on Philip's forehead, a wave good-bye. The hallway alive with some fragrant draft from outdoors, the stones cool beneath her back as she slumped against the wall, her womb hot beneath her hand as she clutched it.

Weak. Wicked. Filled with unnatural lust.

She wanted him so much. What torture it had been to

walk next to him, to feel the heat radiate from his body, and not make a single movement toward him. Her skin had flushed, had burned with the desire to tumble with him on the grass, to press his beautiful flesh against hers, naked in the sunshine.

Her eyes screwed shut. His kiss, oh God, his marvelous mouth on hers. The yearning streaking down her limbs, melting between her legs. She would burn in hell; she would die of shame. She'd given in, again, *again*. She'd kissed him back regardless, and cradled his arousal between her hips.

She'd agreed to meet him tonight and complete her ruin.

"Signora Somerton? You are not well?"

The warm scent of baking bread drifted across Lilibet's nostrils, at the same instant as the gentle voice reached her ear.

She started upward. "Oh! Signorina Morini! No, no. Quite well. It's just . . . such a warm day . . ."

The housekeeper stood near, quite near, her face creased with sympathy. "You need perhaps a cup of the tea? I am making very good tea, now. Signorina Abigail is doing the teaching."

Refusal hovered at the tip of Lilibet's tongue. What she said, however, was: "A cup of tea would be lovely, signora. Thank you."

She followed the slender white-shirted back of Signorina Morini down the hallway and into the kitchen, where the fire had been banked low and the loaves of bread stood cooling on the table. Next to them, a teapot and a cup waited expectantly.

Lilibet picked up the pot and poured into the cup. Steam drifted upward in fragrant spirals; she buried her nose in them and dropped into a chair with a sigh.

"You see?" Morini eased herself into the chair at the head of the table. "Is better now, yes?"

"Very nice. It's kind of you, to adapt to our English ways. The breakfast, and tea."

The housekeeper smiled and shrugged. "Not so many things. The lunch, the dinner, they are all very much of

Toscana, of the hills and the valleys. The things we are growing here, from the earth."

"It's delicious. In England everything is either roasted or boiled within an inch of its life. I never knew artichokes had such flavor."

Another shrug. "You are leaving behind many unpleasant things in England, I think."

Lilibet looked into her cup. "Yes."

"Signora, you have still the tear in your eye. You are not happy. Why is this? You have the beautiful child, the love of the kind signore. You have soon his baby. God is smiling on you."

Lilibet jerked her head up. "Signorina!"

Morini was smiling, her face eased into kind lines. "Is true. I am knowing these things. You meet him tonight, yes?"

"How did you . . . who . . ." Lilibet's mouth stumbled around the words, unable to form a logical connection with her brain. *Ghosts*: The word echoed unexpectedly between her ears, in Abigail's eager voice. She pushed it away.

Morini shook her head, still smiling. "I am knowing, that is all. Signora, I help you. I watch over the young signore tonight. You go to meet your love. He is making you feel better, making you happy."

"He is not." Her voice broke. "He's making me miserable. I can't . . . I shouldn't . . . I have a husband already, signorina! Philip's father."

Morini laid her hand flat on the table and spoke sharply. "A bad man. He is not your husband."

"Neither is Lord Roland. And I don't mean him to be, signorina. I don't mean to marry him. That's the trouble, you see. I want him . . . oh, I want him so much . . . and I can't have him." She choked back a sob.

"Shh. Shh. *Povera donna*. Drink your tea. Is foolish, this not marrying him. He is a good man, such a handsome man. He is loving you so much."

Lilibet gulped at her tea, taking pleasure in the way it scalded the back of her throat. "For now. But after a year, two years . . ."

"I am not thinking so. The way he is looking at you. The way he is learning your boy." Morini folded her hands together and smiled wisely. "Go to him, signora."

"I can't resist him. I can't. I'm so weak, signorina. It's bad enough when things are normal, but when . . . when I'm expecting . . . I can't bear it. It's as if I'm going to burst from my skin. I want him so much, the way he smells and the way he feels . . ." Her face burned; she tried to stop her words, but they kept flowing from her, like a river in full flood.

"Of course you do, signora. It is the way of nature. You were like this before, no? With the young signore?"

"Yes." She whispered the word. "I didn't even *like* my husband, and still I wanted . . . I couldn't help it . . . I stared at the door between our rooms, desperate and ashamed and . . . I'm beyond hope, aren't I? Why do I feel these things? I want so badly to be good. I do, signorina. And this lust, this animal urge, it fills me up until I can't think." No use holding back the sobs, now. She could only muffle them against her handkerchief, undignified, a common slut filled with emotion instead of reason and virtue.

"Shh, signora. Oh, *mia povera signora*. You are young; you are a woman. When you are having a baby, it is like this. Your body is wanting a man, wanting him close. Is nature. Is the way of life." Morini's hand reached across the table, the slender toughened fingers not quite touching hers. "Is not this shame. Is beautiful."

"It's horrible." Lilibet sniffed, choked back another sob, lifted her cup, and put it down again. She took in a deep breath and forced her voice into calm. "I'm trying to make a rational decision, to decide what's best for my son and for me."

"And the baby. The signore's baby."

She didn't bother to deny it. "I tell myself I'll be stronger, that I'll resist him next time. And then I see him, and these urges, this carnal lust, I can't help myself."

"The body, the heart is knowing what the mind does not accept."

"I can't accept it. I can't marry Roland. Even if I were free, I couldn't. Somerton . . . if he knew, my God! He'd kill Roland. He'd take Philip. You don't know his wrath, signorina. You don't know what he's capable of." She spoke coldly, dully, the knot of fear tightening in her belly.

"I am thinking Signore Penhallow is knowing how to fight."

Lilibet shot her a condescending look. "Oh, I'm sure he does. In the boxing ring or the fencing studio, all civilized and formal. But Somerton . . . he's . . . professional." She drank another large sip of tea and closed her eyes. "He fights to win."

"Perhaps you are not knowing Signore Penhallow as well as you think."

Lilibet flashed her eyes open. "What do you mean?"

Morini shrugged. "I am not meaning anything. I say only, go to your love tonight. Do not throw aside this thing, this beautiful love. The future, it is taking care of itself. This love you are holding inside, this desire for Signore Penhallow, it is a thing of God. Is a gift. You must not keep holding it inside; you must give it back. You are growing his love; you are growing his baby. Is not wrong. Is not shame. Is your glory." She stood with unnerving abruptness. "I am calling the maids, starting the dinner. Tonight, I come to your room, I knock three times, very soft. I watch the young signore for you."

"I can't. I shouldn't."

"You must, signora. For the signore, for the baby. He is a good man. He is making a good husband."

"I have a husband already."

Morini shook her head firmly and smoothed her hands on her apron. "Not before God, signora. No longer before God. Is a truth higher than the words writing on the page. Is higher even than the church. Signore Somerton, he is breaking his vows, mocking at his vows. This marriage between you, is like this." She snapped her fingers. "Is no longer."

"You can't mean that. You're Catholic."

Morini snapped her fingers again. Her dark eyes flashed with authority. "Is no longer. Is no true marriage. Signore Penhallow, he is always your love, your true husband. Now let him be as God is wanting."

Lilibet curled her fingers around her empty cup and stared up at Morini. The woman had taken on a glow, an unearthly glow, her certainty so intense it crackled around her. "How do you know so well what God is wanting?" she whispered.

Morini's eyes narrowed slightly, even as a smile tipped the corners of her mouth. "You trust me," she said. "I am knowing."

Roland saved Lilibet's note for last, because he deserved the reward after the long labor of composing a suitable note to Sir Edward in a code that his lust-befuddled brain had difficulty dissecting.

He got it out at last: *LS resides here with son. Earl of S unaware. Highest confidentiality.*

Brevity was his friend, in this case.

But the note to Lilibet was another matter. No doubt she'd be having second thoughts about now, her scruples getting the better of her; she had little faith in him to begin with. He had to convince her of his steadfastness, bowl her over with his passion.

He propped his feet on the bed and stared out the window at the weightless blue sky.

My darling love, I am seized with rapture at the . . .

Er, no.

Sweet Lilibet, I await the touch of your ruby lips with . . .

God, no.

He chewed on the end on his pen, shook the ink loose, let it dry on the nib. He looked down at the new sheet of paper, blank and neutral.

Eleven o'clock in the peach orchard. My heart is yours.

There. After all, she wanted deeds, not words.

And by God, he'd show her deeds tonight.

* * *

The letter that lay before Lilibet on the writing desk was not a new one.

She'd written it over five years ago, after discovering her husband engaged in sexual intercourse with a tenant's wife during her charity rounds about the Somerton estate in Northumbria, a few months after Philip's birth. He hadn't even noticed she'd entered the cottage. She'd simply stood there in shocked paralysis for a full minute or two. The woman had been naked, though Somerton had merely removed his coat and adjusted his trousers; they'd been sitting in a chair, the woman on top, at such an angle that Lilibet could actually see her husband's organ slide in and out between the woman's flour-white thighs, exercising its droit du seigneur with vigorous application. An infant, not much older than Philip, had been squalling fretfully from a wooden cradle near the window; perhaps that was why they hadn't heard her enter the room. Or perhaps it had been the frantic noises issuing from the woman's throat as she pumped herself up and down on his lordship's well-muscled lap.

At the earl's grunt of release, Lilibet had dropped her basket of food and knitted baby clothes on the table with a thump. She'd gone back to the nursery in the great house, held tiny Philip in her arms, and cried into his silken fuzz of hair. His milky baby scent had surrounded them both in a halo of comfort.

Shock, then grief, then anger. After a half hour or so, she'd gone to her study and taken out a few sheets of writing paper and begun a letter to her father's solicitors, the ones who'd represented the Harewood interests in her marriage settlements.

Dear Sirs,

I regret to inform you that, owing to the infamous behavior of my husband, it has become necessary for me to instruct your firm to initiate a Suit of Divorce on

*my behalf, in order to dissolve a Union that has become
intolerable. Firstly, I have discovered him in criminal
conversation with . . .*

At which point the door had opened with a bang, and
Somerton had plowed into the room in a gust of saddle
leather and wet wool. She'd folded the letter with shaking
hands and hidden it in her drawer; over the ensuing years,
as the incidents had accumulated in number and flagrance,
she'd taken out the paper, reread it, made additions and
substitutions, refined the language.

But she had never posted it. At the last instant, her courage had always failed her. *Divorce*: The word was so ugly,
so final, so immense with consequences. Who would stand
by her against the might of the Earl of Somerton? She'd face
ostracism, reduced circumstances, the loss of her son. The
sordid details would be dragged through the popular press,
ruining her good name, even though the crimes themselves
had all been committed by Somerton.

Until that night at the inn, of course.

Adulteress.

Outside her window, afternoon was settling into evening; the faint glow of sunset echoed in a thin line above
the mountains to the east. The cooling air rushed into the
room, making her skin pucker beneath the thin linen of her
dress. By nighttime it would be quite chilly. She'd have to
wear her shawl of India cashmere, or perhaps even her coat,
when she went to meet Roland.

She thought of him as he'd looked this afternoon, leaning
against the boulder by the lake as if he were Atlas, holding
it up. Could he really stand up to the Earl of Somerton?
Would his family support him in such a scandalous act?

Did it really matter?

Somerton would find them, anyway, before long. She'd
already left him, already disgraced him. The consequences
were already in motion.

*Is a truth higher than the words writing on the page. Is
higher even than the church.*

She'd been a coward. She ought to have divorced him long ago. She had justice on her side; she was strong, she was fierce, she was quick-witted. Let him try to take Philip away. Let him try to intimidate her, to hurt those she loved.

Is no longer. Is no true marriage. Signore Penhallow, he is always your love, your true husband.

She thought of Philip, atop Roland's shoulders, smiling and reaching for her. She thought of Roland, bending over Philip's hands to study the grasshopper within.

The way his lips had met hers as if they belonged there; the way his body had bracketed hers, strong and solid.

The child that grew within her, Roland's child; their child, created in love.

A glimpse flashed before her, a possibility, radiant with hope.

Can you not have the slightest particle of faith in me? he'd asked.

Her eyes dropped again to the paper before her. She set it aside and drew out a fresh sheet, and with a steady hand she made a clean copy in her copperplate writing. By the time the horizon had sunk into darkness, and Philip's excited voice rose from the stairway near her door, she had folded it into an envelope and addressed it to Bellwether and Knobbs, Esq., Stonecutter Lane, London.

FIFTEEN

Roland had anticipated many delights from the evening, and not one of them had involved the long shanks of Phineas Burke gleaming through the moonlight between the peach trees.

Damn it all. What was the old fellow doing here at this hour?

Meeting Lady Morley, probably. As if Burke couldn't just as easily arrange for assignations within the sheltered comfort of that damned workshop of his. No, he had to go wooing his lady-love with fragrant blossoms and moonlight and whatnot, muscling in on other chaps' midnight frolics.

Peach bloody orchard. Come to think of it, what had Roland himself been thinking, naming such a place to meet Lilibet? Of all the damned romantic clichés. Probably half the village was lurking about the trees, drunk with spring-time passion, ensuring the population of the valley would remain at a healthy replacement level the following year.

Roland set the champagne bottle and glasses on the ground—champagne did such lovely things to feminine scruples—and slid his watch out of his pocket to hold it up to the moonlight. He was quite early. Lilibet wouldn't be about for another hour.

He glanced again at Burke's lingering figure. No, really. He shouldn't. Too wicked of him.

He patted his jacket pocket and found the scrap of paper and pencil stub he usually carried about him, in case of emergency. Then he cast about before him for a crisp old stick and stepped on it. Loudly.

A hasty rustling movement took place up ahead.

"Still, still, still," he murmured, projecting his voice forward. "Pill? Kill? Oh, God, no. Mill? Hang it all. Shall have to try something else."

He peered above the top edge of the paper and saw a sliver of tweed jacket along the edge of a tree.

He continued with enthusiasm. ". . . *the memory is with me still . . .* no, *the memory is with me* yet. *The memory is with me yet*, there's the ticket. *The memory is with me yet, and something something . . . shall forget? Or regret? And never shall my love regret?* Oh yes. Very good."

The most jolly awful poetry he'd ever composed, in fact. He was quite proud. He arranged himself against the knobbled trunk of an ancient peach tree and gazed up in rapture toward the blossom-crossed midnight sky.

From the corner of his eye, he caught a slight movement, as a splash of ginger hair spilled in and out from behind the tree. Well, he assumed it was ginger, in any case: In the tree-shadowed darkness, even Phineas Burke's head of bright newpenny copper had dulled to a kind of faintly bronzed gray.

Poor fellow. Though Roland considered himself a far superior companion to the Dowager Marchioness of Morley—certainly a better hand at piquet—he doubted Burke would agree, under the circumstances.

Not that he intended to show any mercy.

"*The memory is with me yet, and never shall my love regret,*" he went on, with a dramatic heave of his chest.

A muffled groan, faint but unmistakable.

Roland made a little start, as if shaking off a lovesick

reverie. He looked down at the blank sheet of paper in his hand, cleared his throat, and took a deep breath. "Excellent," he said, in his most sonorous voice. "From the beginning, then."

Burke's despair seemed to reach out through the air like a spread-fingered hand, aiming for Roland's throat.

Roland went on, constructing line after awful line with deep pleasure, enjoying himself so deeply that he committed that most elementary of errors: He ignored his surroundings. Until . . .

Snap, snap.

At the sound of approaching footsteps, Roland moved by instinct, ducking behind the tree in a single lithe movement. He pressed himself against the rough bark and gathered the sound into his ears.

Heavy, long strides. Not a woman's footsteps. Not Lilibet, then, or Lady Morley. Some fellow from the village? One of the stable lads?

Roland ventured his eye to the side of the tree and saw the dark familiar outline of the Duke of Wallingford progress against the shadows.

Bloody hell.

What the devil was going on here? First Burke, now Wallingford.

There is no such thing as coincidence, repeated Sir Edward in his ear, and his mind darted at once to Lilibet. Had she set him up again? Had he mistaken the passion in her kiss, the anticipation in her eyes?

Wallingford marched on in his straight-backed ducal way, footsteps steady and confident, making no allowances for subterfuge. He passed his brother by a scant yard, so close Roland could have reached out and brushed the tips of his fingers against the light superfine wool of the duke's evening jacket.

That would have given the old fellow a start.

Wallingford came to a stop not far from the tree behind which Burke was undoubtedly cursing.

"I know you're there," he announced, in his booming

voice, rattling the branches of the nearby trees. "You may as well come out."

Roland rolled his eyes. Blasted dukes. What exactly did his brother expect? That everyone would emerge from behind the trees, heads hanging with guilt, limbs shaking in their boots under the irresistible weight of his authority?

Silence seethed around them, broken only by the occasional trill of a nightjar, made uneasy by this invasion of his back garden by a parcel of idiot Englishmen. Wallingford cast about him: stunned, apparently, by the lack of response to his perfectly reasonable request.

He continued in a more conciliatory tone. "I have your message. There's no need to hide. No need for any more tricks."

In the distance, from the direction of the castle, the sound of footsteps—yet more footsteps, picking their way through the orchard—caught Roland's finely tuned ears.

"Now look here," Wallingford said. "You asked me to meet you tonight. Don't be afraid, my brave girl." His voice was lower now, persuasive, so that Roland could hardly distinguish the syllables through the cool, fragrant air. Besides, he was paying attention to the progress of the newcomer.

These were lighter steps than those of Wallingford. Less certain. A woman, probably. He closed his eyes, concentrating his senses on the sound of her, the vibration of the air and the ground she caused, the first possible traces of her scent.

He felt her pause at Wallingford's voice, and then continue, more boldly, using the sound to guide her.

Snap, snap went the twigs beneath her feet, and Wallingford arrested. His neck craned upward, searching her out.

Lilies.

The scent of lilies touched his nose. Roland sagged, ever so slightly, against his tree. Lilies were Burke's problem. Not his.

Lady Morley walked past him, her skirts swishing about her legs, brushing the ground. She turned her head one way and another, trying to make out the figure before her.

Roland saw the exact moment when she recognized Wallingford. Her back straightened; a little gasp came from her throat. His mind, trained to absorb all the tiny details of behavior that gave away human thought, perceived her instant of panic, her grasp for composure, her recovery.

A thoroughbred, Lady Morley, for all her faults.

Wallingford addressed her first, in his drawling voice. They were too far away for Roland to distinguish the conversation; all he could make out were the tones of their voices.

His eyes shifted to Burke's tree, from which no movement came. Good old Burke. He was probably gnawing his own feet to stop himself from jumping in to defend Lady Morley. Of course, by the very act of jumping in, he would only incriminate them both.

A pretty scene indeed.

Roland looked down at the champagne bottle nestled in the grass by his feet, at the pair of glasses nicked from the pantry, and swore to himself.

Couldn't a fellow get five minutes of privacy around here?

Three soft knocks sounded on the door.

Lilibet stole a final look at Philip, tucked beneath a striped woolen blanket in his trundle next to her bed. One arm had fought free to rest on the pillow next to his head; his face turned away, toward the rough plaster wall. The blanket moved, slow and regular, with the pulse of his breathing.

She smiled, blew a kiss in his direction, and opened the door.

Signorina Morini stood outside, a look of mischief crinkling the corners of her face. "The peach orchard," she whispered. "I see him leave, it was almost an hour. He has the champagne."

"The peach orchard. Thank you, signorina. Thanks ever so much." Lilibet tucked her shawl about her shoulders and danced into the corridor and down the staircase. Her body hummed with confidence, with purpose, as if in that single act of sealing a plain white envelope she had restored power to her once lifeless limbs.

The peach orchard. Blossoms, moonlight, champagne. What a dear old romantic he was.

She moved so silently between the trees, Roland almost missed her.

"Darling!" he whispered, as loudly as he dared. "Over here!"

She stopped, turned, hesitated. A stray piece of moonlight, finding its way between the peach blossoms, touched the top of her shawl-covered head.

The breath left his chest. He'd spent the last ten minutes in a panic that he'd missed her, that she'd heard the voices in the trees and fled back to the castle. The heated exchange between Wallingford and Lady Morley hadn't lasted long, but Wallingford had stood staring after her for a long while afterward, his tall body blending into the shadows until he was hardly distinguishable from one of the trees around him, except perhaps less knobby and sweet smelling. At last, with an angry oath, he'd turned around and marched away, and Burke had emerged from behind his tree, shaking his head in a dazed motion.

Poor old fellow. Devil of a disappointment, having one's rendezvous interrupted by a bad-tempered duke.

Burke had gone off in another direction, presumably toward his workshop, and Roland had slumped against his tree trunk to recover, inhaling the cool, rich air in an attempt to clear his head.

Devil take them all. Arranging a moonlight assignation with one's ladylove ought to have been child's play for a man of his experience with clandestine appointments. Instead he'd been thwarted at every turn, and by his own side, at that.

Now, with Lilibet's shadowed figure finally before him,

he was ready to burst from the lust dammed up inside him. He'd consider himself lucky if he didn't disgrace himself like a schoolboy.

He closed his eyes for an instant, gathering his composure. Patience. Every movement counted. If he were to win Lilibet, he had to have his every wit at his disposal. He had to put on the greatest performance of his life. He needed to drunken her with passion, drench her with pleasure, blind her with love. Nothing else would overcome her inflexible virtue.

He flexed his fingers.

"Darling," he whispered again, and strode out from behind the tree, arms outstretched.

She murmured something unintelligible and took a few tottering steps forward to clasp his hands. She'd wrapped her shawl snugly about her head and shoulders, against the growing chill of the evening. "Sweetheart," he said. "At last."

He drew his fingers along her darkened cheek and bent to capture her lips in an eager kiss.

Recognition flashed across his brain an instant too late.

Not Lilibet.

In the light of the waxing moon, Lilibet found the steps cut into the terrace wall without any trouble. She tripped down them, her feet hardly touching the stone. The cool air flew past her cheeks as she hurried along the flat meadow, filled with the scents of evening: the breeze blowing off the mountains, the green things pushing up from the earth, the flowers exploding from the trees and shrubs. Ahead, the whiteness of the peach blossoms glowed like a bank of fog smudged against the darkness.

She quickened her steps, until she reached the first of the peach trees, and the heady scent of blossom enfolded her. She paused and peered ahead, into the shadows. Where would he be? Not far, surely. Waiting for her near the edge of the orchard, with his champagne and his kisses.

She had just started forward, her heart beating in her throat, when the sound of voices froze her foot in the air.

Roland tore his lips away. "Good God!" he said, forgetting to whisper.

"Signore!"

He reached over her head and pulled down her scarf. The moonlight disappeared into a pool of black hair; her arms clutched his. "Signore!" she said again.

"You're the . . . what the devil . . ."

"Signore?"

"Francesca?"

"*Si*, signore." A little sob broke from her throat. "You ask . . . you . . . letter . . ."

"Letter?"

Her hand disappeared from his arm and made some movement at her skirts. His brain spun around in dizzy circles. The letter. The letter for Sir Edward. He'd given it to Francesca to post in the village.

Hadn't he?

A piece of paper entered his hand. He looked down. It was heavy, folded over twice. He opened it with numb fingers. In the shadows, he couldn't make out the words, but he recognized the shape and size of the lines, could even read it to himself from memory.

Eleven o'clock in the peach orchard. My heart is yours.

Francesca's voice crept into his ears, pleading. "Maria . . . she know the *inglese*, she say . . ."

"Oh God." He crushed his fist against his skull.

"Signore . . . you no . . ." Her voice dissolved into another sob, more desperate this time. Her shoulders bent forward beneath her shawl.

"Oh, damn. Poor girl." He straightened her shawl back over her head and tucked it in. "I'm sorry. It's the devil of a . . . a mistake, you understand? Mistake." He bent forward and placed a kiss on her forehead. "You're a lovely girl, Francesca. But I . . ."

Sobs wracked her shoulders. From her mouth came a series of hiccups and Italian phrases: none of which, he suspected, were particularly complimentary to himself.

He took out his watch, glanced at it, and turned it up to the moonlight.

"Look here, sweetheart," he said, patting the edge of her shoulder. "I'm awfully sorry. But . . . do you think perhaps . . . oh, damn. Here." In a few long strides he reached his tree, and the bottle of champagne propped against the base. He grabbed it by the neck and popped it open.

"Here," he said, handing her a foaming glass. "Drink. All better, eh? Nothing like a spot of the old bubbly, in times of trial."

She took the glass, drained it, and held it out again with a choking hiccup.

"Ah. Yes. Bottoms up." He refilled her glass to the brim and set the bottle back in the grass. "Well, in any case, and as I said before, I'm frightfully sorry about this. Dreadful cock-up. Appears I gave you the wrong note, ha-ha. No doubt we'll all have a jolly laugh about it in the morning, eh?"

She glared at him over the rim of her glass.

He cleared his throat. "But I'm afraid, if you're quite all set up with the champagne and whatnot, I really must . . . must be off."

She said nothing, all her concentration apparently fixed into her champagne glass.

He took an experimental step away, and another. "Well, then. Farewell. Much luck. Enjoy the . . . er . . . the champagne."

Another backward step, and he turned and bolted for the castle.

The wrong note. He'd given the bloody housemaid the *wrong note*.

Which meant Sir Edward's letter lay underneath Lilibet's door. Unopened, he hoped. God, how he hoped.

Sir Edward would have his head, if Lilibet didn't have it off first.

He ran across the meadow, up the terrace steps, across the flagstones of the courtyard to the door. The hall was still and dark, illuminated only by a shaft of moonlight beaming through the high windows along the stairway. He went up the steps two at a time, arriving at Lilibet's door in a breathless gust. After a quick thrust of his hands through his hair, he lowered one fist to knock.

And stopped, just in time.

Philip slept in the room with her.

His hand swung downward to crash against his thigh.

He stood there a moment, chest still gently heaving from the effort of reaching her door. A cold trickle of sweat trailed down his back, disappearing into his shirt. He put both hands on his head and turned to walk down the succession of hallways to the west wing, where the gentlemen had their rooms.

Inside his room, he lit a candle and removed his jacket. Light flickered about the furniture and the few items atop the bureau. Norbert's makeshift cage had been covered with cloth before he left, on Philip's orders, so that the grasshopper could settle down and get some rest in his new surroundings.

An unwilling smile nudged up the corners of Roland's mouth. He went over to the chest of drawers and lifted the edge of Norbert's cloth. The grasshopper did, in fact, appear to be resting along one side of his cage, contemplating a blade of grass with one drowsy eye.

Roland lowered the cloth and looked about the room. He'd no desire for bed; energy still looped about his body, disappointment and panic and general annoyance at himself. He walked back out of the room and locked the door behind him.

Perhaps a swim in the lake. That should clear his mind a bit, help him consider his options. God knew his mind needed clearing; he'd been making mistake after mistake ever since he'd crossed the border into Italy.

He went back across the meadow at a jog, mind already pursuing his next course of action. There would be hell to pay in the morning, of course. Flowers? What blooms had emerged already? Well, except for the all-damned peach blossoms, may the bees inflict a mighty plague on them all. He'd go out early, before breakfast, and find something.

The quickest way to the lake lay through the peach orchard, but he'd be damned if he ventured back in there. Instead he skirted the trees, along the terrace wall, keeping a baleful eye on the downward slope. The moon was now directly overhead, cold and distant, casting a precise glow across the grass, just enough to pick out a path.

A sound came out of the darkness ahead.

He staggered to a stop.

There it was again. Odd sort of noise, a bit high-pitched and uneven, almost like . . .

Giggling.

Roland frowned. His eyes narrowed to slits, trying to pick out details from the shadowed shapes before him.

Another giggle.

He took a step forward, and another. A few more.

He came upon them so quickly, he nearly stumbled over their outstretched legs. "What the devil?" he stammered.

"Why, Roland! Is that you?" One of the shadows shifted against the wall. "We thought you'd gone back in."

His mouth opened, then closed. Then opened again. "Lilibet?"

"Come join us, if you like. Though the champagne's nearly finished." He felt something hard and cold bump against his leg. The champagne bottle.

"We?" he asked, voice dry. "Who's *we*?"

Another voice, through the darkness. "Signore!"—hiccup—"You come again?"

"Francesca." He sighed. "Of course."

She's really very nice, you know," Lilibet said. She slung her arm through his, savoring the sturdy warmth of bone and muscle beneath her hand. "Though she drinks a great deal. I hardly had half a glass."

He grunted. "Just as well, in your condition."

"Yes, that's so. Wine turns my stomach at the moment. Was she awfully upset, in the orchard?" Roland was walking quickly; she had to take a few jogging strides to keep up.

"Only for a minute or two." He stopped abruptly and turned to her, his face a mere outline in the night. "And you? You don't seem so awfully upset."

"Well, it was rather awkward for a moment or two. I saw the two of you, and I thought . . ."

"The worst, I expect."

"Just for a minute. Then I realized what had happened and had a good laugh. And poor Francesca. She really is madly in love with you, you cad. It must be a terrific problem for you, having women swooning at your feet all the time, left and right."

"Rather a nuisance, yes." His voice was stony.

"Are you angry with me?"

"I am . . ." He paused, apparently searching for a word. "Bemused."

She smiled. She felt invincible tonight, flooded with power and ecstasy. She reached up and caressed his cheek, the bold, perfectly set bones of his face. He'd shaved before coming down; the skin sprang sleek and dewy beneath her fingers. How she longed to bury her nose in that skin, to inhale its clean, male scent. Instead, she said: "I have a confession for you. I wasn't going to go to bed with you tonight."

His face tensed beneath her hand. "What's that?"

"I'm sorry." She let her hand trail down his shoulder, his arm, until she was holding his stiff hand in hers. "I'd only come down to tell you something. Something rather important; something I want you to know."

"What's that?"

"I sent out a letter today, to my solicitors. I've asked them to initiate a suit of divorce."

His gasp came out of the darkness. "Wh-what? . . . But Lilibet, that's marvelous! Have you really done it, at last?" He took her elbows and drew her against him. "You darling! We must celebrate! We must . . . oh Lord!" His arms came around her, lifting her up, swinging her around in a circle. "By God, darling, my own darling, I'll see he doesn't harm you, or Philip. I'll stand by you like a champion; I shan't leave your side . . ."

"Hush! Stop!" She couldn't help laughing. She put her hands to his shoulders and pushed, gently but firmly, until he set her down on her feet again. "No. You're getting dreadfully ahead of yourself. This has nothing to do with you, Roland."

His fingers pressed into her back. "What do you mean, nothing to do with me? It has *everything* to do with me. With us. By God, Lilibet, you're carrying my child . . ."

She put her finger to his lips. "This is between me and my husband. Well, and all the women he's gone to bed with, whom I shall have to list and name, with dates and places and all sorts of tiresome things. I shall have to prove not only that, but cruelty as well."

That checked his annoyance. "I'm sorry about that, darling," he said, kissing her forehead. "Jolly awful business for you."

"Yes, it will be. It will be a dreadful ordeal, Roland." She took a deep breath and grasped his hands, which still rested at her back. She brought them around front and squeezed them. "Which is why we must stay quite apart until it's finished. Until I have Philip in my legal custody, clear and sound, I can't take any chances. You must stay away."

A nightjar trilled softly from the direction of the orchard. Roland's hands lay heavy in hers. "Stay away?" he repeated.

"Yes. I can't force you to leave the castle, of course, but it would be best."

Another long, heavy pause, and then his hands slipped up her arms to grip her shoulders. "Leave? Are you mad? Good God, no. If he discovers where you are . . ."

"Then I'll deal with him, Roland. But there can't be any hint of impropriety, on my part, or the whole thing will fail. Not a hint." She looked into his shadowed eyes. "Do you know what I mean?"

"Yes." His fingers pressed harder.

"Because if he finds out, if he can prove . . . *that* . . ."—she couldn't quite bring herself to say the word *adultery*, not aloud—"then my suit will be disallowed. The divorce won't go through. The petitioner must be blameless, you see, or else the courts will say I've no grounds for complaint."

"I say, you've studied the law rather carefully, it seems."

"Of course I have. I've done nothing else." She peered up into his face. "Is it . . . is it all right?"

He thrust her away and ran his hand through his hair. "No! It isn't all right! What the devil are you saying? It's not all right, Lilibet. For God's sake, the damage is already done! You're *expecting*! Do you think you can *hide* it? It won't matter if we're as chaste as monks from now on, if your belly is bumping up against the judge himself!"

She shook her head. "I know. I realize that. Which is why I'll stay here until it's all finished. Refuse any visitors. I'll endeavor not to see anyone, until it's final. And if he *does* find out, there's no proof . . . The dates are close enough . . . He can't say for certain . . . and everyone *here* will support us, will say we haven't been together."

"It could be months. Years. The birth, my God, if something goes wrong . . ." His voice was hard, desperate. How she wished she could see his face through the darkness! Somehow it was all harder, talking to a voice in the void that had all the characteristics of Roland, and yet seemed a stranger.

"Then I'll deal with it, Roland," she said. "I have to. Don't you understand? You can't be involved, not at all. Every moment we spend alone could damn us in court. It could ruin everything."

He stepped forward and seized her hands again, pulling her against him. "No. I don't understand. We've waited more than six years already. And now that you're finally here, in my arms, with Somerton at last behind us, you can't possibly expect me to stay away. I'll go mad, Lilibet."

She couldn't make out his face, but she could feel the weight of his eyes, drenching her with the intensity of his

emotion. That magnetic allure of his, pulling at her, drawing her under his spell; the sweet madness taking over her
brain again. She squeezed her eyes shut and placed her
hands against his chest. "No, you won't. And neither will I.
We are human beings, Roland, not animals. We won't do
this. Not yet."

He said nothing. The warmth of his skin gave her an
instant's warning before his lips, firm and tender, brushed
against hers: once, twice. "Lilibet." He touched his forehead
to hers and drew his hands up to cradle her face. "Please. I
can give you so much pleasure, darling. So much love. Just
let me. Allow me the privilege. Just once. Just tonight. Who
will know?"

"Roland, please . . ." she murmured into his lips, every
cell of her body whirling and aching at his touch. He felt so
right; so exactly fashioned for her alone.

"I want you so much, so deeply." His voice rumbled in
her ear as his thumbs caressed her cheekbones. "You can't
imagine how hard it's been, waiting for you."

No doubt about that, she thought. The physical evidence
pushed like a fire iron into her belly.

"Yes, I *can* imagine," she said, pulling back. "Do you
think I don't want it, too? I want you desperately. I long for
you, every night. I . . ." She could hear the hoarseness, the
plea in her own voice, and stepped outside the circle of his
arms to breathe the air in great cleansing gasps. "You asked
me to have faith in you," she went on quietly, at last. "And
I'm showing it to you now, Roland. I'm trusting you with
everything right now. Don't you see?"

He turned away a few degrees, staring up at the castle.
"You're serious, aren't you?"

"Quite serious. Please understand."

"Oh, damn," he said. "Oh, damn."

Silence spun about them. She felt his acquiescence seep
into the air, reluctant and agonized and . . . well, rather
sulky.

She couldn't really blame him.

"Very well," he said at last. "I won't touch you, if that's

how you want it." He leaned close, so close she could feel his warm breath on her face. "But I'm not leaving, Lilibet. Not on your life. I'll stay, and keep watch on you and the baby and Philip. And Norbert the damned grasshopper, I suppose." He tilted his head and spoke into her ear. "And I will not, for one moment, stop trying to change your mind."

"You won't succeed."

"Yes, I bloody will," he growled.

She reached up and pushed away the lock of hair on his forehead. "Oh, cheer up," she said. "It's not as desperate as that. After all, if you give up on me, there's always Francesca."

"Francesca," he muttered.

They walked back to the house, arms held rigidly away from one another. At the doorway, just before they parted, Lilibet remembered something.

"Oh, I meant to tell you. I had the oddest note under my door this afternoon. Do you perhaps know where it came from?"

"Haven't a clue," he said. "I advise you to burn it."

He strode past her, up the wide stone stairs to the western wing, where the gentlemen slept.

SIXTEEN

Midsummer's Eve

There were times, while acting as a *de facto* tutor for a boy of five, that Roland looked back with yearning on his tranquil existence as an intelligence agent for Her Majesty's Bureau of Trade and Maritime Information.

"Uncle Roland," said Philip, in perhaps his fiftieth question during the past hour and a half, "how old is the castle?"

Roland put his hands behind his head and stared up at the library ceiling. "Haven't a clue, old boy," he said, "though I daresay we could find out."

"Do you think one of the Medicis lived here? That would be smashing," Philip said. He jumped up from the rug and began to slash with his imaginary sword. "Fighting off the . . . well, whoever it was."

"Various parties, through the ages, I believe," Roland said. "Shall we look it up?" It was defensible research, after all. They were supposed to be reading history at the moment, not that Philip's course of study was what Roland's own boyhood tutor might have called structured.

He hadn't planned on spending his hours teaching Philip his Latin grammar and English kings. He'd only been looking for a diversion, a way to keep his mind out of Lilibet's bed, where it had a disturbing tendency to burrow if left unchecked. He'd begun by taking the boy out riding and swimming, thinking that he ought to get to know the little fellow better, if he planned on marrying his mother. It would please Lilibet to see them getting on, and he rather liked Philip. He had a certain ardent and ingenious charm to him, always taking things full tilt, always sticking up for underdogs.

Then Abigail had taken to disappearing in the afternoons, right around lesson time, and Roland had shrugged his shoulders and pulled out the books himself. What else had he to do, after all?

"Are you certain?" Lilibet had asked, her eyes turned up to his like a pair of anxious cornflowers. "I can do it myself. You really don't mind?"

"Not at all," he'd said. "You need your rest." Because really, he'd do anything she wanted at the moment. Anything at all to promote a sense of obligation, which might at any point (so he hoped, against all hope) be returned in the form of sexual favor. Over the past few months, he'd discovered that all previously known forms of physical torture were nothing, compared to the agony of watching the woman one loved grow round and ripe with one's child, without being allowed to touch her.

Well, that wasn't quite true. He'd stolen the odd kiss, now and again, but only after excruciatingly exact planning and cunning subterfuge, combined with excessive outpourings of the legendary Penhallow charm. Worth it, every time, even though her kisses had only made him burn even hotter.

Given the incentive, the prospect of teaching Philip his conjugations and sums seemed a small price to pay. He'd plunged into it with a sort of haphazard method, moving from Scottish history to the Chinese abacus in the course of an hour, and somewhere along the way he'd realized he was enjoying himself. Immensely, in fact. He kept spotting little bits of Lilibet in the boy, expressions and habits that stopped his breath in astonished rapture, until spending time sprawled on the library rug with slates and books became, improbably, the next best thing to spending it sprawled in bed with Lilibet.

Not that he had any prospect of the latter, at the moment.

"Where would we look it up?" Philip asked, casting his eyes about the library walls.

"I suppose there must be an estate book of some kind, lying about," Roland said. He heaved himself up from the rug and went to the nearest shelf. "Wallingford has them in his library, collecting dust, all the way back to the first duke. Land grants and revenues and dowries and all that rubbish. Makes me dashed glad I'm not the heir."

"I know," Philip said, with a mournful sigh.

Roland glanced downward. "Oh, buck up, old boy," he said. "It's not so bad, being an earl. Proper title, you know, not like this flimsy pretend one I've got."

"Pretend title?"

"Well, I'm not lord of anything, am I?" Roland read the faded gold letters stamped on the leather spines. Italian history, Italian letters. Where the devil would the estate books be kept? Here, or elsewhere? He knew next to nothing about this Rosseti who owned the pile. "I'm just Lord Roland of Nothing."

"Really?" Philip went silent for a moment, digesting this morsel. "So if Mama were married to you, she'd be Lady Nothing?"

Roland's finger froze on the binding of a Machiavelli. "No," he said slowly. "She'd be known as Lady Roland. Lady Roland Penhallow."

"Oh. Well, that's rubbish. What would happen to her real name?"

Roland's finger resumed its travels along the leather bindings. "Well, you'd still call her Mama, and her friends would still call her Elizabeth."

"What would you call her?"

"I'd call her Lilibet. Or darling, or sweetheart. All those tedious names husbands are obliged to call their wives."

"My father doesn't call her those. And what about the baby in her tummy?"

Roland spun around. "How the deuce did you know about that?"

Philip looked up at him, perfectly composed. "I asked her last night why she was getting so big in her tummy. And she told me there was a baby inside, and I wasn't supposed . . ." His hand flew to his mouth.

"Exactly. See that you don't tell anyone else, young man." Roland ran his hand through his hair. "Your mama wants to keep it a surprise, for now."

Philip's eyes narrowed. "Then how did you find out?"

Roland moved on to the next shelf, thinking fast. "Well, she had to tell someone, didn't she? To run for the doctor and all that. Not an easy job at all, having a baby."

"Oh." Philip followed him without speaking, eyes cast down to the worn rug beneath their feet.

"Let's see here," Roland said. "This looks a bit more promising. Might be ledgers, here." He glanced down. "Everything all right?"

"Uncle Roland," Philip said, in a quiet voice, "is my father dead?"

Roland started. "Dead! No. No, Philip. Good God, no. Alive and well. Just . . . well, just very busy. Earls have all sorts of responsibilities."

Philip looked up at him steadily, his dark eyes round and doubtful. "Are you sure?"

"Quite sure."

"Is he sick?"

"No. Not sick." Christ. He wasn't prepared for this at all. He'd no idea what Lilibet had told the boy about his father, no idea at all how to corroborate her story. Philip continued to examine him with those preternaturally wise eyes, as if he could see right through Roland's fine speeches to read the truth behind them. "I suppose you miss him a great deal," he said at last, crouching down to look Philip straight in the eye.

"Yes." The word was brief, uncertain. Philip looked as if he wanted to say more.

"Yes, but?"

"Well, I didn't see him much. And when I did, he always seemed angry at me." The words tumbled out and then stopped, like the closing of a sluice gate.

"He wasn't angry at you, Philip. I'm sure he loves you very much." Roland fisted one hand, wishing Somerton were here right now, so he could drag him into the hallway for the thrashing of his life. The other hand he placed gently atop Philip's slender shoulder. "You're a fine lad. Any father would be proud of you."

Philip shrugged.

"Look here." Roland gave the shoulder a last pat and rose to his feet. "I think I've found what we're looking for. Looks ancient enough. Ledger-like." He drew a wide, slim volume from the shelf. "I can't make out the Italian properly, but I recognize a bit of Latin in there. Let's take a look, shall we?"

He carried the book to the wide table near the windows— he pictured Medici princes, spreading out their maps of conquest atop the worn wood—and opened the pages to the middle. "Accounts, all right. Good God, it's frightfully old. Look at this, Philip: November the third, 1597. Double-entry bookkeeping, even. Didn't know they had that sort of thing back then."

"What's double . . . double . . ."

"Double-entry bookkeeping. It's how we keep track of incoming and outgoing funds, keeping everything in its proper order. You make an entry in the credit side and an entry in the debit side, to show where the money went." Roland thumbed through the pages. "Household receipts. Seems to have acquired a great deal of silver."

Philip made a restless movement at his elbow, boredom radiating from his small body.

"Let's try something else." Roland closed the book with a snap and went to the shelf again. "Ledgers, ledgers. Now, that's odd. This one looks more like a portfolio." He pulled it out. "Stuffed with papers. A good sign. I keep a few of these myself, for official papers and whatnot."

"What are those?"

"Deeds, that sort of thing. I've a pair of estates in the Mid-lands, part of my mother's dowry. Look here." He spread the papers out on the table. "My God. These must date from the building of the castle. Look here, the deed of gift, from the Pope himself. Ought to be in a museum, really."

"From the Pope? Really? Can I touch it?"

"I daresay you won't burst into flame, though the Arch-bishop of Canterbury won't want to hear of it." Roland turned the pages over, marveling at the paleness of the sheets, the crispness of the ink. As if the papers hadn't aged at all. "In any case, it answers your question. The original deed's dated in 1567; I expect they started building the castle shortly afterward. Here's where they added on, in the next century, if my Latin roots are up to the challenge. And here . . ."

Roland's hand arrested the page in midair.

"What? What is it?" Philip crowded his shoulder and peered over the line of his arm.

He set the paper down on the table and straightened it. The familiar name jumped out at him again, its plain En-glish syllables projecting from the lines of Italian like a tav-ern chorus at a grand opera. "Well. That's odd."

"What's odd? Tell me!"

Roland put the paper back in the stack, slid the lot back into the portfolio, and tied the ribbons in sharp, tight strokes. "Nothing, really. Transfer of ownership, that's all. Happens often enough. I expect they ran out of heirs. But see here!" He rose to replace the portfolio in the shelf. "We found the answer to your question. The castle's as old as Good Queen Bess. Aren't you impressed?"

The library door swung open with a crash against the wall. "There you are!"

Roland looked to the door. Abigail stood there, hair escaping in wild locks from the pins at her nape, energy snapping around her like an electric charge. She held out her hand. "Come along, Philip! We need your help with the party masks."

"Party?" Roland slid the portfolio between a pair of led-gers and turned around. "What party?"

"The Midsummer's Eve festival tonight. Don't tell me you haven't noticed."

"All that rumpus in the courtyard, with the tables and the lanterns?"

"Oh, it will be such fun, Lord Roland. Do say you'll come. Lilibet and Alexandra and I will be dressing up as serving girls, and everyone's going to wear masks, with dancing and music." She made an impatient movement with her hand, still outstretched. "But we're badly behind making the masks, Philip, and we need you to glue feathers for us."

"Look here," Roland said. He leaned back against the library shelves, in an irrational urge to protect the contents from her view. "We're engaged in serious academic endeavors and all that. Can't one of the maids be called in?"

Philip turned to him and snatched his hand. "Oh, can I go, Uncle Roland? Please? We can study an extra hour tomorrow."

"The maids are busy getting the feast ready. You don't mind, really, do you?" Her eyes sparkled. "I'm sure Lilibet will thank you for it afterward."

Roland wasn't quite sure at which point in the past three months he and Abigail had become allies. Like Wallingford's loss of interest in the matter of the wager, it had come on gradually, in tacit gestures, until only the thinnest of polite veneers remained over the obvious fact that love seethed like springtime in the air of the castle and its environs, with the active encouragement of Abigail herself. "In that case," he said, with a slow wink, and a firm squeeze of Philip's hand, "take him, with my blessing."

Philip ran to Abigail, shoes striking in eager thumps against the rug-covered wood.

Roland stared at the open door of the library, leaning against the shelf, legs crossed at the ankles, for a long time after Philip and Abigail had disappeared around the corner into the hallway. His fingers traced the edge of the shelf behind him, back and forth, brushing against the bottoms of the books inside.

There is no such thing as coincidence.

At last he straightened, pulled his watch out of his waist-coat pocket, and gathered his jacket from the back of the armchair by the desk. Nearly four o'clock. He'd most likely find Wallingford out riding at this hour, taking out his frustrated longing for Miss Abigail Harewood in endless bouts of physical exercise.

The duke, he felt certain, would want to know the name of the legal owner of the Castel sant'Agata.

Particularly since it appeared to belong to their own grandfather.

"There," said Abigail, giving Lilibet's bodice a last straightening. "You look perfect. You've filled out so beautifully with Morini's cooking, I'd hardly recognize you."

Lilibet narrowed her eyes, but couldn't detect a spark of mischief in Abigail's eyes. Was she blind? Was the entire castle blind? Her breasts were spilling from her bodice, her hair and skin glowed like patent electric bulbs, and her belly had taken on a decided curve. Did everybody really think it was only the result of the favorable Italian air and Morini's irresistible *panettone*?

People see what they expect to see, her mother had once told her, with a shrug.

Presumably nobody expected to see the legendarily virtuous Lady Somerton with child by her secret lover.

She'd have to tell them soon, of course. What would she say? Would she allow them to assume the baby was a parting gift from her husband, or would she tell them the truth?

"You don't think I've grown too plump?" she asked, with a downward glance at her telltale bosom.

"Lord Roland certainly doesn't seem to mind." Abigail adjusted the apron at her waist. "The way he looks at you! You might take a little pity on him, you know."

Lilibet nudged Abigail's hands away. This morning, she'd felt the first tiny flutters inside her womb, and the hands she craved nearby so private and flawless a miracle did *not* belong to Abigail. "How do you know I don't?"

"Darling, your room's next to mine. If I can hear Mr. Burke bringing back Alexandra at the crack of every dawn, I'd certainly notice you. Does mine look all right?" Abigail twirled before her.

"Quite adorably fetching. You'll have to keep your distance from poor old Wallingford."

"I doubt poor old Wallingford will be in attendance," Abigail said, with a trace of smugness.

She was right. The courtyard burst with people—farmers, villagers, a local philharmonic playing lilting favorites with surprising skill, the towering ginger-topped figure of Phineas Burke—but no sign of the tall, black-haired English duke. Francesca appeared, wearing a white-feathered mask and leading Philip by the hand; he spotted her at once and ran over.

"Do you like my mask, Mama? Do you? It's bully, isn't it? I colored the feathers red myself." He squeezed her around the middle and fingered one particularly spectacular feather, arching outward and upward from the right side. "And this one's the eagle feather Uncle Roland found for me on his ride this afternoon. Isn't it cracking?"

"It's a glorious mask, darling. I adore it. But run along with Francesca; I've got to help Abigail and Lady Morley serve the food. It's the Midsummer's Eve tradition, apparently." She planted a last kiss on the top of his head and returned to the kitchen, where her cousins were lifting trays of antipasti from the broad wooden table.

"I don't know why I let Abigail talk me into these things," said Alexandra, with a regal frown. Lilibet saw with relief that even her own ripening bosom couldn't match the abundance of Alexandra's: released at last from the confines of proper English clothing, it swelled above the low neckline of the servant's dresses with a lushness that put Lilibet to shame. "Have you a handkerchief about you, perhaps, to protect my modesty?"

"Not that large, I'm afraid," Lilibet said. "Abigail, where did you find these costumes? They're hardly decent. Not at all what Maria and Francesca wear."

"Oh, Morini brought them out. Didn't you, signorina?"

Lilibet narrowed her eyes at the housekeeper, who was placing stuffed olives on a tray with a hint of a smile hiding at the corners of her mouth.

"They are seeming so perfect for the *festa*," said Signorina Morini. "Here are the olives, Signora Somerton. Go now, before they are turning cold."

Lilibet heaved a sigh and picked up the tray, following the backs of Abigail and Alexandra down the hall and into the warm, noisy courtyard. Sunset was just deepening into the twilight, and the torches were being lit, one by one, about the perimeter. She scanned the mobile crowd for a familiar tawny head, and found it at one of the long tables, leaned in conversation toward a young woman who looked as if she came from the village. He wore no jacket, no waistcoat. His face bore a white-feathered mask, and a broad smile below it.

Blood rushed to her cheeks. She began to turn away, but the movement caught his eye and he rose to his feet, white shirt billowing in the evening breeze off the mountains.

She couldn't see his expression, hidden behind the half mask, but she felt the rake of his eyes as they took in her face, fell to where her breasts swelled upward just above the platter of stuffed olives, then climbed back up to her eyes. His mouth sagged into a helpless O of shock.

That should teach him to flirt with village girls.

She angled deliberately away and carried her tray to the table next to Roland's. He moved just as quickly. Just before she reached it, he interposed his formidable figure between her and the nearest occupant. "May I help you with that, signorina?" he asked.

"You may not," she said.

"You shouldn't be carrying trays. You shouldn't be carrying anything."

"It's nothing. Besides, I understand it's the worst sort of bad luck, if the Midsummer guests aren't served by the ladies of the castle."

He raised his eyebrows. "According to whom?"

"Morini, of course. Now let me pass."

He leaned forward, until his wine-scented breath warmed her ear. "Only if you promise to meet me, later tonight," he said, his voice low and intimate.

"I'll promise no such indecent thing. Now let me pass."

"Hmm. Are you certain?" His tone dropped even further. "I assure you, I'll make it worth your while."

She nudged him aside with her elbow. "Reminding me of your skill with women doesn't improve your case, your lordship."

He laughed. "Not women in general, Lilibet. Only you." But he stepped backward, allowing her past, and she set her tray of olives on the thick trestle table and tried to settle her racing heart.

When next she saw him, an exhausting half hour later, Philip was at his side, tugging at his hand. Roland bent down to hear him, and then nodded and hoisted the boy onto his broad shoulders with a natural ease that made her eyes ache, made every vein in her body pulse with love. He couldn't know, he couldn't possibly realize how deeply it moved her to see them together, even as it wracked her with guilt. She saw, now, what a dreadful father Somerton had been, always brusque and dismissive; but he was still Philip's father, being upstaged effortlessly by his wife's lover.

What had she done? Was it right?

What if she failed? What if Roland decided he couldn't wait any longer, and left them?

She'd come a long distance from that first surge of elation, following the posting of her letter to Bellwether and Knobbs. A brisk correspondence had ensued, and by early May the solicitors had enough information to send a formal notice to Somerton that his wife had initiated a suit of divorce against him, on grounds of cruelty and habitual adultery.

There had been no response.

Letters to Somerton's lawyers had been met with a terse acknowledgment of receipt of correspondence, dated the 10th instant, the 14th instant, the 19th instant. But that was all. It was like dueling with a ghost.

She'd instructed them to proceed with the legal formalities. Perhaps, after all, Lord Somerton wouldn't contest her. Perhaps the whole matter would glide through the courts without any opposition, and she'd be free in months.

Or perhaps his silence meant something more sinister.

As she watched, Philip clutched at Roland's hair, laughed, and bounced atop his lordship's shoulders with happy confidence. Roland's hands, sure and capable, wrapped around her son's legs, anchoring him safely in place. He tilted his feather-masked head upward, smiling, saying something to Philip that made the boy laugh even harder.

Please, God, she prayed, the empty tray in her arms sagging below her waist. *Keep him safe. Keep them both safe. Somerton has the heir he needed; let him be satisfied, let him be merciful, let him leave us alone to raise Philip into manhood.*

"They make a lovely pair, don't they?" Abigail's soft voice, next to Lilibet's shoulder, made her startle and turn.

"Yes . . . no . . . I . . ."

"I must say, I never expected Penhallow to take an interest in anything other than a horse or a lady," Abigail went on, folding her arms, "but I'm happy to find myself so mistaken."

Lilibet sank down onto a nearby bench, her bones and muscles sighing with relief. "It's very kind of him. Philip's just at the age where he appreciates a man's influence."

"Hmm." Abigail settled next to her. "A lovely party, isn't it? Morini's done such a splendid job, arranging things."

"I'd no idea the village held so many people. Rather nice to see the old pile so merry." Lilibet stretched out her legs and flexed her feet.

"Quite. It hardly seems cursed at all, does it?"

Lilibet straightened. "Cursed? What on earth?"

"Didn't you know? Good gracious. I thought I'd told everybody. The most delicious story, hundreds of years old, to do with a naughty Englishman who happened to be mucking about Italy and ruined the signore's daughter."

Lilibet began to laugh. "Oh, Abigail, really. Next you'll

be telling me his ghost is the one you've sensed haunting about the castle."

"No, not at all. It turns out it's rather more complicated than that." Abigail plucked idly at her fingers. "The old signore came to a suitably bloody end, but not before cursing the castle and its occupants."

"With what?" Lilibet laughed again, more hollowly. Not that she believed in curses, of course. Not that she was subject to irrational beliefs of any kind. "Drafts in the hallways? Because I rather like them, you know. They add to the atmosphere."

"That's the thing. I don't know. I can't get it out of Morini, not after hours of trying." Abigail reached across the table to pluck an overlooked sweetmeat and pop it into her mouth. "I've tried all my powers of persuasion. Because of course it can't be coincidence."

"What can't be coincidence?"

Abigail turned to meet her gaze, her eyebrows raised in amusement. "Why, that we're English, of course. Just like the naughty fellow in Queen Elizabeth's day." She lifted herself up from the bench and surveyed the eddying crowd. The philharmonic was starting up again, after a short rest, and dancers were gathering in the center of the terrace. She turned back to Lilibet's astonished gaze and winked. "And after all, if *I* were the lingering spirit of the old signore, I'd be racking my ghostly brains to plot my revenge."

SEVENTEEN

Pirates and harem girls probably weren't the most appropriate subjects for a young boy's bedtime story, Roland suspected, but they were a dashed sight more interesting than a family of rabbits taking tea in a lettuce patch.

Well, after a bit of judicious bowdlerization, of course.

"And what did the pirates do with the harem girls, once they sank the sultan's ship?" asked Philip eagerly. His fingers clutched the blanket in two enormous fistfuls.

Roland closed the ends of the book firmly together. "I daresay they all sang a few merry songs and went to sleep," he said. "And for that matter, so should you, before your mother comes up to check on you."

Philip sighed and settled back on his pillow. "I expect so. I do like that one, Uncle Roland. Much more exciting than Mama's books. Can you read my story every night?"

"Afraid not, old fellow. That's your mother's favorite job, and she'd be awfully cross with me if I took it over. I'm just filling in while she's busy with the party." He pulled the blankets up to Philip's round chin and tucked in the sides beneath the mattress. "Is that all right?"

"A bit tight," Philip squeaked.

"Oh. Sorry, old man." Roland loosened the bedclothes a trifle. "Better?"

Philip nodded, face solemn in the center of his white linen pillowcase. "Uncle Roland," he said, rather quiet, "do you have any children?"

Roland placed his elbows on his knees and knitted his fingers together, atop the book. "No. No, I don't, I'm afraid. Not yet."

"Why not?"

"Haven't . . ." Something like a choke caught the back of Roland's throat. Rather odd. He swallowed hard to dissipate the unfamiliar sensation. "Haven't been lucky enough, I suppose."

"Oh." Philip's eyes were cast down. He appeared to be studying the weave of the blanket, thick and soft in the flickering glow of the candle by the bed. "Do you want to have children?"

"Do you know," Roland said, "I never used to give the matter much thought. But now I believe I do. I'd like it a great deal."

Philip's jaw worked. "I suppose . . . if we stay here in Italy forever . . . perhaps . . . you could have the baby in Mama's tummy. If you wanted it."

Oh, Christ.

Roland blinked away the ache at the back of his eyeballs. "I daresay that would be very nice. If your mother doesn't mind, naturally."

"Would you love it very much?"

"I'd love it very much, of course."

"I think . . . I wish . . ." A round, fat tear formed at the inner corner of Philip's left eye. "I wish I were the baby."

Roland felt himself falling, as if the pirates in the story had bound his arms and legs and forced him off the plank, into the middle of the wide blue ocean. There were no rules for this. No damned list of instructions, no commandments. Thou shalt not steal the love of another man's child. Thou shalt not refuse thy love to a child who needs it.

He'd have to go on instinct alone.

He laid his hand on the top of Philip's dark head. "Look here," he said, "I'm quite glad you're *not* that baby in your mother's tummy, because I love you well enough the way you are."

Philip's eyes shot up to meet his. "Really?"

"After all, you can't take a baby fishing, can you? He can't even hold the rod. And who'd keep me on my toes with all those clever questions, eh? No, Philip." He leaned down to kiss the boy's forehead. "I love you quite as much as a child of my own, which is to say very much indeed. Now go to sleep, or your mother will have my guts for garters."

Philip turned his cheek to the pillow and yawned. "Don't worry. I'd stop her. I'd tell her it was my fault."

Roland ruffled his hair. "I daresay you would. I daresay . . ."

The door creaked open. "Signore?"

He rose from the chair. "Francesca? Everything all right? He's just going off to sleep right now."

She gave him a slight frown as she picked through his words. She'd learned a great deal of English in the past few months, looking after Philip and dealing with the ladies, but she still tended to become flustered in Roland's presence and forget it all. "I watch now. Is all right?"

"Oh yes. Quite all right. I'm just leaving."

"Signore, there is man. He wait for you. In the . . ." She motioned downward with her hand.

"The great hall?" he guessed. His blood accelerated through his body. A visitor? For him? At this hour?

Not a good sign.

"Yes. The hall, down the stair. He . . ." She stopped again, looking frustrated.

Roland pressed her. "When did he arrive? When did he come here?"

"Now. Is five minutes. He say his name is Bee . . ." A scrunch of her forehead.

"Beadle." Relief filled him—not Somerton—and then apprehension. What would bring the Bureau's Florence agent out to see him, instead of sending a message? He looked down at Philip, who was blinking drowsily at them, too tired even for curiosity. "I'll be down directly. Good night, Philip."

"Good night, Uncle Roland."

Roland closed the door behind him and raced down the stairs, the pirate book still clutched in his hand.

B eadle stood at the back of the great hall, in one of the bench-lined window recesses, watching the festivities in the courtyard. He wore a plain wool suit, the jacket of which lay slung over the seat to his right, topped by a round bowler hat.

"Beadle!" Roland advanced swiftly. "What brings you out here, old man? Come to celebrate the Midsummer with us, eh?"

Beadle spun around, feet scraping against the worn gray flagstones. "Penhallow! Thank God. I've been riding all day."

"Not an emergency, I hope? Would you like a bit of water? Wine? We haven't much stronger, I'm afraid." Roland's mind and body were already switching back into that well-remembered state of hyperawareness, calm and swift, that had seen him through countless crises in the past seven years. Whatever errand had brought Beadle out to the Castel sant'Agata so late on a June evening, he could settle the matter.

"No, no. The maid brought me a glass, a moment ago." He gestured to the window ledge, on which a half-finished tumbler of water shone gold in the reflected torchlight. "Look, Penhallow, you've got to be square with me. I've brought serious news. Rather a shock. Is Lady Somerton about?"

"She's outside." Roland narrowed his gaze. He'd made Beadle aware of the basic facts of the case, including Lilibet's suit of divorce against her husband, during his fortnightly trips into Florence to update himself on the situation at home. Indeed, the agent knew little less than he did at this point, other than the personal details: that Roland and

Lilibet were in love, that she was expecting his child, that they planned to marry once the divorce was finalized. That last piece of information he'd withheld with some indecision; it was Lilibet's private matter, of course, but it did have some bearing on the object of Sir Edward's investigation.

Loyalty to Lilibet had won out, in this instance.

"You've got to find her straightaway and hustle her out." Beadle snatched the glass from the window ledge and took a large gulp. "Lord Somerton arrived in Florence yesterday, off the train from Milan."

"Good God." A rush of panic went through his veins. He forced it down. "Where did you hear this?"

"I asked the officials in Florence to keep me apprised." Beadle set the glass back down and dabbed at his mouth with his handkerchief. "As a precaution, of course. I didn't think it would come to this."

Roland shook his head. "Bloody damn. Does Sir Edward know?"

"I've cabled him. Look, Penhallow, what the bloody hell is going on here? What's Somerton after?" Beadle folded his arms and fixed Roland with a steady gaze. A lazy-seeming chap, Beadle, quite happy to dawdle away his middle years in the relatively sleepy Florentine air, but Roland gathered he'd been a crack agent in his prime. That thinning hair, combed in long, neat strings over the top of his head, concealed a more penetrating mind than it appeared.

Roland put his fist to his forehead. "His wife and son, I think. I hope to God he doesn't know I'm here as well, or he'll have no mercy on her."

"But I was made to understand . . . Sir Edward's opinion is that he has some sort of plot against you." Beadle's voice took on a hint of silk. "Why would that be, Penhallow?"

Roland met his gaze directly. "I don't know. I'm sure you're aware I shared a brief flirtation with Lady Somerton, but that was before her marriage. Until March, until after she'd arrived in Italy, I'd had no contact with her at all. I assure you"—his tone went icy—"I took the most rigid precautions to ensure we didn't enjoy so much as a drawing-room handshake."

"Then why the devil is he attempting to bring you down?"

"I don't know." Roland went to put his hands behind his back and realized he still held the pirate book in his left fist. A fierce surge of protectiveness filled him, for Lilibet and for Philip. He paced a short distance down the hall. In the near-darkness, the arches at the end loomed like mountains. "That's the deuce of it."

A brief pause. "Penhallow," Beadle said, in a low voice, "I feel I must ask, for the sake of the investigation, whether there's anything at all of an improper nature between you and Lady Somerton."

Roland bit back an angry retort. After all, in Beadle's place, he'd want to know the same thing. His hands knotted behind his back, clutching the book. "My reply to your question, Mr. Beadle," he said, quite calmly, staring at the distant wall, "is that there's nothing at all *improper* in my relations with her ladyship. Quite the opposite."

"I see." Beadle gazed at him with full understanding, and perhaps a hint of compassion.

Roland closed his eyes. "The question is, where did he learn about Lady Somerton's whereabouts? Or mine, if he's after me? Damnation. If I knew what was in his mind . . . Has Sir Edward found anything new, since our last meeting?"

"No. The fellow's covered his tracks well. Only that hint of his involvement in Johnson's escape to Argentina last winter, and that secondhand. The Navy office claims he'd never worked with them at all. Laughed at the idea."

"That means nothing." Roland turned and strode back in Beadle's direction. "If he wanted to keep his involvement secret, the Navy boys would damned well keep their mouths shut for him. They're fiercely loyal."

Beadle shrugged. "Then I've no bloody idea." He took his watch out of his pocket and examined it in the faint light from the window. "Look, I'd best be off, if I'm to be back in Florence by dawn. As I said, I'd encourage you to take her ladyship somewhere away. Somewhere distant. Only do let us know where you've gone, eh? I can alert the local Bureau man, if I have enough warning."

"Yes. Thank you. Thanks very much for coming out, Beadle. I appreciate it." Roland reached out to shake his hand. "Anything I can do for you, only ask. If you'd like to exchange your horse for something fresher, the stable's yours."

"That's good of you." Beadle picked up his jacket and hat from the window seat and turned to leave. "Oh, there's another thing. Dashed odd. Somerton sent off a telegram, from his hotel, soon after his arrival. Wasn't able to intercept the contents, but I did discover the recipient."

"Who's that?"

Beadle replaced his hat on his head and gave it a reassuring pat. "Your grandfather, Penhallow. The Duke of Olympia."

The hand on Lilibet's shoulder roused her from reverie. She looked up into the face of Signorina Morini, alive with the shifting glow of the nearby torches.

"Signora, the signore is finish the story. My Francesca, she is watching the boy." The hand on Lilibet's shoulder squeezed gently. "You find him now, yes?"

Lilibet smiled and turned her gaze back to the mass of dancers, laughing and moving with the rhythmic chorus of the musicians, feathered masks fluttering in the air. Abigail was leading a reluctant Alexandra into the throng, her chestnut hair shining in the torchlight. "Why ever for, signorina? I'm sure he's exhausted."

"Not so tired, signora. Not so tired. He is thinking perhaps of love, eh?" Morini sat down next to her at the table and placed a tray before them. On its surface rested two small glasses, half-full with a clear liquid. "He is hoping, I think. Hoping to find you, to dance with you."

"I'm far too tired to dance, Morini," she said. "I've been

serving food all evening. My feet are aching. I only want to go to bed."

Morini gestured to the glasses before her. "I bring you a little something. Is our tradition, on the Midsummer. Is a kind of limoncello, a special mixture."

"Oh, I must refuse. Wine and spirits turn my stomach, at the moment."

"Is not spirits. Is not harming the baby." Morini took one of the glasses and held it out to her. The liquid swished along the sides, cool and alluring. "Is tradition. Is good luck. You drink this, you are finding much happiness in the year. Much love."

"I have quite enough love already, thank you," she said. But her fingers reached toward the glass anyway, as if compelled by some unseen power. She glanced back at the dancers on the courtyard flagstones, looking for Abigail and Alexandra, but they had disappeared into the crowd, into the rhythmic *oom-pah* of the enthusiastic philharmonic.

"You will like. Is not hurting the stomach, the baby." Morini nudged the bottom of the glass. "Drink a little."

Lilibet returned her eyes to the glass before her and shrugged. "Very well," she said, and took a sip. It trailed enticingly down her throat, cool and hot all at once, the lemon fragrance wafting upward to fill her head. "Oh, it's lovely!"

"You see? Is very nice. It is bringing you good luck."

Lilibet tilted the glass and finished it. Energy seemed to flood through her body, coursing down her limbs. "Marvelous. The good luck and the drink. I feel quite better already."

"Ah, is working. I am so glad, signora. Perhaps I give the other drink to Signore Penhallow?" Morini rose from the table and picked up her tray.

"Yes, I rather think you should. He'd like it very much." Her brain began to dance, a clear, shining, joyful dance. She rose next to Morini and smiled at the dancers, the dear, kind villagers and musicians and cousins. How she loved them all.

"Signora, perhaps you like walking? You walk to the lake, signora. I send Signore Penhallow to follow you, yes?"

"Oh, would you, Morini?" She kissed the housekeeper on the cheek. "That would be darling of you. It sounds just . . . delightful."

Roland strode out into the courtyard, filled with determination, his mind humming with plans and contingencies. If they left straightaway, they might be in Siena by daybreak. From there, Rome or perhaps Naples, where they could lose themselves in the bustling streets of the metropolis. Or perhaps the other direction? Venice, or even across the sea to Greece. An island, Crete or Rhodes or Corfu. Large enough to have a decent doctor for Lilibet, of course. Oh, damn. The baby. What if something went wrong? Could he trust the local hospitals?

"Signore?" A hand touched his arm.

He spun around. One of the housemaids. Not Francesca, the other one. Maria? Her hair was bound in a red scarf, and a plain feathered mask covered the top half of her face. "Yes? What is it?" he asked, a little more brusquely than he intended.

She took a half step backward. "You are looking for Signora Somerton?" she asked, in a tentative voice.

"Yes. Yes! Have you seen her?"

"Signorina Morini . . . she say . . . the signora is go to the lake. She wait for you."

"To the lake?" He shook his head and cast a quick glance into the darkness, where the terraces dropped down one by one to the lakeshore. "Why the devil?"

"She wait at the lake, Morini say to me. She say, give you drink." She held out a small tray with a glass. "Is a tradition."

"Oh, damn it all." Roland snatched the glass without thinking and tossed down the contents. A pleasant burn filled his throat and belly, scented with lemons and some sort of unfamiliar herb, some note of flavor he couldn't quite identify. "I say," he murmured, holding up the glass to the torchlight. "That's jolly nice."

Maria shrugged. "Is tradition. You go to the lake, Morini say. Is . . . ah . . . is *must* . . ."

"Important?"

She nodded her head with vigor. "Very important!"

"Well, then." He smiled and set the glass on the tray. A tide of good humor seemed to engulf his body. The urgent need to find Lilibet remained, but the worry and anxiety had fled. Everything would be quite all right. Everything would sort itself out. "I'd best be on my way, hadn't I?"

The moon shone high and bright above him, lighting the meadows and the rows of grapevines, bursting out with bunches of tiny new grapes; the great mass of the peach orchard, thick with leaves and growing fruit; the rows of corn, already reaching his knee. All of it was familiar to him, from his daily walks and rides with Philip, his solitary rambles, his swimming and fishing and reflection. He whistled as he walked, savoring the delicious sense of well-being, of anticipation that tingled his nerves.

Perhaps he might even tease a kiss out of Lilibet, before they left.

It would be lovely, this journey of theirs. Like a honeymoon. She couldn't cling to propriety any longer, not with Somerton breathing down their necks. They'd take Philip, of course, and explain things to him somehow. Once his little family was safely hidden, in some idyllic Mediterranean haven far from the tyranny of London society, he'd go out and find Somerton and end this mysterious game, by force if necessary. He'd do whatever was required to ensure that Lilibet and Philip no longer had anything to fear, anything to dread, from the Earl of Somerton.

He'd marry her, of course, the instant the divorce came through, but the ceremony would be a mere legal convenience. She was already his, in every moral sense, with an inalienable claim to all the love and loyalty and protection he could give her.

Yes, everything would sort itself out.

He reached the olive trees that rimmed this stretch of lakeshore, small leaves glinting silver green in the moonlight. Between the branches, he could just glimpse the tranquil waters of the lake, reflecting the light. A dark shape blocked the ripples: the boulders, he thought. "Lilibet!" he called.

"Here!" she sang out, from somewhere ahead. He caught a flash of movement.

"Where are you?"

"On the rocks! It's lovely, all warm. I'm going for a swim."

A swim?

He emerged from the trees and his breath stopped in his chest.

Lilibet stood atop the boulder, just as she had in April, when he'd brought Philip back to her. Only this time she was naked, or nearly so, just stepping free from her chemise. The moonlight bathed her body in silver, gilded the tips of her heavy round breasts, outlined the slight perfect swell of her belly and the curve of her hip. She stretched out one slender leg to the edge of the boulder and looked over her shoulder at him. "There you are! Isn't it glorious?"

"Glorious," he whispered, frozen to the pebbles beneath him.

She smiled and turned back to the lake and leapt off the boulder.

The water rushed cool and silken against her skin. She touched her feet to the bottom and surged up again, until her face broke the surface. She treaded water for a moment or two, enjoying the sensation, and turned back to the boulder.

Roland was scrambling up to the top. "Come in!" she called. "It's delightful! Much warmer than last month."

"You've been swimming?"

"Of course. Every day, while you're giving Philip his lessons." She kicked her legs, feeling her own strength, and floated onto her back. The stars glittered above her, millions of them, distant and friendly. Though the air was warm, she could feel her nipples pucker as they rose above the level of the water.

"Good God," came a mutter from the shore. She turned

her head. Roland was shucking off his jacket, his waistcoat, his shirt; his muscled chest gleamed in the light from the moon. So beautiful, so perfectly proportioned, every detail sculpted by some loving creator. His hands moved to his trousers; she watched dreamily as he peeled them off, as he let his drawers drop to the ground and kicked them off. His feet were already bare. She had a lightning glimpse of his legs, of the jut of his aroused masculine flesh, before he dove off the boulder in a clean arc, scarcely disturbing the water at all.

She closed her eyes and smiled, waiting for him to appear next to her. Seconds passed by, ticking off some invisible clock.

She opened her eyes just before a warm hand emerged from the water to cover her breast. *Oh!* she exclaimed, and then *ah!* as the hand drew her backward into the solid wall of his chest.

"Water sprite," he murmured next to her ear. "I'd no idea you could swim."

She turned and put her arms about his neck, tangling her legs with his as they treaded the water. The tips of her breasts just touched his skin. "There's a great deal you don't know about me, Roland Penhallow."

"I'd like to find out." He kissed her, his mouth warm and soft and lemony as it mingled with hers. His hands stole around her waist under the water, melting her skin, melting her entire body.

She whispered into his lips. "Roland. I think . . . I think . . ."

"What do you think?" He kissed along her jaw, her ear.

"I think . . . I don't want to wait any longer. It might be ages, it might be never, and I want . . . I want you so much . . ."

"We can't," he said, his lips hot and alive against the hollow beneath her ear. "Not now. Not tonight. I've come to fetch you. We've got to leave here, straightaway."

"What?" The information didn't disturb her, for some reason. "Why's that?"

"Your bloody husband," he said, kicking his legs, draw-

ing her with him inexorably toward the shore, "is in bloody
Florence at the moment."

"Oh." She leaned into him, letting him carry them along.
He was so warm, so strong beneath her. She kissed his
throat. "That's an awful nuisance. Can't we simply stay and
fend him off, if he comes here?"

"Darling love, I'd like nothing more, if it were just me.
But I can't take a chance that he'll harm you, in your condition. Or Philip, God forbid." He feathered kisses along her
cheek, her temple. Her body lay atop him as they stroked
through the water, her breasts pressing against his chest,
her hips tucked into his. Even in the cool embrace of the
water, he wanted her. She could feel his arousal, hard and
urgent between her legs.

"You're terribly gallant."

"Rather a coward, really," he said softly. "I ought to stay
here and fend him off. Finish him, once and for all. But he's
Philip's father, and things would get off rather on the wrong
foot if I killed the old earl outright. Not that he doesn't
deserve it."

The air seemed to still in her ears. "What things?" she
whispered.

"Being Philip's stepfather. Raising him with you, if God
grants me such a privilege."

His words stole across her heart. She pulled at his neck,
drawing them upright. Her toes just dragged the bottom of
the lakeshore. "Make love to me, Roland. We don't need to
leave right away. What's an hour or two?"

"Shh." He pushed her wet hair away from her face. She
could just see his eyes in the moonlight, gazing at her with
tender joy. "I'd like nothing more, darling. As you can
plainly see. Have thought of little else, these past months.
But you were quite right about waiting. At least until you're
safe, at least until I've got you somewhere he can't find us."

"No." The lemony charge of Morini's drink surged
through her body, giving her confidence and purpose, the
pure certainty that this man had been designed for her
alone, and she for him. She put her hands to his wide cheek-

bones and held him between her palms. "Make me yours, Roland. Before anything else. Before we go back to the castle, before we step out of this lake."

He laughed softly. "Well, strictly speaking, my dearest love, we've done that already." His hand slipped around her waist to rest on the curve of her belly.

"You know what I mean, Roland. That was . . . that was passion, lust. That was for the old days. For what we used to share, young and fragile. This"—she kissed him, parted his lips, and kissed him more deeply—"this is for the future. Our future. For what we share now, a thousand times stronger and deeper."

"Ah, Lilibet," he murmured. His hands moved upward to cover her breasts, to brush his thumbs against her hardened nipples.

"Please, Roland. Now. What's an hour or two?"

"Everything, possibly." But he kissed her again, stroked his tongue against hers. He rolled her nipples lightly between his thumb and forefingers. Sensation snaked through her body, sharp and electric.

"That's nonsense. He's in Florence. Ages away, even if he knew where to find us." She raised her buoyant legs and wrapped them around his hips.

"I suppose," he said, between kisses, "we could leave at dawn. But no later, Lilibet."

"Yes," she said. "Yes. Oh, now, Roland. Please."

He chuckled against her skin. "Eager Lilibet. Darling girl. No, not now."

"What's that?"

"Mmm. You see, I promised myself, that if I were so fortunate as to have you in my bed again, so to speak . . ."

"Beds are for dull married couples."

"Quite right. Stables and lakes much more to the purpose." His fingers went on massaging her nipples with exquisite slowness, just the right pressure, and her head fell back in delirium. "But as I said, I promised myself I'd do the thing properly. No mindless coupling, no swift conclusion. I'd give you the bedding—again, so to speak—you deserved."

"And what is that?" She could hardly speak; she could hardly think. Her torso floated in the water, anchored by her legs about his waist and his fingers on her breasts; the stars winked happily at her from the silvery black sky. She felt as if she were in another world.

Heat flooded her right breast as his mouth replaced his fingers. "Pleasure, darling," he said, into her skin. "All the pleasure I can possibly lavish on this lovely body of yours. I mean to show you just how a man makes love to the woman he adores. I mean to leave you in no doubt at all to whom you belong."

"I don't have any doubt about that. Not any longer."

His mouth tightened about her nipple, suckling fiercely. She gasped at the sensation it evoked, the way his heat seemed to spread through her body. His hands moved to her back, resting on her shoulder blades, holding her up for the tug of his lips. "Ah, God, they're so beautiful," he said, his words slurring together at the ends. He kissed his way to her other breast. "So sweet, so soft and endless. In my dreams, I'm doing this. Feasting on you for hours."

Her hands traveled up his face to his hair, tangling in the wet strands, and then swept down again to explore the line of his broad shoulders, the ridge of his clavicle, the hard, flat planes of his chest. She couldn't quite believe she was doing this, that Roland's body lay before her, that she could touch him at will, feel his skin beneath her fingers; could see the light scattering of downy hair glinting in the moonlight. His bones felt sturdy and solid beneath her legs; the thick hardness of his member settled snugly into the crease of her buttocks, unbearably tantalizing. She wanted him inside her, part of her; she wanted it with an immediacy that made her shudder.

She pulled herself upward and found his lips with hers. "Roland, I'm ready," she whispered. "You're ready. Please. I can't bear it."

He shook his head, his smile growing beneath her lips. "Yes, you can, darling. You're going to have to bear a great deal more. I haven't shown you nearly enough." His hands slid down her waist and cupped her hips, his spread fingers encompassing the tops of her thighs. He drew her apart from him, loosening her legs from their death grip around his waist. Not once did his mouth move away from hers. He kissed her gently, relentlessly, his silken tongue ranging about in loving strokes.

Sensation rushed at her everywhere: from his kiss, from the rub of his chest against her sensitized breasts, from the firm roundness of his buttocks against her hooked heels; from his fingers, spiraling along the inside of her leg, closer and closer to the juncture between her thighs. One hand slid to the small of her back, supporting her, while the other roamed deeper, sending currents of water eddying about her loins. She held her breath: waiting, wanting.

His thumb brushed against her curls at last, and a gust of air released from her lungs.

His chuckle warmed the skin of her throat. "You liked that, did you?"

"Yes," she said. "Oh yes."

His thumb brushed her again, delicate and deliberate, until she thought she might perhaps go mad; she strained against him, desperate for more. He began to probe with exquisite care, working his way between the folds of her flesh, parting her, sliding so slowly along the slickness of her lips within that she threw back her head and cried out. "Hush," he said, pressing kisses into her neck. "Be patient, darling. Let it come to you."

How could she be patient, when his thumb was so maddeningly slow? How could she hush and wait, when his thumb at last reached the bundle of nerves at her core and began to circle it, as if they had all the time in the world, as if she weren't bursting from her skin? How could she not simply explode, as he increased the pressure and the rhythm and then backed away, over and over, knowing exactly when she approached each brink, reading every nuance of her body with fine precision.

"Please," she sobbed, rubbing her cheek against his rough wet hair. "Please, Roland."

He drew his thumb away, and it was like the sun slipping

behind the mountains. She gave a bereft little cry and opened her eyes. He gazed down at her, smiling, lifting his thumb to his mouth and tasting her.

"Roland," she said, "I'm going to die, right now, right now . . ."

"Trust me."

His hand moved to her buttocks, cupping them, and then slid along her thighs to her knees. "Swim for me," he said, lifting her legs up to his shoulders, one by one, easing her torso against the tender lap of the water. She shivered at the loss of contact, at the anticipation of the next. Her arms swayed in the water, keeping her afloat. He would take her now; he would thrust inside her at last; he would . . .

Her body jumped out of the water with an inarticulate *Oh God!* as his mouth descended between her legs, so hot and lush she felt her insides melt and rush toward his waiting lips. He held one knee firmly with his hand; the other hand he placed in the center of her back, supporting her, as his tongue swept her hidden flesh with velvet strokes. Cool water lapped against them, mingling with his heated mouth, making her gasp and cry out and shudder, outside her own body with the pleasure engulfing her. His tongue began to work at her exposed bud, flicked back and forth in a relentless rhythm, and she could not stop saying his name, could not stop the waves of release. They crested and broke and ran down her body, until the only thing keeping her afloat was Roland's hands, Roland's arms, Roland's unyielding shoulders beneath her legs.

He thought he might die from the sight of her.

She came and came, contracting in ripples against his tongue, her heady musk rich in his nose and her voice crying his name into the evening air. Before him, the gentle slope of her ripening belly merged with the fullness of her breasts, and her long wet hair tangled with his hand underneath her back. She lay helpless with release atop the water, trusting everything to him.

He remained still, knees bent, feet planted solidly on the lake bottom, letting her body drift down from the peak in its own time. With his hands he supported her, kept her head above the surface, kept her sweet quim just at the waterline, where the lapping waves would meet the dying aftershocks of her climax. He ignored his body's urgent shout to take the magnificent woman laid out before him; this was their wedding night, their true joining, and he wanted everything perfect for her.

At last her arms began to move, waving in the water. She reached for him, and he helped her upright, covering her cooling flesh with his own before she had a chance to shiver. She buried her head at the base of his neck. "I won't ask where you learned how to do that."

He kissed her hair, smoothing away the dripping tangles. "In my dreams, sweetheart. You've sentenced me to more lonely hours in my bed than I care to remember. I think I've plotted out every last possible detail, by now."

A soft gurgle of laughter. "Oh, well said."

He put his hands to her cheeks and lifted her head. "You don't believe me?"

"It doesn't matter anymore, does it? You're mine now. I believe *that*." She moved her hips against his, and this time he couldn't resist her. Even in the cool embrace of the water, his cock was hard and huge with need; the nudge of her body against his engorged flesh knocked away the last tenacious remnants of his self-control.

He kissed her, long and deep. His hands slid down her neck and sides to her bottom; he lifted her buoyant body and positioned it above the eager tip of his staff. With a soft groan he pulled his mouth from hers and met her gaze. Her lips were open, her eyes half-closed; she was breathing in shallow little gasps, grinding downward against him.

"Are you certain?" he managed. "Because I can't . . . Lilibet, this is final. We can't go back . . ."

Her hands gripped his waist and pulled him to her. "Yes. Yes! For God's *sake*, don't stop!"

Slowly he eased himself inside her. The slick channel

clasped him like a fist, hot and snug where the water had been cool and light. His arms shook; his fingers dug into her skin. "Lilibet," he groaned, and with a final thrust he was buried fully within her body, joined with her in the most intimate way, the pulse in his neck throbbing like a dynamo against hers.

She wrapped her legs around him, securing herself on his cock; her hands traveled up his chest to his face, slipping into his hair, and kneaded his scalp. She laughed aloud. "Oh, God, Roland. It's really you. It's really *us*." She stretched her neck backward, dipping her hair in the water behind her, offering her breasts up to him. He bent his head to suckle one dark peak and then the other, rotating her hips in a corkscrew motion, until she gasped and shivered, straining against him, urging him deeper.

He lifted his head and began to thrust in a heavy rhythm, unable to contain himself any longer. She responded at once, coordinating her movements with his, meeting the plunge of his cock with the push of her hips between his hands. The water rushed and eddied about them, creating resistance and friction even as it lightened her body, making him reach and grasp to bring her back for each plunge. It had been too long; he was too desperate. Release began to push past the iron bands of his self-control, and he freed one hand from her hip to circle the little bud just above their joined flesh with the broad pad of his thumb.

Her body jumped against his. She gave a throaty cry and ground down against him, fighting against the water to quicken the rhythm. Her heels dug into his back, anchoring her as she met his thrusts with such vigor, such passion, he thought he might burst with joy. He squeezed his eyes, concentrating, finding the exact movement of his thumb and his cock to please her, and in that instant she reached her climax. She shuddered and collapsed against him, and in two quick thrusts his balls contracted, his release burst forth, and his shout echoed off the rocks and rippled across the lake.

EIGHTEEN

They drifted against each other for some time, still joined, too replete to move. "Am I too heavy?" she whispered at last against his neck, and he shook his head.

"No, you're perfect." She felt his kiss against her hair, her temple. "Perfect, darling." His voice was soft, hoarse.

She raised her head and laughed. "No, I'm not. Your legs are shaking."

"Merely passion, darling. I'm as strong as an ox, I assure you." He sounded just a bit defensive.

"Yes, with a lifeless heifer clinging to his hips." Gently she eased herself away from him and felt him slide out of her in a slick rush. She was boneless, weightless in the water, her legs floating inexorably to the surface until she forced them downward to grip the pebbled lake bottom with her toes. She reached up and kissed his smiling mouth. "Mine," she said.

"Yours." He nibbled at her lips. "Let's get you out of the water, shall we? Before your skin turns a most unsightly prunelike texture."

"Bite your tongue. I'm a legendary beauty. My skin never wrinkles."

They scrambled and staggered to shore, bodies still wobbly from the intensity of union. He dried her with his shirt, dressed her, did her buttons; she helped him with his trousers and jacket. "Your shirt's quite soaked," she said, holding it up before him.

"No one will notice. Come along." He took her by the hand and led her into the olive trees.

"Where are we going?"

"My room."

They stole up the terraces, hand in hand, pausing only when a dark figure crossed their path at the bottom of the peach orchard. "Wallingford or Burke, probably," whispered Roland, "looking for your cousins."

"Really? He didn't seem tall enough. One of the villagers, I expect, taking the short way home."

The courtyard was still full, the band still playing. They crept around the edge of the torchlight and slipped through the door and up the stairs. She paused by the door to her room.

"Don't worry." He tugged at her hand. "Francesca's there. He's quite all right."

"She'll worry, if I don't return."

"I expect she'll figure things out. Come along."

She followed the pull of his hand down the hall, her feet slapping softly against the stone floor, until they reached the west wing and Roland's door.

Inside, he lit a single candle, and without a word, without even a kiss, unwrapped her clothes from her body and carried her to the bed. "Rest," he said, drawing up the blankets around her. "We leave at dawn."

She burrowed herself into the mattress, inhaling the clean scents of linen and Roland, the trace of his soap still on the pillow. He undressed before her, without the slightest hint of self-consciousness, slinging his jacket and trousers over the chair, and then dropped into the bed next to her and gathered her close.

By necessity, in fact: The bed was quite narrow.

She lay there a moment, eyes closed, not quite believing

she was in Roland's room, Roland's bed, his hard body molded around her and his arm across her waist. His thumb fiddled with her nipple and she laughed.

"What is it?"

She turned in his arms and drank in the sight of his face, inches from her own. "You really expect me to drop right off to sleep? Just like that?"

"Why not?" He smiled intimately and rested his hand along her hip. "You should be exhausted, by God."

"So should you." She couldn't resist touching him, couldn't resist the luxury of lifting her hand to caress the side of his face. She ran her fingers along the slope of his cheekbone, the firm line of his jaw, the tiny lines etched his forehead. "But you're not, are you? You're worried."

He turned his face to kiss her palm. "No more than any groom on his wedding night."

"Don't hide from me, Roland. Don't pretend. You may have the rest of the world fooled into thinking you haven't a care in the world, but I know better." She kissed him tenderly. "I know you, darling. There are a thousand things you're not telling me, and I want to know them all."

The corner of his mouth bent ruefully. "Of course you do." But he said nothing else, nothing to enlighten her. He only stroked his hand along the side of her hip, the curve of her bottom, while his eyes searched her face.

"Roland, what is it? Are you worried about Somerton?"

"Yes. I rather resent the fact that the key to my happiness lies in his beastly paw. But I've been thinking also . . ." His voice drifted.

"Yes?"

"Well, we've got to run off, probably to some godforsaken hole, no doctors to speak of, and I can't help feeling . . ." He paused again, frowning.

"Tell me."

His hand settled against her bottom, urging her closer. "Listen to me, darling. When I'd heard you were expecting, all those years ago, so soon after your wedding, I . . . well, I went rather mad. Bad enough you'd married, but that!"

His eyes closed tightly for an instant. "I was rather off my head for a bit. But when the time came, when you were confined . . ."

"How did you know about that?" Her throat was dry.

"I bribed a housemaid," he said, matter-of-factly. "I had to know you were safe. I was most awfully worried. I kept thinking, what if something goes wrong? Women die all the time, having babies. That was when I stopped being angry at you, I believe. All that mattered anymore was that you were safe, that you were alive." His voice took on a strained note, hushed and husky in the flickering air between them. "That night I prayed. On my knees I prayed. I asked God to spare you, that I'd accept everything, anything, as long as you still existed, somewhere on this earth."

"Oh, Roland." She buried her head in his chest. "Oh, Roland. I was fine. Never any danger. I mean, it hurt most terribly, of course. They wanted to give me chloroform, but I refused. And . . . well . . . it was a great deal of effort. It wasn't easy." She lifted her head. "But I was fine. He came out beautifully. The doctor said I was built for it. Like a peasant woman."

His hand went to her hair, stroking. "Darling, if something goes wrong, I'll never forgive myself. For being so careless as to get you with child to begin with, and then in such circumstances. Not having married you. Not having given you my name, to protect you and the baby."

She worked herself upward, supporting herself with one elbow. "Roland, listen to me. I want this child. Do you hear me? I'm not the slightest bit ashamed. Not anymore. As long as you're with me, as long as Philip is with me, the rest of it doesn't matter. Whatever happens, whatever the future holds, I'll always have this part of you, created from you. And I am grateful to God for that."

He turned her on her back and rose above her. His eyes were fierce, glowing. "Don't speak as if we won't be together. Don't even think it, by God. When this child is born, Lilibet, we'll be man and wife. I swear it on my life."

She cupped the back of his head with her hands. "Don't

say that. It doesn't matter, Roland. I'm long past the point of caring what anybody else thinks. I've been married, and it was meaningless. A sham, a travesty." She drew his face down to hers and kissed him. "This is what's real, Roland. *This* is what's sacred. This bond, this union between us."

"But legally, he's still your husband. Legally he still has dominion over you, and I won't allow it. By God, not a moment longer than I can. As soon as I've hidden you and Philip safely away, I'm going to find him and end this."

"No. No, you're not!" She pushed herself out from underneath him, levering herself upright in the narrow bed. "What are you talking about? He's a dangerous man, Roland. You don't understand."

He rose up with her, the blanket falling away from his body to expose the broad reach of his chest, burnished gold in the candlelight and curving with hard, bladelike muscles. "I assure you," he said, his voice low and growling, "I'm capable of holding my own against Somerton."

With one fist she pounded the sheet next to her. "No, you're not. Listen to me, Roland. He's a professional. He's a . . . I can't explain it . . . He does things for the government, secret things, brutal things . . ."

He captured her wrist with his hand and brought it to his lips. "It doesn't matter. I'll win. I've cunning of my own, strength of my own. More than you realize. And more than that: I've *you* to fight for. You and our family."

"Don't do it, Roland. Please," she said, in a whisper. A cold pool of fear spilled through her body, spreading to her fingers, her toes. "I've seen what he can do. It's worse than you can imagine, a different *world* from ours. Listen to me. I followed him one night, thinking he was off to some strumpet's bed, and instead . . . It was unspeakable, Roland, what he did. I saw him kill a man."

"What did you see?" He caught her other hand and spoke with urgency. "Tell me, Lilibet. When was this? What did you see?"

She shook her head back and forth. "A year or so ago. I can't say more; it doesn't matter. I don't want to remember it. But it was horrible, Roland. If he did that to you, I'd die. I couldn't live, knowing it was because of me." She twisted her fingers around, until she was gripping his hands. "Don't go after him, Roland. We'll find some quiet place, some secret place. He'll never find us. When he's dead, when Philip inherits, we can return to England . . ."

"And meanwhile live our lives in fear of discovery? Looking over our shoulders for him? No, Lilibet. I won't give him that power. And I'll be damned if I allow you and our child to be exposed to the narrow-minded cluck-clucking of beastly provincial burghers and their wives . . ."

She freed her hands, laid one finger on his lips, and curled her hand around the back of his neck. "Roland, no. I don't want to hear it, at the moment. I don't want to think about it. I want you to make love to me again, and I want to fall asleep in your arms, and in the morning we'll ride off with Philip, and everything will be fine."

"Lilibet . . ."

"Shh." She leaned her head into the hollow of his throat and kissed him there, savoring the salty-sweet taste, the hint of soap, the unexpected softness of his skin: tender and masculine all at once. Desire flooded her, pure and carnal. She rose on her knees, kissed his lips, and rubbed the aching tips of her breasts against him. "Please, Roland. We can decide all that tomorrow. Let's not spoil another moment of this night. *Our* night."

His hands crept up her back. "Oh, darling . . ."

"Again." She kissed him, all over his face, tracing each beloved feature and the fine, rough texture of his midnight beard. She could not stop kissing him, could not stop reassuring herself that he was real, that he was hers. "I want to feel you inside me again. Connected with you, part of you. Please, Roland."

"You *are* a part of me, darling. You always have been." He was still stiff, still trying to resist her. Still wanting to resolve things.

"Shh. You know what I mean." She kissed her way to his ear and drew her hands down to the curve of his buttocks, guiding him toward her. "You know what it's like when we're together. Don't you feel it?"

He groaned. "God, yes."

"Consummation. Communion. As if our souls were somehow speaking to each other. And don't say it's rubbish. You know it's true." She took his hand and placed it around her breast, his fingers dark and strong next to her pale skin. "Please. Work your magic on me again, Roland. All those lovely feelings. I want them again. I want *you* again."

A low growl came from his throat, a noise of surrender. He eased her backward, into the mattress. "Here? But it's just a dull old bed. For married couples, you said."

"Oh, well. We'll make do. Since there's no lake nearby." She closed her eyes and concentrated on the feel of him, trailing his lips down her throat to her bosom.

"The stables aren't far."

"Too late." She wove her hands through his hair. "I want you *now.*"

He made love to her with painstaking care, until she was nothing but sensation, made of light and air and Roland's body pulsing with release above hers. *Memorize this,* she thought. *Remember it.* Whatever the future held, whatever might come tomorrow, in this eternal instant they existed as a united whole, before God. This act had occurred, a solid physical fact, and no one could change it. No one could erase it.

Not even Somerton.

He remained inside her for long minutes afterward, remained joined with her, the silence wrapping about them like a benediction.

When at last he leaned over her to blow out the candle, she noticed the glint of light on the fine hair of his forearm in the instant before the darkness swallowed him up. She remembered, later, thinking how strong his arm looked, how invulnerable, how fully capable of protecting her.

NINETEEN

Roland awoke abruptly: one instant buried inside a cocoon of sleep, and the next bolt-upright in his bed, every nerve alive, his heart striking a staccato beat against his breastbone.

Outside the window, a gray yellow dawn crept over the crest of the mountains. Five o'clock, at the latest. He swept the room with his eyes, catching every detail, finding nothing awry.

His gaze dropped to the empty hollow in the mattress beside him.

She was gone.

Gone back to her room, of course. Gone back to Philip, before the boy woke and missed her. Packing her clothes, no doubt. Readying herself for the journey.

He sprang from the bed. A vague nervous dread rattled in his head, sending shots of energy into his blood, into his muscles and limbs. He should have packed up the night before, while she was sleeping. He'd meant to, but his body had been so heavy with languor, so muzzy with bliss at the feel of her body in his arms, he'd sunk under the weight of it.

Now dawn had arrived; time ticked away. He'd dress and

pack, then go to Lilibet's room to gather her and Philip. Leave some note in the kitchens, perhaps, so the others wouldn't worry.

He reached for his trousers and drew them upward in swift tugs. His limbs protested the movement. Hardly surprising, after such a night. Passionate Lilibet, all her restraints fallen away, all her beauty bare and breathtaking in his arms. The way she'd arched her back and cried out her climax; the way she'd curled her body into his, afterward, entangling their fingers, while her breathing drifted off into regularity.

He shut his mind to the memories, to everything but the list of actions before him. Love and passion and pleasure belonged to the moonlight. Cold, sharp reason: That was all he needed this morning.

His hand closed around his shirt and lifted it from the back of the chair. A button was missing from the collar, after its hasty removal on the lakeshore last night. He stared at the dangling thread, at the wilting linen, attempting to trace in his mind the source of the anxiety sunk into his bones.

With an oath he strode to the door and whipped it open.

His long legs shifted into a jog: down the corridors, around the corners, past the rough stone walls, the floor cold and hard beneath his bare feet. Just a quick look. Just to reassure himself that she was in her room, readying herself and Philip for departure. Just to still the unnatural fear hammering through his body.

He turned the last corner and found her door. The thick wood sat in place, silent and immutable. He raised his fist to knock, and then reached for the doorknob. If Philip were still asleep, he didn't want to wake him. The boy would need all his strength for the journey ahead.

The door swung open easily. In the split second before Roland peered around the edge, he heard a soft noise quaver through the air, directly into his thrumming heart. A choked keening sound, almost like . . .

A sob.

"Lilibet?" he whispered.

But Lilibet wasn't there, and neither was Philip. Francesca sat on the narrow bed, her headscarf a startling white against her black hair, with her face pressed into her hands. She looked up as he lurched through the doorway.

"Signore . . ." Her voice quavered. "Oh, signore!"

"Francesca, what . . ."

She shot up from the bed and flung herself in his arms. "*Perdonami*, signore! Oh, signore!"

"What is it? My God! Where are they?" Roland grasped her shoulders, set her away, and stared desperately into her weeping face. "Tell me, by God! Where are they?"

"The man, he come last night, middle of night. He take the boy! Oh, signore! I can do nothing! He is big man, angry. I run to find the signora. I know she is . . . she is . . ."

"With me."

"Yes! I come in, I wake her, I tell her."

"Good God!" He raked his hand through his hair, half-mad. "Good God! And you didn't wake me? Good God!"

"The signora say no. The signora, she follow me, she get her . . . her dresses, her things."

"Good God!"

"She tells me, stay here. Wait for Signore Penhallow. Tell him . . ." Another choking sob. "Tell him not to follow. To wait here. She return."

"Good God! Good God! You should have told me! You should have found me!" He just stopped his hands from grabbing her shoulders again and shaking her.

The tears broke loose from her eyes. "But the signora! She say to wait! I go to you two times, three times, and stop. I . . . I . . . Morini . . . she is not here. She . . ." Francesca shook her head and fell to her knees. "Forgive, signore!"

"How long ago? How long ago did she leave?" He strode about the room, eyes stripping the walls, the chests, the wardrobe. Dresses still hung from the rail; a brush still sat on the chest of drawers. She hadn't taken much.

"One hour ago, I think."

He turned. "Did she walk? Did she ride?"

"I think she go to the stable. I hear voice. The horses."

The stables. "Giacomo. I'll find Giacomo. He'll know, blast him!"

Roland raced from the room, toward the stairs, straight into the tall, jacketless figure of Phineas Burke as it emerged from Lady Morley's bedroom.

"Good God! Penhallow! What is it?" Burke demanded, in a fierce whisper.

Roland clutched his shoulders. "Have you seen her?"

"Seen whom?"

"Lilibet! Lady Somerton!"

"No, I haven't. Not since last night. What's the matter?"

Roland flung him away and ran down the stairs, into the silent chasm of the entrance hall, through the still, lichen-crusted courtyard. The sharp stones in the driveway cut into his bare feet, but he didn't pause, didn't slacken his pace, not until he ducked through the stable door and called Giacomo's name in his most thunderous voice.

"All the night, all the night, it is noise and talking and fires!" The groundskeeper emerged from some dusty corner, brushing at his trousers. "Now *you*, signore! No peace for Giacomo! The dawn, it is hardly here!"

"Look here, Giacomo! It's an emergency! You must tell me . . ."

Giacomo shook his head. "I am not understanding. What is this emer . . . this thing?"

"Oh, for God's sake! Never mind that! Lady Somerton, was she here? About an hour ago? Did she take a horse?"

Giacomo removed his hat and scratched his hair. "Lady Somerton. She is which one?"

"The beautiful one, the . . . the . . ."

"The women, they are *all* beautiful." Giacomo scowled, as if the general attractiveness of the visiting Englishwomen were something to be deplored rather than celebrated.

"Good Lord! The *most* beautiful one! The one . . . oh, blue eyes, dark hair. The one with the child."

"The child, he is not with her. The father is taking him, before."

"Blast it all! I know that! But the *mother*! Did she take a bloody *horse*?"

Giacomo looked puzzled. "No. The horse, he is not bloody. Why the signora take a horse that . . ."

"I don't mean *blood*! I mean, did she take a horse at all?"

The Italian rolled his eyes. "Yes, of course she take a horse. You are thinking she walk? She take the horse of the duke, the best horse. She put on the saddle, she ride him away at a . . . at . . ." He moved his fingers on his opposite palm, mimicking a horse.

"At a gallop! Oh God!" Roland pressed his fists into his head. That damned horse of Wallingford's, fast and spirited. Images filled his brain, lurid images of Lilibet falling off, of the horse throwing a shoe or stumbling on a rock, Lilibet launching over its head. "And Philip? The boy? The man who took him, what did he say? Was he riding or driving?"

Giacomo shrugged. "He is saying nothing. He drive in a carriage, a fast carriage. I hear the noises, I go outside, I see them in the moonlight."

"Was he hurting the boy? Tell me, Giacomo! Was Philip all right?"

Another shrug. "I cannot see. There is no screaming, no . . . no fighting."

A deep gust of relief shook Roland's chest, the first in some time. At least Philip had gone willingly and hadn't tried to struggle. At least Somerton hadn't hurt him or taken him by force.

The panic in his brain was settling now. He had the facts: Somerton in a fast carriage with Philip, Lilibet following on horseback. Headed where? Florence, he guessed. That was where Somerton was staying. Easy connections to Milan, eventually to London. Somerton was only an hour or two ahead of him. He could catch them.

He braced his hands on his hips. "Look, Giacomo. Listen carefully. I've got to go inside, to pack a few things, and then go after them. I'll need a horse saddled, the fastest we've got, and . . ."

"Oh no. No, no, signore." Giacomo's head swung back

and forth in emphatic fashion. "I am not saddling the horses. I am grounds keeper." He separated the words, as if to emphasize their meaning.

"Then tell the stable hands! I don't bloody care!"

"Signore, it is a very long night. There is the fire in the carriage house, there is . . ."

"Fire? What the devil?"

Giacomo waved his hand in the direction of the valley. "The place, the work place of the Signore Burke. Is a fire."

Roland started. "A fire? When? But I saw him a moment ago . . ."

"Is out now. But then there is the father, making all the noise. And then the signora, with the horse." Giacomo placed his hand atop his heart. "Is a very long night."

Roland drew in a steadying breath. "Yes. I daresay it's been a long night. Rather a long night for me as well. But regardless, old man, you'd better listen up. Because when I emerge from that castle in approximately twelve minutes, I want a horse saddled and waiting for me, right where you're standing now. I don't care how tired you are. I don't particularly care who does it. But I want it *done*." Roland leaned closer and lowered his voice to a menacing purr, suitable for threats of all kinds. "Is that clear, Giacomo, my friend?"

The groundskeeper's eyes narrowed into petulant slits. "Is clear."

Roland wheeled about and plunged through the doorway, into the brightening stableyard.

"Signore Penhallow?"

He turned back. "Yes, Giacomo?"

The groundskeeper nodded to Roland's naked chest. "Is better if you are wearing the shirt."

She'd forgotten her gloves, and the reins cut into her palms as she drove Wallingford's horse along the hard-packed road toward Florence.

She didn't notice.

The sun rose fully above the mountains at her back,

casting long shadows across the ground before her, warming the clothes against her skin, but her only response was to urge the horse faster as the road became visible.

The duke's saddle chafed at the tender skin between her legs, and she could only think, *Damn Somerton, damn him to hell*, because while she'd known this would happen, had known he would eventually track them down, she'd never imagined he'd choose to strike in the hours after she'd engaged in repeated acts of carnal union with her vigorous and well-endowed lover.

Bastard.

She could only pray that she wasn't harming the baby, that the tiny precious life would remain tucked inside her, safe and well cushioned from the jolting ride.

She could only hope that Somerton was taking Philip to Florence and not in the opposite direction. She could only repeat to herself, over and over, that Somerton was a brute but not a devil: that he loved Philip, in his way, and wouldn't hurt him. Philip was his heir, after all. His future.

Just let him be all right. Just let Somerton be rational, be humane. Let him be just, and not blame Philip for his mother's sins.

The track wound on through the hills, unrecognizable from her journey in March, now warm and verdant where they'd been dank and gray and sterile. She crossed a bridge and realized it was the same one bordering the inn where they'd stayed that fateful night. She caught a glimpse, as she trotted smartly past, of the long, red-roofed stable in which she and Roland had come together for no more than ten frenzied, tender, secret minutes, during which the baby now inside her had been conceived. Months ago, a lifetime ago. Then, she'd been rigid and proud and fearful; now she was brimming with love, with strength, with plans for the future.

In March, the ascent from Florence to the inn had taken all day in the rain and mud; descending now in fine summer weather, Lilibet cantered through the sun-soaked outskirts within a few hours, crossing the Ponte Vecchio as the clock tower in the Piazza della Signoria tolled noon.

The midday sun blazed against her shoulders; the horse beneath her nodded his head in weary resignation, waiting for her next command.

What that command might be, she had no idea.

She'd reached Florence. What the devil did she do now?

Roland had taken the road to Florence several times since arriving at the Castel sant'Agata. Every fortnight, he'd ridden into the city to meet with Beadle, discuss Bureau affairs, and update himself on any developments in the search for evidence of Somerton's activities. There hadn't been much to discuss on that count, so they'd soon moved on to wine and *bistecca* and gossip at some discreet trattoria near the Arno, and watched the sun climb down behind the round red globe of the Duomo.

He knew the road well, and he knew where to cut off from the main track to wind his way into the city using the back alleys. He pushed his horse to a drumbeat pace, crossed the Arno not long after Lilibet, and made his way straight to Beadle's rooms near the Santa Croce.

"Penhallow! What the devil!" Beadle's face split open in a punishing yawn through the crack in the door.

"Let me in, you fool!" Roland pushed the door wide enough to allow himself through. "We're found out. Somerton came to the castle last night and took the boy."

"The devil you say!" Sleep vanished from Beadle's face. He tore off his nightcap and tossed it on a nearby table. "And his wife?"

"She was with me." Roland said it without hesitation, without apology. Nothing about his liaison with Lilibet was dishonorable, and he'd kill the man who dared to suggest otherwise. "The maid woke her, and she slipped off after them. I saddled a horse as soon as I discovered them missing."

Beadle dropped down to his desk and unlocked the

drawer. He drew out a stack of papers and began riffling through them. "How far ahead were they?"

"As best I can judge, Somerton arrived about three-thirty in the morning, and Lady Somerton left shortly thereafter. She couldn't have left earlier than four, as the moon was gone." He paced to the window and drew aside the curtain. Outside, the ordinary life of Florence went on: street vendors, beggars, students, flocks of tourists with Baedekers clutched in their hands. A monk strode through the courtyard, toward the church, his brown robes fluttering with motion. Busy, teeming city: How the devil were they to locate Somerton? Had he even come this way at all? Roland turned back to Beadle. "We'll start with the hotel, I suppose. Somerton's hotel. See if he had the cheek to return, or if he's gone straight to the railway station."

Beadle shook his head. "If he'd left by rail, I'd have had a message by now. My contact's sharp as the devil."

"Then we'll start at the hotel. Where's he staying? The Grand, I expect?"

"Yes, of course the Grand. A ten-minute walk, I should think." Beadle consulted his watch. "You'd better run along without me. I'll dress and run by the Palazzo Vecchio, see if my contact's heard anything. In the meantime, inquire for a desk clerk named Sartoli, and tell him you're a friend of mine. He'll know if Somerton's been through or not."

"Very good." Roland sounded calm, matter-of-fact, even to his own ears. This was territory he knew, territory he owned. He knew how to run men to earth. "Barring further developments, I'll meet you in the lobby at, say, two thirty. Can I leave a message with this Sartoli of yours, if I'm unable to make the rendezvous?"

Beadle rose from his chair. "Yes. I'll do the same. Have you eaten?"

"Not since last night."

Beadle moved to a small cupboard in the corner. "Here's a bit of bread and cheese. Stale, I expect, but it should hold you over. There's water in the pitcher. I'm off to make myself decent." He disappeared through the doorway into the other room, with more swiftness than Roland could have imagined from his softened body.

Roland poured himself a glass of water, drained it, and poured another. He stuffed the bread and cheese in his pocket and ducked once more through the doorway, closing the old wood behind him with a confident thump.

TWENTY

The soaring lobby of the Grand Hotel strained its utmost to shield guests from the aesthetic infelicities of modern life, and Roland's handsome face only just saved his unkempt body from being barred from the premises by a dubious doorman.

The desk clerk, however, looked ready to reach for a pistol.

"Good afternoon, my good man," Roland said, in his most drawling upper-class manner. He extended a blinding grin. "Lord Roland Penhallow. I was hoping I might speak to a fellow named Sartoli, if he's about."

At the word *Lord*, the clerk's sallow face relaxed a fraction of a degree. He paused a single telling instant, and said, in a voice nearly devoid of accent: "If his lordship will be pleased to wait a moment."

"Of course." Roland placed his worn tweed elbow on the polished marble counter and arranged his body into an aristocratic slant, feet crossed at the ankles. Only the most minute observer would have detected the keenness of his gaze as it passed over the room; to everyone else, he looked exactly like the negligent, laconic, wooden-headed Lord Roland Penhallow the world supposed him to be.

The ormolu clock above the sprawling marble mantel read one forty-five in the afternoon, and most of the hotel guests were enjoying luncheon in the splendor of the dining room. A pair of middle-aged ladies formed a white linen fortress at one end of a nearby sofa, heads conspiring over a Baedekers guidebook; at the other end of the room, three light-suited men sprawled across a set of armchairs, with a morning's vigorous sun-soaked sightseeing written across their pink faces. Above their heads, the ceiling fans stroked a lazy rhythm, doing little to disturb the somnolent afternoon air.

No sign of Somerton's large dark-haired figure; no hint of Lilibet.

"Sir."

Roland turned his head to find a black-suited man behind the counter, his collar a spotless starched white against the dark tan of his neck. His eyes glittered with considerably more intelligence than the previous fellow. "Ah," Roland said. "Sartoli, I believe?"

"Yes, sir. May I be of service?"

"I hope so. A dear friend of mine suggested I speak to you, regarding a matter of mutual interest to us. An English fellow, by the name of Beadle."

"I know Mr. Beadle well." The clerk folded his hands atop the counter. If the previous man's accent had been slight, Sartoli's was almost indistinguishable from the Queen's own tongue. "What seems to be the matter?"

"You have, I believe, a guest on your books by the name of Somerton."

"The Earl of Somerton?" The skin beneath Sartoli's eyes released a faint twitch. "I am sorry to report that Lord Somerton checked himself out of his rooms an hour ago."

"Did he?" Roland spread the fingers of his left hand across the marble. "Was he alone, or did he have a companion?"

An instant's hesitation. "He was alone, my lord, at the time."

"At the time?"

Sartoli's voice dropped discreetly. "He has had a companion in the rooms, sir. Another Englishman; his secretary, I believe."

"And no sign of a woman? Or a young boy, of about five years?"

"No, sir." Sartoli's voice was firm and sure; his eyes did not betray any hint of deception. His fingers continued to rest on the counter, lean and brown against the russet marble.

"Very good. Thank you, Sartoli, for your trouble." Roland lifted his palm from the counter long enough to reveal the gold coin hidden beneath it. "I was wondering, my good man, if I might perhaps be allowed a short visit to the rooms previously occupied by his lordship."

Sartoli's eyes flickered downward, and back up to meet Roland's steady gaze. "I believe that can be arranged at once."

"Another thing, Sartoli. If his lordship, or his secretary, or a five-year-old boy, or a young woman with blue eyes and dark hair—a beautiful woman, you'll note her at once—should appear at any location in this hotel, I would most gratefully receive that information at your earliest convenience, either directly or through Mr. Beadle." Roland slid his palm, with the coin underneath, two further inches in the direction of Sartoli's closed hands.

Sartoli tilted his head and nodded. "I shall be more than happy to be of assistance, my lord." His fingers extended to envelop the coin Roland had left behind. "If you will be so good as to step toward the lift, sir. His lordship's rooms were on the sixth floor. I shall ensure you're met there with a key."

"Thank you. I shan't be more than a few minutes," Roland said. The blood raced through his veins, carrying this new information to every point in his body. Before he stepped away from the counter, he pressed a single finger into the cold stone. "I shall, I believe, require a hackney on my return to the lobby. And Sartoli?" He leaned inward.

"Yes, sir?"

"Perhaps, when you're giving the doorman the instructions, you might inquire whether he has any knowledge of Lord Somerton's destination. Do you understand me?"

Sartoli nodded and met his eyes. "With all possible haste."

* * *

Roland moved swiftly through the well-appointed sitting room, scanning the gilt furniture and gleaming parquet floor for any sign of its previous occupant.

His instincts had been correct; Somerton hadn't gone straight to the train station with Philip. The boy was merely a pawn to him, an object, of the same status as a diamond: valuable, investment-grade, even useful, but hardly human. No, he wasn't simply going to whisk Philip back to England and raise him alone. He had to know that Lilibet would follow them, would do anything for her son. Somerton had other plans, larger plans.

And Roland was determined to find out what they were.

He hadn't much time. Somerton had left the hotel an hour ago, alone. That meant he was keeping the boy somewhere else, *with* someone else. Had Lilibet found him already? Had Somerton already managed to threaten her into submission? Roland forced down the fury in his blood and aimed his concentration at the objects around him. Beadle was at the train station. Beadle would have them stopped if they tried to leave Florence.

Nothing seemed out of place. He checked the wastebaskets: empty. The desk drawers contained only blank hotel stationery; the blotter was clear of any marks. Roland hadn't expected anything else; Somerton was an intelligence agent, after all. He knew how to cover his tracks.

Light flooded through the gap in the curtains; Roland went to the window and peered between them. The room faced south, toward the placid gray brown Arno and its succession of stone bridges reaching across to the hills beyond. Six floors below, a hackney pulled up to the front entrance, and the doorman stepped forward to meet its driver.

Time to go.

Roland turned away and walked to the door along the eastern wall, leading presumably to the bedroom. It was slightly ajar; he pushed the heavy wood and stepped forward.

The room was dark, the curtains tightly shut, and instantly Roland knew that someone was there. He could feel it in the air: the light pulse of breathing, the faint crackle of human energy, close and expectant.

Roland paused in the doorway, reviewing his options in a rapid fire of thought. He might turn the switch on the wall—the Grand Hotel had recently installed modern electric lighting, for the convenience of its well-heeled guests—but the occupant might just as easily turn it off again. Or he could, of course, simply wait in the stillness until his eyes adjusted.

The devil take it.

Roland strode to the window and swept aside the curtain. The room filled with afternoon sunlight.

"You must be Lord Roland Penhallow."

The voice came from the opposite side of the room. A figure rose from a deep armchair in the corner, a man's figure, slim, medium height. His hair, slicked back with pomade, shone a deep auburn in the diffuse light just beyond the reach of the shaft from the windows.

Roland leaned back against the broad windowsill, muscles coiled for action. "I am, sir. And whom, may I ask, do I have the honor of addressing?"

The man stepped forward. He was a handsome fellow, clean-shaven, startlingly young. Not more than twenty, Roland judged. "My name is Markham. I'm Lord Somerton's private secretary."

"I see." Roland ran his gaze up and down the man's slight, well-groomed figure, each button correctly fastened, each fold precisely ironed. A very pretty young man, in fact. Somerton's private secretary, was he?

Roland smiled and folded his arms. "I expect you're waiting for me, Mr. Markham."

The young man cleared his throat. "I've been instructed to give you this letter, upon your arrival in town."

"And you knew I would arrive here? In his lordship's former suite?"

"I had been told it was likely." Markham's voice had a

schooled quality, the voice of a young man who wishes to appear older than his years. Beneath those well-tailored clothes, a kind of adolescent gawkiness seemed to lurk, layered in padding and artifice. How old was he, really? What the devil were Somerton's proclivities? A little eddy of alarm grew in Roland's chest, quite apart from the general sense of urgency he'd felt since discovering Lilibet and Philip's absence this morning.

"By Somerton, of course."

Markham inclined his head and drew out a folded paper from his jacket pocket. He walked forward, holding it out before him like a shield.

"Thank you," Roland said, in a silky voice. He took the note. It was folded in thirds and sealed with a large pool of black wax.

"Aren't you going to open it?" asked Markham.

Roland shrugged. "Generally speaking, I endeavor to read my correspondence in private, Mr. Markham."

"I've been instructed to wait for a reply."

"Hmm." Roland ran his finger along the edge of the paper. The young man—boy, really—had a fine-boned face, an almost dewy cast to his skin, a slight blush staining the upper reaches of his cheekbones, but his eyes were old and brown and serious. A ripple of compassion went across Roland's heart. "You're a remarkably conscientious secretary, Mr. Markham."

"I endeavor to give satisfaction, your lordship." The blush on the boy's cheekbones intensified, but his eyes remained steady.

"Yes, I expect you do. Very well. You may wait in the chair."

Markham retreated to the chair in the corner with long coltish strides and sat, one slender leg crossed over the other. The shadows swallowed the dull fire of his auburn hair, leaving it an anonymous brown atop the pale skin of his face.

Roland broke the seal.

Your presence is cordially requested at the Palazzo Angelini, in the via Ducale, to decide the fate of the wife and son of the Earl of S.

His fingers clenched at the paper's edges. A dizzy spiral wove through his brain, before he righted it with brute force.

He did not fear the threat implied in the letter. Whatever Somerton's skills, Roland could outwit him; he had years of training at the feet of Sir Edward; he was strong and agile and clever, and he had justice on his side.

The location of the palazzo, on the outskirts of town, did not trouble him. The suburbs had tactical advantages; he could bend any circumstance to his need.

No, the facts of the letter, the bare sentence itself, left him unmoved. He'd received countless such instructions in the course of his career, and dealt with them summarily. What made his heart strike against his chest, what made alarm snake through his body, was the fact that the words on this particular page had been formed in the unmistakable curves and angles of Lilibet's handwriting.

Y ou do understand, my good fellow, what it is your employer has done?" Roland reached up one hand to the leather strap hanging from the roof of the hackney, as it swung around a corner with a particularly reckless lurch.

Markham did not flinch. "Yes, I do. He's recovered his son, who was taken from the family home some months ago."

"By his own mother." The hackney lurched back into balance, but Roland kept his hand looped around the strap. The other hand he slipped into the folds of his jacket, where a small pistol lay concealed inside an inner pocket.

"Who gave Lord Somerton no forwarding address, no indication at all as to her direction, or even the country to which she had absconded." Markham's brown eyes didn't waver from his own, didn't betray so much as an atom less than total conviction.

"Because she feared his reaction. She feared he might harm the boy, or her."

At last Markham turned away, gazing out the small window of the cab with an inscrutable expression. "Then she doesn't know him."

Roland made an astonished noise. "Bollocks, young man. You of all people should know what Somerton's capable of. You of all people . . ."

The young man flashed back to Roland's face. "He wouldn't strike her! Nor the boy!"

Roland leaned forward. "Not physically, perhaps. But there are worse things a man can do."

Markham's lips parted, drew in a little breath, and paused.

Roland sat back. "You see what I mean. And I warn you, Markham, that if so much as a particle of harm comes to Lady Somerton or her son, I shall hold the two of you directly responsible. I shall make no allowances for your youth."

"The boy is perfectly fine," Markham said sharply. "I left him smiling and content, not an hour ago."

"You saw him? When? Where?" Roland's hand fisted around the strap, biting painfully into the leather. The air inside the hackney had grown warm and stale; it pressed like clay against his face and neck.

"Upon his arrival in town. A fine boy. He was delighted to see his father. I was quite moved."

Roland rotated the words in his mind, attempting to assess their sincerity. Markham's face had resumed its impassive stillness; his words hadn't conveyed any particular emotion. "And her ladyship?" he asked at last.

Markham's eyes seemed to harden, in the rectangle of sunlight penetrating the window. "Her ladyship is in perfect health."

"Then how was she persuaded to write this note herself?" Roland patted his jacket pocket. "It could only have been by force, moral if not physical. And I swear to you . . ."

"I don't know anything about that." Markham spoke sharply.

Roland considered him. "Is she with Philip?" he asked.

An instant's hesitation, and then: "They are both at the Palazzo."

Roland looked out the window. The hackney was slowing, tilting upward as it climbed the sloping road. The Palazzo Angelini, he knew, sat atop one of the low hills along the river, to the east of town; to his right, the hillside dropped away in a succession of green terraces, overflowing with the bounty of summer. At the bottom, the gray yellow city clustered around the river, the bridges like long, gnarled fingers spanning its width, the great red bowl of the Duomo shimmering above everything like the sun. Already Florence looked quite distant, quite remote. He'd managed to drop a message at the front desk for Beadle, but even if it found his colleague, he could expect no help for at least an hour or two. He was on his own.

He turned back to Markham and spoke in a quiet voice. "Come now, young man. You must know he's in the wrong. You must know what he's done. A beast of a husband, a damned incompetent father."

"He loves his son."

Roland shrugged. "As one might love a dog, perhaps. Or a valuable painting in his gallery. Tell me, how long have you been in the earl's employ?"

"Something over a year."

"Have you, at any time, seen Lord Somerton embrace his son? Show him the slightest sign of affection?"

Another slight hesitation. "He's not a demonstrative man, it's true . . ."

"He's a coldhearted corpse, and you know it!" Roland slid his hand from his jacket and pounded the hard seat next to him. "That boy has the most open heart in the world; he'd do anything for a mere crumb of affection from his father, and he's had nothing but rebuffs and shouting and coldness, when he's been noticed at all. Thank God, thank God his mother is the most loving angel on God's earth!"

Markham's dark eyes flashed anger at last. "Oh, indeed!

A most loving angel! One who fled the country, into the arms of her lover? One who introduced her own son into that illicit . . ."

His voice ended in a choke. Roland had reached across the space between them and gathered up Markham's pristine white shirt and neat wool lapels into his single fist. "Do not," he whispered, "profane Lady Somerton's name again."

Markham's eyes grew into large brown saucers.

"I will not," Roland continued, in an icy voice, "betray her confidence with a recitation of Somerton's crimes against her. It should suffice that he has betrayed her a thousandfold more, and long before she entertained so much as a disloyal thought in her head." He released Markham's shirt and let his hand fall back in his lap. "She owes him nothing. Not her fidelity, not her loyalty, and certainly not her love."

Markham lifted his hand and brushed at his collar. "I take your point."

Roland folded his arms and regarded the young man: his expression, which had fallen into sullen lines; the slope of his shoulders; the slow movements of his hand. "Tell me, old man," he said, in the Penhallow drawl, "do you happen to know his lordship's plans here today?"

Markham cast him an upward glance. "As it happens, I don't."

"Do you know, I think I believe you," Roland said. The hackney was crawling now, edging around a corner. A stone gatepost glided past the window. "I believe you've no more notion of what's in Somerton's head than I do. And I suspect you rather resent me for it. Heigh-ho. We're in this together, it seems."

Markham straightened his shoulders and lifted his torso. He spoke coldly, even scornfully. "We are not, your lordship, *in this together*, as you put it. The telling difference is this." The hackney lurched to a stop; he put his hand on the door handle. "*I* am Somerton's trusted aide, and *you*"—he swung the door open, hopped outside, and turned back to glare at Roland—"are merely his wife's lover." His eyes traveled up and down Roland's body, and he smiled. "Though not, I expect, any longer."

He strode away, across the graveled courtyard.

Roland eased thoughtfully out of the cab and turned to pay the driver. *"Attendere l'angolo,"* he said, sliding an extra ten-lire note into the man's hand.

"Grazie, signore," the driver said, eyes wide, tipping his cap. He snapped his whip and the horse moved smartly, across the courtyard and back out the open gate into the road, the wheels crunching the gravel as they went.

Roland turned. Markham stood waiting for him at the entrance of the square Palladian building, his feet slightly apart, his hands behind his back. Odd sort of chap, Markham. Not a bad fellow at heart, clearly, and yet devoted to that rotter Somerton, and not particularly enamored of Lilibet. What sort of hold did the earl have over the boy?

For an instant, Roland allowed his eyes to slide over the windows of the facade, wondering whether Lilibet or Philip were behind one of them, staring down at him. He began walking across the courtyard to Markham, taking in every possible detail, in case of later need: the height of the windows, the distance to the nearby trees, the composition of the high stone walls surrounding the property, the direction in which it faced.

At the door, Markham stood aside and allowed him to enter first. He passed through the doorway into a soaring entrance hall, beautifully proportioned and quite empty. His eyes flashed about the creamy walls, the doors, the curving staircase, and the row of French doors at the rear, bright with sunshine and the hint of a broad stone terrace beyond. His ears picked up the crisp echo of his own boots on the old marble tiles and nothing else.

He stopped, folded his arms behind him, and turned to Markham. "So?" he inquired. "You've brought me here. Where, my good man, is Lord Somerton?"

And more importantly, where the devil was Lilibet?

TWENTY-ONE

Two hours earlier

Lilibet sat in her chair, in the center of the room, on the second floor of the Palazzo Angelini, and waited for the Earl of Somerton.

The ritual was not entirely unfamiliar to her. Early in the evening of the last night before Lilibet had left her husband, Lord Somerton's private secretary, Mr. Markham, had knocked on the door of the nursery, where she was reading Philip his bedtime story. "His lordship requests the honor of an interview in his study," he'd said, in that quiet voice of his, eyes dark and emotionless. Or something like that, anyway; something formal and correct, that somehow managed to convey a world of foreboding behind its commonplace words.

She'd gone to the study, and found it empty. She hadn't been surprised; he'd always done that, kept people waiting for interviews, sweating and shifting in the chair before the desk, until he entered at last to deliver some rapier thrust. So she'd settled in the chair in question, arranged her skirts, folded her hands in her lap, and concentrated on keeping her pulse at a slow, even pace. On loosening the thread of alarm that wound through her chest and belly; on remembering

that she was a countess, a lady, a woman of dignity and virtue. That she had nothing to fear.

With her mind so occupied, it had taken her several minutes to realize that the elegant gilt jewel box in the center
of her husband's desk belonged to her. And while she was
still contemplating this fact, and before she'd begun to feel
more than a dawning sense of outrage that it had been taken
from her room, had been opened without her permission,
and now sat on Somerton's broad gleaming mahogany desk
with its lid hanging ajar, her husband had entered the room.

She knew, therefore, that her presence in the Palazzo
Angelini was all part of Somerton's plan. Every detail around
her had been arranged with care, from the moment she'd
seen Markham's face emerge from the crowd of tourists clustered around the Ponte Vecchio.

This large, empty room, devoid of any furniture, except
for an armchair, an escritoire, and the tall straight-backed
chair in which she now sat.

The lamp, the pen, the sheet of writing paper lying upon
the escritoire.

The sound of small running feet, of muffled voices, of
occasional laughter, of scattering blocks and thumping
objects, coming from the room directly above.

The windows, shut and locked, allowing not a breath of
fresh hilltop breeze to disturb the mounting heat in the
room, as the afternoon sunlight pressed full force against
the many-paned glass.

The clock now ticking above the mantel.

Just as she had that evening, many months ago, she now
maintained her posture with care. Her back remained
straight, her muscles steady. She could wait, too. She had
time. She had power.

After all, she wasn't without wits. She'd anticipated this
possibility. Lying with Mssrs. Bellwether and Knobbs this
minute was a piece of paper listing every liaison in which
Somerton had taken part, every foul encounter, every shady
association, with instructions to submit the information to
the Queen's own secretary should Philip set foot in En-

gland in the earl's company. She had compiled it with pains-taking care over the past year. She'd followed Somerton and noted everything. She'd kept track of every man who entered his study; she'd bribed a footman at his club to dis-close the names of his companions. Ammunition: She'd been stockpiling it for some time.

This time, she would win.

By the time Roland tracked her down, she'd have Somer-ton's signed agreement to accept the divorce.

Why, then, did her pulse continue to throb in her throat?

She stared at the ceiling, where Philip's little feet raced just a few feet away, and tried not to count the loud scratches of the clock as it ticked through the minutes. Every particle in her body longed to dash up the stairs, to capture Philip and cover him with kisses, to carry him out and away with her. Away from this cold, symmetrical villa and back to the dear Castel sant'Agata baking in the June sun, and to Roland's waiting arms.

But she couldn't allow herself that luxury. She had to settle with Somerton first. She had to end this.

A bead of sweat made its way between her shoulders and her back. She could try to unlock one of the windows and push it open, but they were enormous: twelve panes over twelve, as tall as a man. Besides, the very act would betray her nervousness. Better to sit here calmly and perspire.

A slight pause interrupted the flow of noise above her, and in the gap she felt a vibration through the floorboards, strong and regular.

Footsteps.

She drew in a deep breath, filling her lungs with the hot, musty smell of sunbaked plaster and old wood. For an instant she closed her eyes, trying to determine the source and direction of the disturbance. *Thump, thump.* She could hear them now, heavy booted feet, striking the marble staircase with purpose and deliberation.

Louder, now. Unmistakable.

At the last instant, she leaned back in her chair, laid her elbows upon the armrest, and turned her gaze to the window, where a long line of cypress marched across the glass, each tree exactly identical to the other.

The door made a low creak as it opened, and a smart crack as it closed again.

"My dear Lady Somerton," said a familiar voice. "You're looking very well indeed. Italy appears to agree with you."

Lilibet counted off a second, two seconds, three, and turned her head to the doorway. "I find it agrees with me very well indeed, sir. Thank you."

He hadn't changed, not by so much as a turned hair. Tall, broad, massive, black-haired, black-eyed, he stood before her like a block of granite, on which a sneer had been carved with utmost precision.

He walked toward her, stopped, reached out his hand, and tipped up her chin. "Remarkable," he said. "I hadn't thought it possible your beauty could be improved. Yet so it is." He tilted his head and regarded her from another angle. "Yes, remarkable. Pity it's all thrown away on that ass Penhallow, of course, but your tastes always tended to the common side."

"He's worth a thousand of you."

Somerton laughed. "How gallant! Really, my dear, you're terribly amusing. Almost as if you thought I cared for your good opinion."

"Generally, husbands do."

"Ah, but you no longer consider me your husband, do you? You wish to divorce me." He said the word *divorce* with a keen sharpness, like the crack of a whip, leaning forward as he did so.

She did not flinch. "Yes, I do."

He smiled, or rather sneered, and turned to settle himself in the armchair a few feet away. "Very well, then, my dear. I've no objection to a divorce." He crossed his legs and draped his arms over the armrests. "What are your terms?"

She stared at him in astonishment. "My terms?"

"I'm more than prepared to meet any reasonable request. An allowance, of course. A house. You're quite welcome to take the boy, though I shall expect regular updates on his progress, and perhaps an annual visit. You look amazed."

"I confess, I am." Her back, damp with perspiration, was beginning to stick to the chair. She lifted herself upward, out of her indolent pose. "I thought you meant to contest me."

"Never in life. Why on earth should I wish to remain married to a woman who shares another man's bed?" He said the words with cold deliberation, while his eyes bored into hers, without so much as a blink.

Heat prickled in her cheeks and at the tip of her nose. "If I have, it's because you drove me there. You've sinned a thousand times more than I have, ten thousand."

"Have I? I've enjoyed a greater variety, perhaps, but the relative *quantity* of sin is a matter of question."

"That's not true! I never . . . He was never my lover. Not until . . ."

"Come, my dear," he said, in soothing tones. "Let's not waste time on meaningless denials. His photograph in your jewel box, all these years." He leaned forward and placed his spread hands, spiderlike, on his knees. His voice darkened and intensified. "In your *jewel box*."

Lilibet blinked her eyes, hard. She hated the way he could make her weep, with just a few words in that cutting voice of his, a single menacing look from his black eyes. With enormous mental effort, she brought her jumping nerves under control. "You know Roland and I admired each other, once. It was common knowledge. Then I became your wife, as God willed. But I never betrayed you, Somerton. Not in word or in deed, not until after I left England. Not until chance brought him my way again . . ."

A dry chuckle escaped Somerton's lips, and he leaned back in his chair. "Chance! Oh, my dear! *Chance!*"

"Chance!" she said fiercely. "I had no idea he was in Italy, no idea he was bound for the same castle! We answered an advertisement in the *Times*, for heaven's sake!"

"I saw no such advertisement."

"Then call it an act of God. Of destiny." She gripped the armrests, straining her fingers around the carved wood. "All this time I denied myself, Somerton. I tried so hard to be a good wife. I wanted so much to love you, to forget the past, to forget my lost dreams. To make new ones with you. But you raised your fist and you crushed them, just like that, with your deceit and your infidelity, your women without number, your temper and your coldness. And so I lived six years in winter, *six years* in bitterness and solitude, with only Philip to bring the slightest warmth to my heart. I lived like a nun, like a penitent for your sins, until that last night, that dreadful night, the night you accused me of adultery. *Me!* Of consorting with a man I'd given up for you, a man I hadn't seen in years."

He rose from his chair in an abrupt movement and strode to the window. With a single heave he opened it, letting the afternoon breeze flood into the room. "His photograph, my dear! Among your jewels!"

"I'd put it there long ago," she said quietly, watching him. "I never disturbed it. It only gave me comfort, to know it was there."

He stood there by the window, drawing in the air. "Among your jewels," he said again, almost inaudible, the breeze snatching away the words.

"I never betrayed you."

A bird began to sing outside the window, eloquent and exuberant, perched somewhere in that row of identical trees along the garden border. The smell of outdoors, of spicy cypress and sweet flowers, of sunshine baking into green leaves, swirled around them both.

A thump sounded from the room upstairs, and a high trill of laughter. The sound made Lilibet's chest strain with yearning.

"I presume you have a nursemaid of some kind with him," she said.

He turned from the window and leaned against it, bracing his hands against the old wooden sill. "Of course. His old nursemaid, the one you left behind in Milan."

"After I discovered she was carrying your child."

He shrugged. "Not mine, in fact. I always take the most

scrupulous care to avoid such nuisances. A footman, I suppose."

She felt the heat invade her cheeks again, and spoke in a high, matter-of-fact voice to cover her embarrassment. "In any case, I suppose we should return to business."

"Business?"

"The terms of our divorce. I should like to conclude the matter as swiftly as possible."

"Yes, of course." He pushed away from the window and returned to the chair, placing his hands atop the back and regarding her with his dark gaze. "Will a thousand pounds a year be sufficient?"

"I don't require your money."

"Should you remarry, of course, or accept another man's protection, I shall be obliged to cease payment. But with your face, I should imagine you'll find a deep enough pair of pockets to keep you in style, even with a divorce attached to your name." He spoke steadily, but his knuckles were white against the curved gilt back of the chair.

"I told you, I won't accept your money."

"I shall provide you a house in town, if you like, though I expect Philip to spend at least six months a year in the country, both for his health and for his moral development, until he begins at school."

"Moral development? Oh, that's rich," she said. "Coming from you."

"The dowager's house, on my estate, shall be made available, if it suits you. As the future earl, Philip ought to know something about the land he will inherit. I will assume, for legal purposes, he is in fact my son."

"You may submit all these matters to my lawyers. They will be happy to draw up an agreement to our mutual satisfaction." She rose from the chair. "Really, I don't see why any of this was necessary. You had only to send a letter, not kidnap my son and force me to ride through the hills on a . . ."

"Wait a moment, my dear." He held up his hand. "I

haven't quite finished. In exchange for my cooperation, I shall expect a few concessions."

Something about the way he said the word *concessions*—the hint of a silky drawl in his voice, the accompanying gleam of light in his eyes—made her blood turn to ice in her veins.

She twisted her fingers together. "What sort of concessions? If you mean visits, I will of course allow Philip . . ."

With one hand, he waved at the escritoire, and the pen and paper lying on its well-polished surface. "First of all, I should like you to write me a letter."

"A letter? What sort of letter?" she asked warily.

"I shall dictate it to you, if you don't mind."

She hesitated. "For whom is the letter intended?"

She knew the answer in an instant, even before he replied. She saw it in the faint satisfied curl of his lip, in the triumphant arch of his eyebrow.

"Why, to your lover, of course. To Lord Roland Penhallow, our gallant hero, valiant debaucher of other men's wives." Somerton made another wave of his hand, in the direction of the escritoire. "I think he deserves at least a friendly note of thanks for his exertions in my marital bed, don't you?"

"Leave him out of this, Somerton. He has nothing to do with the ruin of our marriage. I knew, long before I saw him again, that I could no longer live under your roof."

"Tell me," the earl said conversationally, returning his hands to the back of the chair, "did he please you? Did he make you cry out, in that demented way you have, when you reach your culmination? Did he . . ."

"Stop it! Stop it at once! How dare you!"

"Was he gratified to discover your whorish appetites? Tell me, Elizabeth. I want to know every detail. Did he suckle on your teats? Did he put his tongue between your legs?"

She put her hands to her ears. "Stop it! Stop it!"

He lifted the chair and flung it across the room with a crash of splintering wood. "Was his cock as satisfying as mine, Elizabeth? Did you scream with pleasure when he thrust it inside you, as you did with me?"

She stood her ground and let her hands drop to her sides. Her pulse knocked against the side of her throat. "Stop it," she said, in a low voice. "You disgrace yourself."

He stood still before her, broad and furious, chest heaving, eyes glittering in his rough-hewn face. His right fist began to clench and unclench in a steady, expectant rhythm, as if his heart were beating outside his breast.

She went on, more gently. "Can we not be civilized about this, Somerton? Can we not simply agree to part, and wish each other well?"

He took another deep breath, and another. His voice, when he spoke at last, had been schooled back into calm. "The easiest thing in the world, madam. Only write that note, as I requested, and we may proceed."

"I will not. Roland Penhallow has nothing to do with this." Her palms were growing damp; she closed them around the folds of her dress.

A smile crept across Somerton's lips. "My dear, dear wife. Did you think I had brought you here, brought your son here, merely to discuss our divorce in amicable terms?"

"I've no idea why you brought me here."

"Or did you think I hoped to lure you back? To have you again as my wife? Or that I meant to take Philip home with me, and raise him myself?"

She said nothing, only returned his gaze, waiting with dread to hear his words.

He reached out to grasp her chin between his thumb and forefinger, and leaned in close, his brandy-laced breath brushing against her nose. "Far too late for that, my dear," he said. "I don't want you back in my bed, another man's whore. I don't want your brat clinging to my legs."

She slapped his hand away. "Then what *do* you want, you damned insufferable bastard?"

His eyebrows lifted at her words. "Such language, Elizabeth." He chuckled.

He went to the escritoire, picked up the pen and paper, and held them out in her direction. The expression on his face glowed with triumph. "I want Penhallow, my dear. I want your lover. And if you want to see young Philip again—if you want, in fact, to see him leave this building alive—you will agree to serve as the bait."

TWENTY-TWO

Of course, she'd capitulated.

What else could she do? She knew, as a matter of logic, he wouldn't kill his own son. Not even Somerton was as deranged as that. True, he'd expressed doubt about the boy's parentage, but that had been intended merely to insult her; no one, looking at Philip's black eyes, could possibly think he sprang from the loins of any man other than the Earl of Somerton.

She also knew, as a matter of logic, that she had her tidy, well-annotated list on file with Bellwether and Knobbs, that she was not without her own power.

But the fear in her heart could not be ruled by logic. She was, at that moment, within Somerton's physical power, and so was her son. And Roland, she'd reminded herself, was at least a day away, assuming he were still at the Castel sant'Agata and hadn't tried to follow her. Somerton would have to find him, wherever he was, and he'd have to make his way here. Plenty of time for her to change the earl's mind; hours and hours for her to plot an escape.

"I want to see Philip," she said, when she handed him

the note. She looked him full in the face, to let him know she couldn't be cowed this time.

"But of course." He folded the note with a single sharp crease, put it in his pocket, and went to the door. "Madam," he said, swinging the paneled wood wide and stepping aside.

He led her upstairs, up twenty-two broad marble steps (she counted each one, to keep herself steady) and around the stairwell to a door, on which he rapped his knuckles twice.

She didn't bother waiting. She pushed past him, flung open the door, and ran forward to swing Philip into her arms. His warm body fit into hers, smelling of bread and jam and new linen. "Darling," she said, into his hair. "Darling."

"Mama! Mama! There you are! Look, it's Miss Lucy! She's back!"

Lilibet shifted her eyes to where Lucy Yarrow stood deferentially next to the window, the sunlight outlining the swollen curve of her pregnancy.

"Madam," she said, bobbing a supremely awkward curtsy.

Philip whispered in Lilibet's ear. "She's going to have a baby, too!"

The blood left her limbs. She looked quickly at Somerton, but he hadn't seemed to hear: His fingers tapped against his jacket pocket, and his gaze wandered around the room, until it came to rest on her.

She felt his eyes on her face, on her figure. She wore her traveling suit, jacket still buttoned; Philip's body still pressed against her front. Could he see her thickening waist? Did he discern the bulge of her bosom, the bloom in her cheeks? The changes seemed so obvious to her.

She nodded at Lucy to break the silence. "She must be tired. I'll watch him myself."

"Very well." Somerton nodded curtly at the nursemaid. "Wait downstairs, in the kitchen. I'll send for you when you're required."

"Thank you, sir." She bobbed another unbalanced curtsy and fled, as quickly as her body would allow her.

Somerton turned back to Lilibet. "I expect you're hungry. A tray will be sent up in due course."

"Where have you been, Mama?" Philip asked, next to her ear. "Where's Uncle Roland? Did he come, too? Does he know Father?"

"*Uncle Roland,*" said Somerton, locking eyes with her. "Dear old Uncle Roland. He'll be along shortly, I expect. And to that end, I suppose I must beg your permission to retire. Markham waits below." He gave his jacket pocket another satisfied pat. The tweed strained under the movement of his powerful arm; his shoulders squared with confidence. Every organ in her body seemed to sink downward in despair at the sight of him, at the strength of his body and the cunning in his eyes. How could she ever think to outmaneuver him? How could she have betrayed Roland to him?

Courage, she thought. Faith and courage. He was a man, no more.

"Take as long as you need," she said coldly. Philip was getting heavy; she allowed him to slide downward to the floor and took his hand tightly in hers.

Somerton went to the door and inclined his head toward her with courtly formality. "I shall, of course, apprise you at once with any news."

He left with a firm slam of the door, and the soft snick of a key turning in the lock.

Damn him for that.

"Father seems very cross," said Philip softly.

She turned to him and knelt on the floor. "Did he hurt you at all, darling?" she asked, fighting to keep the question as gentle and unassuming as she could.

He shook his head. "No. But I can tell when he's cross."

"Yes, a little cross, I suppose." She drew in a deep breath of relief. "But you mustn't mind that. Your father's just . . . well . . ."

"He hates me, doesn't he?" Philip's voice was startlingly matter-of-fact.

"No! No, of course not, darling. He loves you very much."

"No, he doesn't." Philip put his arms around her neck. "He didn't say anything to me, in the carriage. I don't think he likes children."

"He doesn't know what to say to them, that's all. But he does love you." She embraced him back, resting her chin on his head.

"Uncle Roland is much nicer. Uncle Roland . . ."

She stroked his hair. "Uncle Roland what, darling?"

"I wish . . . I think . . ." He sighed and drew back. "Was Father telling the truth? Is Uncle Roland coming?"

"I . . . Well, he might be."

"Father doesn't like Uncle Roland, does he?" Philip reached out and began plucking at her sleeve, his little fingers just brushing the skin of her wrist.

How had he known that?

She swallowed. "Not very much, no."

"Is he going to kill him?"

Lilibet froze. She tried to laugh, but it came out rather more like a choke. "Goodness, no! Where do you get these ideas? *Kill* him, really. People don't just kill each other, dear."

Her words didn't sound convincing, even to her own ears. What did Somerton mean to do with Roland, after all, if not to kill him?

Philip leaned silently back against her, the slight movement of his breath merging into hers. "If I go back to England with Father, will he not be angry with Uncle Roland anymore?"

"Oh, darling. It isn't that. It isn't your fault. Sometimes people just don't like each other." She set him away, so she could look at his face. The skin was pink, the eyes heavy, as if he were trying hard not to cry. "Uncle Roland will be just fine."

Philip's eyes narrowed into two worried slits. "Are we going back to England with Father?"

She hesitated, taking his hands into hers. "Do you *want* to go back?"

"Yessss," he said reluctantly, as if it were an unwelcome duty, and then: "But I wish . . . Why can't . . . I think . . ." He flung himself back at her chest. "I'm going to miss Uncle Roland! And Norbert! And fishing in the lake!"

"Oh, darling. Hush. It's all right."

"And Father's so angry, and England's cold and rainy . . ."

"Not now. It's summertime. And Father . . . well, he . . . we won't see him so much. Only when you want to. We'll . . . we'll find a house of our own, and you can visit your father . . ."

The little body tightened into a knot within her arms. "We won't . . . we won't live with Father?"

Oh, damn. Bloody damn. She didn't want to talk about this, not yet. She hadn't had time to prepare. She hadn't practiced the words yet. She was consumed with worry for Roland, consumed with worry for herself and Philip. How the devil did one tell a five-year-old boy that his parents' marriage was over?

"Darling, I think . . . well, your father wasn't in the house very often before, was he? It won't be so different. It's just . . . because he was away so much, and so very busy, we thought . . . well, that it might be better if we had our own house. And you and your father would be great friends, and see each other whenever you liked. Sometimes that's easier, when you're living apart. You don't get angry so much." She stopped, trying to gauge his reaction.

He didn't speak for a long moment. His cheek pressed against her breast, and his eyes seemed fixed on some far corner of the room. "Does Father want to marry someone else? Like that king?"

"Which king?"

"The one with all the wives. Uncle Roland told me about him. He had six of them, I think. And they were all named Katherine, which is rubbish, because how could he tell them apart?"

She couldn't help laughing. "They weren't *all* Katherines." Her knees were beginning to ache on the hard wood;

she settled herself on the floor and drew Philip into her lap, with her chin resting comfortably atop his head. "And your father's not a king. I don't think he wants to marry anyone else. He just . . ."

"He just doesn't want to be my father anymore?"

"No! No, it's not that at all. He'll always be your father, darling. He'll always love you." She gazed across the floor, across the endless parquet pattern stretching into the wall. Sunlight flooded the enormous window opposite, warming her face and hands.

"I don't want him to take me back!" Philip said, with sudden fierceness. "I don't want to leave here! If he tries to take me back, I'll . . . I'll run away!"

"Shh. No, you won't. You'll . . ."

"I will! And Uncle Roland will come and get me, and . . ."

"Don't say that!"

"Why not?" He struggled out of her arms and stood up, facing her. His dark eyes were bright with passion. "I want him to get me! I want to live with Uncle Roland! He's much nicer, and he loves me. He told me so."

"Hush, darling. Don't say that. Your father may hear you; he may be standing outside . . ."

"I don't care! I want him to hear me! I want Uncle Roland to come here on his horse and take us both some-where where Father can't find us. And if Father tries to stop him, he'll . . . he'll hit Father! He'll shoot him with his revolver and . . ."

"Oh, heavens, Philip! No!" She reached for him, but he slipped away and ran to the window. "Philip, you mustn't! Your father may be . . . be difficult, but . . ."

"I'll bet he's out there right now, looking for a way to spring us free." His little head craned forward, straining to see the ground below.

She took him by the arm and pulled him away from the window. "Nonsense. He's back at the castle, waiting for us. He . . ." She stopped. What could she say about it? She couldn't lie, couldn't tell him the truth. Couldn't assure

Philip that Roland was perfectly safe; couldn't tell him she'd just written Roland a letter, luring him into Somerton's clutches. "We'll just wait and see, won't we?" she finished lamely. "I'm sure everything will sort itself out."

"Uncle Roland would lick Father for us," Philip said confidently. "I know he would."

Her heart sank. "Oh, Philip. Uncle Roland . . . he's very clever, but he's not . . . We'll just hope he stays away from your father, won't we? We don't want any fighting. I'm sure we can all sort it out."

"Uncle Roland could lick Father," Philip said. "He knows a lot of things. And he's big and strong."

"Don't say that," she whispered. "Don't say that. We don't want them to fight." She gazed into her son's eyes, into the martial light burning in their depths, and felt a cold helplessness creep over her chest. Because of course they would fight. They were men, and that was what men did. They'd fight, on Somerton's terms, and Roland—her Roland, her beautiful, clever, huge-hearted Roland—would be no match for Somerton's cunning, Somerton's brute strength and bloody-minded ruthlessness.

And it was all her fault.

She glanced at the locked door, at the window. The walls of the high-ceilinged room seemed to loom over her, pressing against her and Philip, like the bars of a prison. In the heat of the afternoon, the air had grown stuffy, heavy with the scents of wood and plaster and paint and sunshine.

How much time did they have? It all depended on Roland, on whether he'd stayed at the castle or not. Somehow she doubted it. Roland would have come after them, the instant he discovered what had happened. He was probably on his way to Florence this very moment, galloping like the wind, his tawny hair curling from the edges of his cap and his hazel eyes fierce with determination. Galloping to save her, galloping straight into Somerton's well-laid plans.

Hours, then. She had only a few hours to find a way out of the villa with Philip, to escape Somerton and his vengeance.

Only hours in which to save Roland from the trap she'd laid for him herself.

From the expression on Markham's face, Roland might have supposed he'd asked for an audience with the Queen herself. No butler's nose could have tipped any farther upward as he said, thrusting an arm in the direction of a shadowed doorway off the staircase: "Lord Somerton asks that you await him in the study."

Roland smiled and folded his hands behind his back. "My dear fellow, I'm afraid I must decline the honor."

Markham gave a visible start. Evidently Somerton's pronouncements were not usually met with refusal. "What's that?"

"I must decline," Roland said, with a regretful shrug of his shoulders. "I shall remain here in the hall. Charming sort of foyer, really," he went on, pronouncing the word *foyer* with an exaggerated French accent, "all classically proportioned and whatnot. Fiendishly clever, that fellow Palladio. Should trade this in an instant for the old pile back home."

Markham stared at him, brown eyes wide with shock. "Sir, the study," he stammered.

"Very kind, I'm sure," said Roland, still smiling, "but I much prefer things where I am. Sunshine, clean air, lovely elegant staircase—look how it stretches upward, the clever thing—yes, quite content right here."

Markham's eyes narrowed, compressing from amazement into determination. "Sir, I must command you to await his lordship's arrival *in . . . the . . . study.*"

Roland blinked. "I beg your pardon, dear fellow. I must have misunderstood you. Some trick of the acoustics, I daresay, made it sound almost as though you used the word *command.*"

"I did." Markham's chin jutted. "I *command* you to retire to the study and await his lordship."

Roland chuckled. "Oh, my dear Mr. Markham. How

droll you are. Ha-ha. *Command*, indeed." He removed his handkerchief from his pocket and dabbed at his eyes. "You're a dreadfully amusing fellow. *Command*, ha-ha. Tell me, what's Somerton paying you, eh? I'll double it, just for the enjoyment of hearing you rattle off these comic ideas."

Markham's fists clenched into two decidedly unamused knots at his side. He lifted one booted foot and stamped it against the marble tiles. "I am *not* amusing. I am perfectly serious. You must go to the study at *once*, sir, or . . . or . . ."

"Or what?" Roland asked gently.

"I will . . . His lordship will . . ." A slow flush spread upward and across the elegant bones of Markham's face.

"Exactly," Roland said, in the same soft voice. "So you see, I shall stay exactly where I am, feet planted firmly on the floor, until Lord Somerton does me the honor of a meeting."

"That's . . . impossible. He . . . he'll never meet you like this. He . . . These things must be done properly, must be done in a civilized fashion." Markham's voice descended to a low hoarseness, heavy with desperation; his hands plucked at the sides of his jacket. The sunlight from the back window slanted across his face, exaggerating the delicate line of his cheekbone, the reddish glint to his sleeked-back hair. He looked like an angel caught in the very act of falling.

"Civilized fashion? Egad, that's rich," said Roland. "Frightfully civilized, kidnapping a young boy from his room in the dead of night, in order to exact one's medieval revenge on his mother. Done properly, there's the ticket."

"You twist everything around," said Markham. "You make it sound as if you're just an innocent man, minding his business, instead of . . . of . . ."

"At a loss for words again, my boy? Yes, you've got yourself into quite a muddle, swearing fealty to Somerton and all that." Roland folded his arm across his chest and allowed his head a sympathetic tilt. "Look here, why don't you leave off all this philosophizing—tiresome stuff, that;

I avoid it above all things, myself—and do something useful and revolutionary. Such as telling your sainted master I've arrived."

"I can't do that. You'll disappear, the instant I'm gone."

"I say, that's a brilliant idea! You trot off after Somerton, and I'll dash around all the rooms and rescue Lady Somerton and his little lordship. Solves everything, really: You're pulled away from the moral chasm yawning at your feet, and her ladyship continues in the independent and dignified life to which, I believe, as a subject of the British Empire, she's properly entitled." Roland spread his hands and smiled. "You see? Brilliant!"

A slow thunderous clapping cracked down from above.

"Very good," boomed the voice of Lord Somerton, his broad shoulders blocking out entirely the light from the window on the first landing. He leaned forward and placed his hands on the iron railing. "Very well played indeed, Penhallow. You've almost convinced me yourself."

"Ah! If it isn't the villain of our story," Roland said cheerfully. "Good afternoon, Somerton. Kicked any puppies yet today?"

A slight narrowing of the black eyes, and Somerton straightened from the railing. He turned to the final flight of stairs, stretching down in stately procession to the entrance hall, and descended each step with a deliberate ceremony. "Yes, well played. You have, however, left out one crucial element in this elegant calculus of yours."

"Really? How frightfully careless of me."

Somerton reached the bottom of the stairs and walked up to Roland, his booted heels clacking on the marble like the tick of some monstrously demented clock. He stopped, mere inches away, and bored his charcoal eyes straight into Roland's. "The most crucial element of all, really."

Roland raised his eyebrows. "Hmm. What's that?"

"Me."

TWENTY-THREE

R oland snapped his fingers.
   "You! Of course! How muddleheaded of me." He gave his chin a thoughtful tap. Lord Somerton stood unnaturally close, and a slight trace of lavender seemed to drift, for just an instant, from his burly person. The scent shot straight to Roland's heart, made it pound in a desperate rhythm, made him fight to keep his voice confined within the Penhallow drawl. "Lord Somerton . . . let me think . . . oh, that's right. You, I believe, are meant to return to England and devote yourself to good works for the rest of your unlamented existence, in hopes of perhaps earning your way into some higher circle of hell than the one currently reserved in your name." His eyes slid to Markham's white face. "I daresay your secretary would be delighted to assist you in the endeavor."

   A flash of something—anger? fear?—crossed Somerton's expression, so quickly that a less observant man than Roland might have missed it entirely. "Mr. Markham," the earl said, in a silky voice, "is a man of high standards and unimpeachable loyalty. Unlike, for example, my wife."

   "Oh, unimpeachable loyalty, without question," said

Roland, "though I must beg respectfully to differ on the matter of his high standards, eh what?"

"Look here," burst out Markham.

Somerton half turned in the secretary's direction and quelled him with a single look: not fierceness, not anger, but some sort of fleeting tenderness, an exchange of mutual understanding. Markham's eyes cast down, and he took a half step backward. "What an arrogant little coxcomb you are," the earl said, turning to Roland.

Roland shrugged. "One does what one's feeble wits permit."

"Hmm." Somerton stepped away and glanced up the staircase. "And are you not the least bit curious as to the whereabouts and good health of your stolen whore?"

"Egad, old man. I don't quite follow your logic. This dashed old bean of mine. I don't suppose you can possibly refer to that angel, Lady Somerton, whose honor I would defend to my death?"

"The very same."

Roland tapped his forehead and took a few thoughtful steps in the opposite direction, head bent at a pensive angle. "But that means . . . well, my good man, it don't add up. For if the countess, who calls only one fortunate man her beloved, and that only *after* she's decided to end her travesty of a marriage . . . if *she* can be called a whore . . ." He let the sentence dangle.

"Yes, Penhallow?"

Roland straightened and turned back to Somerton, with his most open and innocent expression. "I beg your pardon, but what does that make *you*?"

"Me?" Somerton thundered, incredulous.

"Why, yes. You. Do you deny you've had carnal knowledge of any number of other females, throughout the course of your marriage?" A quick glance at Markham. "Or, as the case directs, *persons*?"

Somerton's right fist crashed into his left palm. "What are you implying, sir? You damned whelp! Say that again!"

Roland spread his hands before him. "Come, now. Common knowledge. I daresay the count must be in the hundreds. Dashed loose behavior, if you ask me."

Somerton stared at him, fist still clenched in his hand, eyes narrowed into slits. The air between them vibrated with tension. Markham took a step forward, hesitated, then took another step.

Something eased in Somerton's face. The flush left his cheeks by gradual degrees, and the hard line of his mouth settled into something that might be called a smile, at least in puppy-kicking circles. "Surely, Penhallow, we're both men of the world. A bit of the pot calling the kettle black, isn't it?"

"What's that? I beg your pardon. I don't quite follow."

Somerton's hands went behind his back. He ambled in Roland's direction, eyes gleaming. "How many wanton beds have you visited in the past few years, eh, Penhallow? Dozens? Hundreds?"

"Oh, that's easy enough." Roland grinned broadly. "None."

The earl threw back his head and laughed. "None! The great Penhallow, debaucher of London's women! Ha-ha. None, indeed."

Roland shrugged. "Awfully sorry to disappoint you, old fellow, but I'm afraid you're barking up the wrong tree. From the day I met Lady Somerton until now, I've known no other woman except her."

The earl's laughter withered into nothing. His eyes searched Roland's face, as if desperate to find something to contradict the ring of sincerity in his words. "Impossible," Somerton said at last in a dry voice.

"No, no. Solid fact, I'm afraid. Tried, a few times, but . . . well, things weren't quite the same as before. Couldn't keep her face out of my mind long enough to perform the deed. Oh, I suppose I might eventually have managed it. Drunk up a bottle or two of brandy, found myself a willing widow." He smiled at Somerton's horror. "But my luck was in, I expect. Her ladyship collided with me on the doorstep of an Italian inn, and even my thick old wits grasped that I'd been given another chance."

"Impossible," Somerton said, without conviction.

"Impossible!" spat out Markham. "We know your reputation. You've paraded your conquests all over London, you damned cur!"

Roland looked past Somerton's shoulder and nodded at the secretary. "Well, I didn't want word getting around, did I? Kept up appearances, that sort of thing. In the end, though—droll, isn't it?—it seems I was truer to Lilibet than you were." He drew close to Somerton, close enough to see the tick of the earl's pulse at his throat, hard and swift. "If I'm not mistaken, that's what they call irony, old chap."

Somerton wet his lips. "For more than six years?"

"Over seven, really, since the day I met her. Seven long, bloody years. A most painful period of penitence. Of which the only good thing I can observe"—he gave Somerton a gentle chuck under the chin—"is to thank God it's finally over."

In the next instant, he was flying across the floor, propelled by the hard crunch of Somerton's fist against his jaw.

H e'd expected it, of course, but the expectation hardly softened the blow. He lay on the marble tiles for a moment, adjusting to the shock, rubbing his jaw. Not broken, at least. He studied the octagonal pattern in the ceiling, elegant plaster scrollwork, looking as if it had recently been repainted, and counted the repeats. "Well, now," he said at last. "I'm frightfully glad *that's* out of the way." He raised himself on his elbows and flashed a smile in Somerton's glowering direction. "Now that the tiresome formalities have been completed, we can get down to business, as the Americans are fond of saying."

Somerton's lip curled into a snarl. "The only business between the two of us, you mongrel, is that which I plan to administer to you. You shall not, I'm afraid, depart this house alive."

Roland sprang to his feet and laughed. "Oh, brilliantly said! I think I heard that in a play, once. Have you perhaps considered a career on the stage?"

Markham's voice, low and worried, emerged from behind Somerton's heaving chest. "Sir, I don't think . . . Surely you don't mean . . ."

Roland spread his arms wide. "There, you see? Have a go at me. Pistols, what? Or perhaps your taste runs to sabers. You've a jolly dramatic streak to you, after all."

"Don't be an ass, Penhallow."

"You wish to kill me? I won't stop you from trying."

"You admit you're in the wrong, then," the earl flashed back.

"Not at all," Roland replied. He let his hands drop to his sides. "But I'm not going to fight you, old man."

A contemptuous look settled into Somerton's austere features. "A coward, then. Just as I thought. You don't even love her well enough to fight for her."

"Oh, I do. If it were only her, you'd be dead already. But there's someone else to consider, you see."

Somerton's brow furrowed. "Someone else?"

"Young Philip. Your son, if you'll recall," said Roland, quite softly.

"You'll not speak to me of my son!" Somerton's fist swung again in reckless fury; Roland dodged it with ease.

"A fine boy, young Philip," Roland went on. "Clever, curious. Rather fancies stories about pirates." He sidestepped another blow. "And the thing is, regardless of the whole sorry wreck of your approach to parenthood"—he skipped away just in time to avoid a vicious cut to his left eye—"I can't quite face the prospect of explaining to Philip how I've managed to kill his father."

Somerton stopped, chest heaving, eyes glittering. "You won't have the chance, by God. You'll never lay eyes on the boy again."

Roland shook his head slowly. "No, no. You've got it all wrong. If you think I'm going to leave Philip in *your* tender care for the rest of his childhood, your poor old noggin must be in even more desperate straits than your fists."

"You *dare* to . . ."

"Here's how it works, Somerton." Roland slid his right

hand to his hip, near his waistcoat pocket. "You're going to give Lilibet her divorce, and I'm going to marry her, and you're going to leave us alone to raise that son of yours into the sort of man who'll recover all the honor the title's lost through you."

Somerton began to laugh, a harsh guttural sound, unlike any other laughter Roland had ever heard. "Oh, splendid! Fascinating! I always knew you were an arrogant young fool, Penhallow, but now I begin to wonder how you managed so long, even with that pack of idiots at the Bureau!"

"Oh, dumb luck, I expect." Roland fingered the edge of the waistcoat pocket in an idle gesture.

"And you suppose—you really suppose—I'll simply bow to your commands? When Lady Somerton and my son remain firmly within my power? When you yourself lack the courage even to raise your fist against me?" Somerton shook his head and laughed again. "Give up, Penhallow. You'll never take me, and you'll never have my wife unless you do." He leaned forward with a skull-like grin. "Checkmate."

Roland smiled and shrugged and sidled away. "But there it is, old chap. I don't have to take the king, in this little match. I only have to take"—he sprang toward Markham, secured the man against his chest, and drew the slender knife from his waistcoat pocket, all in the same fluid motion—"your knight."

From the panic in Somerton's face, from the unguarded lunge he took in their direction, Roland knew he'd chosen his target wisely. He pressed the tip of the knife into Markham's collar and dragged him backward. "Not so close, Somerton. You've led me the devil of a dance, and I should hate to lose my wits and cause one of those messy sorts of accidents, so common in our profession."

"You wouldn't dare."

"Oh, damn," Roland said, "I believe the knife just slipped. I'm so dreadfully clumsy."

"Sir . . ." Markham squeaked. His body pressed slight

and rigid against Roland's chest, no movement whatever. A tiny drop of blood welled up against the tip of the knife.

"What soft, pale skin he's got," Roland went on amiably. "Does he scar easily, do you think? I once knew a man like that. Every little nick left a mark. I expect his mistress could scarcely bear to look at him."

"Bastard," growled Somerton. His face had calmed into wary readiness, eyes trained on Roland's, fingers flexing at his sides.

"You're a reasonable man, Somerton. You know how much she means to me. How little this fellow *here*"—he gave Markham a friendly jiggle, causing Somerton's breath to draw in sharply—"means to me. Is your silly vengeance really worth poor Markham's young life? So much promise, such a handsome new seedling torn from its roots, such a perfect stain blotted out . . . no, hold a moment, I've got that wrong . . . such a . . ."

"*Stop.*" The earl's voice was dry, hoarse, fierce. The fear had returned to his eyes and to the slant of his brows. The force of it surprised even Roland.

"Oh, I've no *wish* to slit his throat," Roland said. "But I've no wish to have my own slit, either, or to see the woman I love suffer one more jot by your hand. So I suggest you make haste, my good man, up that staircase. I'll follow along with our friend, at a discreet distance, until we reach the room where you've got—let me see if I've understood this properly—an innocent woman and her helpless son imprisoned."

Somerton's lips parted. He stood there a long moment, perfectly steady, as if the mind behind his masklike face weren't engaged in the battle of its life. He glanced briefly, almost pleadingly, at Markham's face, and then back up to Roland. "You're a damned bloody bastard, Penhallow," he said at last.

"No more than you," said Roland kindly. "Lead on, then."

Somerton turned and trod to the stairs, taking each step as if it led to the scaffold. Roland followed him with Markham in tow, keeping a good ten stairs below the earl, keeping his eyes fixed on Somerton's broad shoulders for any sign of unexpected movement. The shoulders always betrayed a man first.

But no muscle so much as twitched along the vast expanse of tweed jacket, as they climbed to the first-floor landing and the second. Somerton walked to the end of a wide hallway and came to rest in front of a door.

"It's locked, of course?" Roland inquired.

Somerton nodded and produced a key.

"Unlock it," said Roland.

Somerton raised his hand like an automaton and then shook his head. "No. Release Markham first, and I'll give you the key."

"Oh, rubbish." Roland laughed and shook his head. "I've been at this game for seven bloody years. I know better than that. Unlock the door and produce my fiancée—unharmed, I hardly need add—and you'll have your precious secretary back."

"No. Release him first."

Roland pressed the knife against Markham's throat, causing a yelp of distress from the secretary.

Somerton stepped forward. "Damn you! You'll pay for that!"

"Hardly," Roland said. "A drop or two of blood is easily removed with a good soak of cold water. *Cold*, mind you. Anything warmer and it's set for life."

Somerton's face had gone as pale as a parsnip. "Release him *now*, Penhallow. You have what you want."

"No, I haven't."

"For all I know, you'll kill him . . ."

Roland rolled his eyes. "Oh, for God's sake," he said, and stepped forward, raised his booted foot, and crashed the door down.

"What the bloody . . ."

Before Somerton could react, Roland flung Markham before him into the room and jumped after him over the broken door.

He dragged Markham back onto his feet, back against his own chest, and cast wildly about the room.

A rocking chair, a ball, a stack of toys in the corner. A settee, a few chairs, a table with a lamp. A faint hint of lavender in the air, mingling with the spicy scent of cypress drifting from the open window.

But no Lilibet. And no Philip.

TWENTY-FOUR

The Palazzo Angelini might have been designed by Palladio, Lilibet thought grimly, but the garden was pure Machiavelli.

At least Philip was enjoying himself.

"This is a jolly splendid maze," he said cheerfully, running back to her after looking around the next corner. "Can we plant one at our castle? I'll bet Uncle Roland could lay out a cracking big maze."

She tucked a tendril of hair behind her ear. She'd left her hat back in Philip's room—who thought of hats when shimmying down a length of rope to the balcony below?—and the sun beat down against her uncovered head, causing perspiration to trickle along her temples and down the front of her dress. She could only hope the dark color of her hair would blend in with her surroundings better than a pale straw hat and make her less visible from the villa behind them.

Though she doubted Somerton himself could find them in this maze.

"The thing to do with mazes," Philip said importantly, "is to turn right at every corner." He trotted along at her side, apparently untouched by heat or exhaustion or confusion.

"Really? Are you sure?"

"Dead sure. It was in a book, I think. Uncle Roland read it to me, so it must be right. Look at that bird!"

She gripped his hand. "Stay with me, darling. We can't get lost." She rounded the next corner, and a new set of tall dark green walls loomed up around them, exactly the same as before. Her heart gave a desperate stab. Who knew if they were heading the right direction? The ground was flat, the hedges high. Dashing across the stone terrace to the lawn, she'd seen the red-tile roof of the Duomo just peeking up above the trees to her left; now, in the middle of the maze, it had slipped away from view. Were they making progress? Were they backtracking? The sun made a hot white light in the pale sky; too high yet to find her direction.

She hurried forward with Philip's hand firm and damp in her own. She'd thought herself rather ingenious, unwinding the long length of rope from a spool on one of Philip's toys. Slender rope, designed for playtime, but strong: secured to the heavy settee, it had borne her weight down to the first-floor balcony, and then Philip's little body as she waited anxiously for him at the bottom, arms outstretched to receive him. She'd flown through terrace and lawn with a surge of elation at her easy escape from Somerton's clutches—how astonished, how mortified he'd be, when he found them gone—and now here she was, stumbling through the shrubbery without the faintest idea where she was headed.

Keep turning right, Philip had said.

She was trusting their lives to his five-year-old memory.

A wall of green leaves reared up before her: blind alley. "Come along," she said, almost jerking Philip backward and then to the right, to the right again, blind alley, right turn, the air still and hot around her body, the smell of leaves and cypress heavy in her nose, the sunbaked dirt like pavement beneath her feet. She turned right again, wheeling them both around the corner, and with breathtaking suddenness a vast green lawn opened before her, descending in a gentle slope to a crumbling stone terrace overlooking the sluggish mud brown waters of the Arno.

* * *

Roland's shocked arm released Markham, who slid to the ground with an inglorious thump. He spun around to face Somerton. "Where the devil are they? Speak up, man! What the devil sort of trick is this?"

But he could see, already, that it was no trick. The last drop of blood had drained from Somerton's face, and his eyes were wide with astonishment. The earl strode to the window, picked up the length of rope stretching from the leg of the settee, and leaned his broad shoulders out the window. "It appears," he said, straightening, sounding unnaturally calm, "they've outmaneuvered us both."

"Outmaneuvered *you*, you mean," Roland said. "Both of us, indeed. I refuse to accept any blame for this. What the devil were you thinking, keeping a length of rope in the room? Why not the proverbial series of bedsheets to knot together, for God's sake? They might have been killed!"

Somerton rolled his eyes. "There's a balcony below. They were in no danger at all."

Markham stood up and dusted his sleeves. "Shall I go to the garden and fetch them?" he asked.

"The devil you will!" Roland said, starting for the door. "I'll find them myself, by God, and end this damned charade."

"Though not, of course, if I find them first."

Roland stopped and spun around just in time to catch the top of the earl's head as it disappeared below the window, dragging the settee with a pane-rattling crash against the wall.

"Bloody hell," Roland shouted, and ran for the door.

He flew down the stairs, not caring whether or not Markham were following him, his legs moving in a blur. Fear gave him agility; at the next landing, he launched himself over the banister to land midway down the next flight, and leapt down the remaining stairs two at a time.

At the last step he nearly tripped, and staggered into the entrance hall with his feet just under him. He rounded the corner of the staircase and ran to the row of French doors at the back of the hall, rattled the knobs, found one that opened with a groan of old hinges, and lurched through and onto the terrace.

A wide, shallow lawn stood before him, followed by a formal garden exploding with June blooms, crisscrossed by an elegant symmetry of graveled pathways. No sign of Somerton nor Markham. Had they already passed through? Were they headed in another direction?

He hesitated an instant, raising his arm to shield his contracting pupils from the white glare of the sun. Where would Lilibet have gone? To the road, or through the gardens and down to the river?

She'd want to stay hidden, he knew intuitively. They'd be spotted straightaway on the road. Along the riverside, away from the bustle of traffic, they had a much better chance of making their way back into town unnoticed.

Decision made, he bolted across the terrace and down the lawn to the garden, weaving his way around the burgeoning beds, gravel crunching and splaying beneath the hard soles of his riding boots. The ground before him was marred with footsteps: Lilibet and Philip? Somerton and Markham? Both?

He reached the back of the garden and a tall hedge stood before him; to the right, he thought he saw a gap in the dense thicket of leaves. He ran toward it, ducked through, and cursed.

A maze. A bloody maze. Just like the ones back home, in every damned stately home worth its salt; just like the one in the formal gardens of his brother's magnificent old pile in Cumberland.

Clever way to keep the riffraff from the river away from the house, of course. He couldn't blame its ancient owner.

He just wanted to rattle the man's throat.

He knew his way around a maze, of course. The trick was simple: Keep your right hand out, brushing the leaves, and follow it along. Sooner or later you'd emerge at the end.

Preferably sooner, of course, than later.

He took off at a trot, right hand outstretched, skipping

the obvious blind alleys. Around he went, feeling by instinct as he drew closer to the center of the maze, then outward again. The heat of the day began to soak through his jacket, prickling against his skin. He'd lost his hat somewhere—the entrance hall, probably, when Somerton had laid him on the floor—and the sun seemed to penetrate all the layers of hair and scalp to bathe his brain in suffocating warmth. He took off his jacket, slung it over his shoulder with his left index finger, and strode on around the next right-hand corner.

As if by signal, some eleven thousand or so nearby birds began to clamor all at once, hard and shrill, and he burst from the maze to another lawn, another terrace, the Arno a strip of dull brown silk beyond; and Somerton, dragging a kicking Philip in one arm and a pleading Lilibet in the other, looking as if he'd much rather drown them both in the river behind him.

L ilibet saw Roland's hair first, returning the light of the sun like a halo, or a golden helmet. Like Apollo, except corporeal and frightfully late.

Joy, fear, relief, exaltation: The rush of emotions stopped her breath in her chest. Somerton's arm wrapped around her shoulders like a band of steel; she fought to crane her neck, to see Roland better, to reassure herself that he was really there.

"Oh, look!" she exclaimed in triumph. "Roland's here!"

Somerton's body went slack for an instant, and she swung her fist with all her might into the general region of his kidneys. Philip dropped like a stone into the grass.

"Run, Philip!" she shouted. "Run for the maze!"

"Uncle Roland!" the boy called, and pelted up the slope, arms outstretched. Roland knelt and took him full force, wrapping his long arms around the boy, bending his head to Philip's ear. Lilibet's eyes stung with tears. All at once the pieces fell into place, the world adjusted itself on its axis, the doubts and qualms dissolved into a sense of almost painful rightness.

"You see!" she hissed at Somerton. "You see how he is with him! He loves him!" She couldn't help it, couldn't help wanting to taunt her husband, to force the bitter cup to his lips and make him drink. At the moment, she had nothing in her heart for the Earl of Somerton except anger and vengeance.

She started forward, but Somerton, recovering from the blow, reached out and snared her. "Vicious little thing, aren't you," he said, his voice still raw with physical pain, and yet oddly calm. As if the sight before his eyes didn't bother him at all.

"Let me go!" she panted. "Can't you see it's hopeless? Can't you see you won't win?"

"He shan't have you," Somerton said in her ear. "By God, he shan't."

"Then kill me! Kill him! Kill us all! What the devil do you mean by all this? Do you think to save your pride with revenge?" She took in a short breath, and another, her lungs unable to catch themselves in the fear and panic overwhelming her. "It won't work. It never works. Revenge is hollow; don't you know that, by now?"

He gave her a shake and didn't reply.

"That's it, isn't it?" she whispered. "You haven't a clue what to do with us. You can't bring yourself to let us go, but you can't bring yourself to end it all. You're a coward, Somerton. A bully and a coward."

A look of fury crossed his face. He raised one arm, and she closed her eyes, expecting the blow to land on her cheek, her head, her jaw.

But nothing happened.

His arm remained stiff underneath her, holding her firmly. She opened her eyes and saw that he was staring into the distance, down the side of the river, his thick black eyebrows raised high with disbelief.

Hands grasped her—warm, tender hands, Roland's hands, she knew without asking. She gave herself up to them, and Somerton's arm relinquished her without a fight.

"Lilibet," came Roland's familiar voice in her ear, low

and full with emotion, and she turned herself into his hot, sun-drenched chest with a sob. "You're all right, darling?"

"Yes," she managed to whisper.

He pulled her away, out of Somerton's reach, and held her in place. His body rang with tension against hers, taut and ready, smelling of soap and horses and perspiration. He felt like a hunting dog, poised for the kill.

"Philip?" she heard herself say, in a voice too thin and high to possibly belong to her.

"Hush. At the top of the lawn." His arms loosened; his lips pressed against the top of her head, against her temple. "Go to him, darling. Now."

"But . . ." She lifted her head, confused.

"*Now*. Run." He wasn't looking at her at all; he was gazing with narrow eyes in the same direction as Somerton had, down along the side of the river.

She turned and looked.

A man was walking down the riverside path, stepping just now onto the flagstones of the terrace, tall and straight-backed and steely, his hair liberally peppered with gray and his body clothed in English tweed.

Behind his broad figure, Lilibet could just glimpse the familiar slight shape of her husband's secretary, Mr. Markham, before he disappeared into the brush.

S omerton's voice cut through the heavy air like a saber. "What the devil are you doing here, Olympia?"

"Your grandfather!" exclaimed Lilibet, against Roland's chest.

"Go *now*, sweetheart," he hissed in her ear. He loosened his arms and gave her a little push. "Go to Philip."

His grandfather's familiar voice rang out from the edge of the terrace. "I might ask the same of you, Somerton. Good God, what a cock-up you've made of things."

"Things? What things?" demanded Roland. He stepped forward and crossed his arms. What had Beadle said? That Somerton had sent a cable to the Duke of Olympia after arriving in Florence? And his connection to the Castel sant'Agata: What was that about? He understood his grand-father well enough to know with certainty that these scraps of information didn't constitute a mere coincidence.

The duke came to a stop and leaned on a gold-knobbed walking stick, his eyes flashing back and forth between Roland and Somerton. It was a pose, of course; Roland knew he needed no assistance to stand upright. His grand-father had the strength of an ox.

"What *things*, Grandfather?" Roland demanded again.

The duke's gaze shifted to him. "Perhaps our good friend the earl would care to explain. Eh, Somerton? What of it?"

"I don't know what you mean," said Somerton. Roland couldn't see his face, but his stance was all belligerence: legs spread, arms crossed, brow jutting forward like an ancient warrior.

The duke sighed. "Come now, my good man. I'm far too old and cantankerous for gamesmanship. When I agreed to clear the field for you, all those years ago . . ."

"What's that?" Roland took a step forward. "What did you say? Clear the field?"

"Somerton?" the duke inquired, but the earl only shook his head in a brief violent motion.

"Somebody *talk*," Roland said, in his most menacing growl: rather like his drawl, really, except in a much lower register. He glanced up the hill to see Lilibet kneeling with Philip in her arms, brow furrowed with worry. Could she hear them?

"Very well. If the earl is reluctant to speak of it himself." The duke placed his other hand on top of the first, as if set-tling down for a long story. "I expect you'll be rather cross about this, Roland, my boy, so spare me your imprecations until I've finished."

"*Talk*, Grandfather."

A shrug. "Quite simple, really. Somerton, my friend and colleague, approached me seven summers ago with what seemed, at the time, a fine proposal: that I should put your

name forward to the Bureau as a recruit of exemplary promise. That he had a sensitive matter arising in Norway, in
which the Navy must not, at all costs, appear to be involved,
and for which you, Roland, were ideally suited."

"By God!" Roland ground the words out.

Olympia held up one hand. "Old as I am, I'm no fool," he
said, "and I quite perceived the real motivation behind my
colleague's suggestion. But you see, I rather agreed with it."

Roland's hands balled into fists. The enormity of it all
began to unfold before him, with all its consequences. "You
agreed? You let me fall into his trap, let me leave, knowing
full well that . . ."

"You were far too young for marriage, my boy," the duke
said sharply. "Far too young. You were idle, purposeless.
Not a fit husband at all for a woman like that." He nodded in
Lilibet's direction. "Within a year, you'd have become bored
and restless. You'd have made her miserable."

"Not so miserable as her husband did," Roland bit out.

Somerton burst out at last. "Damn you for that!"

"It's true! She's had six years of hell, all because you
thought I wasn't ready for marriage! What the devil were
you thinking, delivering her to a man like that? We were in
love, we . . ."

"Yes, yes. In love and all that rot; quite moving. In hind-
sight, perhaps I might have done better. But you can't deny,
my dear boy," the duke went on, his voice softening, "it's
been the making of you. You're ten times the man you were
before. You'd been indulged, had nothing but privilege and
entitlement. You needed challenge. You needed hardship."

"Who were you, to decide that for me? Who were you,
to decide for Lilibet?"

The duke replaced his hands on the knob of his walking
stick, curling them around each other. His blue eyes seemed
to reach into the distance. "I was married at eighteen," he
said. "The results were not happy."

"I am not the Duke of Olympia," said Roland quietly.

"No, you are not." The duke turned his gaze to Somerton. "And you, young man. You've made a regular botch of

things, haven't you? I lay a prize like that at your feet"—he waved his hand up the slope, toward Lilibet—"and you haven't the faintest notion how to treat her. You and your damned whores, by God. Ought to have you thrashed."

"See here . . ." began Somerton.

"And then there's the matter of how you came to be plotting against my grandson." The duke stabbed his walking stick into the ground with a violent thrust. "The same man you recruited for Bureau work; the same man from whom you had me steal your own bride! You've a great deal to answer for, by God!"

Roland's hand smacked into his palm. "You've both a great deal to answer for! *You!*" He spun to Somerton, gathered the man's shirt in his fist, and snarled in a most un-Penhallow-like manner. "You *stole* her from me, you filthy scoundrel! Wronged husband, my arse! She was *mine!*"

"Say that again," Somerton said, in a menacing growl. His black eyes lit with fury. "Say that again, Penhallow."

Roland tightened his grip, until his nose nearly touched the earl's. "I'll say it till doomsday. I'll . . ."

The duke's walking stick poked sharply between them. "See here, you young fools," he said sharply. "We'll have none of this. Not in front of the women and children."

Roland gave Somerton's jacket another shake and released it. The men stepped apart, hackles raised, steps wary, like two dogs in a ring.

"The sins of the past are finished," said the duke. "Irrevocable. Nothing to be done about them."

"I'll tell you what's to be done about them," said Somerton. "I'm going to tear his every bloody limb . . ."

"You won't. What the devil use would it be? It's finished, Somerton. You had your chance with her."

"*Honor*, Olympia." The earl sneered. "A foreign notion to the two of you, perhaps, but one I happen to prize highly."

"Honor? You don't know what it means," said Roland. "What sort of honor demands ruining the lives of others in order to salve one's wounded pride? An honorable man would do the opposite. An honorable man would allow his unhappy wife to make her own choice. An honorable man would act in generosity, not in meanness."

"I . . ." Somerton faltered. He looked between Roland and the duke, shoulders braced as if under siege, and then glanced up the hill, where his wife and son stood huddled at the entrance to the maze, gazing down at them.

"Give up, Somerton," said the duke, in a low voice. "Bow out gracefully, while you can. For if you don't, you know . . ."

Somerton's shoulders, improbably, relaxed. He straightened his legs and his back, and raised one thick eyebrow at the duke. "If I don't? The so-honorable Penhallow, here, has already refused to fight for the woman he professes to love."

"If you mean that I won't face down the father of a five-year-old boy at twenty paces, you're right," said Roland. "But be warned, Somerton: If I must, I'll defend Lilibet and Philip, by whatever means."

His words dangled in the air, quiet and heavy.

"But there won't be any need for that sort of thing, will there, Somerton?" The duke's voice wrapped around them like velvet. He stared at the earl with eyes such a bright, clear blue they seemed to leap forth from his lined face. His hand tightened around the knob of his walking stick.

"I don't know what you mean," Somerton said, in a guarded voice that signified he knew exactly what the duke meant.

Roland shifted his stance, sent a lightning glance toward Lilibet and Philip, and returned his gaze to his grandfather and Somerton. Understanding began to dawn within him, that they'd only scratched the surface of what lay between these two. That in the endless coils of intrigue that made up Her Majesty's intelligence services, the Duke of Olympia and the Earl of Somerton were deeply entangled.

And he wasn't going to be told the least bit about it.

At last, as if by some predetermined agreement, the duke reached into his pocket and removed a roll of papers. "Do you know what this is, Somerton?" he asked.

The earl folded his arms. "I expect I do."

The duke tapped the edge with his right forefinger. "You never contested it, did you? You never planned to contest it."

"Of course not. Why should I? That wasn't the point."

"What does he mean?" Roland demanded. He took a step forward, reaching. "What is it?"

The duke shook his head. He looked up the hill to Lilibet and beckoned with one finger.

"By damn." Roland glanced at Somerton's impassive face. He'd turned his attention to the river, where a boatful of tourists was passing by, laughing and raucous, their voices traveling with incongruous clarity across the still air. The water rippled behind them in silken brown waves.

Roland looked up the hill. Lilibet had risen and was bending down to instruct Philip. *Stay here*, he imagined her telling him. *Don't wander off. I'll only be a moment.*

Her arrival cracked the brittle silence among the three men. "Here you are, my dear," said the duke, more kindly than Roland had ever heard him speak. He unrolled the papers and placed them in her outstretched hand.

She stared a moment, scanning the page before her, and looked up at Somerton, at the duke, her face helpless with shock. "I don't . . . I don't understand . . ."

"What is it?" demanded Roland.

Her blue eyes found his at last. "It's the decree nisi," she whispered.

"What's that?"

"The preliminary decree of divorce," said the duke. "Granted four days ago, at the court in London. I met privately with the judge, a right old fellow; my fag at Eton, as it happens. He's agreed to issue the decree absolute in one month, if there are no objections lodged."

"*One month?*" Lilibet asked. Her eyes went round, staring at the duke as if he were mad.

"What does that mean?" asked Roland. He grasped her shoulder. "What does that mean?"

She looked at him. "Six months. It's usually six months, except in extraordinary circumstances." Her eyes returned to the duke. "How did you . . . ?"

"My dear," he said, looking wise, "don't you think these circumstances are extraordinary indeed?"

"And you . . . you spoke to him . . ."

He took her hand. "I had a word with your husband's solicitors, my dear. With my old friend, the judge. He kindly agreed to move the suit through as quickly as possible, to spare both petitioner and respondent any unnecessary pain."

She turned to Somerton. "And you agreed?" she asked, in a hoarse voice. "You allowed the petition to continue, unchallenged?"

Somerton made a mocking little bow. "As I believe I informed your ladyship, I had no objections to the divorce itself. Your facts were all quite in order. I have committed adultery. I have, I suppose, been cruel."

"You only object to *me*, then," said Roland sharply.

"Yes." The earl met his gaze, and the hatred in his eyes seemed to scour Roland's face, pure and ruthless. "Lord Roland Penhallow. Pretty, brilliant Penhallow, born under Fortune's star, adored by all England. I saw her first, did you know? At the river party in Richmond, dazzling, outshining everyone else in her beauty and innocence. A rose unplucked, its petals yet unfurled. But before I had the chance to beg for an introduction, you'd swept her away into the shrubbery, with your damned golden smile and your *charm*." He said the word *charm* with a snarl, as if it were an obscenity.

"You're mad," Roland said.

"She hadn't a chance, after that. I watched her fall under your spell, you silly ass, all summer long. Do you know how close I was to murdering you? I might have done it a hundred times, as you walked back from your club, from a ball, from a dinner. No one would have known."

"*I* would have known," said the duke, "and by God I'd have seen you hanged for it."

Somerton didn't seem to notice. "Until I hit upon the perfect scheme. The Norway caper fell into my lap like a ripe plum, and your grandfather"—he spared a sneer at the duke—"went along with things more easily than I might have dreamed."

"What's this? The *Norway* caper? I thought . . . But he

was fishing for *salmon*!" Lilibet's voice was incredulous, desperate. She said again, in a whisper: "Salmon."

"Fishing for salmon!" Somerton laughed. "Good God, madam. Haven't you discovered it yet? It only took you a month or two, with me."

Roland put his hand on her arm. "Darling, I couldn't tell you . . ."

Her white face turned to his. "You can't mean . . . all this time . . ." Her stammering voice, the disbelief in her eyes, cut Roland to the quick.

"It's what I've been trying to explain. That my conduct, since that summer, since your marriage, was all part of the disguise. To cover . . ."

"To cover, or rather to excuse, his activities as an agent for the Bureau of Trade and Maritime Information," said Somerton, in a bored voice, staring at Roland. "An inferior organization, of course, but I could hardly propose an untried boy for anything more sophisticated. But Sir Edward took him in, at His Grace's urging. It all went exactly according to plan, except . . ." He shrugged, his mouth curling with disgust.

"Except?" demanded Lilibet, hands on hips.

He turned to her. "Except he wasn't supposed to survive it, my dear. I must admit, I gave the boy too little credit. I forgot that Fortune forever smiles on the Penhallows of the world. Yes, he outwitted Europe's most deadly assassin, rot him, and returned home in triumph, the Bureau's most promising new agent in years. And not a moment too late."

Quick as a flash, Lilibet's hand struck Somerton across the face, nearly knocking him sideways with its unexpected force. "Damn you!" she hissed.

Roland stepped before her, shielding her with his body before Somerton could strike back. But the earl merely touched his finger to the corner of his mouth, wiping away the tiny smear of blood that appeared there, and smiled at her. "I suppose I deserve that," he said, looking not at all penitent. "In any case, I had you. He was too proud, or too cowardly, to attempt to win you back. Yes, I had you first," he finished softly.

"And never will again," she whispered.

He looked on her a moment longer, his expression inscrutable, his eyebrows drawn together as if in deep thought. The blood coursed angrily through Roland's veins. What was he thinking? Of his wedding night? Of all those other nights with Lilibet, with his stolen bride? Roland's fingers itched to close around the earl's thick throat, to strangle the life out of him. Only the thought of Philip stopped his hands. Philip sitting cross-legged on the lawn, picking idly at the grass, glancing up at a passing cloud. Had he seen his mother strike the earl?

Roland closed his arm around Lilibet's shoulder, drawing her next to him, and took a step backward. "Stay out of our lives," he said. "I don't want to see you again. I don't want to see you near Lilibet, or the boy."

Somerton's face flashed awake. "Spirited words, my boy. But you forget, we have a score to settle, you and I. Perhaps I won't have our dear Elizabeth again, Penhallow. But neither will you."

"I believe the score's already settled, Somerton. And you've lost. I *shall* have her, if she'll have me. Shall have her and hold her, with all the love you've denied her, all these years."

"Will you?" Once again, his eyebrow lifted. Roland felt an urge to pound it off his face. "Must I remind you that the document in her ladyship's hands is merely a decree nisi? A month remains, before our union is dissolved. A month in which new evidence can be brought before the court, to dismiss the suit out of hand."

"There is no new evidence," said the duke, a little too sharply.

"Isn't there?" Somerton turned to him with an air of surprise. "Why, I have Lord Roland's own assurance of carnal knowledge with my wife. I have her corroboration. Adultery by the petitioner nullifies any claim of matrimonial causes against the respondent, does it not?"

"Hardly admissible proof, a private conversation," said the duke.

Somerton's eyes narrowed. "I say, Your Grace. I believe I detect a certain air of unease." He looked back at Roland, at Lilibet. "Is there something the three of you wish to disclose?"

"Nothing," Lilibet said, too swiftly.

"Don't talk rot, Somerton," said Roland.

Somerton spun back to the duke. "What is it, man? What are you hiding? This haste of yours. Special circumstances, you said. What are they, then?"

"Nothing!" Lilibet snapped.

Roland could feel her rising panic. He squeezed her with his arm, trying to reassure her. She'd give them away, if she didn't calm down. Somerton would look at her closely, would search her . . .

But it was too late. The slow rake of Somerton's eyes began at her forehead and worked slowly down, noting (how could he not?) the bloom in her cheeks, the fullness of her bosom, the strain of her jacket buttons over her rounded middle. Roland tried to turn her away, to spare her the inspection, but it was the sort of thing one couldn't hide. To a suspicious eye, the evidence was obvious.

"By God," whispered Somerton. "By God."

The duke's cane interceded just in time, pushing him back. "You've no right, Somerton," he said quietly. "Penhallow, my boy, keep her back!"

Roland turned her about, keeping her shaking body under his arm, urging her back up the hill to make her safe, out of Somerton's reach. He could deal with the earl later.

"Is it mine?" Somerton demanded, behind him. "Is it mine, by God?"

Roland felt the change in her body an instant too late. With sudden resolution, Lilibet ducked under his arm, before he could grab her back. "No!" she screamed. "It's *mine*! It's mine and Roland's, our baby, and you shan't have it! You miserable beast, you . . . you . . ." She heaved for breath, as Somerton's face grew purple with rage. "It's

Roland's baby, you cuckold, you monster! Roland's, do you hear me? And every baby after it, every one, will be his, and you can take that knowledge to hell with you!"

The duke stood before Somerton, holding his walking stick at each end, pressing it against the earl's burly chest in an effort to restrain him. Roland started forward, just as the duke gave way, slipped in the grass, and Somerton burst free, his black eyes wild.

Roland slipped his knife out of his pocket and held it in his hand, balancing on the balls of his feet, waiting for Somerton. He heard Lilibet scream behind him, but he kept his eyes steady on the earl's approaching body, tracing his every move, every flick of his eyes. Readiness: the first thing Sir Edward had taught him.

But at the last instant, Somerton pulled back.

"What's this?" he asked. "A knife?" His gaze traveled behind Roland, to rest on some distant object. He nodded and smiled. "Why, I believe Philip can see us. How edifying a spectacle for a young boy. Tell me, where are your principles now, Penhallow?"

Roland straightened. The earl's face had lost its fury; he looked merely amused, that faint sarcastic smile lifting the corner of his thin mouth. Everything behind him had gone still. He wanted to look around, to see if Lilibet had gone up to Philip, but he couldn't take his eyes off Somerton for an instant.

Behind the earl, his grandfather was rising slowly to his feet, shaking his head, his hair a white shock against the backdrop of brown water and distant shore. He turned to face them, taking in the situation. He met Roland's eyes and nodded, once.

Roland felt his shoulders ease with relief. Now he had only to distract Somerton. "You're right," he said. He tossed the knife into the grass. "No blood. No fighting. No . . ."

He hadn't the chance to say more. Somerton bent down in a fluid motion, picked up the knife, and charged.

Right past Roland, toward Lilibet and Philip.

TWENTY-FIVE

She heard the footsteps behind her in a strange slowed-down rhythm, each noise distinct, *thump thump thump* on the dry, sun-beaten turf.

She knew what was happening. She knew she couldn't stop him. The impact drew near, raising expectant prickles on her skin. She bent, wrapping her arms around her middle, protecting the tiny life inside her.

A loud thump, a muffled shout. Something blunt, an elbow perhaps, knocked her between her shoulder blades. She staggered forward, just keeping her feet, and turned around.

The two men rolled around in the grass, Roland and Somerton, wrestling for control of the knife that flashed in and out of her vision, in Somerton's thick fist. "Stop!" she screamed. "Stop!"

Useless, of course. They rolled down the hill together, pulled by gravity and the inexorable rhythm of the fight, of the shifting balance of power. They fought like boys, she thought wildly. Fingers poked into eyes, knees shoved into groins. She would have rolled her eyes and let them go at it, except for that knife, that slim, deadly knife, clutched in her husband's hand and wavering like a snake between them.

"Stop them!" she screamed at the duke, past the dry taste of fear in her mouth, but he only stared, ready and watchful. They were moving too fast, of course. He couldn't do anything, for fear of hurting the wrong man.

The combatants reached the flat stone surface of the terrace, and Roland sprang away, landing on his feet in a movement of pure athletic grace. Somerton rose and lunged, knife outstretched toward Roland's gut, but he dodged the thrust. He backed away in wary movements, each step farther away, closer to the edge of the water. *He's leading Somerton away*, she realized. Away from her and Philip.

"Go!" someone yelled at her. Amid the grunts and shouts of the fighting, she couldn't tell if it was Roland or the duke or . . . was it someone else? "Run! Take the boy!" She cast about and saw her husband's secretary, Mr. Markham, standing at the opposite edge of the terrace, hands cupped about his mouth.

She swayed with indecision, unable to leave Roland, desperate to keep Philip safe, to protect him from the sight of his father fighting with the man he'd grown to love. Motherhood won out. She turned up the hill.

It took her a second or two to realize that the entrance to the maze stood empty. No sign of Philip, no sign at all.

"Watch him! Watch him!" someone yelled from behind her, the duke or Markham, and she spun around.

Her son was pelting down the hill, toward the terrace.

"Philip! No!" she screamed.

He went on running, screaming something incoherent, his little legs churning like pistons in the grass. Roland turned, with a father's instinct, to the sound of the boy's voice, and Somerton took instant advantage, thrusting forward to his unguarded middle.

"No!" Philip yelled. He rammed into Somerton full force, pushing him off-balance. The earl took a staggered step sideways, and another. He put his hand out on the crumbling stone balustrade, and it gave way beneath him, sending him tumbling downward with a shout into the swift muddy waters of the Arno.

They hung arrested, all four of them, shock running in a tangible current between their bodies: Lilibet, Roland, the duke, Markham. A bird squawked angrily into the silence, erupting from a nearby tree in an explosion of feathers.

Philip picked himself up from the terrace, looking dazed, and stared off into the gap in the balustrade. Another piece of stone broke off and fell into the water with a gulping splash. "Father?" he squeaked.

"Good God," said Roland. He leapt to the edge of the terrace and glanced down.

"Is he . . . is he . . ." Lilibet couldn't get the words out.

Roland turned to the duke. "My boots," he said, but Markham moved first, flying to Roland's feet and tugging at the dusty scuffed leather with expert hands. The right one came off, and the left, and Roland rose, his white shirt blinding in the sun, and dove into the water.

The clean sound of the splash sent a spark of life through Lilibet's frozen body. She rushed to the river, gripping the edge of the balustrade with both hands, Markham at her side.

Somerton's body had already floated some ten or twenty yards downstream in the brisk current. He was either dead or unconscious; his arms and legs made no movement to keep him afloat, no attempt to direct his progress down the river.

Roland stroked with mechanical speed, using the current to launch himself toward the earl. He reached him in less than half a minute, thrust out his long arms to enclose Somerton's chest, just below the arms, and lifted his head from the coursing water.

Lilibet gasped. Blood rolled down, red and livid, from a wound at his temple. His head slumped to the side, against Roland's arm.

A hand settled on her shoulder, and the duke's voice murmured in her ear. "Don't fret. A head wound bleeds more than it's worth."

Roland made for shore, swimming on his back as he supported Somerton in his arms, his legs moving powerfully through the water. Markham turned and ran along the terrace, down the steps, on the path by the riverside. Lilibet made as if to follow them, but the duke's hand tightened on her shoulder. "No," he said softly. "Let Markham do it. Stay here with the boy."

She looked downward, where her son clutched at her legs, his fingers gripping her tightly through the thin wool of her skirt. "Oh, darling," she whispered, and bent to pick him up.

His head burrowed into her shoulder, warm and wet with tears. "I'm sorry," he sniffed. His voice was tiny, lost within the weave of her jacket. "I'm sorry. I didn't mean it. He was hurting Uncle Roland. I'm sorry."

"It's all right, darling, it's all right. My brave boy."

"Is he dead? Is he dead?"

"No! No, of course not! He's not dead, darling. Uncle Roland's got him. Uncle Roland will bring him in. He'll be just fine."

Please, God, let him be fine.

She craned her neck to see the riverbank, twenty or thirty yards away, where Markham stood knee-deep in the water, no regard at all for his boots, arms outstretched. The end of the balustrade blocked her view of the river. She saw Roland's wet head appear above the smooth stone, gold muted to brown; saw Markham move forward to meet him; saw them struggle, presumably with Somerton's bulky body. The two heads moved together, bobbing and flashing between the pillars of the balustrade, and then all three of them came into view on the riverbank.

Roland's arms were still bound around Somerton's chest; Markham set his feet down with a heavy thump in the beaten path. She pressed Philip's head into her shoulder. "They've got him out now, darling," she said.

"Is he dead? Is he dead?" Philip's face squirmed against her, unable to look for himself.

She opened her mouth to reply. Somerton's body hung limply from Roland's arms. Roland was saying something to Markham, and was thrusting upward with his arms, against Somerton's chest, again and again. Markham had taken out his handkerchief and was pressing it into Somerton's white forehead, wiping at the streaming blood. "No, of course not," she said faintly. Her veins felt as if they were full of air instead of blood. Her legs began to wobble. This couldn't be real; it couldn't be happening. "Of course he's alive. Of course he's alive. He's just resting a moment."

Please, God, let him be alive.

The duke started forward to join the men on the riverbank.

In a sudden movement, Roland heaved Somerton around, face forward, and water gushed from the earl's mouth in a torrent of coughing and sputtering. His fists clutched, his back heaved. The sound of his groan wavered through the air.

Alive.

The relief began at the top of Lilibet's head and poured through her in a flood, so immense that her legs gave way at last beneath her. She sank to the ground, clutching Philip in her arms, unable to speak.

"He's dead, isn't he?" Philip murmured.

She forced her voice to work. "No! He's alive, darling. I see him now. He's swallowed a bit of water, but he's alive." She bent her head and let the tears disappear into Philip's dark hair. The warmth of the stones seeped through her clothes and into her body, like a comforting hand.

"Is he all right? Is he bleeding?"

She peeked upward. Roland and Markham were settling the coughing Somerton on the ground. The duke had reached them, had taken out his handkerchief, was helping Markham with his forehead, loosening Somerton's jacket and collar as the earl vomited with astonishing gusto into the tall muddy grass by the river.

"A little," she said. "But he's fine, now. He'll be just fine. We'll all be just fine."

A breeze, the first of the afternoon, fluttered through the loose strands of her hair, mingling with her sigh of bone-deep relief. Behind it came a sheet of white paper, sliding along the terrace stones as if by its own power. Another followed, and another.

Lilibet shifted Philip onto her right hip and rose. She trapped the papers, one by one, beneath her shaking fingers, and placed one of the broken stones from the balustrade atop the little stack, to secure it against any further threat.

TWENTY-SIX

When Lilibet emerged at last from Somerton's bedroom, the house was quiet, and the sun had already begun to slip behind the western hills.

"Lady Somerton." The Duke of Olympia rose from one of a pair of armchairs beneath the hallway window; Markham, in the other, hesitated an instant before rising, too.

"Your Grace." She held out her hand, and the duke stepped forward and clasped it with an old-fashioned courtliness. "He's asleep now; the doctor's going to watch him a bit longer. It was rather a bad concussion, apparently, but he seems confident of recovery."

Markham made a stiff bow. "I shall be happy to watch him tonight, your ladyship. I expect you're fatigued."

She looked at him. Faint circles smudged the skin beneath his eyes; his hair, ordinarily combed back with immaculate sleekness, hung down about his face. "You seem rather tired yourself, Mr. Markham. Are you quite certain?"

"Yes, madam. I'm used to late hours."

She nodded at the door. "Very well, then. Thank you."

He nodded and went through the door, with disarming silence.

"Tell me," she said, before the duke could open his mouth to speak, "who, exactly, does Mr. Markham work for? I confess I'm at a loss."

The duke shrugged. "You have *me* at a loss, madam."

She folded her arms and sent him her sternest glare, designed for Philip at his naughtiest. "I'm beginning to think everyone in the world is an intelligence agent, and they all dance to your tune, Your Grace."

A small smile grew at the corner of his mouth. He was not an unhandsome man, really. He must have been nearly seventy, and yet his face and upright figure—the athletic ease with which he moved, the surprising strength in his arms, holding back Somerton with his own walking stick— might have been that of a man twenty or thirty years younger. "My dear girl," he said, in a soft voice, "you aren't nearly so gentle as you seem, are you?"

"I am not," she replied, "and I beg you to remember it. Do not"—she edged closer and lowered her voice—"involve me, or the members of my family, in any of your schemes again."

"Ah. Tell me, this family of yours. Does it perhaps include my grandson?"

"I am not at liberty to say."

He nodded, with gentlemanly discretion, at her middle. "And yet, I suspect we may soon be related, you and I. By ties of blood, if nothing else."

She hesitated, but only for an instant. "I won't deny that, Your Grace. You know it already, I believe. How you learned, I can't begin to imagine."

"I have my sources. And Roland owns it as his? Without reserve?"

"He does."

The duke nodded. "If he didn't, of course, I'd bring him to his senses without delay. Shan't allow my great-grandchild to be born in shame."

"How good of you to look after my interests so thoroughly," she said coldly.

His smile grew. "I gather you dislike me, Lady Somerton. And yet I admire you very much. I have, I hope, your best interests at heart."

"If only you'd had them there seven years ago."

"Ah." He put his hands behind his back, like a statesman preparing for oration. "But then you'd not have your son, madam. And Roland . . . well, he's turned out rather well, all things considered, but I wonder whether he might have done so well for you at twenty-two as at twenty-nine."

"All true, perhaps. But Your Grace will forgive me for observing that it was hardly your place to decide."

"Lady Somerton." He held out his hand; she placed hers, reluctantly, atop it. His other hand moved to cover them both, the fingers curling firmly, wrapping her in an unshakable grip. "The past is past, my dear. You have now my unswerving loyalty. You are the mother of my great-grandchild, which by itself entitles you to all the protection I can give you." He brought her hand to his mouth and kissed it.

"You will not," she whispered, "entangle him further in your schemes."

He gave his head a tiny shake and looked steadily into her eyes. "That, my dear, is for him to decide, though it seems to me he'll do nothing without your consent. Your power over him is great, madam, and I trust you'll use it in wisdom."

She returned his gaze, searching his bright eyes, saying nothing. She had so much she wanted to ask him; to interrogate him with, really: Roland's intelligence activities, the duke's own involvement, Markham's role, Somerton's. What had really happened that summer, seven years ago; what had really happened these past months. But could she trust his replies? What sort of game was he playing?

Did she really want to know?

The duke nodded again at her belly, and she realized

she'd placed her other hand atop her womb. "Go to him," he said. "He's in his room, now. Waiting for you, I expect. Go." He brought her hand, which still lay clasped in his, to his lips, and kissed it again. "You have my blessing."

"I don't need your blessing."

"You have it, in any case."

She pulled her hand away and inclined her head. "Good night, Your Grace," she said, and turned to the staircase.

The knock sounded on his door just after nine o'clock, as twilight cast an indigo glow about the horizon outside the window, and Roland's eyelids were drifting downward into a much-needed sleep.

He removed his hands from behind his head and sat up in the bed. "Come in," he said softly.

Lilibet slipped through and closed the door behind her with a gentle click, leaning backward against the fine carved wood. In the light of the single candle by the bed, her face was deeply shadowed, drawn with fatigue. She wore a loose dressing gown, a few inches too short, and her hair was coming free from its pins.

She was beautiful.

He rose from the bed. "How is he?"

"Resting comfortably." Her hands seemed to be fiddling with the knob behind her back. "All stitched up. Markham's watching him. I've just tucked Philip into bed. Miss Yarrow's with him." A flush rose in her cheeks; she looked down. "How are you?" she asked the floor.

"Well enough. A bit rattled, I suppose. But I've bathed and shaved. Feeling more human." He went to her and reached around for her hands. "How are you, darling? A dreadful shock for you. Have you bathed? Eaten?"

"Yes," she said, staring at the buttons of his shirt. "Miss Yarrow gave me a few things to wear. I . . ." Her voice cracked.

"Shh." He drew her into his chest, as gently as he could. Her breath stirred his shirt in a warm cloud; he could feel the thump of her heart at the bottom of his ribs. "It's all right. He'll live, I daresay. Men like that always pull through. And I doubt he'll be contesting anything. He'd better not, by God, after I took on half the mud in Florence to save his miserable hide."

She gave a little choke of laughter into his shirt. "No, he won't contest. Markham promised me. He . . . well, he's been rather nice, Markham. I can't . . . I can't quite make him out. I saw him with your grandfather, and yet . . ."

Roland sighed. "I suspect he's been working with the duke all along, and . . . well, things can get complicated, more or less, in tight quarters."

She nodded. "I suppose so. I suppose you know all about these things. As my husband did."

"Not quite like Somerton. I assure you, I relied whenever possible on my wits, rather than my fists."

"I'm sure you did. Putting your life in danger every moment, of course."

He kissed her hair. "My life held little value to me, at the time."

"And now?" She looked up and spoke in a steady voice, the one he knew disguised her deepest emotion. "Are you going back to the Bureau?"

He sighed. He'd been doing his best to avoid the subject of his future with the Bureau. "I can't simply abandon it all, darling. There are men who depend on me. But I promise you, I shan't go on as I did before. I've too much to live for." He caressed the side of her face. "Others whose claim on me is even stronger."

She searched his face with anxious blue eyes, and he would have given his left arm to know what she was looking for. At last she laid her head against his chest and laughed again, a dry chuckle. "All this time, you were an intelligence agent? For heaven's sake, Roland. You hid it well. I still can't quite wrap my mind around it."

"Well, that's the point, isn't it? To hide oneself in plain sight. I did rather a thorough job of it, I flatter myself. Turned old Penhallow into the most feckless, foolish gadabout . . ."

". . . warming every bed in London . . ."

". . . when in fact," he said, drawing her away, so he could look in her eyes, "there was no one but you, Lilibet." He drew his finger along the line of her cheekbone to smooth the fine hairs above her ear. "Only you."

"Really?" she asked, breathless. "I can't believe that."

He shrugged. "You don't need to believe it. It's simply the truth." Her body felt so fine and fragile in his arms, so right and perfect. He wanted to hold her, to protect her, to ravish her. To make up for all the lost years in a single passionate, sleepless night. A night for the ages.

Except that he was ready to drop dead from exhaustion. He decided he'd settle for a kiss, for now.

He bent his head and brushed his lips against hers. She hesitated, and then put her hands around his neck and kissed him back, gentle movements of her mouth, almost tentative, as if they were kissing for the first time.

His loins ached, his entire body ached for her, but he pulled back. "All right?" he asked.

She nodded, without smiling.

He sighed. "It's not all right, is it?"

She looked down again, slid her hands back to his chest, and fingered the buttons of his shirt. "It's not that, darling. It's just . . . well, it's been a long day, very tiring, and . . ."

He picked her up in a single swoop and carried her to the bed.

"Roland!" she gasped.

But he didn't lay her down in the middle, didn't peel away her clothes with his lips, as he wanted to. Instead he sat with her, on the edge, facing the window, settling her in his lap with her head tucked comfortably into the notch between his chin and shoulder. "Look out there," he said. "I've been watching the sunset. Isn't it beautiful? The sky's glowing purple, and there's the Duomo towering up against it, with its red tiles. I think you must have assigned me the best room in the entire palazzo."

She laughed. "Purely by accident, I'm afraid. And I'm quite sure Somerton doesn't know you're still here."

"It's none of his business, is it? He's no longer your husband."

Her laughter died. "Well, we aren't quite divorced yet. Not until the final decree, in a month's time."

He kissed her temple. "Legal details, darling. The truth lies right here." He picked up her hand and placed it on his chest, atop his heart. Her fingers curled and stretched, caressing him. "This truth. The one between us; the one that's always lain between us."

She said nothing, only watched her hand as it rose and fell with the rhythm of his breathing.

"What is it?" he asked. "Do you doubt me?"

"No," she said, in a strangled voice, and he realized she was too full of emotion to speak.

He held her for a moment longer, watching the last of the sky's color darken into night, and the Duomo's red roof fade to a mere smudge on the horizon. He breathed in the scent of her hair, felt her soft body nestle into his, and at last had to shift himself, as discreetly as possible. "So, my dear," he said, kissing her temple again to cover the awkwardness. "What next?"

"I suppose I should be getting back to my room," she whispered.

He cleared his throat. "Well, we can discuss that, too, but I rather meant the next few days. Weeks. Months. That sort of thing."

"Oh!" She stiffened in his arms, a movement that caused another necessary and rather painful adjustment to his lap. "Yes, of course! I . . . well . . . I suppose . . . that . . ."

"Yes, darling?"

"I suppose that depends on you," she said in a rush.

"On me?" He began to smile.

"Well, I'll be staying here for a bit, just to make sure everything's all right, and then . . . well . . ." Her words dangled in the air.

"Lilibet." He delivered the Penhallow drawl directly into her right ear. "Darling. Are you waiting for something?"

"No! I . . . No! I . . . I mean, well, the course is quite clear. I suppose I'll take Philip back to the castle, and we can resume our lives with . . . with the goats and . . ."

"Lilibet." He edged out from beneath her—things were getting rather too uncomfortable, anyway—and kissed her nose, and her mouth, and her chin. He worked his way downward, kneeling onto the hard wooden floor, pressing kisses into her throat and bosom and a particularly tender one on the swell of her belly. He took her hands into his and looked up into her face, luminous with the rising moon, heavy with fatigue, surrounded by the haphazard strands of her loosened hair. "Lilibet, my sweet Lilibet. My dear and rather rumpled love. Mother of my scandalously illicit child. Will you do me the very great honor of becoming my wife, in, shall we say, a month's time, in order to properly legitimize our offspring?"

She was laughing and blushing, trying to pull her hands back. "Oh, Roland. You silly thing. This is quite improper. I'm not really divorced, not yet . . ."

He held firmly to her hands, kissing them hard enough to brand them. "What's improper, darling, is the round belly you'll be parading about Florence as a nearly divorced woman. You've already done the improper thing, my strumpet, so it seems to me the sooner we're formally engaged, the better."

"Oh, Roland," she laughed.

He rose and urged her backward, inexorably, parting her dressing gown with eager fingers. "To say nothing of the improper way you invited yourself into my room just now. One would think your intentions were rather less than pure."

"That's not true. I . . ." She broke off in a sigh.

Her right breast lay exposed before him, round and plump and dark-tipped. He kissed it reverently, ran his tongue around her nipple, admired the way it puckered at his touch. "One would think you had *designs* on me, you shameless wanton."

"I had no such thing. I merely . . . I wanted to inform

you . . . Oh!" She groaned at the hungry enclosure of her left breast by his hand.

"You do realize the sort of ideas a man gets, when a woman visits his room after dark?" He trailed his lips across the divine canyon between her breasts, and suckled on the other.

"It . . . it wasn't quite dark, after all . . ." Her hands wound into his hair.

"It was decidedly twilight, my dear. The question does not admit doubt." He eased the dressing gown over her shoulders, exposing the entire tempting reach of her torso to his eager eyes. With one hand he lifted her bottom and slid the rest of the gown away from her body and onto the floor.

She wore nothing underneath.

"Look at you," he breathed. He ran his hand along her smooth skin, across the rise of her womb, caressing her. He covered the mound with his hands, imagining the tiny miracle that lay beneath, not quite able to believe it. Had they really done this? Created a child together, Roland and Lilibet?

"A fallen woman," she said, the laughter fading from her voice.

"The most beautiful woman I've ever known," he said, kissing her belly again, and then lifting himself to kiss her lips. "The most honorable. The cleverest. The bravest."

"I'm not brave at all."

"Yes, you are. Even to contemplate a future with such a sorry rapscallion as myself . . ."

"Rapscallion?" A giggle burst from her lips. "*Rapscallion?*"

"Rapscallion. Scapegrace." Another kiss, long and dissolute and, he hoped, representative of rapscallions, which the ladies always loved. "Marry me, Lilibet. You really must."

She rolled her eyes. "Of *course* I'll marry you, Roland Penhallow. For heaven's sake, it's not as if you've left me any choice, half-gone with child. I'm not *that* immune to shame, I hope."

"My thoughts precisely." He kissed her again, with an emphatic smack. "And now that *that's* settled . . ."

She moved so quickly he couldn't finish, turning him over and swinging her leg over his hips, looking outrageously decadent with the fresh, newly risen moonlight bathing her naked breasts. She leaned in close to his face, letting her hair tumble over her shoulders to enclose them. "Now that *that's* settled," she said, "I can ravish you as you deserve. My noble Roland, my beautiful and quite irresistible Roland, composer of poems and savior of drowning passersby." She kissed him and leaned back, unbuttoning his shirt with nimble fingers. "Passionate lover, daring spy." She slid the shirt from his body, as, entranced, he lifted each arm with obliging promptness to assist her with the sleeves. "Faithful admirer. And oh, my darling"—she slid her hands up his chest, his throat, until she cupped his face—"the most important, the most wonderful Roland of all. The loving, openhearted father, for whom I can only thank God." She lowered her face to his and kissed him, deeply and passionately.

The blood roared in his ears. His lips returned her kiss, while his hands went to his hips and shimmied off his trousers, taking particular care not to dislodge his love from her quite satisfactory post above him. At his expert kick, flicking the last of the offending garment from his right foot, her laughter bubbled up from her chest. She lifted her head and grinned at him. "I don't believe you," she said.

"What's that?" he mumbled, his wits not altogether at prime performance.

"That was far too well rehearsed a maneuver for a man of chaste habits."

He assumed an angelic expression. "My agility is legendary in intelligence circles, madam, and quite up to the challenge of disrobing under pressure."

"Pressure?" Her eyebrows lifted.

"The most immense and painful pressure." He ran his hands down her back to cup her round bottom. "For which I humbly beg your most earnest efforts in relief."

She smiled, a knowing, dreamlike smile, and reached down to caress the tip of his cock. His answering groan nearly rattled the window.

"Hush," she said. "You'll wake the house, and then where will we be?"

"For God's sake, madam," he ground out, grasping her hips, "do your duty."

She laughed and went up on her knees, positioning herself just so, and came down hard, impaling herself to the hilt. This time her groan mingled with his, deep and heartfelt: acute physical pleasure amplified by the knowledge of connection, of oneness, of his body plumbing the depths of hers, soldering himself to her.

He fought the instinct to close his eyes and simply revel in the sensation of her hot embrace, slick and tight around his cock; he lifted his eyes to her face and found that she was watching him, too, her blue eyes dark and unfocused, her skin flushed and ready. "Move with me," he whispered, and she began to slide upward, slow and a bit uncertain, examining his face as if for clues how to proceed. He let his hands travel upward, along the soft skin of her waist and belly to her breasts, warm and heavy under his fingers. "Ah, God," he said, "you're so beautiful, so damned alluring." He circled the tips in a languorous pattern, keeping time with the rise and fall of her body along his, holding himself in check as she stretched and arched above him for long exquisite moments, trying him out at every angle until her eyes widened and her breath caught in her throat.

"That's the spot, is it?" he said, smiling.

"Oh God."

He moved his hips beneath her, increasing the pace, rolling her nipples gently between his fingers. He could see she wanted it faster, that she'd found the key and wanted to unlock the door, but he wasn't quite ready to let her go. Instead, he dropped one hand to her bottom, guiding her, helping her find the precise rhythm to keep her shimmering just on the edge of release, to coil the tension like a fine tight spring, higher and higher, until she panted and moaned into the dark air, until her skin glowed with heat and her fingers dug into his chest.

How had he lived without this? How had he survived without her, all these years, so passionate and beautiful, so essentially Lilibet, her keen spirit seething under its layers of serene perfection, like a flame behind a fire screen? Her head tilted back, her breasts danced before his eyes, her skin branded his fingers; he couldn't hold on any longer, as the intensity of pleasure threatened to kill him. With his hips he urged her on, harder and faster, and it seemed she felt it, too, felt as desperate as he did. In mere seconds her body stiffened and her silken walls rippled with release along his length, and her stifled cry of joy sank like the music of heaven into his ears.

With an answering shout Roland let himself go, let the climax overtake him in long, luxurious pulses. Lilibet collapsed against his damp chest, her hair spreading and tumbling around them, and through the thick and now-familiar treacle in his brain he thought he heard her murmur something rather important.

He stroked her hair and blinked several times. The treacle remained, however, and so he pushed out, with great effort, "I say, darling, *what* was that?"

She stirred comfortably. "What was what?"

"What you just . . . You said something just now . . ."

"Mmm." She pressed a kiss into the hollow of his throat. "I said I love you."

He closed his eyes. The mattress gave gently beneath his back; the bedclothes caressed his flushed skin, soft and fragrant with lavender.

Or was that Lilibet?

"I thought so," he said, and went to sleep.

EPILOGUE

The sun burned high and hot in the blue August sky as they made the turn from the main road, past the faded wooden sign that read CASTEL SANT'AGATA 1 KM.

Philip, riding a few yards ahead on his new brown pony, shouted back over his shoulder. "I can see it! Just behind the trees! There's my window! Do you think Norbert misses me?"

Roland cleared his throat. "Well, in the matter of grass-hoppers, old boy, it's entirely likely . . . well, given the length of our absence . . ."

". . . Norbert may be out playing with his grasshopper friends in the meadow," Lilibet said quickly. "I'm sure Cousin Abigail wouldn't have wanted him to be lonely, with you away."

"Oh." Philip's shoulders sagged beneath his rather wrinkled cotton jacket.

"But we'll head out into the meadow directly after lunch and find him," Roland said.

"Oh, yes!" Shoulders up again. "I'm sure he'll come when I call. He's a jolly nice grasshopper. He's dom . . . domis . . ."

"Domesticated. Yes, quite," said Roland. He glanced at Lilibet, his hazel eyes gleaming with humor and his handsome face now tanned from a month of Florentine sunshine, despite the protection of his straw boater. The sun adored her new husband. His skin had only to pick up a few errant rays to mellow into a rich and quite unfashionable glow.

"Papa, may I ride on ahead? It's just a little ways." Philip looked up at Roland from beneath the brim of his hat with a kind of hero worship in his eyes.

"Yes, of course. Keep to the road and mind the rocks."

"Yes, sir!" Philip nudged his pony into a businesslike trot and headed down the familiar drive toward the castle. She was eager to follow him, eager to throw her arms around her cousins and tell them everything, but Roland had proven unshakable in his insistence that she keep to a sedate pace. She looked down at her hands on the reins, at the ridge beneath her glove where Roland had placed a plain gold band four days ago, and smiled.

"I expect you're desperate to tell the whole tale to your ladies," Roland said, as if he could read her thoughts. She turned to him, and her smile broadened.

"They'll be quite shocked to see me swing off the horse, for one thing. I've grown out scandalously these past few weeks."

"More beautiful every day," Roland assured her, his gaze traveling down the curve of her body with a look of deep and appreciative sincerity. He moved his horse closer to her, until his leg nearly brushed her skirts.

She laughed. "I'll be bumping into everything. Anyway, Philip will have told them every detail before we've even dismounted. His new baby brother and his new papa."

"He'll have the devil of a shock if it's a girl. I've tried to explain . . ."

"Well, at least *you're* not going to disappoint him." She reached out and touched his gloved hand, curling her fingers around his, because the love between Roland and Philip made her heart draw breath and expand into every corner of her body.

She and Roland had taken Philip out for a picnic, three weeks after Somerton had returned to England and the day after the telegram arrived, confirming the issuance of the decree absolute of her divorce from the earl. Together, they'd told the boy that he and his mother and Roland and the new baby were going to be a family, and that even his father thought this was a good idea, and would see him during the holidays when he was home from school.

She hadn't known quite how he would react. He loved Roland, of course. Loved spending time with him, insisted on holding his hand during walks, looked up to him as a kind of god among men. But how would he feel about Roland marrying his mother? How would he feel about his father—unpleasant, unaffectionate, but still his father—being supplanted in his world? She'd held her breath as he looked between the two of them, eyes wide and mouth open with disbelief, not quite able to speak at first.

And then: "Uncle Roland's going to be my father? And the baby's father?"

Roland had knelt next to him in the crisp summer grass. "Your father will always be your father, Philip, old boy. But I'd like very much to live with you and your mother, and help her with the baby, and do all the things that a papa would do. If that's quite all right with you, of course."

"Oh." Philip had looked at him uncertainly, brow creased with thought, evidently turning over something of great weight in his head. "But . . . if Father's still my father, but you're marrying Mama . . ."

"Yes?"

"Well, what will I *call* you?"

Roland had looked at Lilibet. Lilibet had looked at Philip. Philip had looked between the two of them in deep perplexity.

"You can call me anything you like," Roland had said at last.

"Hmm." A pause. "Will the baby call you Papa?"

Roland's voice had roughened. "Yes, I expect it shall."

"Then I'll call you Papa, too," Philip had said, with an

air of settled decision, and he'd flung his arms around Roland's neck. That night, as Lilibet had tucked him into bed, he'd said, in a small voice, "I'm afraid to go to sleep, Mama. I'm afraid it was a dream, and I'll wake up and it won't be true."

She'd kissed him and reassured him that it *was* true, every bit of it, and a week later he'd held Lilibet's hand in the small chapel as she said her marriage vows, with Beadle and the Duke of Olympia sitting behind them in a pew, and Roland had lifted him into the carriage afterward for the long ride back to the Palazzo Angelini, where his new pony awaited him in the stables.

That had more or less won him for life.

Now, as they watched him trot ahead, into the clear, warm Tuscan air, Lilibet saw the familiar turrets of castle appear from behind the trees and wanted to sing with joy.

"What is it?" Roland asked.

"I was just thinking how miserable and apprehensive I was, riding up this same road in March, with you by my side. How empty and forbidding it all was, how mysterious. And Morini, appearing like a ghost in the hallway, frightening us to death." She laughed.

"Ah yes. The fabled Morini. Everyone goes on and on about that dashed housekeeper, and I've never even met her. Only poor old Francesca."

"That dreadful first night! Cold and rainy and lonely. And now it will be full of love and laughter. They'll be so happy to see us. I expect Mr. Burke and Alexandra will be engaged by now, and . . . do you think your brother . . . ?"

He laughed. "What, with Abigail? I hope not. She's far too good for him."

"The grapes will be ripening, I think. They'll be picking them by the end of the month. And the apples and peaches. Oh, Roland, how I love it here! Let's go swimming in the lake tonight. Let's never leave. Let's see if we can find the owner—what was his name?—Rosseti. Let's see if we can renew the lease. Do you think we could?"

Roland shifted in his saddle and lifted one gloved hand

to rub his upper lip. "Well," he said, "I believe that could be arranged, without much difficulty."

Something in the tone of his voice caught her attention. She tilted her head and peered at him, at the evasive look in his eye. "What do you mean?" she asked.

"Didn't I tell you? I thought I must have said something. Rather busy few weeks, I suppose. Perhaps I said something about it to Beadle, and assumed . . ."

"Roland." She invested the word with as much doom as its two brief syllables would allow.

"Hmm. Yes. Well, it's a funny old story. Odd, really. A sort of coincidence, you might say. The day before we left, Midsummer's Eve, as you no doubt recall, that marvelous party with all the masks and whatnot, and then of course . . . well, afterward was lovely, too, the loveliest night of my life really, except perhaps our wedding night, which will live forever in my memory as . . ."

"Roland!"

"Yes. All right. So there I was, going through the estate documents with Philip, as a sort of research project, and it turns out . . . quite funny, really, how you'll laugh . . . you'll never guess who . . . well, at any rate, he *seems* to be the actual owner, according to the deed . . ."

"The *actual* owner? You mean it's not Rosseti?"

He looked down at his hands, fingering the reins. "Yes, rather funny, that. Rosseti's name was never on the deed. The castle was built by the Marquis di Monteverdi. But it was transferred, quite some time ago, to another man entirely."

"Who, Roland?"

"Oh, look! Is that Giacomo up there? Ha-ha. He doesn't look at all pleased about the pony."

"I don't see anyone. Who, Roland?"

"What, you don't see Giacomo? He's right there, darling! Got his hand on the bridle, scolding Philip . . ."

"Enough of your *jokes*, Roland. Who owns the castle?"

He cleared his throat and stopped his horse. His voice lost all hint of laughter. "The property was transferred in 1591 to the Earl of Copperbridge."

"Are you certain? An Englishman? The Earl of Copperbridge?" She stopped her horse beside his and knit her brow, trying to remember where she'd heard that name. "But that's . . . isn't that the courtesy title of . . . ?"

"It was my uncle's title, before he died. It's the family title used by the heirs of the Dukes of Olympia."

She knew she was staring like a wide-eyed idiot, but she couldn't seem to adjust her face from its shocked expression. "Then your grandfather . . ."

". . . owns the castle. Apparently."

She sat still in her saddle, absorbing this. A breeze went by, warm and fragrant with the scents of summer, rustling in the nearby cypress. "The old bastard," she whispered. "I knew he was playing deep, but this!"

"Yes, the old . . . *What* did you just call him?"

"Never mind." She nudged her horse forward. "Let's find the others. I've an idea Abigail might find this information even more interesting than I do."

She pushed the horse into a trot, raising puffs of dust at every hoofbeat, despite Roland's pleas—escalating into orders, which she ignored—that she take care, for heaven's sake, and think of the baby. She dismounted in the courtyard, handed the reins to an emerging stable hand, and waited only just long enough for Roland to swing himself to the ground before she hurried on to the door.

"Philip!" she called.

"I expect he's gone in through the kitchen entrance," Roland said. He tugged open the door and followed her along the short passage into the inner courtyard, with its dry fountain, and through the entrance to the main hall.

"Philip!" she called again. "Abigail! Alexandra!"

Her voice echoed about the room, loud and clear in the vast stone-lined emptiness. She turned to Roland and put her hand on his arm. "Where is everybody?"

"I don't know," he said. "Didn't you send a telegram?"

"Yes, a few days ago. I told them we were returning. I didn't say anything else; I wanted to surprise them."

His hand slipped into hers, solid and reassuring. "Perhaps they're finishing luncheon. Or perhaps they're out."

"Let's try the kitchen. Morini will be there, I'm sure." She started off in that direction, leading Roland by the hand, but before she'd gone more than a few steps, Philip ran into the room, hatless, his jacket unbuttoned and covered with crumbs.

"Mama!" he said, jumping in her arms to spread his crumbs all over her new black riding habit from the Florentine tailor. "Morini gave me a slice of *panettone*, and you'll never guess!"

"Guess what, darling?"

"Nobody's here!"

She set him down on the floor. "What's this? What do you mean?"

"They've all gone away! Our cousins and the duke and Mr. Burke. She doesn't know when they'll be back, either. Would you like a bite of my *panettone*?" He held the remainder out to her.

"I . . . No, thank you, dear." She wiped absently at the crumbs and glanced uneasily about the room. Despite the warmth of the day, a chill seemed to have invaded the air.

"Well, that's odd," said Roland. "Jolly odd indeed. But at least we'll have the old pile to ourselves for a bit, eh what? Like a honeymoon, really, except for Norbert the grasshopper."

"Will you be sleeping in our room?" Philip stuffed the remaining *panettone* in his mouth with a notable lack of elegance.

Roland scratched his forehead. "Well, as to that, old boy, there may be some adjustments in order, in the matter of sleeping arrangements. You did have your own room in the palazzo, didn't you? Because you're such an awfully big boy now?"

"Roland," Lilibet said, in a low voice, "may I have a word with you?"

"Oh no," said Philip. "You'd better watch out, Papa.

That's what she says to me when I'm in trouble." He turned and trotted back in the direction of Morini's *panettone*.

"Now look here, Philip. Leaving the field of battle, are you? There's a word for that sort of thing in the army, and it isn't a nice one . . ." He turned from Philip's disappearing figure and smiled at her. His warm smile, laden with the Penhallow charm, which never failed to settle her world on its proper axis. "What's wrong, darling?" he asked, taking her hands. "Aren't you happy to be here?"

All at once her fears slid away. Curses, really! Mere superstition. The others were probably off sightseeing, bored of the summer routine in the remote castle. Didn't Mr. Burke have some sort of automobile exposition in Rome? Likely they were enjoying themselves too much to leave. Or perhaps they'd gone on to see Pompeii, or Capri.

As for the involvement of the Earl of Copperbridge, it could only be a coincidence, surely. The duke had said nothing about the Castel sant'Agata, in all the time she'd spent with him during the past month.

She brought Roland's hands to her lips and kissed them. She leaned forward and kissed his lips, warm and dry after the long morning's ride from the inn, where they'd spent the previous night in the landlord's best bedroom and taken a midnight stroll through the stables. "Nothing's wrong," she said. "Nothing at all. We're home, that's all."

He grinned. "Are we? In that case . . ."

Before she could do more than gasp, he'd bent down and swung her up into his arms and carried her back through the courtyard and out into the brilliant Italian afternoon, where the sun caught his eyes in a hazel glow. "What are you doing?" she demanded, clutching at his shoulders.

He set her on the ground, straightened his cuffs, adjusted his lapels, and picked her up again. "I'm doing this properly, by God," he said, and carried her over the threshold and into the courtyard, where he placed her on the lichen-crusted edge of the fountain and tossed his hat on the ground.

"Welcome home, Lady Roland," he said, and kissed her senseless.

Turn the page to read an excerpt from
the next book in the trilogy

A DUKE
NEVER YIELDS

London
February 1890

The Duke of Wallingford, as a rule, did not enjoy the sound of the human voice upon waking. Not that of his valet, nor his mistress—he never, ever spent the night with a woman—and certainly not the one that assailed his ears just now.

"Well, well," said the Duke of Olympia, to the prostrate form of his eldest grandson. "For an instrument that has cut such a wide swathe of consternation, it appears remarkably harmless at present."

Wallingford did not trouble to open his eyes. For one thing, he had a crashing headache, and the morning light already pierced his brain with sufficient strength, without his giving up the additional protection of his eyelids.

For another thing, he'd be damned if he gave the old man the satisfaction.

"Who the devil let you in?" Wallingford demanded instead.

"Your valet was kind enough to perform the office."

"I shall sack him at once."

Olympia's footsteps clattered in reply along the wooden floor to the opposite end of the room, where he flung back the curtains on the last window. "There we are! A lovely day. Do examine the brilliant white of the winter sun this morning, Wallingford. Too extraordinary to be missed."

Wallingford dropped an arm over his face. "Rot in hell, Grandfather."

A sigh. "My dear boy, may I trouble you to consider a dressing robe? I am not accustomed to addressing the unadorned male member at such an early hour of the day. Or any hour of the day, as a matter of habit."

Arthur Penhallow, Duke of Wallingford, twenty-nine years old and assuredly not a boy, flung his unoccupied arm in the direction of his dressing-room door. "If the sight offends, Grandfather, I recommend you to the wardrobe. The dressing gowns, I believe, are hanging along the right-hand side. I prefer the India cashmere, in wintertime."

"I must decline your gracious invitation," said Olympia, "and ring for your valet instead. Have you never considered a nightshirt?"

"When *I* am sixty-five, and without hope of tender feminine attention upon my withered person, I shall remember the hint." This was not quite fair. Wallingford knew for a fact that his grandfather's person, withered or not, currently enjoyed the tender feminine attention of Henrietta, Lady Pembroke herself, who did not choose her lovers for mere whimsy.

On the other hand, the opportunity was too tempting to pass up.

"And yet, Wallingford, your own person exhibits no evidence of feminine attention of any kind." A delicate pause. "Quite the contrary, in fact."

"Bugger off."

"What a crude generation my children have spawned. Ah! Shelmerstone. You perceive His Grace stands in need of a dressing gown. In a manner of speaking, I hasten to add."

Wallingford heard the door close behind his valet and the soft tread of the man's feet across the thick Oriental rug toward the dressing room. "Shelmerstone," he said, "once you have dressed and shaved me, you may collect your things and vacate your position. I am not to be disturbed before nine in the morning, and certainly not by so intolerable a character as His Grace, my grandfather."

"Yes, sir," said Shelmerstone, who was accustomed to being sacked several times a day, as a matter of course. "I have taken the liberty of putting out the gray superfine, sir, and your best beaver hat."

"Why the devil? I ain't contemplating church this morning."

"I chose it, sir, as being more suitable for calling upon a lady, on a matter of such unprecedented delicacy."

This caused Wallingford to sit up at last. "What lady?" he demanded, shading his eyes against the merciless abundance of light. Was it his imagination, or did everything smell of stale champagne this morning? "What . . . *delicacy*?" He said the word with a shudder of distaste.

"Madame de la Fontaine, of course." Shelmerstone emerged from the wardrobe's depths with a dressing gown of fawn brown cashmere and an air of irresistible moral authority, laced with cedar.

"See here." Wallingford rose from his bed by the sheer force of habit and allowed Shelmerstone to fit his arms into the robe.

Olympia, impeccable as ever in sleek morning tweeds and riding boots, squared his arms behind his back and cast his grandson his most withering smile. Wallingford had loathed that look since childhood: Like an ill wind, it blew no good. "My dear boy, there's no use pretending ignorance. The entire town knows of last night's charming little farce. I don't suppose you'd consider *belting* that robe? At my age, one's digestion is so easily upset."

Wallingford lashed his robe into modesty with vigorous jerks of his arms. "There was no *farce*, Grandfather. The Duke of Wallingford does not condescend to *farces*."

"Shelmerstone," said the Duke of Olympia, his bright blue eyes not leaving Wallingford's face for an instant, "may I beg your indulgence for a moment of private conversation with my grandson?"

"Of course, Your Grace." Shelmerstone set down the shaving soap and departed the room without a sound.

Wallingford attempted a smile. "I'm to be scolded, am I?"

His grandfather turned back to the window, fingered aside the curtain, and gazed out into the forest of white pediments that was Belgrave Square. The light fell across his features, softening the lines, until he might have been taken for a man twenty years younger were it not for the shining silver of his hair. "I don't object to your taking the woman to bed," he said, in the preternaturally calm voice he reserved for his most predatory moments. "French husbands are tolerant of such things, and as a diplomat, Monsieur de la Fontaine must be aware of the advantages of the liaison. It is why such a man marries an alluring woman."

Wallingford shrugged. "He has been all that is accommodating."

"Yes, of course. And in return, one expects that you would demonstrate a certain degree of respect. A *modicum*"—here Olympia's voice began to intensify, signaling the approach of the attack—"a *modicum* of good breeding, which would prevent your indulging that wayward prick of yours with another diversion, whilst you remained the acknowledged lover of Cecile de la Fontaine." He turned to Wallingford, eyes ablaze. "Under her own roof, no less, and at her own party. How else to humiliate her so thoroughly?"

"I never made Cecile any promises." Wallingford's insides were turning rapidly to stone, defending him against onslaught. Of course he had been wrong; he'd known it even as he was committing the very act—up against the wall of the de la Fontaines' elegant conservatory, quite efficient, quite pleasant, if rather oppressively drenched with the scent of Cecile's prize orchids—and to quit the lady in question (what the devil was her name, anyway?) with so little ceremony had represented the height of stupidity. Every lady, even one willing to take an uprighter with her hostess's own lover against her hostess's own conservatory wall, required a little ceremony.

But who would have expected her to confront him so publicly, and so half-nakedly, and with such quantities of fine French champagne flung at his head? His hair was still sticky with it.

"No, of course you did not. I'd have expected nothing else," said Olympia, in a voice laden with scorn. "But there's a promise implicit in taking such a woman to bed, a respectable woman, a woman of position. Indeed, a woman of any sort, though I should hardly expect you to possess the chivalry to go so far as that."

No one wielded scorn so brutally as the Duke of Olympia. Wallingford felt it pound against the hard stone of his innards in a familiar rhythm, searching for weakness. He added a few buttresses for support against the assault and hardened them into granite. When he had finished, and felt sufficiently confident of the results, he idled his way to the carved wooden bedpost and leaned against it, arms crossed. "A bit of the pot calling the kettle black, isn't it, Grandfather?"

"I don't deny I've taken many women to bed," said Olympia, "and, on the whole, a far more interesting lot than *you* have troubled yourself to assemble, but I have always had the decency to finish with one lover before taking another."

"Except your wife."

The words snapped and spun in the pale morning light. Wallingford regretted them instantly.

Against Olympia's hand, where it fisted atop his waistcoat, a gold watch chain caught the sun with a sudden glitter. "In the future," he said evenly, "you will avoid any mention of Her Grace in vulgar context. Do you understand me?"

"Of course."

"I have often wondered," Olympia went on, relaxing his fist, "whether a wife might not have civilized you, or at least contrived to soften your worst instincts."

"I am perfectly civilized. I am a perfectly good duke. My estates are in excellent order, my tenants prosperous . . ." He sounded like a schoolboy, Wallingford realized angrily, desperate for some crumb of approval.

"Yes, for which I give you full credit," Olympia said. "Your father, that scapegrace, was not capable of so much. I often wonder at my daughter's lack of sense in marrying him. A duke, to be sure, and a handsome one, but . . ." He shrugged his shoulders expressively.

"I beg you to remember that the scapegrace in question was my father."

Olympia lifted the watch and flipped open the case. "You have an abundance of natural qualities, Wallingford. It grieves me to see so much promise go to waste."

"I beg your pardon," drawled Wallingford. "Am I keeping you from an appointment? Do not stand on ceremony, I implore you."

"I will come to the point. I understand Mr. Burke has laid a certain proposal before you."

Wallingford rolled his eyes and left his post at the bed to sprawl in an armchair. "What, his mad scheme to retire to Italy for a year of monastic reflection?"

"You cannot imagine yourself capable of such restraint?"

Wallingford leaned his head against the forest green damask and laughed. "Oh, come, Grandfather. Why should I? What use would it be? I have never understood this religion of self-sacrifice among the Burkes of the world."

"Do you not? Have you never contemplated the peculiar difficulties of his life?"

"His life as your bastard son, do you mean?" Wallingford said.

Again, the silence echoed about the room; again, Wallingford wished his words back. Phineas Burke was an excellent fellow, after all: a bit tall and ginger haired and taciturn for some, but a genuine scientific genius, an inventor of the highest order, building electric batteries and horseless carriages and whatnot the way other men tinkered with watches. A colossus, really. Moreover, he had none of your tempers and thin-skinned resentments, your vain strivings and artificial manners, so common in well-bred bastards. Burke simply went about his business and did not give a damn, and as a result he was received everywhere. In his heart, Wallingford counted Burke as his closest friend, though of course one could never publicly admit such a thing of one's natural uncle.

Really, Burke was so steadfast and clever, so stalwart in any crisis, Wallingford could almost forgive him for being the apple of Olympia's eye.

"You see," Olympia said softly, "I know how it is. You've always been a duke, or else in daily expectation of a dukedom. You have been blessed with a handsome face and a sturdy figure. You take these things for granted. You think that you have *earned* all this around you"—his arm, at a wave, took in the splendid furnishings, the army of servants moving soundlessly behind the walls, the rarefied pavement of Belgrave Square outside the windows—"instead of having it dropped in your lap like an overripe peach. You think you deserve to enjoy sexual congress with some mere acquaintance, against the wall of your own mistress's conservatory, simply because you can. Simply because you are His Grace, the Duke of Wallingford."

"I recognize my good fortune. I see no reason not to enjoy its fruits."

"Its *fruits*? This woman, this lady of good family, with a mind and soul of her own—she is reduced to a mere vegetable, in your calculus?"

Wallingford turned his attention to the sleek cashmere sleeve of his dressing gown, searching for a piece of lint at which he might brush, laconically, to show his disinterest. But Shelmerstone was far too efficient a valet to allow any flaws to disturb the impeccable line of the ducal sleeve, and Wallingford was reduced to brushing phantom lint into the dustless air. "I seem to recall," he said, "that the lady in question was enjoying herself."

"Really?" Olympia's voice was cold. "I rather doubt you would have noticed either way. In any case, I've decided that all this nonsense has gone far enough. You are nine-and-twenty, and a duke. With regret, I must demand you *not* to accept this proposal of Burke's, however edifying, and turn your attention instead to marriage."

Wallingford looked up, certain he'd misheard the old man. "*Marriage?*" he asked, as he might say the word *castration.* "Did you say *marriage?*"

"I did."

"Are you *mad?*"

Olympia spread his hands. "Surely you recognize the necessity."

"Not at all. We still have Penhallow, who would make an extraordinarily decorative duke, should I have the misfortune to choke on a chicken bone at dinner this evening."

"Your brother has no interest in your title."

Like a pitcher turned upside down, Wallingford found his patience had run abruptly out. He rose from the chair in a bolt of movement. "Have we come to the point at last? Is *this* why you came to see me this morning? I am to be a stud? My ability to breed another duke constitutes the sum total of my usefulness to you, does it?"

"My dear boy," Olympia said, "has the entire conduct of your adult life ever suggested your usefulness for anything else?"

Wallingford turned to the tray of coffee and poured himself a cup. No cream, no sugar. He wanted the drink as black as his mood. *Marriage,* indeed. "I have many talents, Grandfather, if you ever bothered to count them."

Olympia waved that away. "Don't be a child, Wallingford. In any case, you need not concern yourself with the tiresome matter of choosing a wife. I've done all the work for you. I have, in my deep and abiding regard for you, found you the perfect bride already."

Wallingford, in the very act of lifting the cup to his lips, let it slip instead with a thump to the rug below. Such was his astonishment, he did not bother to retrieve it. "*You* have found *me* a bride?" he repeated, in shocked tones, clutching the saucer as if to a life buoy.

"I have. Charming girl. You'll adore her, I assure you."

"I beg your pardon. Have I gone to sleep and woken up two hundred years ago?"

Olympia patted his coat pocket and withdrew a slim leather diary. "No," he said, examining a few pages. "No, it remains February of 1890. Thank goodness, as I've an immense number of appointments to make today, and I should hate to have to wait so long to complete them. If this is all agreeable to you, Wallingford, I shall invite the girl and her family around at the end of March, when they return to town. A private dinner would be best, I think. Allow the two of you to get to know each other." He turned a few more pages in his diary. "A wedding around midsummer would be ideal, don't you think? Roses in bloom and all that?"

"Are you mad?"

"Sound as a nut. I must be off, however. I'll send in Shelmerstone on my way out. No doubt he stands ready at the keyhole. And Wallingford?"

"Yes?" He was too stunned to say anything else.

"Do contrive not to embroil yourself in any further scandal before then, eh? The Queen doesn't like it, not a bit. Oh yes! And orchids."

"Orchids?"

"Orchids to Madame de la Fontaine. It seems they're her favored blooms."

Olympia left in a flash of tweed coat and silver hair, and Wallingford stared at the door as if it were the gate to Hell itself.

What the devil had come over the old man? He'd never so much as mentioned the word *marriage* before, and all at once it was brides this and weddings that and bloody *roses*, if you will! He looked down at his hand, holding the blue and white porcelain saucer, and saw it was shaking.

The door slid open in a faint rush of well-oiled hinges. "Your shave is ready, sir," said Shelmerstone. He took in the faintest of breaths at the sight of the pool of coffee settling into the priceless rug, surrounded by long ambitious streaks of brown and, at their tips, the final tiny droplets, still winking atop the rug's tight woolen weave. Without a pause, he snatched the linen napkin from the coffee tray and fell to his knees, blotting, going so far as to murmur a reproachful *Sir!* in the depths of his distress.

Wallingford set down the saucer. "I beg your pardon, Shelmerstone. His Grace has delivered me the devil of a shock."

"What was that, sir?" Shelmerstone asked, covering a sob.

"Marriage," Wallingford said. He then added, for clarification, "Mine."

A dreadful pause. "Sir."

"Yes. Most distressing. He's picked out the bride, the date, the damned flowers. I daresay he's chosen her a dress already, and embroidered the pearls himself, God rot him."

Shelmerstone cleared his throat. His face was white, either from the coffee or the bride or some combination of the two. A funereal gravity darkened his voice. "Her name, sir?"

Wallingford squinted his eyes. "It was . . . something like . . . By God. Do you know, Shelmerstone, I don't think he even saw fit to tell me."

"Sir."

"Not that it matters, of course. I shan't do it. I shall tell my grandfather exactly where he can stash his arranged brides." His words sounded hollow in the great cavern of a bedroom, and he knew it. He could hear Shelmerstone's thoughts, as he bent over the coffee stain.

Ha. Like to see him try. No going against His Damned Bloody Grace Olympia, when he has one of them ideas in his noggin.

"I believe I shall fetch the bicarbonate," Shelmerstone said faintly, and rose to his feet.

Wallingford fell into the armchair, staring blankly at the room around him. His familiar room, grand and yet with a certain worn comfort, bare of unnecessary decoration, not a flower in sight, his favorite books piled on the nightstand, his aged single-malt Scotch whiskey at the ready. The very notion of a woman inhabiting this sanctum made his mind vibrate with dissonance.

No. No, of course not. Not even the Duke of Olympia would dare such a thing.

True, he'd hand-selected more than one prime minister in the last half century. And the Queen herself had been known to change one or two of her notoriously firm opinions after an hour of private conversation with His Grace.

And there was that time he traveled to Russia aboard his private steam yacht and told the tsar in no uncertain terms . . .

Good God.

Wallingford leaned forward, put his elbows on his knees, and covered his face with his hands.

There had to be a way out.

He spread his fingers and peered through them. The scent of last night's tossed champagne still hung in his hair, pressing against his nostrils, making him feel slightly queasy. Champagne. Orchids. His brain sloshed about with the memories of last night: the impulsive coupling, banal and sordid, the work of a mere minute or two, and then the sour distaste as he had wiped himself with his handkerchief and looked at the lady's flushed face and perspiring bosom and tried to recall her name.

He needed more coffee. He needed . . .

Something caught his eye, in the stack of books atop his bedside table, next to the coffee tray. Something that was not a book at all.

A tickle began at the base of Wallingford's brain, as if a pair of fingers were nudging him. It felt . . . it felt . . . almost like. . . .

An idea.

He rose, paced to the table, and lifted the three topmost volumes.

There it was, beneath the Dickens, atop the Carlyle. A folded newspaper, given to him a month ago, the edges already beginning to yellow under the inexorable poison of oxygen.

Wallingford picked it up and smoothed the page. There, circled in thick black ink, the print as crisp as it had been when Phineas Burke had handed it to him in the breakfast room downstairs, read an advertisement:

English lords and ladies, and gentlemen of discerning taste, may take note of a singular opportunity to lease a most magnificent Castle and Surrounding Estate in the idyllic hills of Tuscany, the Land of Unending Sunshine. The Owner, a man of impeccable lineage, whose ancestors have kept the Castle safe against intrusion since the days of the Medici princes, is called away by urgent business, and offers a year's lease of this unmatched Property at rates extremely favorable for the discerning traveler. Applicants should inquire through the Owner's London agent . . .

A year, Burke had proposed. A year of study and contemplation, free from the distractions of modern life and the female sex. Four weeks ago, Wallingford had laughed at the idea, once he had overcome his initial shock that such a notion should even occur to a sane and able-bodied man, in full possession of his youthful animal spirits.

A year, free of the interference of the Duke of Olympia, and his brides and his June weddings. A year—it must be said—free of recriminations from Cecile de la Fontaine and her vindictive French temper.

A year free of temptation, free of ducal trappings. In a remote Italian castle, where nobody knew him, where nobody had even heard of the Duke of Wallingford.

Wallingford slapped the newspaper back down on the books, causing the topmost volumes to tumble to the floor in surprise. He poured himself a cup of coffee, drank it in a single burning gulp, and stretched his arms to the ceiling.

Why, it was just the thing. A change of scenery from gray and changeless London. He could use a change. He'd been dogged with a sense of dissatisfaction, of restlessness, long before his outrageous indiscretion last night, long before Olympia's unwelcome visit this morning.

A year with his brother and his closest friend, both decent chaps who minded their own business. Tuscany, the land of unending sunshine. Wine in abundance, and decent food, and surely a discreet village girl or two if absolutely necessary.

What could possibly go wrong?

ETERNAL
ROMANCE

FIND YOUR HEART'S DESIRE...